Mike Dellosso is a storyteller extraordinaire. It's a rare writer who has the chops—or the courage—to lead readers into hell so he can show them heaven. In *Scream*, Dellosso does exactly that. *Scream* is an expertly crafted thriller that combines a tight, twisting plot with intriguing characters, primarily an imperfect but genuinely likeable protagonist, and one of the wickedest villains this side of a nightmare. Toss Dellosso's brilliant word-smithing into the mix, and *bam!*—you got yourself a story that'll keep you reading well into the night…and thinking about it long afterward.

—Robert Liparulo
Author of *Comes a Horseman*, *Germ*, and *Deadfall*

Mike Dellosso turns up the heat in his edgy and gripping thriller *Scream*. Never predictable, always riveting, and superbly paced, this novel is impossible to put down—and impossible to ignore.

—Kathryn Mackel
Author of *Vanished*

In *The Hunted* and now in *Scream*, Mike Dellosso speeds readers along the twisting back roads of rural settings, where characters struggle with personal anguish and spiritual questions. Hold on for a fast-paced journey that satisfies on a number of levels.

—Eric Wilson
Author of *Field of Blood* and *Haunt of Jackals*

Mike Dellosso has once again brought us an engaging thriller full of gut-wrenching suspense and strong spiritual truth. *Scream* will have you breathlessly flying through the pages and closely exam-ining your heart at the same time. Mike Dellosso is a bright new talent who demands to be noticed.

—Jake Chism
TheChristianManifesto.com

Mike Dellosso, an astonishing new voice in supernatural thrillers, cer̲̅ ̲̅ ̲̅ h the likes of King and Peretti ̲̅ *Scream*. Dellosso's

D1372519

sophomore effort is packed with wonderfully flawed characters, a very creative plot, and a strong spiritual message.

—SUSAN SLEEMAN
THESUSPENSEZONE.COM

Mike's writing is full of suspense. Once you've started his book, it's hard to put down. More importantly, there is a truth that comes through loudly and clearly. Heaven and hell are real. In light of the brevity of life, the time to tell people about Christ is not tomorrow; it's today. *Scream* reminds each believer of the need to reach out—NOW!

—DR. LARRY MOYER
PRESIDENT AND CEO, EVANTELL

scream

Mike Dellosso

REALMS
A STRANG COMPANY

Most STRANG COMMUNICATIONS/CHARISMA HOUSE/CHRISTIAN LIFE/
EXCEL BOOKS/FRONTLINE/REALMS/SILOAM products are available
at special quantity discounts for bulk purchase for sales promotions,
premiums, fund-raising, and educational needs. For details, write Strang
Communications Book Group, 600 Rinehart Road, Lake Mary, Florida
32746, or telephone (407) 333-0600.

SCREAM by Mike Dellosso
Published by Realms
A Strang Company
600 Rinehart Road
Lake Mary, Florida 32746
www.strangdirect.com

This is a work of fiction. Names, characters, places, and incidents
are products of the author's imagination or are used fictitiously. Any
similarity to actual people, organizations, and/or events is purely
coincidental.

Design Director: Bill Johnson
Cover design by Justin Evans

Library of Congress Cataloging-in-Publication Data

Dellosso, Mike.
  Scream / Mike Dellosso. -- 1st ed.
      p. cm.
  ISBN 978-1-59979-469-3
  I. Title.
  PS3604.E446S35 2009
  813'.6--dc22

                                        2008042882

First Edition

09 10 11 12 13 — 987654321
Printed in the United States of America

For Darrell, whose near-appointment with death
first inspired me to turn to the written word

For Dan and Judy Dellosso (Dad and Mom),
for always believing, never doubting

Acknowledgments

So this is the part of the book where I get to thank all those who played a role in the production of this story. If I thanked everyone, this volume would compete in page tally with some of the great epics in history. I won't do that to you. So to keep things reasonable, I'll limit my acknowledgments to the core contributors. This in no way diminishes the role or contribution of everyone else, but sometimes frugality is necessary, and in an effort to spare a few trees and do my part in saving the planet, I must practice self-control. Here goes:

Thank you, Jen, my dear wife and constant supporter, for praying for me, loving me, and (let's be honest) putting up with me. In short, for being the best doggone wife a man could ask for. You deserve an award. Seriously.

Thank you, Laura, Abby, and Caroline, my sweet trio of giggles, for bringing so much brightness and laughter into my life. You're the best daughters any daddy could want.

Thanks, Mom and Dad, for your prayers, encouragement, and love.

Thank you, Les, my wise and knowledgeable agent, for your guidance and counsel. I know I couldn't have done this without you.

Thank you to my editors, Debbie Marie, Lori Vanden Bosch, and Deb Moss, for your sharp eyes, careful suggestions, patient ways, and constant encouragement. Another sweet trio.

Thanks to all those who have prayed for us, encouraged us,

supported us, and fought this battle with cancer alongside us. You are dear to me, and I really can't say thank you enough.

Thank you to everyone else who encouraged me in my writing, offered advice or assistance, and urged me onward and upward. Sorry I can't mention each of you by name, but hey, you're joining me in sparing a tree. That's something.

And lastly, thank You, Jesus, for saving me. Your promises make that appointment with death a sweet reunion waiting to happen.

Preface

THEY SAY GOD WORKS IN STRANGE AND MYSTERIOUS ways. Well, I'm not going to argue with that. I've seen my fair share of the strange and mysterious coming from the hand of God.

As of the writing of this preface (which happens to be occurring during the editing phase of this book), I am in a battle with colon cancer. It's not what I ordered, not what I had in mind, and definitely was never part of my plans, but it's what I got. It's funny (not *ha-ha* funny, but *strange and mysterious* funny) how life can change with one phone call. It was March of 2008, and I was at work when I received a phone call from the gastroenterologist, the doctor who, days earlier, performed a colonoscopy on me. I'll never forget the feeling of utter solitude, the way the world seemed to literally stop spinning on its axis, when he said, "I'm very sorry, but you have colon cancer."

I was thirty-five at the time, excited about preparing to release my first novel, *The Hunted*, planning my future, and suddenly I was thinking about death. That vapor that is my life had been disturbed and had taken on a new shape.

Now I think about death all the time. Cancer has a way of doing that, of reminding you of the frailty of your existence, the brevity of life. Of reminding you that we're all just walking on a thin sheet of ice that can crack or break at any moment.

But thinking about death is a good thing. The wise king Solomon wrote, "We must all die, and everyone living should think about this." (See Ecclesiastes 7:2.) Good advice. Thinking about death forces us to think about life, something most of us don't do nearly enough. And thinking about life forces us to think about how we're *living* our life, something all of us should do a lot more of.

Anyway, I don't mean to bore you with all this macabre talk of death, but honestly, it's what's on my mind now. And ironically (here goes that whole strange and mysterious thing), it's what *Scream* is about. I find it funny (again, not in the *ha-ha* way, but in the *interesting* way) that I'm battling cancer, being reminded of the brevity of life and the imminence of death, experiencing firsthand how quickly life can shift on us and *everything* can change, while I'm reworking my novel about just that…the appointment with death we all must keep.

Strange and mysterious.

—MIKE DELLOSSO
HANOVER, PENNSYLVANIA
AUGUST 2008

There's nothing certain in a man's life except this:
That he must lose it.

—AESCHYLUS, *AGAMEMNON*

Death is a debt we must all pay.

—EURIPIDES

Now, this bell tolling softly for another, says to
me: Thou must die.

—JOHN DUNNE, MEDITATION 17

It is appointed unto men once to die, but after
this the judgment.

—HEBREWS 9:27, KJV

Chapter 1

❶

MARK STONE COULD STILL SMELL THE GREASE ON his hands.

No matter how hard he scrubbed or what fancy soap he used, the residue remained, stained into the creases of his fingers and caked under his fingernails. In a way, though, it was comforting. At least something in his life was still predictable. He gripped the steering wheel of his classic Mustang with both hands and willed his eyes to stay open. The hum of rubber on asphalt was almost hypnotic. It had been a long day at the shop, and he was ready to go home, soak in a hot shower until he puckered like a raisin, and get cozy with his pillow.

Outside, the headlights cut a swath of pale yellow light through the dense autumn darkness. Stars dotted the night like glitter on black felt. A pocked moon dangled low in the sky in front of him, a cratered carrot on the end of an unseen string, leading him home, home to the comfort of his bed.

His cell phone chimed the theme from *The Dukes of Hazzard*. Mark turned down the radio and flipped open the phone. It was Jeff Beaverson. "Jeffrey."

"Hey, buddy. How goes it?"

Mark glanced at the dashboard clock—10:10. "Kinda late for you, isn't it?"

Jeff laughed. "You know me too well. I was at my parents'

house installing a new hot water heater, and it took longer than I thought it would. I'm heading home now. Gonna walk in the door and drop myself right into bed. You in the car?"

"On my way home."

"Boy, you're putting in some late hours."

"Yeah, business is good right now. Keeps my mind off... stuff. You know."

"I know, buddy. I've been thinking about you. Thought I'd check in and make sure we're still on for tomorrow."

Tomorrow. Saturday. He and Jeff were scheduled to meet for breakfast at The Victory.

On the radio, John Mellencamp was belting out "Small Town."

"Yeah. Seven o'clock. You still... kay with... at?"

"Sure. Where are you? You're breakin' up."

"Mill Road. Down... oopers Hollow... lasts a... ittle."

Mark paused and tapped his hand to the beat of the music. Jeff's voice boomed into his ear. "Am I back? Can you hear me now?"

"Yeah, I can hear you fine now," Mark said with a laugh.

Jeff snorted into the phone. "I always lose my bars along that stretch. Hey, I've been meaning to ask you..."

Jeff's voice was suddenly drowned by a hideous screaming. Not just one voice, but a multitude of voices mingling and colliding, merging and blending in a cacophony of wails and groans, grunts and cries. A million mouths weeping and howling in bone-crunching pain. Agony. As if their skin was being peeled off inch by inch and their burning anguish was somehow captured on audio. It rose in volume, lasted maybe five, six seconds, then stopped just as abruptly as it had started.

Mark clicked off the radio and pressed the phone tighter

against his ear. Goose bumps crawled over his arms. "Jeff? You OK, man?"

There was a pause, then, "Yeah. Yes. I'm fine. What the blazes was that? Did you hear it?"

Mark massaged the steering wheel with his left hand. "Yeah, I heard it. Sounded like something out of some horror movie." *Or hell. Weeping and gnashing of teeth.* "Weird."

"Maybe our signals got tangled with something else. Weird is right. Anyway, I've been wanting to ask you—and we can talk more about it tomorrow if you want—how are you and Cheryl doing?"

Mark clenched his jaw, pressing his molars together. Cheryl. *Don't make me go there, Jeff. It's too soon.* "I don't know. I think it's over."

"Over?"

Over. Finished. Kaput. I blew it, and now I have to live with it. "Nothing official yet. But she pretty much made it clear she doesn't want anything to do with me."

Jeff paused and sighed into the phone. "Man, I'm sorry. Is there anything I can do?"

Mark slowed the Mustang around a hairpin turn. He didn't want to talk about this now. He wasn't ready. And besides, it was late, and he was tired. "No. I don't even think there's anything more *I* can do. Can we talk about it in the morning?"

"Absolutely. I just...wait. Hang on a sec. What's this guy—"

The sound of screeching tires filled the receiver. Rubber howling against asphalt. Then a low earthy rumble...Jeff grunting...crunching metal and shattering glass.

Mark leaned heavy on the brake, and the Mustang fishtailed to a stop. The engine growled impatiently. "Jeff? You there?"

Nothing. Not even static. His pulse throbbed in his ears.

Mark dialed Jeff's number. Four rings. "Hello, this is Jeff."

Voice mail. Great. "You know what to do." A woman's voice came on. "To leave a voice message, press one or wait for the tone. To—"

Mark's thumb skidded over the keypad, dialing 911.

Sheriff Wiley Hickock sidestepped down the steep embankment, sweeping the light from his flashlight to and fro in a short arc. Up above, a couple of firefighters were winding a hose; two others were stripping out of their gear. Lights flashed in an even rhythm, illuminating the area in a slow strobe of red and white. Red, red, white; red, red, white. The pungent smell of melted rubber and burnt flesh permeated the air. Three towers holding four floodlights each lit up the area like a baseball stadium during a night game.

When he reached the bottom, Hickock surveyed the ball of twisted, smoldering metal that had once been a Honda Civic before it bulldozed ten feet of oak saplings and wrapped around the scarred trunk of a mature walnut tree. Tongues of smoke curled from the misshapen steel and licked at the leaves of the walnut. A large swath of ground had been dug up, exposing the dark, rich soil.

Deputy Jessica Foreman headed toward him. Her dark russet hair looked like it had been hastily pulled back in a loose ponytail. Her uniform was wrinkled, a road map of creases. Her hands were sheathed in blackened latex gloves.

Wiley frowned as she approached. "Sorry to get you out here on your day off, Jess. Thanks for helping out, though."

Jess tugged off the latex gloves and swept a rebellious lock of hair away from her face and tucked it behind her ear. "Do what's gotta be done, right?"

Wiley squinted and ran a finger over his mustache. "That's

what they say. When did fire and EMS get here?" There were still some firefighters milling around the wreckage, poking at it with their axes. Two paramedics were standing off to the right, talking and laughing.

"'Bout twenty minutes ago. Didn't take long to douse the fire." She glanced at the paramedics. "No need for those guys. Did you notice the skid marks on the road?"

Wiley nodded, keeping his eyes on what barely resembled a car. The driver was still in there. He could see his rigid, charred body still smoldering. Mouth open in a frozen scream. Lips peeled back. Back arched. Fingers curled around the steering wheel. He'd seen it only once before—a burned body. It was revolting, and yet there was something about it that held his gaze, as if the burnt stiff had reached out with those bony, black fingers and grabbed his eyeballs—*Look at me!*

He shut his eyes tight, trying to push the memory of the *other* burnt corpse from his mind. He knew it would never leave, though. It was seared there by some psycho-*something* branding iron.

Wiley opened his eyes and blinked twice. *Concentrate.* "Yup. Two sets of 'em. But only one car. I don't like it. Loose ends. What's your take?"

Jess shrugged and nodded toward the wreck. "Got run off the road by a drunk or sleeper, lost control, and met Mr. Tree."

"You sound fairly certain. Got a witness?"

Jess turned and pointed over her shoulder. "Almost. See that guy over there?"

Wiley looked up the embankment and saw a thirty-something average joe in a faded gray T-shirt and grease-stained jeans leaning against a classic Mustang, hair disheveled, arms crossed, shoulders slumped, eyes blank. "Yeah. Who's he?"

"*He* was on the phone with—" She jerked her thumb toward

the wreck and the stiff. "Said he heard the accident happen and called it in. Got here before anyone else, but the car was already a torch. Name's Stone. Mark. Said our friend here said something like 'What's this guy doin'?' then he heard the wheels lock up and busting up stuff, then nothing."

Wiley eyed Stone again. In the light of the cruiser's strobes, his eyes looked like two lifeless chunks of coal. His mouth was a thin line, jaw firm.

Wiley turned his attention back to the Civic. "Anything else?"

"No. Not yet anyway."

They both stood quietly, studying the remains of the car, until a man's high-pitched voice from their right broke the silence. "Sheriff."

Wiley turned to see Harold Carpenter, volunteer fire chief, high-stepping through the tall grass, his chubby jowls jiggling like Jell-O with each movement. With his sagging cheeks, underbite, and heavy bloodshot eyes, the man looked like a bulldog.

Carpenter stopped in front of Wiley, flushed and out of breath. "Sheriff. What'd ya think?"

Wiley didn't even look at him. He kept his eyes on the corpse sitting behind the wheel. "Just got here, Harry. Don't think much yet."

Carpenter shoved a singed, brown leather wallet at Wiley. "Here's the driver's wallet. One of my guys retrieved it from the...uh...back pocket."

Wiley took the wallet and handed it to Jess. Opening it, she slipped out the driver's license. It was singed around the top edge. "Jeffrey David Beaverson."

"Did you run the plates yet?" Wiley asked.

Jess nodded. "Sure did. Same Beaverson."

❸

It was a perfect day for a funeral. If such a thing existed.

The sky was a thick slab of slate suspended over the small town of Quarry, Maryland, coloring everything in drab hues of gray. A dense mist hung in the air, a blanket of moisture, covering the region in a damp clamminess. The air was cool but not cold, and there was no wind whatsoever.

Mark Stone walked from his car to the grave site, his black loafers sinking into the soft ground. With the exception of their little cluster of about twenty people, the cemetery was empty. Still and quiet. Eerie, Mark thought. For acres, granite headstones protruded from the ground like stained teeth, each memorializing somebody's loved one, lost forever. In the distance, maybe a hundred yards away, stood a mausoleum, a concrete angel perched on the roof above the doorway. Mark shuddered at the thought of a body lying inside. Dead and cold.

Mark looked to his right then to his left. The other mourners—friends and family of the Beaversons—were climbing out of their cars and making their way across the wet grass, shoulders slumped, heads bowed low. Men held black umbrellas against their shoulders; women held white tissues to their noses. A few trees dotted the landscape, their twisted, half-barren branches reaching into the gray sky as if begging for even a glimmer of life. But there was no life in a place like this. Only death.

Mark swallowed the lump that had become a permanent fixture in his throat and ran a sleeve across his eyes.

The reverend (Mahoney, was it?) stood beside the black, polished casket, faced Wendy Beaverson, and opened a little black book. He cleared his throat and began reading, "Jesus said to her, 'I am the resurrection and the life. He who believes in Me, though he may die, he shall live. And whoever lives and believes…"

Mark looked across the casket at Wendy. Her red, swollen eyes leaked tears that coursed down her cheeks in long rivulets. Her honey-colored hair was pulled back in a tight bun, accentuating the sharp angles of her face. She wore a black knee-length overcoat buttoned to the collar. In her left arm sat little Gracie, clinging to her mommy's neck.

Poor kid. She'll never remember her daddy. He was a great guy, sweetheart.

Wendy's right arm was draped over Sara's shoulder. The eldest daughter, just five, leaned against Wendy's hip, her head fitting perfectly in the dip of her mother's waist.

A sob rose in Mark's throat, and he struggled to keep it under control. Death was a beastly thing. Showed no mercy at all. A daddy torn from his family; children left confused and empty; wife suddenly bearing the burden of raising two daughters by herself, no one to share joys and heartbreaks with. What a crock.

Reverend Mahoney continued talking, his monotone voice a fitting backdrop to the dismal atmosphere. "And so, as we bury Jeffrey today, it is true to say we bury one of us. We bury him in a cemetery…"

Cheryl had an arm around Wendy's shoulders, holding her tight. She always was the caring type. A real Mother Teresa. Mark wiped at his eyes again and watched his wife comfort his best friend's wife. Widow.

"…I have never yet heard anyone say there is a different heaven for each faith…"

A splinter of guilt stabbed at Mark's heart, and he was suddenly glad he and Cheryl had not yet had kids. He'd hurt her enough. Ripped her heart out and tossed it in the garbage like last week's leftovers.

—*It's over, Mark. Done.*

—*Cher—Cheryl, wait . . . I—*

—*No! Wait? Wait for what? Wait for what, Mark? Your apology?*

—*Cheryl, please don't go—*

—*Shut up! You think saying you're sorry can make up for what you . . . what you did to me? To us?*

He would have never been able to bear knowing he'd not only betrayed Cheryl but betrayed a son or daughter, or both, as well. Hurting Cheryl was enough. More than enough. Seeing her now, he could barely stand to be in his own skin. If only. That's what he'd told himself a million times since she'd found out. If only this. If only that.

" . . . we are all the same before God . . . "

Life was full of *if onlys*, wasn't it? But the kick in the gut is that those *if onlys* become a phantom, a haunting, relentless ghost that clings to the soul like a parasite, slowly sucking the life from its host. But there's not a thing to be done about it. No one can change the past. What's done is done. Live with it.

Mahoney was still droning, " . . . we take nothing with us when we die . . . "

Cheryl looked up, and her gaze met Mark's. A knot twisted his stomach at the sight of her hollow eyes. They were once so brilliant, so alive, so . . . blue. The color of a Caribbean surf on a cloudless day. From somewhere deep in his *noodle* (that's what Cheryl would say) a memory surfaced. Mark didn't want it to surface, not now. Save it for some lonely time when he was parked on the sofa in front of the TV with a microwave dinner on a little folding tray.

The memory: sitting on a blanket in the park, Cheryl by

his side, her head on his shoulder, a cool breeze playing with her hair, bringing the scent of her shampoo so close he could almost smell it now. Cheryl tilts her face toward his.

—*What d'ya know, babycakes?*

—*I know I love you.*

—*Really? Forever and ever, cross your heart and hope to die?*

—*Forever and ever. Cross my heart and hope to die.*

But now those eyes were dull, muted by the pain of betrayal and the ache of death. Her face was drawn and pale, thinner than the last time he saw her.

I'm sorry, Cheryl. So sorry.

He wanted to scream the words, run to her and drop to his knees, but she would never forgive him. She held his stare for mere seconds, her eyes piercing his with a loneliness that he'd brought on.

Cheryl. Baby. Babycakes. I'm sorry.

"...So as we bury Jeffrey, we bury one of us..."

Mark shifted his weight, clasped his hands behind his back, and lowered his head, letting the mist cool the back of his neck.

When Mahoney finally finished, the mourners slowly cleared, whispering to each other. "Isn't it a shame." "What a horrible tragedy." "The poor woman. Two little girls with no daddy, but didn't they look precious."

Back to life as they know it. Life goes on. For some.

Wendy approached the casket and rested her hand on the glossy surface. She whispered something Mark couldn't quite make out. Little Gracie turned her head to look at the box that held her daddy, and Sara choked out a sob, her tender mouth twisting into a broken frown.

As Wendy passed Mark, she rested her hand on his forearm and squeezed. She didn't say anything, but her eyes said it all: *Thanks for coming.*

Mark forced a smile and nodded.

Cheryl followed Wendy. As she passed in front of Mark, he took her arm in his hand. "Cheryl, I—"

"Don't, Mark," she said, her voice strained with grief. She looked at the ground and her chin quivered. "Don't."

Mark let his hand fall to his side and let his wife walk out of his life. Again.

Ten minutes later he was sitting behind the wheel of his Mustang, tiny raindrops pattering on the windshield. The mourners were mostly gone now, heading to the Beaversons' home for the wake. He didn't want to go but knew he had to at least make an appearance...for Wendy. His mind wasn't on the wake, wasn't even on the funeral. It was on the screams. They were as fresh in his mind today as when he'd first heard them a week ago.

He'd raced to Cooper's Hollow after dialing 911. The first thing he saw was the gyrating orange glow of the fire on the horizon, retching a pillar of smoke as black as new charcoal into the night sky. The next thing he saw was Jeff's Civic engulfed in angry flames and Jeff pinned behind the steering wheel, bloated and stiff. The sound of the fire was like a locomotive. The smell of burning fuel and flesh was hot in his lungs.

The rest of the night was a black blur, a nightmare that would surface piece by piece until the whole ghastly affair played itself out like some cut-'em-up horror movie in his head. And he would be forced to watch, eyelids taped open and head held in place. The last thing he remembered was arriving home, falling into bed, and dreaming of Jeff's blackened corpse writhing in anguish as flames licked at his flesh and wrapped his body in hell's chains.

Mark ran his hands over his face, feeling the bristles of his morning stubble, a reminder that he hadn't shaved. He could still hear the screams, awful sounds, like thousands, no, millions, of voices lifted in agony, a chorus of misery and anguish. Every time the sounds of the outside world died and silence crept in like a demon, the screams were there, echoing through his head, filling his ears with the sound of the tortured. If it was nothing more than tangled signals like Jeff had suggested, where was the signal coming from? Hell, that's where.

He shut his eyes and pressed both palms to his forehead. Maybe the wake would take his mind off things.

Judge sat in an old brown metal desk chair in the center of a basement room, elbows resting on the armrests, fingertips lightly pressed together, forming a tent in front of his face. A gray metal desk sat against one wall, its surface covered with photo clippings and notebook paper scrawled with notes. To the left of the desk stood a metal bookshelf, empty except for one stack of spiral notebooks and manila file folders. To the right of the bookshelf stood a gray, metal, four-drawer locking file cabinet.

Everything was metal. Firm. Dependable. Solid.

Fire resistant.

In the center of the room, a single 60-watt bulb dangled from the ceiling, casting sharp shadows on the walls.

All four walls were covered with a collage of photos. A closer look would reveal that all the pictures were of four women in particular. One for each wall.

His four victims.

No, not victims. No way. They weren't victims. *She* was a victim. Katie was. *They* were perpetrators. Guilty and getting exactly what they deserved. Justice.

He stood, walked over to the wall behind the desk, and stared at a photo of a brown-haired woman in a miniskirt and halter top. Amber. He knew everything about her. Probably more than she knew about herself.

She got off work every night at ten. Took exactly thirty-seven seconds to walk the forty-five yards to her car. Drove a late model Chevy Cavalier that she bought from Prairie View Pre-Owned Cars eight months ago. License plate: LUV ME. Drove the five miles to her second-floor apartment in just under ten minutes, depending on traffic flow and traffic light patterns. She was thirty-one, five-six, hazel eyes, and drop-dead gorgeous.

Drop dead, gorgeous.

She *was* lovely, though, wasn't she?

But it wasn't about love. No way. Not even about desire or lust or hunger. He wasn't a pervert like some. Sure, he liked to look as much as the next guy, but when it came down to business, it wasn't about the needs of the flesh. It was about justice. And he was the judge and the jury.

That's why he called himself Judge.

She was guilty. They were all guilty.

He smiled and stroked the tuft of hair below his lower lip. He'd heard somewhere that it was called a soul patch. A fitting name. His soul needed to be patched.

He then smoothed his mustache with his left hand and gently stroked the photo with his right.

Justice would be served tonight. His heart beat a little faster at the thought, and his stomach fluttered. This is what he was born to do. Be an agent of justice. An enforcer of right.

An image flashed through his mind. A young girl, thirteen. Katie. She was innocent, and they killed her.

And he did nothing. Cowering like a frightened kitten, fighting the urge to vomit, struggling to find oxygen, he did nothing but watch in paralyzed horror.

Well, no more.

He glanced at his watch—8:27—and tapped a picture of Amber. "Soon."

The plan was ready, everything down to the last detail. Details were good. He would carefully execute the plan, documenting everything.

Tonight. Justice.

It's gonna be a hot time in the old town tonight.

Amber Mann slipped off her apron and hung it on a brass hook on the wall. She tucked a lock of hair behind her ear, stood on her toes, and looked at herself in the small mirror that someone had hung a little too high for the averaged-height waitress.

"You outta here, hon?" Marge, her co-waitress for the evening, emerged from one of the bathroom stalls and went to wash her hands.

Amber smoothed her eyeliner, puckered her lips, and applied a thin layer of lip gloss. "Yup." She glanced at the clock on the wall—the one with *Bertha's Diner* in fancy script painted across the face. Someone had given it to Bertha for the diner's twentieth anniversary. She didn't particularly care for the style, so she'd banished it to the lady's room. 9:57. "Three minutes and I'm punching out. I need every minute I can get."

Marge chuckled and tilted her head to the side. "You goin' out tonight?"

Amber shot her a sideways look and a devilish grin. "What's it to ya, mommy dearest?" She quickly unbuttoned her uniform shirt, slipped it off, and replaced it with a black tank top with thin shoulder straps. Yanking her pants off, she pulled on a black miniskirt that barely covered her fanny. She then slid her feet into a pair of black pumps.

"Well, if you ain't, you sure look good for just sittin' 'round your 'partment."

Amber laughed. "Yeah, I'm going out. Over to Bruno's, see what kind of action is happening tonight."

Marge put her hands on her hips and gave her a motherly look. "Well, be careful. Bruno's ain't the safest place for a girl lookin' like you to be goin'. Lotsa tough guys tryin' to impress the girls there."

Amber stuffed her uniform in a pink duffle bag. She grinned wide. "Don't worry about me, mommy. I can handle myself around the boys."

"You doin' anything special this weekend?" Marge said, drying her hands with a paper towel.

"Tomorrow I'm going over to my sister's to spend some time with my nephew. You should see him; he's so adorable. I just can't get enough of him. How 'bout you? Got any big plans?"

Marge humphed. "Yeah, right. All Jim wants to do is sit around and watch football. The old goat. I'll keep myself busy 'round the house, though."

Amber looked at the clock again. "Hey, it's time. Gotta run, Marge. Love ya, girl." She pulled on a red coat and gave Marge a loose hug.

"Love ya, hon."

They left the bathroom, and Amber headed for the back door. As she pushed through the door she heard Marge call out one more time, "You be careful now."

She let the door close and breathed in a chestful of cool autumn air. Bruno's should be hoppin' tonight. And Mitch would be there. She could almost feel his thick arms around her waist as they danced, her head on his chest, breathing in his masculine scent. They would stay like that for hours, bodies intertwined, moving in unison to the steady rhythm of the music, then go back to his place. It was perfect, heaven on earth if there ever was one.

She strode across the parking lot toward her car, heels clicking on the asphalt, echoing in the stillness of the evening. She hadn't told Marge about Mitch. He was a tattoo artist, had his own shop downtown. Mommy Marge would never approve. She watched over Amber like a mother hen, closer than her own mom did. Amber could just imagine what old Marge would say if she ever found—

She started and took a quick step to her left. A man was suddenly there, walking beside her, step for step. "Oh, hey. You scared me."

The man stopped and faced her. "Amber Mann?"

She stopped too. One hand rested on her duffle bag, the other hung loosely at her side. Somewhere in the distance, a few blocks away, a car horn honked. "Yes. Is something wrong?"

"Can I ask you a few questions?"

Amber brushed some hair off her face and tucked it behind her ear. She noticed her hand was suddenly shaking. "Uh, sure. Is something wrong?"

"No, ma'am. Nothing's wrong. Just need to ask you a few questions. It's about Mitch Young."

Mitch. Amber felt her stomach twist into a knot, like someone had gut-punched her. She knew what she had with Mitch wouldn't last. It couldn't. Her life didn't work that way. "Um." She bit on a fingernail, not sure if she wanted to answer questions, not sure she wanted to know Mitch's secrets. "I guess."

"Let's walk to your car," he said.

"Oh, OK." She turned and headed toward her Cavalier. She was within feet of the car when something exploded in the back of her head.

❻

It was nearly half an hour later by the time Judge dragged Amber to the barn. He'd had to knock her several times to subdue her enough to get the ether over her mouth and nose. She was quite the feisty one. It was too messy, though, too sloppy. During the time it took, someone could have driven by or come out of the diner. But she was the first. Now he knew; he'd have to be more careful with the others.

He gripped her by the wrists and pulled her into a corner where a bed of straw had been prepared. Outside the barn, the dogs were barking like maniacs, over and over, nonstop. Judge kicked hard against the barn wall. "Quit your bawling! Or I'll roast you!" The racket ceased for maybe five, six seconds—long enough to notice the sound of crickets in the distance—then resumed in a flurry of yelps and coughs.

Removing a pocketknife, he flipped it open and cut the duct tape from Amber's wrists and ankles. Just a precaution during the long ride over. He didn't need her coming to and throwing a hissy fit in the backseat while he was driving. Safety first.

She moaned and tried to roll over, but a grimace twisted her face and she relaxed again, letting out a strained sigh. He could see two goose eggs on her head but knew there were more. He'd walloped her at least three times.

"Sleep tight, beautiful," he said, squatting beside her. "You're gonna have one killer headache when you wake up."

The dogs continued their onslaught, like an old smoker trying to clear fluid from his lungs. Judge stood and kicked the boards again. "Shut up!"

Placing his hands on his hips, he looked around the barn. Enough light from the full moon was seeping through the cracks between the wall planks to dust the spacious interior with soft blue light. Straw, strewn across the floor like a loosely woven carpet, glistened under each moon ray. It was actually a very pleasant evening. What a shame to have to ruin it for little miss LUV ME here.

He stared at her for a moment, taking in her graceful, feminine form. She lay on her side, hand resting on her head, long legs slightly crossed. She was a fine specimen, indeed. But it wasn't about that, he reminded himself. It was about justice and justice only. Nothing more, nothing less. Don't personalize it.

But still, he couldn't deny the fact that she was beautiful. Maybe just a peek under that skirt. She would never know—

No! It's not like that. I'm not a monster.

He went outside, walked around to the back of the barn, and stopped in front of two metal dog kennels. Stooping to unlock them, he said, "Now boys, you keep good watch over our guest. And don't stray too far. She's gonna get lonely, you hear?"

Amber rolled onto her back and lifted both hands to her forehead. Her whole skull throbbed, felt like it would explode any second. She peeled her eyes open and noticed the first rays of light filtering through rough-planked walls, dust swirling in the air. Something crunched beneath her. Where was she? What happened last night? Her mind spun. She winced and ran a hand gently over her head. Where did she get these lumps? So tender. She moaned and tried to push herself to a sitting position, but her body felt like it was filled with lead, and her muscles refused to cooperate. Finally, she settled on scooting herself back and propping up on the mound of straw.

Straw? Wait a minute. She was on a bed of straw. She looked around again. Wooden planks rose vertically on either side of her about fifteen feet into the air, held together by wooden beams. A few slanted bars of sunlight slipped past the gaps in the planks and dotted the floor with golden light. Straw was scattered over the worn flooring.

Amber's mind was slowly beginning to piece things together. Straw. Wood. Beams. She was in a barn. For the first time since regaining consciousness, she drew in a long breath. Yes, definitely a barn. The musty, earthy odor of straw and rotting hay and who-knows-how-old animal dung was unmistakable.

She looked around. The barn was obviously abandoned. There were no stacks of bales, no tools, no tractors, and as she listened, no rustle of animals. As far as she could tell, she was the only occupant. She leaned to her left and pressed her face against a gap between two wall planks. Outside the barn, the ground sloped away toward what looked like an overgrown pasture. On the other side of the field, maybe a quarter mile away, stood a line of trees that stretched as far as she could see to the left and right. North and south. The sun peeked out just over the treetops, and beyond that, fingers of pink light reached into the pale blue sky.

A jolt of panic, like a thousand-volt shock, buzzed through her nerves.

Where was she? How did she get here? And how did her head get so banged up? The questions stood like giant bullies, refusing to leave until answered. Like her dad. An image of him towering over her, thick arms crossed, forehead wrinkled, asking over and over again "How many bales today?" flashed through her mind. How many bales? She was only nine. She just wanted to do a nine-year-old's worth of chores and go play. But he made her work and work and work. And if she didn't make her quota? Well, well, "You're not goin' anywhere, missy, until you finish your chores." He'd corner her and fire questions at her, quizzing her on mundane farm facts—how many square feet in an acre, how many acres in a square mile, how many quarts in a peck and pecks in a bushel—and wouldn't let her eat or sleep until she answered every one correctly. The bully.

But this time she had an answer, one that made her shiver. She'd been kidnapped. Taken against her will. Abducted. Apparently beaten and…she didn't even want to think about what else. Instinctively, she tugged at her skirt, wishing she'd worn pants.

Slowly, like a TV station slowly picking up the signal from a rotary antenna, her memory faded in. She left work last night and a man approached her in the parking lot. She remembered his face, lean and angular, mustache and patch of hair under his bottom lip. But that was all. Just his face. He'd asked her a question, she knew that. But what the question was, was yet another question. Unanswered.

And what about Liz? She was supposed to visit Liz and Christopher today. Surely they'd miss her and report it, right? They'd have cops looking for her before the day was over. Or maybe not. Maybe Liz would just assume something came up, something more important. But if Liz didn't report it, surely Mitch would. She was supposed to meet him last night. Mitch. He must have been worried sick when she didn't show. That settled it in her mind. By the end of the day, there would be a massive search effort underway. There had to be. Somebody would miss her.

She pulled her knees up and looked out between the planks again. Suddenly, a furry, toothy face appeared only inches away, mouth curled into a snarl. A dog! Then another face appeared. Two dogs! Dobermans. Outside the barn. The dogs began clawing at the planks, snarling and growling. Amber tried to push herself away from the wall, but her hand slipped on the straw, and she tumbled to her side. A jolt of pain shot up her neck and pounded in her head, and she let out a scream.

"I see you're awake," a voice said from one of the far corners. A man's voice.

Amber started and sat up straight, her head scolding her for the sudden movement. She searched the far corners of the barn and noticed a man standing in one. He was wearing jeans and tanned leather work boots. The rest of his body was hidden in the shadows.

"Good morning," he said. His voice was in no way cheerful but not altogether sinister either. The voice from last night. This was the man she'd met in the parking lot. And no doubt the man who gave her the killer headache and brought her here.

Amber tried to push farther back against the wall, but she was already pressed against it. She tugged again at her skirt. "Who are you?"

The man shifted his weight and crossed one leg over the other. "No need to bother with names here. Let's not make this personal. You can just call me Judge. There's a gallon of water and bag of apples to your right. That should hold you over for now."

The dogs to Amber's left began chewing at the wooden planks, snarling, their tongues flitting in and out of their mouths. Amber shot them a wary look.

"Don't worry about them," the man said. "They can't get in. They're to keep you from getting out. Don't even think about making a run for it. We're miles from nowhere, and the dogs are very hungry. Do you know what it's like to be eaten alive? Meat pulled from your bones while you're still kicking and screaming? No, of course you don't. And trust me, you don't want to find out."

Amber covered her mouth with her hand and choked back a sob. Her eyes burned with tears, and a lump the size of one of those apples had lodged in her throat. Fear had wrapped its bony fingers around her neck and tightened its grip. "What—what are you gonna do with me? Why am I here? What do you want?"

The man chuckled and uncrossed his legs. "Soon enough, my dear. You'll get answers to all your questions soon enough. You'll be getting some company too. I don't want you getting lonely all the way out here. The dogs are good for some things, but they're lousy conversationalists."

There was a long moment of silence, and though she couldn't see them, masked by the shadow as they were, she could feel his eyes on her. And it made her skin crawl.

Finally, he walked to a cutout door in the middle of the larger, rolling barn door, opened it, and paused, still obscured by a slanting shadow. "Until later, Amber." And then he was gone. She heard a lock slide into place and something large and heavy thud against the door at the bottom.

To her left, the Dobermans continued their gnawing and chewing.

It was almost three o'clock in the afternoon when Mark finally took a break to eat lunch. After the funeral yesterday he'd gone to the wake and numbly stood in a corner of the den in Jeff's home (the same den where he'd spent countless hours playing poker, shooting pool, and rooting for the Washington Redskins) nursing his iced tea and watching Cheryl mingle with their friends. Correction, *her* friends. After she left him and the news became public, *their* friends suddenly wanted nothing to do with him. Jeff and Wendy were the only ones who had remained loyal. The rest had proven to be fair-weather friends—the worst kind.

He'd spent less than an hour at the wake, returned home, fell onto the sofa, clicked on the flat screen, and zoned out. How long he sat there or what he watched he had no idea. But it was late, wee-hours-of-the-morning late, by the time exhaustion finally overtook him. When he'd had enough, he trudged into the bedroom, the one he *used to* share with his wife, and collapsed on the bed, falling quickly asleep still wearing his dress clothes.

This morning he'd debated whether to go into work or not. It was, after all, Saturday. He could stay home and play zombie all day, regretting how his life had turned out, regretting every poor decision he'd ever made, regretting there was nothing he could have done to save Jeff. Or he could go to the garage, lose himself in some engine or transmission, and hopefully keep his mind off the hopelessness of life and retain his sanity for another day.

The prospect of sanity finally won.

Mark sat in a gray swivel chair in his cubicle-sized office and opened his cooler. Ham sandwich, barbecue chips, and an apple. He wasn't hungry, but he unwrapped the sandwich and took a large bite anyway.

Jeff's death was a shock, of course, and Mark's heart ached for Wendy and the girls. Every time he pictured the girls in their pretty dresses standing beside that casket, a lump rose in his throat, and his eyes burned with tears. But one thing that kept hammering in his mind like a hyperactive woodpecker was the phone call he had with Jeff just before the accident. There was that awful scream that had interrupted the conversation. What was it? Where did it come from?

Mark took a long swig of Diet Pepsi, wiped the condensation from his hand, and took another bite of his sandwich. In the main shop area, his boom box belted out some guy singing.

"...you had a bad day..."

23

Mark grunted. That pretty much summed it up. How 'bout bad life?

His mind went back to the scream. At the time he'd thought nothing of it. Just some interference in the cell phone signal or something. But now, for some reason he couldn't explain, he wasn't so sure. But what was it? It was the first time he'd ever heard such a thing, and it just so happened to occur on the same night—only minutes before—Jeff got in a bizarre car accident and died? Not just died, burned to death. Weird. Very weird.

He reached for a chip and flipped it into his mouth just as the phone on his desk rang.

Mark quickly chewed the chip, took a gulp of Diet Pepsi, and answered the phone on the third ring. "Stone Service Center."

"Mark, it's Jerry down at Detweiler's. How's it going?"

Crappy, Jerry, but thanks for asking. That's what he wanted to say, but he had no desire to talk about Jeff's death yet. Play it safe. "'Bout half. What, you working Saturdays now too?"

Jerry chuckled. "When business is good you do what it takes to keep it that way."

"You got a point there."

"Hey, I have that fuel injector you ordered. For the '99 Cavalier. You—"

Screams cut off Jerry's voice like a guillotine. *The* screams. The same ones Mark had heard before—before Jeff died. Hideous, tortuous wails and groans. An image of thousands, maybe millions, of twisted faces, distorted with pain, flashed through his mind and his blood ran cold, as if someone had jammed an IV of ice water into his vein. Goose bumps freckled his skin, and his neck and jaw tingled. His throat suddenly tightened, and he found it hard to breathe.

Like last time, it lasted maybe five seconds then ceased abruptly.

"Mark? Mark, you still there?" Jerry was talking to him, but Mark's mind was not registering it as actual words spoken to him. They were off in the distance somewhere. "Hello?"

"Uh, yeah, Jerry, I'm still here." He had to force the words out past his restricting trachea.

"Did you hear that?"

Mark closed his eyes, willing his muscles to relax. He took a deep breath. "Yeah, I heard it."

"What was it? Sounded like screaming."

Like hell itself. "I know. I don't know what it was."

Jerry snorted into the phone. "Crazy. Anyway, I'll run the injector over to you right now."

Mark still wasn't thinking clearly. He was still hearing the screams ringing in his ears. "O-OK. No, wait! Jerry. Wait."

"I'm waiting. What is it?"

"Are you calling from a landline?"

"You mean a regular phone? Yeah. Why?"

A thought had suddenly occurred to Mark, and it made his heart thump. He was on a landline too. There was no way the screams were some kind of interference, signals crossing with something else. "Um, nothing. Just wondering. You don't have to bring the injector out here. I'll come get it."

There was a pause, and Mark could hear paper rustling in the background. "No, I'll drop it off. I have a couple other parts to deliver, and you're on the way."

Panic seized Mark. He gripped the phone tighter with a sweaty palm, tried to sound calm. This was crazy! "Jerry, really, I insist. I need to get out of the shop for a little. Cabin fever thing, you know? I've been putting in some long hours, and I'm getting stir-crazy. I'm leaving right now. I'll be over in ten minutes. Don't go anywhere, OK?"

"But—"

"Jerry, please." He knew his voice was rising, and he knew Jerry probably thought he'd completely lost his grip on reality, but he didn't care anymore. He pressed his molars together then relaxed them. "Don't go anywhere. I'm coming right over. OK?"

"OK, OK. I'll wait for you. Don't be too long. I got things to do, you know."

Mark blew out a breath and loosened his grip on the receiver. "Thanks. See ya in a few."

"OK. A few."

Mark raced down Broadway in his 1973 Ford Mustang, slowing only for the dips in the road at each intersection. Pineville was a small town, hokey even, and anywhere one wanted to go in any direction was no more than a ten-minute drive—going the posted speed limits. But Mark wasn't anywhere near the posted limit.

His mind raced too. He'd heard it again, hadn't he? Were the screams real? Of course they were. He'd heard them with his own ears. *Weeping and gnashing of teeth.* And Jerry heard them too. So did Jeff. They were real, all right. Too real. Made his skin itch just thinking about it.

Crazy. That's all Mark could make of it. And his bizarre reaction. Just because Jeff died shortly after the screams didn't mean Jerry was in immediate danger. Or any danger at all, for that matter.

Crazy. Jerry had to think he was half out of his mind. Maybe he was.

But what if he wasn't? What if there really was something to the screams? What if Jerry's life really was in jeopardy? He couldn't afford to be wrong. Jerry couldn't afford it. No, he'd done the right thing. Jerry was safer just staying put and waiting for Mark to pick up the injector.

At the intersection of Broadway and Clayton, Mark slowed the 'Stang just enough to keep rubber on asphalt and took the ninety-degree turn at a tire-screaming speed. An elderly man working in his garden jerked his head up and around and yelled an obscenity, flailing his arms wildly.

Up ahead, Detweiler's sat on the corner of Clayton and Monroe. Mark pressed the accelerator; the engine rumbled, tachometer climbed steadily. Just before the entrance to Detweiler's parking lot, he stomped on the brake and jerked the steering wheel hard to the right. The car bounced into the parking lot and came to a stop.

Mark jumped out of the car and ran for the front door. His pulse was pounding out a steady rhythm in his ears, and the adrenaline rush had left him nearly out of breath. He was lucky to make it here without getting pulled over.

Swinging open the glass door, he stepped inside and called for Jerry. When no answer came, he looked around and noticed the store was empty. No customers in the aisles. No Jerry behind the counter.

C'mon, Jerry. Don't tell me you left anyway.

Mark peered out the storefront window and saw Jerry's tan Chevy S-10 sitting in the parking lot, *Detweiler's Auto Parts* emblazoned across the door panel.

"Jerry!" He listened and approached the counter. "Hey, Jerry. It's Mark. You here?"

No answer.

"Hello? Jerry?"

Still no answer.

Mark leaned over the counter and nearly choked on his own

saliva. There, behind the counter, lying prone on the cement floor, was Jerry Detweiler.

Mark rushed around the counter and rolled the large man over. Jerry's empty eyes, like two blank TV screens, bulged toward the ceiling, mouth open, a trickle of blood curling around his nostril. Mark pressed his fingers against Jerry's carotid but felt nothing. No life-giving blood pumping through the artery. No steady pulse throbbing under his fingertips. A groan escaped from somewhere deep in Mark's chest, and he clenched his jaw tight, cursing under his breath.

Jerry was dead. But it couldn't have happened more than five minutes ago. Mark had just talked to him, and the drive here only took seven minutes tops. He reached for the phone on the counter and punched in 911. Then, with phone jammed between his ear and shoulder, he placed both hands on Jerry's barrel chest, one on top of the other, and started compressing.

Chapter 2

❶

BRIGHT RAYS OF WARM MORNING SUN SLICED BETWEEN the planks and landed on Amber, stirring her out of a deep sleep. She rolled to her back, opened her eyes, and focused on the rafters high above. A family of bats hung silently, adjusting their wings to settle in for a day's worth of slumber. Birds sang a cheerful melody from a nearby tree, but other than that it was still and quiet.

Wait a minute. Quiet. No dogs. She rubbed her eyes, sat up, and scooted over to the wall. Leaning her face against the planks, she searched the outside for any sign of the Dobermans.

A gentle breeze rustled through the treetops. Long, cirrus clouds stretched across a bright sky. The pasture glistened like glitter as morning light danced on the dew. It was chilly, and her skin puckered with goose bumps. She remembered the weatherman saying the overnight temperatures were going to be in the upper forties all week.

But all was quiet. Maybe her four-footed prison guards had wandered away in search of food.

She had no idea what time it was, but from the low position of the sun in the sky, she figured it to be about eight or nine. She did know it was Monday morning, though. She'd been in the barn for two full days with no sign of her abductor. Judge, he called himself. Odd. Would he ever come back? Or was he just going to leave her here to dehydrate and rot? Trapped in this musty old barn—a wooden tomb. The first day, Saturday, she'd screamed and screamed until her lungs burned and her voice was hoarse, but no help had come. She truly was in the middle of nowhere. Where *nowhere* was, though, she hadn't a clue. Was she still in Maryland? Did he take her to some remote farm in West Virginia? Or Pennsylvania? Either way, no matter where she was, she would surely die here.

Suddenly, an attempt at escape didn't sound so bad. She didn't know how much longer she could survive here. She tried to drink the water and eat the apples sparingly but found it harder than she thought. Her growling stomach had been very persistent. The result was less than half a gallon of water and two apples left. Add that to the fact that she had no toilet paper, no blankets to keep her warm during the cool nights, a bed of uncomfortable straw she shared with a nest of mice, and the fact that the Dobermans, those demon dogs from hell, were always waiting, and she didn't know how much longer she could hold on to her sanity.

She climbed to her feet, ignoring the pounding headache that only intensified whenever she was upright. The lumps on her head had gone down but were still very tender. She'd concluded the first day that she probably had a concussion, and all kinds of images of blood clots and slipping into a coma swam through her cloudy mind. When she was sixteen, her brother fell from the loft of their barn and landed on his head. He was in a coma for three weeks, then in rehab for three months. The doctors said the only thing that saved his life was the fact that he was only eighteen and his brain was still pliable enough to adapt and compensate for the injured areas.

She was thirty-one and doubted her brain was very pliable. That sent a wave of panic over her. She could easily slip into a coma here and nobody would know. Who knows how long she would last. How long can a person survive without water? Just a few days, she thought. At least she would die in her sleep. Better than being fully aware of the fact that her body was gradually wasting away and life was slowly oozing out of her.

But since the coma, the most attractive option, was no guarantee, she had to try to escape. It really was the only way. She walked over to the wall, stretching her aching back and legs, and leaned against it, scanning the countryside for any sign of the dogs. She then went to the other three walls and peered through them. No dogs. They had to have gone off in search of food. Now was her time. Now or never.

She walked over to the cutout door and placed her hand on the latch. It was locked, but she'd expected that. She jiggled the latch, pushed against the door, rammed it with her shoulder, but it didn't budge. Something was blocking it at the bottom. Looking between the planks, she saw a large cinder block sitting on the ground, snug up against the door. She tried pushing it, lying on her back and kicking at it with both feet, then sticking the heel of her pumps through a one-inch gap between the planks and rocking it, but it didn't move.

Looking around the interior of the barn, she was once again reminded of the futility of her situation. The structure had been gutted, the loft removed. It was literally four walls, a roof, straw, bats, and her. And the mice. A cloud of doom settled over her, and she sat on her haunches and cried. For the first time since waking in this prison two days ago she let the tears flow. And flow they did. Sobs shook her shoulders and burned in her throat for what seemed at least twenty minutes.

When she had wiped her tears with her shirt, she rocked back on her hands and stared at the rafters. A thought suddenly entered her mind. A thought from somewhere deep in her past, her childhood. From where it came she had no idea since she hadn't entertained such a thought in over two decades. When she was a child, her mother had taken her and her brother to a Nazarene church until her father had finally forbid it.

The thought came again: she should pray.

It was a silly thought, she had to admit. A childish thing to be thinking at a time like this. Or was it? She remembered her Sunday school teacher saying that God listened to our prayers. That He cared. But did He care about her? Did He even know who she was?

She wrestled with the thought a few more moments, then settled the matter. If God was God, then of course He knew who she was. Whether He actually cared about her or not remained to be seen.

God, I know I haven't talked to You in some time.

Praying after so many godless years felt awkward. Maybe she should say it out loud. "I'm sorry I sorta forgot about You. That wasn't right." She looked around the barn again, nothing but wood and straw. "I, uh, could really use some help right now. Please show me a way out of this. I want to live." There, it was done. Not the most eloquent prayer He'd hear today, of that she was sure, but it was sincere. She meant every word.

She waited a few minutes for some great revelation to appear, a flood of light, a booming voice, an angel in bright array, something, but nothing happened.

Standing to her feet, she took a step toward the door again when her toe caught on a warped board. Bending low to the floor, she pushed straw out of the way and inspected the board. A chill buzzed down her back. Of course! The trapdoor for shoveling straw and hay to the animals below. Why didn't she think of it earlier? In a barn like this, built on a small hill, there was a basement of sorts where the animals were kept. Feed and bedding were stored on the first floor, animals below. She wiped the rest of the straw from the door and checked the latch. It was open!

Just then the low whine of an engine broke the silence. Amber jumped up and ran to the wall, pressing her face against the boards. A white sedan was bouncing down the dirt lane, a cloud of dust in its wake. She kicked the boards and cursed. Her mind began to race. She looked through the crack again. The car was almost there. It had to be the maniac. Judge. Quickly, she ran to the trapdoor, pushed a thick layer of straw over it, and sat in her corner.

Moments later the engine shut off and a car door slammed. A figure appeared outside the barn door, rolled the cinder block away, fiddled with the lock, and swung open the door.

"Well, well, awake are we?" Judge said, stepping through the cutout doorway. He had a brown paper bag in his arm, but his face remained in the shadows.

"I brought you some things. Water, apples, toilet paper." He set the bag on the floor and stepped toward the door. "Are you finding your accommodations cozy?"

Amber did not answer, did not even attempt to look at him. She had a stubborn streak that ran through her like a vein of cold iron ore, forged from years of withstanding her father's psychological abuse.

"Well, you won't be here long, my dear. And tonight you'll be getting some company." Then he stepped through the doorway, pushed the door closed, locked it, and shoved the cinder block back in place.

Amber dropped her head into her hands.

Outside, Judge began hollering. "Buck! Duke! Get over here!"

In the distance the faint sound of barking echoed over the pasture. The dogs were back. The barking grew closer until it was just outside the barn.

"Hey! Where've you been?" Judge was hollering. He cursed loudly then grunted, and one of the dogs yelped. Then another curse, another grunt, another yelp.

"Do your job and keep watch!"

The car door closed; the engine revved to life, and the sound of wheels rolling over packed dirt ground through the barn. Amber got up slowly, walked to the wall, and watched as the white sedan disappeared over the horizon, leaving a tan trail of dust billowing into the still air.

The Dobermans were circling the barn, noses to the ground, hungrily searching for a morsel of food.

Judge liked the light dim when he meditated. The single bulb hanging from the ceiling gave no light. Instead, an oil lamp, resting on the top shelf of the metal bookcase, cast an orange undulating glow around the small room.

He leaned back in his desk chair, stroked his soul patch, and studied the wall before him. The pictures of Amber had been removed, and a new face had taken their place.

Virginia. Friends call her Ginny.

Now only three walls were adorned with photos—in front of him, to his right, and to his left. Three to go. But the other two would remain nameless until their time came. That was his way. One at a time. Focus on one guilty soul at a time.

Virginia. He was no friend.

He'd already found out all he needed to know about her. Twenty-five. Five-three. Brown hair. Brown eyes—eyes like deep pools of dark chocolate. Single. Drove an '02 Ford Focus. Silver. Plates ABD-6488. Employed for the last three years with Just For You Salon. Cosmetologist. She worked the afternoon/evening shift, got off at 9:30, walked to her car with a friend, took twenty minutes to drive home, and arrived at 42 Broad Court by herself at precisely 9:55. Give or take.

He'd wait for this one at home. Nice and dark, secluded area, and plenty of shade. It had taken him almost two weeks to find her. She'd be easy.

Virginia. He let her name resonate through his mind, focusing on her face, her quick gait, perfect posture, shoulders back, chin up, pelvis tilted just so. He envisioned a hardwood gavel dropping on the bench. The sound of wood on wood echoing through the still courtroom. Guilty! *Sorry, Virginia, but the long arm of the law eventually catches up to all of us. You did the crime, now you must pay the time.*

He knew full well *she* didn't do the crime. Well, she must have committed some crime in her life for which she had yet to pay. Speeding violation. Tax fraud. DUI. Something. But she hadn't committed *the* crime. Those girls were long gone. He'd kept track of them for a good many years, following their movements around the country, their multiple marriages, multiple families, multiple name changes, but they'd scattered too far, become too obscure. With his other responsibilities it was too much to keep up with, and too risky. Someday, though, justice would find them, in its own way, in its own time. For now, for him, it wasn't so much the need to render justice on *them* as it was the need to render justice for justice's sake. For Katie's sake. *Someone* had to pay.

Katie. He closed his eyes, rested his hands on his lap, and let his mind replay the events of so many years ago.

❸

1974

Katie McAfee was a tomboy who lived on a small family farm in western Garrett County. Her strawberry blonde hair was shoulder length and always parted into two perky pigtails. Her nose was spattered with light brown freckles (*sprinkled* is how she used to put it), her mouth permanently bent into a smile, and her blue eyes were brighter than the afternoon sky on a cloudless day.

The first time Judge met Katie, she was hoisting bales of hay into an old '59 Ford farm truck. Rust dotted the side panels, the paint had long been faded, and the front bumper was cockeyed, like it was smirking. Katie later told him, "My dad tried to move the bull with it, but ole Otis just pushed back. And Otis won."

His dad knew Katie's dad through some mutual friend, and they had arranged it so Judge could work the summer at the McAfee farm. He wasn't too thrilled about the idea at first, but after one look at Katie in those worn jeans with the hole in the seat, he was a card-carrying farm boy. Loved it so much he even volunteered to show up on Saturdays and help out for free. "I got nuthin' better to do, anyway," he said, trying to sound casual. But everyone knew the real reason a twelve-year-old boy would volunteer to spend his Saturday mucking out horse stalls had nothing to do with priming his work ethic or an inbred love of animals and everything to do with a certain twelve-year-old girl.

That summer, he and Katie saw each other every day except Sunday. That's when he would attend Heritage Baptist Church with his parents and sit and stand when he was supposed to, say "Amen, brother" and "Praise the Lord" and "God is so good" when it was appropriate, and joyfully place exactly seventy-five cents— one-tenth of his weekly pay—in the felt-lined offering plate.

Yes, Sunday was the Lord's Day, and no work was permitted. They wouldn't even think of going out for lunch after church because his dad said them going out made the people at the restaurant work, and that was "displeasin' to the Lord." Though he never could figure out why it wasn't displeasin' for Mom to spend an hour in the kitchen preparing Sunday dinner. It was just one of those things he never would understand. Like why it was so important to have his hair trimmed short enough that it didn't touch his collar or ears, or why he could never go to the matinee over in Spicerville like so many of his friends, or why he couldn't wear shorts in the summer, even when it was so hot you could fry an egg on the hood of Mr. McAfee's old Ford pickup.

He spent eleven weeks that summer working side by side with the prettiest girl he ever saw, and when the last week finally arrived, a knot had twisted itself somewhere in his stomach and made it hard to even eat. Katie commented on his lack of appetite every day at lunchtime, but he would just shrug his shoulders and say he wasn't feeling well, maybe it was the heat. If she only knew how he really felt about her. Soon, he would only see her on Saturdays if Dad allowed it. That thought made the twist grow tighter, so tight he actually thought he would vomit.

Finally, the last Saturday of the summer arrived. School started Monday. If he remembered right, which of course he did—he would never forget that day—it was a warm, clear day, with a light breeze that rustled the treetops and blew straw around outside the barn. The smell of freshly bailed alfalfa was thick in the humid air. They had spent the day cleaning out the two horse trailers and refilling the water troughs for the cows. At four o'clock on the dot (he remembered it was exactly four because he had been waiting all day for the hour to strike) he looked around and asked Katie to go to the barn with him...

37

"There's something I need to tell you," he says, his voice wavering.

Katie's permanent smile widens, and her eyes sparkle as if she knows exactly what he is up to. (*Is there a more beautiful girl in all the good Lord's creation?*) "Sure. What is it?"

He shoves his hands in his pockets and kicks at some straw on the hard-packed dirt. "Just something I need to tell you is all."

They walk to the barn in silence, he with his hands buried in his pockets to hide the trembling (*this cursed trembling, and I probably have red blotches all over my neck too*), she with her hands clasped behind her back, head turned skyward, watching the clouds as she likes to do.

When they arrive at the barn, they step inside, and he walks to the far corner, where a wall of barley bales stands over ten feet high. He faces her, slips his hands out of his pockets, and wipes his sweaty palms on his jeans. "Um—"

Unexpectedly, the moment Judge opens his mouth a lump rises in his throat, and for a second he thinks he is going to cry. (*Cry! In front of Katie! Don't you dare.*) He swallows hard and tries to continue. He has to say this.

"Um, there's something I been wanting to tell you."

He looks around the barn nervously. The breeze has swung the door shut, and the only light comes from a thick shaft of sunlight pouring in from a missing board in the loft. Dust floats lazily through the ribbon of light, sparkling like glitter. A sparrow flits around up in the rafters, its tiny wings beating against the still air. Judge is suddenly very aware of his heart banging in his ears and the sound of his own breathing.

Katie reaches out and takes his hands in hers. It's the first time they've ever held hands, and it makes his pulse spike. She smiles again (*an angel's smile*), her perfect teeth glowing in the muted light. "It's OK. You can tell me anything."

He swallows and shifts his weight. "Um, well, I just wanted to say that—" His palms are sweating like a spigot. (*Why can't I make them stop?*) She has to be grossed out. And his heart feels like it's in his throat. (*This is not going well at all, I should bail now.*) For some reason, he glances over at the sunbeam and finds the glitter floating carelessly through the air. Oddly, it seems to calm him just enough that he can continue without making a complete fool of himself. "—this summer has been great and, well, and, um—"

Katie gives his hands a squeeze and leans just an inch closer. He can smell her now, all flowers and farm. "Just say it. It's OK."

He forces a nervous smile. "O-OK." It is at that moment, the moment when he determines to just say it, that the world stands still. He swears the earth has stopped spinning on its axis, clocks have stopped ticking, the sun stands still, that floating glitter has frozen in space, and the sparrow has hushed its beating wings. Even his pulse seems to stop. It's a moment that will change his life. (*Nothing will be the same again.*) He will never be the same again. He looks her right in those forever-blue eyes and the words just ease out. "Katie, I love you."

Judge stroked his soul patch slowly, aware that his hand was shaking and his breathing rate had increased. The words sat in his mind like a lump. *Katie, I love you.* He'd really said it, hadn't he? At least she knew how he felt. At least he'd had one chance to speak his mind…his heart.

I'm not a monster.

❺

Here he was again, at another funeral. Jeff's was just days ago and still so fresh in his mind. He didn't have to come to Jerry's; no one expected it of him. Heck, he barely knew the guy, except to buy auto parts from him. Jerry seemed nice enough, though. Always willing to go out of his way to make a delivery. And for that, Mark had given him all his business. Even when that chain store moved into town last year and Jerry lost a ton of patrons, Mark made it a point to let the older man know he'd never lose Stone Service Center's account.

Now Jerry was dead, and Mark would have to go to the chain store. He hated the thought.

The minister was going on about what a religious man Jerry was. What did he know? Just a few months ago, while delivering a carburetor, Jerry had gotten Mark on the subject of religious fanatics and had admitted to not setting foot in a church in over fifty years. Said he was born and baptized Episcopalian, and that's all he needed. Mark had agreed with him, but deep in his heart, where a man really knows what's what, where the soul communicates with the mind, Mark knew he was wrong. There was more to it than that. But who was he to say anything? He was no theologian and definitely no Bible scholar. Unless eighteen years of Sunday school qualified one for Bible scholar status. And he hardly thought it did.

Reverend Wutsisname was still spouting off. "...an honest businessman, a devoted family man, a loyal husband..."

That made Mark flinch. *Loyal husband.* If it were him lying in that brown box, and his loved ones and friends standing around dabbing at their eyes, that part would have to be left out. Mark was a lot of things, mostly positive, but loyal he was not. And it killed him to admit it. But it had killed Cheryl even more.

—Cheryl, when are you coming home? We—

—You don't get it, do you? I'm not coming home, Mark. Not now, not soon, not ever.

—We need to talk about this sometime. You can't just throw our marriage away.

—Me? Throw our marriage away? You're the one who killed our marriage. You killed what we had. Don't you dare try to put the blame on me.

—I'm not blaming you, but . . .

The realization burned in his stomach like an ulcer. How many times over the past few months had he wished he could turn back time, tell Rachel no, avoid her, do whatever needed to be done, anything to save his marriage.

He'd give anything—literally *anything*—to have that one moment back again.

Cheryl. Dear, sweet Cheryl. I'm so sorry, baby. You have to know that.

Mark looked around the small group that had gathered. Jerry's wife—he didn't even know her name—was standing across from him, black dress, black hat, black veil. She was a petite woman with olive skin, small features, fragile hands, and very dark eyes. Through the veil he could see her red-rimmed, swollen eyes and red nose. She kept bringing a laced handkerchief to her nose and struggled to choke back the sobs that wanted to rack her frail frame. Beside her stood a tall man, middle-aged, with jet-black hair. Must be Jerry's son. He talked about him from time to time. An accountant or something. Bob. Or was it Rob? He was wearing dark sunglasses, had his arm draped over his mother's shoulders, and his head bowed low. The bright sun glistened off his silky hair. Beside Bob—or Rob—was a slender, attractive woman that must have been his wife. She leaned into him like a frightened little girl. Like Sara

Beaverson had leaned into Wendy, finding some solace in the strength of her mother.

A gentle breeze tossed Mark's hair to the side, and the sound of children playing in the distance carried across the cemetery. They were screaming and giggling with delight.

Screaming.

The sound of *those* screams suddenly filled Mark's ears again, reminding him again of the two phone calls he'd received. One from Jeff; one from Jerry. Both were interrupted by those screams—*weeping and gnashing of teeth*—and both had died. What they were or where they came from, Mark had no idea. He'd spent the last two days searching for possibilities, probabilities, answers of any kind, and had come up with nothing. They were just screams from somewhere...or nowhere. Maybe some weird crossed-wire thing. Maybe some nut job prank caller with the techno skills to pull it off. But how would he know Jeff and Jerry would die? Maybe the screams were from another dimension. Yeah right. *Twilight Zone* stuff. At the end of it all, he was right back where he started—with nothing.

The good reverend was wrapping it up: "In the name of the Father, the Son, and the Holy Ghost, amen and amen."

Jerry's wife laid a rose on the casket, dabbed at her nose again. Her son gave her shoulder a little squeeze and guided her away from the burial site.

When they came to where Mark was standing, Jerry's wife stopped and looked up at him. There was a look of emptiness and despair in her dark eyes that Mark had never seen before. They were hollow, blank, like someone had sucked the life right out of them and left her with two empty orbs.

She reached out with a thin, shaky hand and took his hand in hers. It was cold and dry and bony. But her grip was surprisingly strong.

"Are you the man who tried to save my Jerry?" Her voice was strained and weak, and she struggled to rein in a sob in the middle of the question.

Mark squeezed her hand gently and nodded, fighting the baseball in his throat. "Yes. I'm sorry."

After calling 911, he'd given Jerry CPR until the paramedics came. When they finally arrived he had collapsed with exhaustion, sucking wind like a man who'd just finished running a marathon.

"Sorry?" Her eyes widened and chin quivered.

—*Sorry? You're sorry? What does that mean, Mark. What does sorry do?*

—*What do you want me to say?*

—*Nothing. Don't say anything at all.*

She placed her other hand on top of his. "Son, you don't have to be sorry. His time was up is all. I've been harping on him for years to get that heart of his checked out, but Jerry was such a stub'rin man." She paused and nearly smiled, and Mark saw, for just an instant, a flash of life in those eyes, like when the sun breaks through on a stormy day, but just for a moment and then is gone again. "He was so stub'rin."

She patted his hand. A tear slipped from her eye and traced a track down a deep groove in her cheek, finally lodging near the corner of her mouth. "His time was up is all. Jerry was never a religious man, y'know. I tried and tried to get him to come to church, but he said he never did like being around churchgoin' hypocrites."

She looked up, and her eyes met his directly. They seemed to bore holes in his brain. Mark tried to loosen his grasp on her thin hand, but she only gripped tighter, refusing to let him go. She leaned closer, and he now noticed a fleck of spittle on her lower lip and the tight set of her jaw. "Everybody has a reck'nin' hour, young man. Everybody has an appointment with God. It was time for Jerry's appointment is all. Is all." She then released her hold on his hand and burst into a fit of silent sobs, nearly collapsing if not for the steady support of her son.

"C'mon, Mom, let's get you to the car." Her son smiled and nodded a thank-you to Mark, then led the old woman away.

Mark was left standing there alone with nothing to comfort him but the screams of the children still bouncing from headstone to headstone and the eerie warning of a grieving old woman—*Everybody has a reckoning hour. Everybody has an appointment with God.* Maybe he should talk to someone about it. The reverend here seemed like he'd be able to help. Maybe he'd make an appointment with him, tell him everything, get his slant on it.

He'd call the church tomorrow—St. Agnes Episcopal Church.

Reverend Dale Mahoney was an imposing man.

At six-three and well over two hundred pounds, his large frame swallowed his leather chair and dwarfed his mahogany desk. His jowls hung over his white collar like a bulldog's, and his nose was bulbous and red. A full shock of ruffled snow-white hair perched atop his large head. Yellow, coffee-stained teeth peeked out from behind thick lips.

"Good morning, Mr. Stone," Mahoney said, his pockmarked cheeks jiggling with each syllable. He stood and stuck out a large, meaty hand.

"Good morning, Reverend," Mark said, shaking the man's hand. Or rather, being shaken by the man's hand. "You can call me Mark."

Mahoney laughed, a hoarse, wheezy kind of laugh, and

rubbed his bulging belly with one hand. "Good enough. Good enough. Have a seat, Mark."

Mark sat in a leather wingback chair across from Mahoney's desk. The reverend's office was equally impressive as the man. Three large, floor-to-ceiling bookshelves sat stuffed with books of all sizes and colors and thicknesses. A large painting of a Middle Eastern landscape framed in gold hung on the wall behind Mahoney. Two wooden file cabinets stood side by side to the left of the desk, and a small wooden computer table sat to the right. A screen saver showing carved images of the Christ flashed every five or so seconds on the screen. On the wall to the left a large gilded crucifix overlooked the entire room, reminding Mark where he was. The office smelled of dusty books and old leather.

Mahoney eased himself back into his chair and laced his fingers across his broad chest. "So what can I do for you?"

Mark suddenly felt very awkward. How should he approach the subject of the screams without sounding like some escapee from the local funny farm? *Well, Father, I've been hearing hell on my telephone.* He forced out a nervous laugh and smiled. "I, uh, was at both the funerals you did for Jeff Beaverson and Jerry Detweiler. Jeff was a friend of mine, and I did business with Jerry. I run Stone Service Center down on Chestnut Street."

"I see," Mahoney said, suddenly looking very serious. "I'm sorry for your loss. They were both fine men, I'm sure. And your purpose for this meeting?"

"Well, I, um, experienced something strange with both Jeff and Jerry right before they died." *Experienced something strange? A little vague, don'tcha think? I'm sure the good reverend will have no problem at all deciphering that one.*

As though he could read Mark's thoughts, Mahoney unclasped his hands and stroked his chin, tapping the deep dimple that parted it into two round halves. "Something strange? Like what?"

Mark shifted his weight in the chair and twisted his hands in his lap. "Like screams. Right before both of them died I was on the phone with them, and I heard screams over the phone. They heard it too."

"Who was screaming?" Mahoney seemed interested, but maybe he was just playing the part of a good minister. Maybe he was really debating on the quickest way to get in touch with the psych ward.

"I don't know. It wasn't just one person, it was…a lot of people, hundreds, maybe thousands. And they sounded like they were in pain…no, agony. Moaning and crying and screaming and carrying on. I went to church a lot as a kid, and it sounded like what the Bible says hell is like—"

"Weeping and gnashing of teeth?" Mahoney said. He had leaned forward in his chair and now rested his elbows on the desk.

"Yeah. Exactly. Weeping and gnashing of teeth."

Mahoney fingered the corner of a piece of paper, sliding the edge under his fingernail. Without looking at Mark, he asked, "What do you think it was?"

Mark shrugged. "I have no idea. That's what I was hoping you could help me with. With Jeff we were on cell phones, so I thought maybe our signals got crossed with something else, but with Jerry we were both on landlines. I've been thinking some pretty far-out things."

"Like what?" Mahoney abandoned the paper and was back to tapping his chin dimple, showing interest. Or at least *pretending* interest.

Mark chuckled and felt a mild warmth touch his cheeks. "Like maybe someone is playing some high-tech prank, or…"

Mahoney leaned closer. "Or what?"

The warmth in Mark's cheeks intensified and spread to the back of his neck. "Or I somehow tapped into another dimension or...or hell itself. I know it sounds crazy. Believe me, I think it's crazy."

Mahoney sat back in his chair. A smile parted his thick lips, revealing those yellow teeth, like two rows of corn kernels. "Hell, huh?" He tapped his chin with a fat index finger. "Personally, between you and me, I have a hard time with the whole concept of hell. Is it real? Is there really a place where the damned spend eternity wallowing in fire and brimstone? Personally, I doubt it. I find more evidence in the Scriptures that God just destroys the wicked. Mark, think about it. How could a God that is pure love, perfect love, sentence someone to hell, a place of unthinkable torment, for eternity? Doesn't it sound a bit contradictory? A little out of God's character, don't you think? Judgment I understand. Punishment I agree with. But torment for eternity? Makes God sound like He's in need of anger management."

OK, so the reverend didn't believe in hell. But he did make a good point. God is love; God punishes people forever and ever. Could the two go hand in hand? "Well, what do you think it could be?"

Mahoney lifted his big shoulders and let them drop. "Don't know. Maybe just some bizarre transmission thing. Like you said, crossed signals or something."

Mark wasn't buying it. He'd been over the possibilities in his head a thousand times. Two thousand times. The chances of him being on the receiving end of some *bizarre transmission thing* and then both men dying mere seconds later was beyond comprehension. What were the chances? He was no statistician, but they had to be astronomically small. "And the deaths? How do you account for them?"

Mahoney shrugged again and grunted. "Coincidence. Believe me, when you've been around people and their problems as long as I have, you see some pretty unbelievable things. I've seen stranger."

Mark shifted in his chair and glanced at his watch. Time to wrap this up. The good reverend wasn't exactly a well of wisdom as Mark had hoped. He'd spouted a few deep words at the funeral, but in person he was about as shallow as a creek in late summer. Time to go. Definitely. "Well, Reverend," Mark said, standing and straightening his jeans. "Thanks for your time."

Showing not even the slightest surprise at Mark's abrupt termination of the meeting, Mahoney rose out of his chair with a grunt and a quick snort and extended his meaty hand over the desk. "Anytime, Mark," he said, grinning broadly. "It was a pleasure meeting you. Do you attend services anywhere?"

Mark shook Mahoney's hand, then released it. "Nope. Church isn't exactly my thing anymore."

"Well, so sorry to hear that," Mahoney said, running his hands along the waistband of his pants before hiking them up over his belly. "If you ever change your mind, you're always welcome here."

"Thanks, Reverend. I'll keep that in mind." Mark turned and exited the ornate office, waved politely to the secretary, and pushed his way through the oversized doors out into the sun-baked parking lot.

That was a waste of time.

Just For You Salon closed its doors at 9:00 p.m. sharp. Last appointments were at eight, eight fifteen if it was just a wash and cut. That gave Ginny Grisham and Jody Landis exactly thirty minutes to clean the scissors and combs, sweep the floor, wipe down the counters and chairs, and take out the trash so everything was ready to roll in the morning. First appointments were at eight o'clock.

"How's it coming, Gin?" Jody hollered from the back room.

Ginny dragged the broom over the green and white tiled floor, gathering the day's hair clippings into a pile of what looked like miniature tumbleweed—tumble*hair*. "Almost done." She glanced at the clock on the wall. "Twenty after. How you doin'?"

Jody, a short middle-aged woman with a perfectly round moon face and upturned nose, appeared in the doorway, her blue purse slung over her right shoulder, navy blue jacket draped over her left arm. "Done. Anything I can help you with?"

"You can get the dustpan and hold it for me."

"No prob." She picked up the dustpan, placed it on the floor next to the heap of clippings, and began humming a lively tune.

Ginny swept the hair onto the dustpan. "You doing anything tonight?"

Jody dumped the clippings into the wastebasket. "Nope. Goin' home and relaxing. Hopefully, Joe will have the kids in bed. He better, anyway." She tapped the dustpan along the side of the wastebasket, then placed it back under the front counter.

Ginny gathered the top of the plastic bag and hoisted it out of the wastebasket. "Does he always put the kids to bed?"

"Ever since I been workin' evenings. He don't like it much, but too bad, with him being laid off and all, we need this job. It's all that's paying the bills right now. Barely paying 'em."

Jody slipped her jacket on, and Ginny did the same with hers. "How's his job search going?"

Jody shrugged and popped a piece of gum in her mouth. She held out the gum pack to Ginny. "Piece?"

"Sure."

"It's going, I guess. He's had a couple interviews, but no one's called him back yet. I think he has one at the quarry over by Ellerslie tomorrow. Sounds pretty promising."

Ginny hit the lights, and the two ladies walked out into the cool evening air. A single streetlamp cast a dim glow over the parking lot. The traffic light on the corner blinked red on one side, yellow on the other. There wasn't much traffic in Mount Savage after nine o'clock on a Wednesday, and the traffic lights were timed to blink stop and caution after seven.

Judge had arrived at 42 Broad Court at nine fifteen and spent fifteen minutes setting his trap. It was perfect. Everything was going as planned.

Now he crouched by the side of the house, hidden in the deep shadow of a boxwood. He lifted his sleeve and pushed the light button on his watch. 9:32. She'd be here in eighteen minutes. Give or take. He had some time to kill, but better to be early than late. Late would not be good at all.

He blew out his cheeks, leaned against the house's concrete foundation, and mentally visualized the events that would unfold in the next hour. It was thrilling and frightening at the same time and made his pulse race. There was a part of him that knew what had to be done, longed for it, anticipated it like a child at Christmas. But there was another part of him that found it revolting, the shedding of innocent blood, one person taking the punishment for another. Two extremes battling within the same soul. Black and white. He loved it and hated it, but he had found a way to make the two coexist. Heaven and hell holding hands.

Of course, regardless of his feelings, it had to be done. Someone had to pay for what they did to Katie.

Unfortunately, that someone was Virginia Grisham of 42 Broad Court.

Unfortunately for her.

❾

"So what's happening in the exciting life of Ginny Grisham tonight?" Jody asked when they arrived at their cars.

"Not much. I'm just gonna go home to my lonely house, put on a movie I shouldn't waste my time watching, and stuff myself full of junk I shouldn't eat. Sounds pretty enticing, huh?"

"You're not goin' out with Brandon?"

Ginny stuck out her lower lip in a pout. "He's working nights this whole week."

"How are things comin' along with him? Gettin' serious yet?"

"I don't know," Ginny said, shrugging. "I'd like to think they are. But I don't want to get my hopes up. I mean, I think Brandon's great. He's kind and caring and responsible and treats me like a queen. But..."

Jody crossed her arms over her chest. "But what? You think he's too good for you?"

"Well...yeah, in a way."

"Ginny—"

"I know, I know," Ginny said, holding up both hands. "I shouldn't feel that way. I should be happy that he likes me and not be so hard on myself. I know. But I've been burned before, you know? And it hurts. I don't know if I can take that kind of rejection again. Besides, every time I look at myself in the mirror, I wonder what in the world he sees in me."

Jody leaned her weight forward and tapped her foot on the ground once. "He sees a kind, caring, responsible, and *attractive* woman. One that makes him happy. One that he adores and just can't live without."

Ginny laughed. "You flatter me."

"It's true. I may be a lotta things, but I ain't no liar."

"Thanks. You always know what to say to make me feel better." She looked up at the clear sky and filled her lungs with the crisp air. The sky was awash with pinpricks of light set against a black velvet backdrop. Stars, like grains of sand, speckled the night sky, reminding Ginny of endless autumn evenings spent lying under the stars with her two sisters, trying to identify the constellations. "It's amazing how when the weather turns colder, the stars just seem to pop out."

Jody leaned her head back and whistled. "You know, I don't think I ever noticed before, or if I did, I never thought about it."

Ginny opened her car door and looked once more at the starry sky. Pointing northward, she said, "Look, there's the Big Dipper and the Little Dipper."

"I got an idea," Jody said. "Why don't you come over to my house, and we can sit out back and watch the stars. It'd be a shame to waste such a beautiful evening sittin' by yourself in your apartment. I have snacks too. We can eat and talk and I'll flatter you some more. How's that sound?"

Ginny felt a smile part her lips. She hadn't tried to smile; the idea of sitting under a star-spangled sky with a good friend—*like a sister*—just brought a smile to her face. "That sounds like an excellent idea."

Judge looked at his watch: 10:28.

Where is she? He dropped his sleeve and shoved his hand in his pocket, rolling a quarter between his middle finger and thumb. Twenty-eight minutes ago he'd thought maybe she stopped for gas or milk. But it didn't take this long to pump gas. Something was wrong.

Change of plans. OK, Virginia. You're one up. Fair enough.

She was out there somewhere. And sooner or later he'd catch up to her. Sooner or later she'd come home on time as planned.

Sooner than later.

He'd come back tomorrow, set the trap again, and wait. Again.

Chapter 3

❶

CHERYL STONE LEANED BACK ON THE PARK BENCH, crossed her legs, and squeezed the wadded tissue in her sweatshirt pocket. Huge, pillowy clouds drifted by overhead. Some were as white as cotton; some were beginning to gray. Behind them, the sky was as blue as she'd ever seen it. The meteorologist was calling for rain later. Severe thunderstorm warning for Allegheny and Garrett counties. But it sure didn't look like rain in the sky.

"Have you heard from Mark lately?" asked Wendy Beaverson, sitting next to her on the park bench. It had been almost two weeks since Jeff's death, and Wendy was holding up remarkably well. For the first few days, she was a wreck. And understandably so. Cheryl had slept at Wendy's house to help with the children. Wendy stayed in bed most of the day, eating little and sleeping less. Cheryl had tried to get her up and out of the house, but it was useless. She just lay in that bed, curled around Jeff's pillow, staring at the wall. Said she could still smell him on the pillow and didn't want to lose that. Cheryl's heart broke every time she looked in the bedroom and saw Wendy's face buried in the pillow, sobs shaking her thin shoulders.

The day after the funeral, though, Wendy was like a new woman. She climbed out of bed on her own, showered, ate breakfast, and finally tore those sheets off the bed and washed them. "I have to get on with life," she'd said. "I miss Jeff and think about him every second of every day, God knows I do, but I need to move on...for the kids' sake."

Now, sitting next to her in a yellow sweatshirt and worn-in-the-seat jeans, hair pulled back in a ponytail, Cheryl came to the conclusion that Wendy no longer needed her daily care. Here she was, just lost her husband, and she was asking about Mark. Remarkable.

Cheryl looked up at the clouds. A flock of Canada geese flew by, honking their intentions to find warmer weather. Little Gracie, just three years old, squealed as she slid down the sliding board, "Mamma, looky look!"

Mark. She really didn't want to talk about him, but maybe she needed to. Maybe it would be therapy of some kind to get things off her chest. And now was as good a time as any. "No. The last time I spoke to him was at the..." Her words trailed off into awkward silence.

"The funeral?" Wendy said.

"Yeah. Sorry."

"It's OK. Are you going to get a divorce?"

That was something Cheryl didn't want to think about, hadn't thought about. At least not seriously. Walking out on Mark was one thing. Moving into her own apartment was another, and difficult. But divorce? There was something about it that was so final. She knew she should divorce him; he deserved it. She deserved it. After what he did, she deserved to be rid of him for good and forget about him. But why couldn't she? Sure, she was angry with him, hated him at times. And, yes, during those times she'd thought that she never wanted to see him again. But there was something there, something that lingered way down deep in her heart, way down in the shadows where even she didn't dare look too long, that felt an awful lot like love. Could she still love him after what he'd done? Of course not! After everything they had shared together—the vacations, the laughs, the struggles, the tears, the intimacy—he had just trampled on it all and disrespected her and *their* love. Yes, she was sure of it: she hated him.

"—Cheryl?"

"I'm sorry, what?"

Wendy placed a hand on her leg, by the knee. "Divorce. Is it on the table?"

Cheryl sighed. "I don't know. I want to, and I don't want to. Sometimes I hate him so much I could kill him. And then at other times…I don't know. I try to tell myself maybe there's some hope. Maybe I can find it in myself to forgive him. But then I feel like I don't want to forgive him. I don't want to see him, or hear his voice, or ever be around him again." She looked at Wendy and tried to force a smile, but a lump had risen in her throat and her eyes blurred from tears. "Am I crazy?"

Gracie squealed again.

Wendy patted Cheryl's leg and handed her a new tissue. She had a look of such compassion and understanding in her eyes that Cheryl almost lost it right there. "It's OK to feel that way. It's only been, what, six weeks?"

"A little over."

"Just take it slow. There's no need to rush into anything just yet. Mark's not looking for a divorce, is he?"

Cheryl shook her head, pressing the tissue against her eye.

"Give yourself some time to sort through your feelings. OK? You'll know what to do."

They sat in silence for a few minutes, watching Gracie climb the steps of the sliding board and whiz down, hands reaching for the clouds, smile a mile wide. Way off to the left, just above the horizon, another flock of geese floated by, their honking just barely audible.

An Allegheny County sheriff police cruiser slowed and eased up next to the curb on the other side of the playground. A nasty glare reflected off the passenger's side window, washing the glass white and blocking any view of the officer behind the wheel.

"Is he watching us?" Wendy asked.

Cheryl shrugged. "Maybe he's just on patrol and decided to sit and see what law-abiding responsible citizens do with their time. We could teach him a thing or two, you know."

Wendy laughed. "What? Like how to stay so busy working and taking care of children that you don't have time to break the law? I'd like one day of irresponsibility." She looked at Cheryl and had a mischievous grin on her face. "I think we deserve that, don't you?"

Cheryl laughed and smiled wide. It'd been awhile since she'd smiled like that. It felt good. "Yes. Definitely. One day would be all it would take to get it out of my system. Then I could go back to being a responsible taxpayer again. You think we could go talk to the officer and arrange something? Maybe convince him to turn his head for one day?"

But as if the policeman behind the wheel had heard her, the cruiser slowly pulled away from the curb, stopped at the intersection, and made a left-hand turn away from the park.

Wendy sighed. "Well, there goes our chance. Looks like we'll have to go on being boring, stressed-out, overworked, under-paid, responsible citizens. Whoopee."

Cheryl patted Wendy's back in mock sympathy. "Maybe some other time. We'll get our chance to play Thelma and Louise someday."

9:44 p.m. 42 Broad Court.

Crouched in the shadow of the boxwood, back against cold concrete, Judge waited for Virginia Grisham to walk into his trap. He'd been hunkered down here for nearly fifteen minutes, and his knees were getting stiff.

Six more minutes. Give or take. She better show up this time.

The air was chilly. Judge rubbed his hands together, fighting off a shiver. His mind went to Amber. He'd have to take her a blanket tonight. He felt bad for not showing up last night like he'd promised. He'd actually laid awake thinking about her, wondering if she'd found a way to stay warm. His concern for her well-being suddenly struck him as odd. Anyone else would never have taken her more food, would never have checked up on her, and would never, ever take her a blanket. They wouldn't care about her comfort, whether she was cold or scared or lonely. But he cared. For the hundredth time, he reminded himself, *convinced* himself that he wasn't like others—and he knew the type. He wasn't a monster.

His thoughts then went back to 1974 and Katie McAfee.

1974

"I love you." There, it's out. As soon as the words leave his mouth he feels a sense of freedom and knows that he meant every syllable of it. Every letter (*every jot and tittle*). He's never really known love from his parents. Sure, being church-going folk they talk about love enough. God is love. Love your enemies. Love one another. Love your husband. Love your wife. Love your parents. But live it? Really flesh it out so there is no mistaking that the love they talk about is as real as the Bible they read it from? Hardly. His father's brand of love is chiseled in stone. Rules. Dos and don'ts. Thou shalt nots (*probably carried down from the fiery mountain in the arms of Moses himself*). And his mother's idea of love is to force food and good hospitality down your throat until you're nauseous (*pig-stuffed*), all the while smiling a plastic grin and slinging Christianese around like it's the gosh-darn national language or something. But when he speaks those three words to Katie—finally speaks them out loud (he's been practicing in his head for weeks)—he knows what real love is. There's no mistaking it.

He takes a small step back, half expecting her to laugh at him, half expecting a hand across his cheek and the sting, both to his face and his heart, that will follow. But neither come. Instead, Katie takes an equally small step toward him, leans in, and presses her lips against his.

The kiss doesn't last more than three seconds, but it seems like an eternity. He wishes it will last for eternity (*forever and ever, amen and amen*). It would be a very satisfactory heaven. And during these three seconds he is intensely aware of three things. One, the tenderness and softness of her lips (*like pillows where angels rest their heads*). Two, the sweetness of her breath (*like a bouquet of the best-smelling wildflowers*), teasing him, drawing him closer, deeper. And three, the fact that in these moments every care he's ever experienced, every worry, every self-conscious thought, fear, and dread he's ever dealt with is suddenly banished, nonexistent, forgotten (*cast into the eternal abyss, the lake of fire, forever and ever, glory to God*). It's like he's re-created, reborn, loosed from the chains of self-recrimination that were forged in his parents' oppressive religion and tightened by legalistic hypocrisy.

He is free! And he is in love.

4

A car door closed, jerking Judge out of his past. She was home. The plan was a go.

Virginia walked up the sidewalk, heels scraping on the concrete, stepped onto the stoop, and slid the key into the lock. Turning the key, she swung open the door, stepped inside, and shut the door behind her.

Fifteen more minutes, max. When the shower came on, he had to move quickly. On the trial runs, she'd averaged about eleven minutes in the shower. Enough time for him to do what he had to do.

Exactly thirteen minutes later he heard the shower spring to life and the steady hum of the plumbing in the walls. Pulling himself out of his crouch, he lifted a small cardboard box from the ground beside him and forced his knees straight, despite their painful protest. His feet tingled. He stamped them to bring back the circulation and feeling.

Walking around the back of the house, careful to stay on the grass and not leave footprints in the soft soil of the garden, he swung open the steel doors that led down a short flight of concrete steps to the basement. Fortunately, she was in the habit of leaving them unlocked. Nice neighborhood and all. A few days ago he'd come during the early evening when the sun was just setting and scouted the house. At the bottom of the concrete stairwell was another door, a wooden manufactured door. It wasn't hard to break into—a simple hook that was easy to lift. Most people didn't realize how easy it was to break into a house through the basement. He slid a credit card between the door and the frame and lifted the hook. The shower was still going strong. So far, so good. He looked at his watch. About five more minutes.

Once inside the basement, he set the box on the concrete steps and closed the door, dropping the hook into its locked position. All set. Now he only had to wait for the shower to shut off, count off two minutes, and place the call. He removed a white cotton cloth from one jacket pocket and a tiny vial of ether from the other, set the two on a rough wooden table obviously used for laundry, and sighed deeply.

The warm water felt great on her back and neck. Leaning over clients all day, cutting hair, curling hair, coloring hair, left her spine aching from top to bottom. Ginny lingered a little longer than usual in the shower, enjoying the massaging effect the pulsating water had on her sore muscles.

Turning off the water, she slipped her hand through the curtain and grabbed her towel. The plush fabric felt like velvet against her skin. She was glad she'd sprung for the more expensive set. She dried off, stepped out of the shower, and looked at herself in the partially fogged mirror. She had to start exercising. Her body had blossomed in all the wrong places over the past five years. She still didn't get what Brandon saw in her. She was fat and didn't even have the willpower to do anything about it. Every year she'd made a New Year's resolution to start exercising, walk around the block or bike or something, anything. But every year she'd made excuses why she didn't have time, and after a few weeks of noncommitment, no longer felt guilty about leaving her resolution in the dust. Some other time. Next year.

She huffed and quickly slipped into her pajamas—a pair of red sweatpants and a red University of Maryland sweatshirt. Her muscles still ached, right between the shoulder blades. She'd seen twelve clients today, did three perms, four colorings, and gave one lady a Mohawk. An odd one, that one was.

She was about to dry her hair when the phone rang. She opened the bathroom door and listened for the machine to pick it up—if it was Brandon she'd answer it; otherwise, it would have to wait till tomorrow.

After three rings her voice came on: "Hello, this is Ginny. Can't pick up right now so just leave a message. Thanks."

Beep.

"Hi. I hope I have the right number. Virginia Grisham of 42 Broad Court. This is Jim Valentino with UPS. I, uh, stopped by your house today, Thursday, to drop off a package and you weren't home. I ran out of Post-it notes for your door so I left the package on your basement stairs around the back of the house. The doors were unlocked. I hope that was OK. I wanted to make sure you got the package, though. Well, um, OK then. Bye."

Ginny walked down the hall and into her bedroom, slipped on her pink velour slippers, and headed down the basement steps. Walking through the den, she opened the door to the laundry room and felt for the light switch. She flipped it up, but nothing happened. She toggled the switch a couple times but still no light. Bulb must have burned out. Great.

There was enough light filtering in from the den that she could make out the obstacles on the painted concrete floor. With arms out in front, she shuffled her way through the laundry room, dodging wash baskets and boxes of detergent. The farther back she went, the darker it got and the harder it was to see, even with her eyes slowly adjusting to the darkness. When she reached the door, she felt for the hook, unlatched it, opened it, and felt for the box. There, about the size of a shoebox. She picked it up, tucked it under her right arm, and shut the door with her left. The box had to weigh at least five pounds. She hadn't ordered anything lately. But her grandmother never sent her a birthday gift last month. Maybe this was it. Better late than never.

She turned and made to leave when someone grabbed her from behind. Someone strong. Arms like iron bands wrapped around her shoulders and waist, pinning her arms to her sides. The box clunked to the floor. She opened her mouth to scream, but a cloth slipped over her face and a strong chemical smell filled her nose. Panic gripped her with icy fingers, and she gasped for air, pulling in more of the chemical. Her legs gave out first, and then a thick numbness spread over her body. Seconds later, blackness overtook her.

Amber had just tucked herself under a blanket of straw in preparation for another chilly, sleepless night when she heard the distant moan of an engine. Jumping up, she brushed the straw from her clothes and hair and peered through the boards at the outside world. Two glowing lights, like the eyes of a running cat, bounced down the dirt lane, illuminating a swath of ground in front of them.

She'd been in this barn for six days now, and Judge hadn't come by last night like he said he would. She had suffered through three cold, sleepless nights, burrowing into the hay in a meager attempt to control the shivering. Yesterday she'd awakened with stuffed sinuses and a dry cough. Today, the cough had deepened, and her throat started feeling a little raw, like it was lined with fine-grit sandpaper. She'd taken to sleeping during the day, catnapping really, anything to beat the cold and fatigue that was wearing on her body.

The Dobermans were around constantly, so exploring an escape route through the trapdoor in the barn floor was out of the question. Unless she wanted to become dog food. She'd drained the rest of the water this afternoon and had one apple left. Her clothes were getting tattered; her hair was a tangled rat's nest, and she stank. The whole barn stank. She'd taken to using a corner for the bathroom, covering her waste with straw in an attempt to control the odor. But it still stank.

The cat eyes grew larger and the engine louder, and the dogs started barking. Amber watched as the lights cut through the darkness all the way to the barn, stopped in front of the barn door, and the engine quit. It was the white sedan. Judge was back.

The driver-side door opened, and a man—she could tell it was Judge by his posture—climbed out and opened the back door. With a loud grunt, he jerked something out of the backseat, bent low, and heaved it onto his shoulder. Amber couldn't make out what it was. It was too dark. The sky had grown cloudy late in the day, and now a thick covering blocked out all light from the moon and stars.

Judge left the car's headlights on to spotlight the front of the barn, and when he stepped into the light with the object slung over his shoulder, Amber almost let out a scream. It was a person, dressed in red. A woman, her body dangling over his shoulder like a rag doll, arms and hair reaching for the ground behind him, bottom sticking up in the air in front.

Amber rushed over to the barn door and stopped ten feet away, waiting, wringing her hands. The cold air burned in her lungs. The cinder block was pushed away, the lock jangled, and the door swung open. She moved back a couple steps when Judge stepped through the doorway, the beam from the headlights backlighting him, pasting him as a chalky black silhouette against the yellow light. He stopped about five feet inside the barn, bent to one knee, and carefully lowered the woman dressed in red onto the floor.

Anger ballooned in Amber's chest. Another woman. She

suddenly had the urge to rush Judge, pounce on him like a rabid cat, and claw his eyes out. She clenched her fists and tightened her jaw, mustering the nerve to throw herself at him. If she was ever going to have a chance, this was it. While he was bent over, his attention fixed on the woman in red. The new woman. She could catch him off guard, put him out of commission just long enough so she could flee the barn and disappear into the night, and then...then what? She had no idea where she was. It didn't matter, though. She'd be free. Or the car. He must have left the keys in there. She could take it and roll. And if the attack didn't work? Then she'd surely die. But she was going to die anyway, right? That was Judge's plan, right? Sooner or later. If it had to be, it might as well be sooner.

When she'd decided on her course of action and set her jaw for action, she dug one toe into a floorboard and tensed her muscles. But just then the Dobermans appeared in the doorway of the barn, crouched and snarling like they had read her mind. They were warning her back, back into her corner.

Without saying a word, Judge stood and glared at the Dobermans. The dogs remained in the doorway, tamping the floor with their paws, coal-black eyes fixed on Amber, tongues flitting in and out of their mouths. Judge turned toward Amber, held both palms up, and motioned toward the woman. The dogs following him, he then turned and retreated from the barn, shut the door, and locked it.

As soon as Judge's footsteps began crunching softly over the dirt again, Amber rushed to the woman and knelt by her side. It was too dark to make out the features of her face, but she seemed to be young. She rolled the new woman onto her back and felt her face for blood and her head for lumps. None. She felt clean. She smelled clean.

Moments later the car door shut again, and Judge's footsteps grew closer. The lock on the door disengaged, and he stepped through holding two paper bags. After setting them on the floor, he straightened himself and faced Amber. "More stuff. Food, blankets, warmer clothes."

With that, he turned and left, locked the door, slid the cinder block in place, and seconds later started the engine. The car pulled away, tires crunching packed dirt, and slowly drifted down the lane and out of sight.

Amber returned her attention to the new woman. She patted her cheek. "Hey. Honey. You OK?" She cupped a hand over her mouth and coughed.

No response. He must have drugged her.

She didn't want to move the new girl until daylight, so she gathered some straw for a pillow, rooted through one of the paper bags for a blanket, and covered her where she lay. She then felt through the bag for the clothes, pulled out a pair of sweatpants and a sweatshirt, and quickly donned them, thankful for the warmer clothes. In the bottom of the bag was a pair of white athletic socks. Checking the other bag, she found another gallon of water, more toilet paper, apples, and a box of cereal.

Amber then made herself a bed next to the new girl and lay close. They could keep each other warm. She lay there, on her back, for a long time, staring into the darkness, listening to the high-pitched chirps of a bat family coming and going. He'd abducted another one. How many more would there be? How long would he keep them here? What was he planning for them? Questions swirled in her head like autumn leaves blown about by a stiff wind until sleep finally overtook her.

Amber was up at first light. She'd actually fallen into a deep sleep last night. The sweats kept her warm enough, and that, mingled with the overwhelming fatigue from three nights of restlessness and discomfort, made it possible to get almost a full night's sleep. She rubbed her eyes, coughed, and swallowed hard. Her throat was worsening. She sat up and suddenly remembered the young woman beside her. She could see her clearly now: brown hair with wide, dark blonde streaks, soft features, plump build. She looked to be late twenties, near Amber's own age.

Amber pulled herself up, stretched her arms behind her back, and shuffled to the wall for a look outside. The sun had just crested the treetops, shooting rays of pale blue into the cloudless sky. The morning was peaceful and quiet. A light haze hovered over the pasture. The trees in the distance almost glowed with spotted reds and yellows. In the sky, three barn swallows flitted about, playing in the chilly, crisp air, diving and climbing like acrobatic jet fighters. The outside world was so serene and calm, Amber momentarily forgot about her predicament, forgot about Judge, forgot about her wooden prison, forgot about the Dobermans.

The Dobermans. Where were they? She held her breath and listened. The only sound was the morning songs of some birds in the distance. Maybe they'd run away again. Maybe—

Before the next thought could materialize in her mind, the dogs were there, just on the other side of the boards, growling, snarling, baring their white teeth, the look of hate in their vacant eyes.

The new girl yelped. Amber spun around to find her sitting up, eyes wide, lips parted, face twisted in fear.

Amber ran to her, fell to her knees, and put her arms around New Girl's shoulders, pulling her close like a mother comforting her frightened daughter. "Shhh. It's OK. They can't get in."

New Girl pulled away and looked at Amber with panicked eyes. "Who—who are you? Where am I? What—what happened?"

Amber stroked New Girl's hair. "My name's Amber. Amber Mann. You're in a barn somewhere. You—"

"A barn? How did I get here?" New Girl looked around, taking in her new environment with a wide-eyed bewilderment. Her eyes fell on Amber and studied her face. Amber thought she must look like a train wreck. What a sight to wake up to. "Who are you?"

Amber tried to smile and be reassuring. She knew the trauma of waking up in this strange place, trapped, scared, and not having a clue what had happened. She didn't want New Girl panicking on her. "My name's Amber Mann. You're safe in here."

The dogs began barking and growling again, pawing at the boards. New Girl shrieked and leaned closer to Amber.

Amber placed a hand on New Girl's head and stroked her hair again. "They can't get in," she said. "They can't hurt us."

After a few seconds, New Girl pulled away, hugged herself, and said, "How did I get here? I remember going home after work last night, taking a shower, and getting a call from the UPS guy. After that"—she looked at Amber and her chin quivered— "nothing. I can't remember."

Amber cupped New Girl's face in her hands. "Honey, you've been taken—"

"Taken? What do you mean, *taken*?"

"I mean abducted. Kidnapped. Taken."

Realization dawned on New Girl's face as tears puddled in her eyes. She laced her fingers through her hair and scanned the barn again, eyes wide. "Kidnapped?" She turned, and Amber saw the wild look in her eyes. She was ready to lose it.

Amber jumped into emergency mode. She had to calm the girl down before she totally cracked and went loco in this confined space. "Shhh. I'm here too. I was taken too. We'll be all right. We'll get out of this."

"You—you were kidnapped too. How long?"

"I've been here a week."

"A week? Who? Who took us?"

Amber frowned and combed a hand through New Girl's hair again, pushing it off her forehead. "I don't know. But he wants to keep us alive. He brings food and water and toilet paper and blankets. What's your name?"

New Girl tugged at her sweatshirt and looked around, eyeing the rough floorboards, the gaping wall boards, the cathedral ceiling dotted with restless bats. "Ginny. Kidnapped? He's gonna kill us, isn't he? He's gonna kill us."

Before Amber had a chance to stop her, Ginny scrambled to her feet, rushed the wall, and began screaming for help, clawing and kicking at the boards.

Chapter 4

❶

MARK STONE SHUFFLED ACROSS THE KITCHEN, FRESH refill of coffee in hand, steam curling from the mug. His morning routine was moving right along. The alarm went off at 5:05; he'd hit the snooze button two times and crawled out of bed at 5:30. The sun wasn't even near up yet, the sky a heavy sheet of navy blue. He stretched, wiped the sleep from his eyes, and stumbled into the kitchen, keeping the house dark for the sake of his eyes. Still in a half sleep, he went through the motions of making a pot of coffee. With mug firmly in hand, held close to his face to absorb the warm steam, he then headed for the bathroom, cranked up the shower, and climbed in.

By the time he stepped out of the shower, shaved, and combed his hair, the sky was beginning to lighten and the trees were no longer just black silhouettes pasted against a dark backdrop. He went for the cupboard, pulled out a granola bar, and seated himself at a small, round wooden table in the kitchen. The clock on the microwave read 6:16. He'd usually be waking Cheryl about this time.

—*Time to get up, babe. Rise and shine.*

—*So soon? Wake me up in ten, OK?*

Eventually, she'd make her way to the kitchen, pour herself a cup of coffee, and sit across from him at the table while she sipped the steaming java. That's what she called it—*java*. It always irritated Mark just a little. Like she was trying to be hip or something. They'd sit for maybe ten minutes, small talk about the day ahead of them, then he'd head for work and she'd head for the shower. When they were first married they'd share the shower in the morning, but that hadn't happened in a couple years.

Now, sitting at the table by himself, he thought of how much he missed Cheryl, what he would give to share a shower with her, even hear her call her coffee *java*. He would give his right arm for ten minutes of small talk and coffee sipping this morning.

He thought about the mistake he'd made. The other woman. Rachel. How did it happen?

—*How did it happen, Mark?*

—*I don't even know, it just—*

—*Oh, no. Don't you even tell me it just happened. That's such a bunch of...*

He never thought he'd be the kind of guy to cheat on his wife. It seemed so callous, so cold, so...ignorant. He knew some guys that had cheated, and they were all jerks. He never thought of himself as a jerk. He loved Cheryl. Really, he did. Even when he and Rachel were growing closer, laughing at each other's dumb jokes, talking about their lives. Flirting. Yes, it had *just* happened so fast he'd neglected to take the time to step back and get control of the situation.

He remembered the first time he met Rachel at Ray's Family Restaurant. He'd gone there for lunch, sat in his usual spot, and toyed with a sugar packet until Melody, the regular waitress, stopped by. When he looked up, though, the waitress standing by his booth, notepad in hand, was not Melody. She was an angel. Tall, lean, auburn hair that fell loosely to her shoulders, full lips, and the biggest, roundest, brown eyes Mark had ever seen, like roasted chestnuts encased in jewels. She smiled, and he stammered, "Hi. Are—are you new?"

"Yes. Started just three days ago. Can I get you something to drink?" Her voice was smooth and clear. Cold mountain water on a sultry summer day.

"Uh, yeah, sure. A large Coke, please, and I'll have the two hot dog lunch special too. It's nice to meet you"—he glanced at her name tag—"Rachel."

Rachel slid her notepad into her apron pocket and smiled. Her eyes flashed like brilliant amber. "Nice to meet you too"— she leaned to the right a little to get a look at the name stenciled on his Stone Service Center shirt—"Marj."

Mark's face flushed hot and he forced a smile. "It's Mark. They stenciled the wrong letter on and I just never bothered to send it back to have it fixed."

She laughed playfully, and the sound nearly took Mark's breath away. He had to hear more of that laugh.

The phone over the kitchen counter rang, yanking Mark out of his painful memory. He shoved the chair back, stood, stretched again, and picked up the phone.

"Hello?"

"Mark?" A familiar voice. Strained. Crying.

"Mom? What's the matter?"

A muffled sob. "It's your father. He had a heart attack last night."

Mark didn't say anything at first. He hadn't held a real conversation with his father in years. They weren't exactly on speaking terms anymore. Sure, they were cordial to one another at holidays and other social gatherings, but when it came time to sit and talk, one of them was always conveniently preoccupied. "Is—is he OK?"

Mom sniffed. "No. It was bad, Mark. He almost died. I thought I'd lost him."

Mark stood by his kitchen counter, silent, listening as his mom retold the story of how his father had complained of a pressure in his chest but refused to go to the hospital. Typical. That was just like him. She called 911, and by the time the ambulance got there, he was almost gone. They were able to get him stabilized enough to transport him to the ER, where they did emergency surgery—triple bypass—and almost lost him on the table. Two times. Two times he tangled with death, she said. As she told the story, her voice grew more and more strained, and Mark could tell she was fighting back the sobs. "Mark, I'm here in his hospital room. He...he wants to talk with you."

The words didn't register at first, sounded foreign, then hit him like a wrecking ball, almost knocking him over. *He wants to talk with you.* Talk with him? Dad didn't talk *with* him, never did, even when they were on good terms, which seemed like a lifetime ago. He talked *at* him; that was just his way. Mark dragged a chair across the linoleum floor and sat in it, pressing the receiver against his ear. "OK."

There was a moment of silence where the only sound was Mark's own pulse tapping in his ear, then a weak, raspy voice. "Mark."

Dad.

"Hi, Dad." It was awkward at best, talking to a man called Dad who was more like a stranger. A stranger who had just dodged the bullet of death two times.

"Well, looks like you got your wish."

My wish? "What do you mean?"

Dad tried to laugh, but it only came out as a gravelly cough. "You once said you wished I was dead."

Mark remembered the time. He was a stubborn, independent,

Mike Dellosso

ignorant nineteen-year-old who thought his dad was the dumbest prude on the face of the earth. He'd left the church, grown his hair long, listened to "worldly" music, and had a non-Christian girlfriend. Those sins combined were enough to place him squarely in the crosshairs of his father's righteous (*self*-righteous was the word Mark had used) indignation. After enduring ten solid minutes of his father's own version of Judgment Day, he'd stormed out of the house, cursing. He'd stopped on the sidewalk, spun around glaring at his father's still form behind the screen door, and hollered loud enough for the whole block to hear, "I wish you were dead!"

He was surprised Dad had remembered. Or not surprised at all.

"Dad, that was a long time ago. I was young and stupid. I never should have said that." He paused, waiting for Dad to say something. When he didn't, Mark said, "I didn't mean it, you know."

Dad coughed again, a raspy hack that filled the phone with static. "Naw, you meant it, but it doesn't matter now. It's gonna happen soon. Your mother keeps telling me I'm gonna be OK. Be going home in a few days. She's wrong about that. I'm not leaving this room. I can feel death creepin' up on me."

Mark thought about that and was surprised by the feelings of remorse that filled him. He'd lost so many years with his father because of anger and resentment. Now he wished he could have those years back. He was about to say something when Dad started up again.

"Mark, listen to me. Are you listening?"

"Yeah, Dad."

"I've been thinking. Not much else to do here." He coughed loudly three times. "I'm sorry, Mark. I did a lot of stupid things as a father, things I now wish I hadn't done. Made a lot of stupid rules, said a lot of stupid things. I need to make it right with

74

you. Now that I'm looking death in the face, I'm not sure where I'm going, and it scares me. But I at least want to leave on good terms with you."

Mark could tell Dad's voice was getting weaker the more he spoke. He ran his sleeve across his eyes, wiping the tears away. Dad's words had plucked a chord deep in his heart. He'd longed to hear his father say those words, longed for it for so many years but thought it would never happen. "Dad, I—"

He was cut off by an eerie sound that sent chills down his back and peppered his skin with goose bumps. Screaming. Painful, pealing screams that rose and fell and collided like two steam engines that had been barreling full throttle toward each other. *Weeping. Gnashing.* Molars grinding. Fists clenching. Bodies writhing. It lasted maybe five seconds, then stopped abruptly.

Mark panicked. The others—Jeff and Jerry—had died almost immediately after he'd heard those awful screams. Dad's words tunneled through his head like a mole. *I can feel death creepin' up on me.* "Dad? You still there?"

"Yeah. What was that?"

"Nothing, Dad. Don't worry about it. I'm coming up to see you." What was he saying? His parents lived outside of Roanoke, Virginia. A five-hour drive. Chances were strong, if this call was anything like his last call with Jeff and Jerry, Dad wouldn't live to see the next five minutes. Five hours now seemed like an eternity. Was an eternity.

"No, Mark. It's too far. I just wanted to say that."

But Mark had made up his mind. He'd close the shop for a couple days. If he was right, and Dad passed before he arrived, he could at least be there for his mother. If he was wrong, he'd get to see his dad maybe one last time. Either way, he needed to go.

He sniffed back some tears and wiped his nose with a napkin

from the counter. "I'm coming, Dad. I'll leave in a couple minutes. And, Dad?"

"Yes?"

"I love you. I want you to know that. In case…well, I just want you to know that."

There was a long pause, then Dad's thin voice came on again. "You can say it. In case I don't make it. Me too, son. I love you too."

Sheriff Wiley Hickock was hoping for a quiet day, and all was going as hoped until Jess walked through the door waving a single white sheet of paper. The look on her face told Wiley that his quiet day was about to end. The sheet of paper turned out to be a missing person report. Amber Mann. Thirty-one. Five-six. Brown hair. Hazel eyes. Last seen last Friday leaving work at Darlene's Diner. Her car was still at the diner.

Wiley sat behind his desk, leaning back in his chair, one leg crossed over the other, lips tight, studying the photo of Amber. "I hate these cases. Nuthin' but bad news."

Missing person meant just that, missing. Disappeared. Whereabouts unknown. Most of the time it was nothing more than a case of miscommunication or so-and-so wandering off to *find* himself in some foreign land. And most of the time so-and-so showed up broke and an emotional train wreck. Rarely did the cases materialize into anything serious like murder or abduction. And when they did, nine out of ten times it wasn't discovered for months, and only then by some twist of chance. That's why he hated them. Too many variables. Too many unknowns. Too many unanswered questions.

He unfolded his legs, straightened in his chair, and set the report on his desk, still studying it. "Good-looking girl too. And you checked with her family?"

Jess nodded, biting at the nail of her index finger. "Yup. They live over near Swanton in Garrett County. Her mom said she hasn't heard from Amber in over two weeks. Apparently she doesn't call home much and visits even less. She was supposed to visit her sister Saturday. Never showed up. Her sister filed the report."

"Where's the sister live?"

"Charlestown."

"Did you interview her yet?"

Jess tapped her notepad. "I'm swinging by this afternoon."

"And her house? Mann's?"

Jess flipped a page on her notepad. "Clean. No break-in. Nothing disturbed. No messages on the machine. She didn't leave much of a trail."

Wiley thought for a moment. No surprises there. "Anything else on her? Friends, co-workers?"

Jess stepped around the chair across from Wiley's desk and lowered herself into it. She leaned forward, rested her elbows on her knees. "Oh, yeah. Marge Anderson. She kinda took to mothering Amber and said when Amber left work Friday night, she was headed to Bruno's Bar over in Frostburg. Seems Ms. Mann had a secret boyfriend there. Mitch Young, a tattoo guy in Frostburg. Amber didn't know that Marge knew about Mitch, tried to keep the fling hush-hush. Marge said Amber left work Friday night all dolled up saying she was going to Bruno's, that's where she would hook up with lover boy. She didn't show up for work the rest of the week. Marge said at first she thought maybe Amber was sick or ran off for a few days—"

"Was that like her?" Wiley asked.

"To run off without telling anyone?"

"Yeah."

"Marge said no. But when someone doesn't show up for work, the last thing you're thinking is kidnapping. She just figured Amber got a little wild and forgot about work for a few days."

"And the fact that her car was still in the parking lot didn't concern her?"

"She said she assumed a friend picked Amber up. Apparently that's happened before."

"What friend?"

"Don't know. Seems Amber kept her life pretty private."

Wiley leaned his elbows on the desk and tented his hands in front of him. "Did you talk to Mr. Tattoo yet?"

"Paid him a visit last night while he was closing the shop. Says he was expecting Amber Friday night; they were supposed to hang out at Bruno's for a few hours, down a few drinks, dance some, then go back to his place. But she never showed. Said he waited until after midnight but no Amber, so he just figured she got sick or something came up, and he went home. The next day he tried calling her, but there was no answer. Tried again the rest of this week, but every time, no answer. He assumed she'd gone away and forgot to tell him."

"Forgot to tell her boyfriend she was going away for a week?" Wiley looked at the photo of Amber again. She was wearing a fitted red tank top, short jean shorts, and sandals. Her brown hair was pulled back in a ponytail. She was smiling ear to ear and holding up a horseshoe like it was some kind of trophy. Good-looking girl. Nice figure.

"I know," Jess said. She was back to nibbling at her fingernail. "Sounds odd, don't it? Lover boy says he's got more than a handful of people that can testify that he was at Bruno's until after midnight last Friday and every night since then. Said he goes there every evening after he closes the shop."

Wiley smoothed his mustache and pressed his lips into a thin line. "And you said you questioned him at his shop?"

"Yes. It's in Frostburg. College Avenue. He gets a lot of clientele from the college."

"Did you notice any snapshots of Amber around?"

Jess thought for a moment. "As a matter of fact, yes. There were a few on the counter of Mitch and her, and a couple on one of the walls. He did a phoenix tattoo on her lower back."

Wiley sat back in his chair again, crossed his arms over his chest. Amber stared at him from the photo on the desk. Her mouth was smiling, but her eyes pleaded with him, begging. All at once the room starting closing in upon him. The walls tightened; the ceiling crouched. His chest constricted, making it feel like he was breathing through a straw. He tried to draw in a deep breath, but his lungs were in a vise. Then the room began to spin, first slow, then faster, faster. But in the center of it all was Amber. Her face. Smiling. Pleading.

"—Sheriff?"

Wiley started and looked at Jess. She was standing in front of his desk, leaning over it.

"You OK? You looked like you were ready to faint or something."

Wiley rubbed his face with both hands, smoothed his mustache. "Yeah. I'm fine. I hate these cases. Get me a list of every client he's had in the past week. Run their backgrounds. See if anything comes up. And keep an eye on Romeo. Visit him every day if you have to. Let him know we're watching him."

"I'll head back over there right now. I have a few other questions I want to ask him too. Better to do it in person."

Jess turned to leave. Wiley cleared his throat, a sign he wasn't finished yet.

"Something on your mind, sir?" Jess said, one hand on her hip, thumb hooked in her belt.

"You dating anyone yet?"

Jess's eyes narrowed. He'd taken her by surprise. Good. It kept her sharp. "No," she said, letting the vowel linger on the edge of her lips. "Is this relevant…?"

"You need a life, Jess."

"I have a life, sir."

"Outside your job."

"I have a life outside my job."

Wiley studied her for a moment. Jess was an attractive girl, smart, responsible, good sense of humor when she wanted one. No reason any guy wouldn't want to date her. He nodded once. "You need a boyfriend."

Jess pursed her lips, a look his mother used to give him when he'd come home late for dinner and run through his list of rehearsed excuses, none of which convinced her of his innocence. "With all due respect, let me worry about my personal life, sir. You worry about the whereabouts of Miss Amber there."

Wiley smiled. He liked Jess's spunk. It was one of the qualities that made her such a good cop. "Fair enough…but you still need a man in your life."

Jess grinned and shook her head. "I believe that's my call." She then turned and walked out of Wiley's office, thumb still hooked in her belt.

Jess pushed through the glass door of Monster's Ink Tattoo Studio. An electronic chime announced her arrival. The place was more art studio than tattoo shop. Jess had been in some of the other shops in Frostburg and Cumberland, and none of them compared to this. The walls and ceiling were linen white, the floor, black and white checkered tile. Framed images of artsy designs hung on the walls, spotlighted by track lighting positioned in strategic locations across the ceiling. A white counter sat in the middle of the large room, and behind it, a small waiting area furnished with four black art deco chairs and a black table stacked with magazines and photo albums of tattoos. In one corner sat a large flat-screen TV flashing a music video. Beyond the waiting area a black curtain hung from ceiling to floor, hiding the work area from prying eyes.

Jess picked up the TV remote and pushed the mute button. She could hear the hum of the tattoo gun behind the curtain. She knocked on the counter. "Mitch Young?"

"Be out in a minute," Mitch shouted.

She took a seat in one of the chairs and flipped through a photo album while biting off the last remnants of the nail of her index finger. This Mann case had her bewildered. Either Amber ran off unannounced, which, according to her sister and co-worker, wasn't like her at all, or there'd been some foul play. And as far as she was concerned, Mitch Young was at the top of the list. Something about him just didn't sit right in her gut. She'd only been a deputy a few years, but she had natural police instincts. She could smell a rat through ten feet of concrete. And Tattoo Mitch emanated the aroma of rat.

A few minutes later the curtain swung open and Mitch stepped out. He was wearing a pair of faded jeans and a white T-shirt. His dark hair was cropped close to his head, and his angular face was framed by a set of jaw-length sideburns and little tuft of hair below his bottom lip. A look of surprise lighted his face when he saw Jess. "Deputy Foreman. What—is Amber OK? Did you find her?"

Jess shook her head. "Not yet. Have a seat, Mitch. Do you have time for a few more questions?"

Mitch looked back through the curtain. "Take a break, Jules. I'll be right back." He then turned to Jess. "Mind if we go outside and talk? I could use a smoke."

"Sure."

When they were outside, Mitch reached in his pocket and pulled out a pack of smokes and a lighter. He smacked the pack against his palm, slid out a cigarette, and flipped it into his mouth. Lighting it up, he drew in a long breath and closed his eyes. "I've been working on Julie in there for over an hour. I needed a break."

He exhaled, letting the smoke filter out of his mouth in a slow, curling ribbon. "So any leads on where Amber is?"

"Not yet," Jess said. "I was hoping you could help us with that."

"I thought I answered all your questions last night. You really think she was abducted?"

"You don't?"

Mitch shook his head and sucked on his cigarette. "Nope. Man, I hope not. I only knew her a couple months, but she was an independent one. The type to do what she wanted and no one was going to change her mind. I learned real quick just to accept it. 'Course, well... never mind."

Jess cocked her head to the side. "Go on."

Mitch tapped his cigarette and a pillar of ash crumbled to the sidewalk. "Well, it's just that, we weren't like, 'boyfriend and girlfriend,' if you know what I mean."

"I don't. Please explain."

"We weren't all lovey and stuff; we just liked... being with each other." He looked at her and shrugged. "You know, *being* with each other. It was a release for both of us. We were good together."

Jess knew exactly what he meant. It was a relationship of

convenience. They both had something the other wanted. At least that was *his* take on it. She wondered if Amber felt the same way. "And you think she got tired of you and left?"

"Yeah." He shrugged it off in an obvious attempt to protect his manly ego. "No big deal."

"And left the area too?"

"I didn't say that. I don't know, maybe she just needed some time alone, maybe she's visiting friends out of state. Who knows? But abducted? Man, I hope not."

"Did she have out-of-state friends?"

Mitch shrugged and tapped his cigarette again, dispensing another pillar of ash. "How should I know? It was just an idea. I'm just saying that she seemed like the type to pick up and leave without saying anything. Abduction seems like such a stretch."

"Her co-worker said that's not like her at all. Said she was a reliable worker, always showed up on time and did her job."

Mitch snorted. "Who'd you talk to, that old gal she works with, Marge?"

"Yes."

"Amber said that old woman mothered her like a hen." He dropped the cigarette and ground it into the sidewalk with his boot. "Then again, she probably knew Amber better than I did. Sorry, Deputy, I guess I can't be of much help. Seems I only knew one side of Amber."

Jess looked at the cigarette butt on the sidewalk. "You gonna just leave that there?"

Mitch looked at the butt, then up at her. "What?"

"It's littering. I could slap you with a three-hundred-dollar fine right here."

Mitch stooped and picked up the butt. "Thanks for the heads-up. I gotta get back to Julie. You'll let me know when she shows up?"

"Do you want to know?"

Mitch nodded and lowered his brow. "I'd like to. Just for the peace of mind."

"I'll keep you updated. This probably won't be the last you'll see of me."

"Great," Mitch said, rolling his eyes.

Jess turned to leave, then stopped. "Hey, Mitch, one more thing. Why do you think Amber would leave her car at the diner? Seems kinda odd for someone running away or just going out of state, doesn't it?"

Mitch held the glass door half open. "Don't know. Maybe someone picked her up."

"That out-of-state friend?"

Mitch didn't say anything.

Jess continued. "I just think it's odd that you were the last person she was supposed to see before she vanished. Just makes me wonder is all."

Again, Mitch didn't say anything. He turned and let the door slowly close behind him.

"Oh, one more thing," Jess said. "Mitch?"

Mitch stopped the door from shutting completely and poked his head out.

"I'll need a list of all your clients in the last, say, four weeks. OK?"

"I don't think you can do that, can you?"

"I could get a warrant, but that would make my life complicated, and if my life gets complicated, so does yours."

Mitch frowned. "I'll see what I can do."

Jess smiled. "Thanks, Mitch. I'll be back tomorrow to pick it up."

She walked back to her cruiser, got in, and looked at the address for her next stop. 2037 Charlestown Road. Liz Fiddler.

Lord, You need to give us a lead on this one. That girl is out there somewhere; I know it. Please keep her safe. And keep her alive.

Show me the way.

She lifted a hand and bit a hangnail from her ring finger.

Jess had no problem finding the Fiddler residence. There was only one potholed road that ran through Charlestown, and the Fiddlers lived a mere half mile outside of town. Their home was a faded blue, vinyl-sided double-wide trailer that sat in the middle of a large level lot surrounded by maple saplings. To the right and left of the home were similar double-wides on similar lots. Across the road was a wide-open field that must have just been harvested. Looked like soybeans had grown there. It gradually sloped upward for maybe a quarter mile until it met a heavy tree line dense with evergreens. Where field met forest Jess noticed a thick-shouldered buck standing tall, head erect, no doubt scanning the area for predators before giving the OK for the rest of the family to venture out into the open.

Jess walked up to the house and rapped on the front door three times. Moments later she heard heavy footsteps inside the house, then the door swung open.

A tall woman with a curvy figure and frizzy bottle-blonde hair stood in the doorway. She was dressed in navy blue sweats and looked like she wasn't accustomed to visitors dropping by. Especially visitors in uniform.

"You Deputy Foreman?" she said in a harsh tone. A blond-haired toddler, no more than two, appeared at her knees, poking his wide-eyed, food-smudged round face between her legs.

"Yes, ma'am, I am. And you must be Liz. We spoke on the phone. I need to talk to you about your sister." Jess preferred to do interviews in person. Telephones were so impersonal, and she liked the advantage of watching body language. Though some could spin intricate tales with words, the body rarely lied.

"Did you find anything out yet?" Liz sounded half concerned, half accusing.

"No, ma'am. Not yet."

Liz opened the door wider and stepped aside. "Well, come on in. You'll have to excuse the mess. Christopher here is a little tyrant. It's all I can do to keep up with him."

Jess laughed politely and entered the house. On Sundays, she worked with the toddlers at church and knew all about *keeping up* with them. Their energy was an endless storehouse of vigor, and it didn't take much for a handful of two- and three-year-olds to have her running in circles and forgetting which way was up. Christopher here looked like a bottle rocket of mischief.

The inside of the trailer was neatly decorated, everything from the waist up had its place, but the floor was littered with toys and books and puzzle pieces.

Liz weaved through the living room with a deftness that said she'd done it too many times, sidestepping and high-stepping through the maze of toddler-sized debris. "I feel like all I do all day is pick up after Christopher and cook and clean." She shot Jess a sideways glance. "My husband likes the place neat and clean when he comes home from work. Have a seat on the sofa."

"Oh, I don't mind the mess," Jess said, trying to put Liz at ease. She could tell by the tone of her host's voice and the posture of her body that Mr. Fiddler was an overbearing person to live with—or live *under*. She'd seen women like Liz so many times she could spot them with her eyes closed. "I work with the toddlers at our church, so I'm used to kids and messes." She sat on a dark brown sofa and removed a small steno pad from her shirt pocket.

Little Christopher waddled over to Jess and handed her a toy car covered in saliva. Jess took the car with two fingers. "Thank you very much. How thoughtful of you."

Christopher squealed and laughed and slapped at his legs, then promptly fell on his bottom.

"So what do you need to know?" Liz said.

Jess studied the woman for a moment. Dark bags hung under her eyes, her colorless lips were drawn thin, and there was an emptiness in her blue eyes that was almost haunting. She'd stopped taking care of herself a long time ago, Jess thought. Her attention was now focused on cleaning up after Christopher and staying out of her husband's doghouse. There was no time for herself. Jess had the sudden urge to steer the conversation in a different direction: *Why don't you tell me about your husband. Tell me why you're so afraid of him.* But she decided against it. Amber was the more pressing issue, and prying into Liz's personal life might erect walls Jess would never be able to disassemble. Instead, she sent a silent prayer to heaven on Liz's behalf: *Father, show this woman Your love.*

"Officer?"

Liz was talking to her. "Oh, uh..."

Liz turned her attention to Christopher, who was about to topple a lamp. "Chris—no! No, no!" She lifted her eyebrows at Jess. "What do you need?"

"Um, tell me what you know about Amber's boyfriend, Mitch Young."

Liz lifted Christopher onto her lap, rolled her eyes, and laughed. "The loser. That's what I call him." She shrugged. "That's what he is. Amber hates me saying that, but hey, it's the truth. I call 'em like I see 'em."

"Do you know anything about him as a person, his character?"

Liz gave another quick shrug. "He's a loser. What more do you need to know?" She bent over and picked up a toy train, handed it to Christopher. "Look, Amber is a good person. Kind. Loving. Softhearted. She'd do anything for anybody. But she's naive and gullible. Met this Mitch guy at some bar, he sweet-talked her, told her how beautiful she was, you know, the regular stuff most of us would just roll our eyes at. Well, not Amber. She fell head over heels for the guy. He knew it and was using her. I could tell. The way she talked about him..." She turned her head and looked out the window at the field across the road. "I know the type."

I'm sure you do. Jess's heart ached for Liz. Women like her had lost all hope. They had been so beaten down—maybe not physically (most of them weren't), but emotionally and psychologically—that they lived in an empty shell, void of real life. "Did she love him?"

Liz laughed. "I don't even know if Amber knows what love is. Real love, anyway. She's been in one bad relationship after another. I think she's in love with the idea of being in love. She's so nice it's easy for men to take advantage of her. And they have."

"Mitch said their relationship was a mutual understanding. They...uh, met each other's needs and didn't expect anything more than that."

Liz rolled her eyes again and shook her head. "And you believed him?"

"Actually, no—"

"He's a jerk. OK? I met him once. Amber brought him by a couple weeks ago. As soon I saw him I knew what he was after. One of these wham-bam-thank-you-ma'am types. He may not care about Amber, but I can tell you she's head over heels for the guy. A sister knows these things. He's using her. Trust me, I've seen it happen to better women than Amber."

Jess was going to question further but decided against it. It was obvious both Liz and Amber grew up in a home where Dad was king and Mom and the kids were his obedient servants. They say women gravitate toward men that are like their fathers. Here were two perfect examples.

"Is it like her to just up and leave?" Jess asked.

Liz's eyes widened. "You think she ran away or something?"

"I don't know what to think at this point. As you know, she just disappeared. We have no evidence to support an abduction, but none to suggest a runaway either. Is she the type to go off on her own for days on end and not tell anyone where she was going?"

Liz shook her head emphatically. "No way. Amber is naive and gullible and stupid when it comes to men, but she's responsible. She would never just wander off and get herself lost. Not her. No way." She laid a hand on Christopher's head, and Jess noticed moisture gathering in the corners of her eyes. "Something happened to her. And if I were you, I'd be lookin' real close at that loser Young. I'd bet my last pair of socks he's involved."

Jess closed her notepad and pocketed the pen. Standing, she smiled at Christopher and ruffled his hair. "For Amber's sake"—she looked at Liz and felt the smile disappear—"I hope you're wrong. But I will be keeping an eye on Mr. Young, and I'll keep you updated."

Liz set Christopher on the floor and stood. "Thank you, officer."

"Let me know if you remember anything else or hear anything we would need to know about. And"—Jess placed a hand on Liz's arm and gave a gentle squeeze—"pray, OK?"

Liz forced a smile and blinked away the gathering tears. "I will."

❺

Mark stood outside his dad's hospital room, leaning against an off-white wall, staring at the black-scuffed beige and brown tiled floor. The hall was busy with activity. Nurses hurried by, flipping through charts and rearranging the contents of their pockets. Food services staff pushed carts with squeaky wheels, and doctors, backs straight, heads held high, cruised by in small herds, whispering intently to one another.

Mark had stock-car'd it down Interstate 81 and in spite of Friday traffic made the trip in just under five hours. He found his dad's room easily enough and parked himself in the hallway, trying to muster the nerve or courage, he wasn't sure which, to enter the room and face his dad. Obviously, Dad was still alive. He could hear Mom chattering on and on about what Mrs. Guthrie, their neighbor, said about so-and-so down the street.

Mark rested his head against the wall and blew out a breath. For some reason Cheryl came to his mind. He wished she were here right now. She knew how to get through to Dad. She was the only one who could hold a real conversation with him and not walk away wanting to strangle him. Her easy-going temperament and quick wit were the perfect balance for his overbearing, opinionated, legalistic attitude. He remembered the first time Cheryl met Dad. She and Mark had gone to his parents' house for dinner, and not five minutes into the meal Dad dropped his fork on his plate with a loud clink and straightened in his seat. He looked Cheryl right in the eyes and

—*Are you fornicating with my son?*

—*Dad, really. I don't think—*

—*Hush, boy, I'm asking her the question, not you. Well?*

—*Dad. C'mon. Cheryl, you don't have to ans—*

—It's a simple question, really. Are you fornicating with my son?

She'd answered just as cool as if he'd asked her if she'd had the tires on her car rotated.

—Not yet.

And it was the truth.

Dad went back to eating his dinner and didn't challenge her again. At least not for the rest of the evening.

A slight smile parted Mark's lips. Cheryl. How he missed her. *Forever and ever. Cross my heart. Hope to—*

Suddenly, Mom was standing beside him. "Mark! What are you doing out here?"

Mark shrugged and gave his mother a hug. "I don't know. Just collecting my thoughts, I guess."

Mom stepped back, leaving her hands on his shoulders. She leaned in close and lowered her voice. The loose folds around her eyes were puffy, and her nostrils were rimmed in red. "He's doing real bad. Took a turn for the worse a couple hours ago. I've been trying to stay positive around him, but even he knows the time is close. Doctor says he could go anytime now. Honestly, I think he's been holdin' on till you got here. He really wants to see you."

Mark swallowed hard. The sound of the screams resonated in his head. The sound of death nearing. "OK." He gave his mother another hug, letting it linger just a little longer than usual, then stepped back. "How are you doing?"

She shrugged and dashed a tear from the corner of her eye. "I'm holding on," she said, but the emptiness in her eyes betrayed her words. She looked old, Mark thought. Older than her sixty years. Sooner or later she'd break down. Probably after Dad was gone. She'd been putting on a front that everything was wonderful for far too long, almost her whole life. At least her whole life with Dad. When he was gone, she'd be able to take the mask off and be herself, and there was no telling what would come out.

Mark released his grip on her and entered the room. The smell of antiseptic, body odor, and urine hit him all at once and reminded him how much he hated hospitals. Dad was lying in his bed, propped up with pillows, a white sheet pulled up to his waist. When he saw Mark, he smiled and waved him over.

If Mark thought his mother looked old, Dad looked even older. He was sixty-four but looked a hundred and four. His face was gaunt, eyes hollow. Transparent skin hung off his frail frame like it was two sizes too big. It was amazing how many years someone aged spending just one day in a hospital.

"Hi, Dad," Mark said as he made his way around the bed and sat in the chair Mom had pulled up next to it. Mom leaned against the wall next to the door, staying out of the way, letting him spend some final minutes with his dad. "How are you feeling?"

Dad tried to laugh but hacked terribly instead, the long, thin muscles in his neck becoming taut chords. "Like death is waiting out in the hall. He's got a book with my name in it. I'm next on the list." He tried to swallow, but his Adam's apple wouldn't bob. Instead, he licked his lips with a dry, white tongue. "I'm glad you came, Mark. I need to tell you something."

Mark sat stiffly, waiting for Dad to say what was on his mind. He wasn't used to heart-to-heart talks with his father, and he had the feeling that's exactly what this was going to be.

Dad reached for his water bottle, took a short swig, swished the water back and forth in his mouth, and swallowed, wincing as his Adam's apple finally broke loose. "Mark." He reached out his thin hand and held it open, palm down. Purple veins wove between rigid tendons. Mark took his father's hand in his.

"Son, my whole life was a lie."

"No, Dad, it wasn't—"

"Yes!" Dad coughed again, a phlegmy hack. His face calmed, and a shadow passed through his darkening eyes. "Yes, Mark. It was. I played the game, you know. The game of religion. I knew all the rules, all the right words to say. But in the end it was just that—words. I didn't mean any of it. Not really."

Mark placed his other hand over his father's. He knew what he was saying was true, of course. He'd known it his whole life. Dad was a phony. Their whole family was phony. Their whole church, in his opinion. It was all just going through the motions. He knew it to be true, but he couldn't stand to hear his father say it. "Dad, please stop—"

"Mark." Dad smiled, a weak grin that barely made it to his eyes. "It's OK. I need to tell you this. I drove you away with all my religion."

He stopped, and tears pooled in his eyes. His jaw shifted back and forth ever so subtly, bottom lip quivering. When he spoke again, his voice was strained and tight. "I'm lost, son. I spent my whole life thinking—fooling myself really—that I was on the right track. Doing, doing, doing. But now look at me, lying on my deathbed, and I'm lost. I don't even know what's right anymore. What the truth is."

Tears spilled out of Mark's eyes and trickled down his cheeks. He swiped at them with his sleeve and tried to swallow, but he couldn't get past the baseball in his throat. Man, he wished Cheryl was here. His father's words were so damning. What was he saying? He'd spent his whole life trying to impress God and everyone that he was religious only to realize now, moments from death, that it was all worthless?

Dad's eyes momentarily rolled back in his head, and he slowly closed them. Mark caught his mother's eye and motioned her over. When Dad's eyes opened again, there was only a flicker of light left in them. He was fading quickly. He licked his lips and reached for Mom's hand. "It's almost time," he whispered.

Mom sat on the bed next to her husband and held his hand in her lap. Tears wetted her cheeks. Mark could tell she was holding back the sobs, damming the river behind her eyes. "Dear, we've had a good life together," she whispered. "And I've loved you the whole time. Like nothing else."

Dad's lips trembled. He blinked slowly. "My love for you never faltered. Not even the gates of hell could prevail against it."

A stab of guilt ran through Mark's heart. He thought once again of Cheryl and how he'd betrayed her, wounded her. The gates of hell had been flung open.

Dad squeezed Mark's hand, but there was no strength left in his once-firm grip. "Son. I love you. I didn't say it much and showed it less, but I always have."

Dad's eyes rolled back again, his irises disappearing almost totally, and slowly closed. His breathing became labored and wheezy; he was struggling for every breath. Mark knew the end was upon him. He leaned forward and whispered in his father's ear, "I love you too, Dad. Always did."

Dad's eyes suddenly flipped open wide like two spring-loaded window shades. He gripped Mark's hand with unusual strength. His whole body tensed, and he fixed his eyes on a spot high on the wall directly in front of him. His mouth gaped, and fear—not just your matinee scary story kind, but staring-into-the-too-gruesome-face-of-death kind—deep-froze his eyes. The sound of screams—*those* screams—echoed through Mark's head. Weeping and gnashing. The gates of hell. It was time. His father was dying right in front of him.

Dad gasped one final breath, then his frail body relaxed, hands losing all strength, eyelids slowly drawing shut.

It was over. Dad was dead.

Mark released his father's hand, rushed past his whimpering mother, and escaped into the hallway. The weight of death in the room was too great for him. He found a padded bench in a small waiting room down the hall and fell onto it. The screams were still there, bouncing around in his head. He sat with his elbows on his knees, head in his hands, fingers laced through his hair, crying.

The scream. It had predicted another death. He tried to think it through, reason it out logically, but his mind was awash with nothingness, like it had been erased clean, an empty chalkboard. He'd think about it some other time. But not now.

His dad just died.

Chapter 5

❶

JUDGE'S ROOM IN THE BASEMENT WAS HIS FORTRESS. His chamber. His sanctuary. Another collage of photos had been removed, leaving two walls still decorated, the one in front of him with snapshots of a short brunette, thick around the midsection, brown eyes, pixie nose, full lips, large white teeth. In one photo she's with a man, his arm around her waist, pulling her close, no doubt preparing to wow her with his romantic prowess. He might have to be dealt with. In other photos she's by herself, climbing out of her car—a gold '99 Pontiac Sunfire. In another she's leaving work, in another entering her dormitory, and in yet another, walking to or from class along a white sidewalk, the sun illuminating her round face. She's attractive in a common, homely sort of way and has a habit of tucking her hair behind her right ear.

The wall to his right was dotted with photos of another woman. In a few days, she'll take center stage, but for now, that honor belongs to Shelley.

Shelley Kurtz, college sophomore.

He leaned back in his chair and stroked his soul patch. It needed to be trimmed soon. If only a soul was easy to patch. His had a few holes.

He focused on one snapshot of Shelley in particular. She's looking at someone off the picture, head turned slightly to the left, no, right, his left, a sinister smile playing across her face. He'd used the photo-editing program on his computer to zoom in on her face before printing if off. There's something about the shape of her mouth, the way the lips part ever so subtly, turn up on the corners, flare the nostrils, crinkle the eyes at the corners. Something familiar.

His mind went back to the barn.

The girl.

The kiss.

1974

With their lips still pressed together and that deep warmth still surging through his bones, the barn door swings open, allowing bright rays of sunshine to flood the interior of the barn.

"Ha! Caught ya!" Four girls enter the barn, arms crossed or hands on hips, chins up, backs straight. Katie's older sister Bethany and her snotty friends. One of them has a cigarette dangling from her lips. (*Daddy calls it a cancer tube, coffin nail, death stick.*)

"Well, well, well," Bethany says, strutting to within feet of Katie and him, hands on her hips. "Looky what we got here, girls. A couple of real lovebirds. Caught in the act."

Releasing his hold on Katie, Judge steps back, cheeks burning, hands beginning to tremble. (*That stupid trembling!*) He looks at Katie. Her face is bright red, but there's anger in her eyes. Anger like he's never seen in a twelve-year-old girl, or any twelve-year-old, for that matter, and though he would never admit it to anyone, it scares him just a bit.

"Shut up, Beth," Katie growls. "It's none of your business."

Bethany, four years older and three inches taller than him, walks over, her feet shuffling through the hay and straw on the floor and shoves him, both hands landing squarely on his chest. He stumbles back but maintains his balance.

"What are you doing to my sister, punk?" Bethany hollers, lunging at him and giving him another push, this time succeeding in knocking him off-balance and giving him a seat on his butt. "Tryin' to feel her up or something? You violatin' my sister?"

He scrambles to his feet, his shirt now clinging to the sweat on his back, and, though he is fully scared now, looks Bethany directly in the eyes (*devil eyes, windows to hell, the eternal pit of fire and brimstone where the wicked weep and gnash their teeth for . . . forever and ever*).

Katie steps between them and pushes out her chest. She looks up at Bethany, meeting her older sister's icy stare with one equally as cold, if not colder. "Leave him alone. Why don't you and your freak friends go muck out the horse stalls?"

Bethany glares, and her nostrils flare. Red spots crawl up her neck and tint her cheeks. She's mad, mad as a wet hornet, as they say. She leans forward and pokes a finger in Katie's chest. "Watch your mouth, you little tramp." She straightens up, seems to tower over both of them. "And I'd watch where I put my lips too." She jabs a thumb in his direction. "No tellin' what kinda diseases this little germ is carrying."

That brings a round of laughter from Bethany's cronies (*the laughter of devils*).

Katie narrows her eyes and stares knives at her sister. "You're such a witch." Then she reaches for Judge's hand. "C'mon. Dad will get rid of these trolls for us."

But before Katie can take a step further, Bethany catches her in the chest with her hand and pushes her backward. A sinister grin splits her face, and the corners of her mouth seem to reach almost from ear to ear. "Oh, no. You're not going anywhere.

Dad's in the far field, and Mom went to the store." She glances at the loft ten feet above. "You know, it's pretty dangerous in the loft. How many times has Dad told you not to goof around up there? I guess you'd get pretty bruised if you fell."

And before his mind even registers it, she smacks Katie full on the cheek. The sound echoes in the silence of the barn (*like the crack of a whip on bare skin*). Katie stumbles to her right and reaches for her face. She remains like that for at least five seconds before righting herself. When she straightens up again there are tears in her eyes, but more than that, there's hatred.

Bethany's hand still hangs in the air; her lips tremble. "Girls, take care of lover boy. I want to teach my little sister a lesson in respect."

The three other girls, all much taller and heavier than he, form a half circle around him, sneering and blocking his view of Katie. One of them shoves him in the chest, and he stumbles back and falls, landing hard on his butt. He hears another smack and a cry of pain. He tries to get up, but one of the girls, the fat one with the cigarette, kicks him in the leg, sending a shock of pain through his thigh.

Trying to look around the girls' legs, he sees only glimpses of two bodies tangled in battle (*a struggle for survival, life or death, winner takes all*). A grunt sounds, then another smack, and another cry. Within seconds the air in the barn is filled with grunts and groans, cries and shrieks. It's difficult to make out who is delivering the blows and who is receiving. Katie is a tough girl; he knows that. He's seen her carry her own weight around the farm for nearly three months now. But pitted against Bethany's size and weight (*four years older, three inches taller, with a fully developed chest and child-bearing hips*), Katie is no match.

He tries to get up again. He has to help Katie. He can't just sit here and let her be beaten unmercifully. (*She's gonna kill her, beat her to death like a bad dog.*) But another blow, this one to the back, puts him on his stomach in the hay.

Anger seethes inside him. No, rage. Pure rage. He jumps to a crouch and throws himself at the girls, releasing a primal grunt. One of them catches him around the neck and holds him while the other two land a barrage of punches to his torso. Numbing pain thuds up and down his rib cage as he tries to fight back. But it's useless; they're too big and have him in such an awkward position.

But in the midst of his own beating, he suddenly becomes aware that the brawl between sisters taking place just feet away has slowed (*a wind-up toy losing its umph*). Someone is on the floor, pinned in the corner, while the other delivers a steady round of kicks. The thudding sound of sneaker against flesh is sickening. He hears one of the girls, maybe the fat one, say, "That's enough, Beth. Geez, don't kill her."

The beatings end abruptly, and he's tossed to the floor. The girls step away from him, laughing and mocking as they turn toward Bethany (*devils gloating in the work of the devil*). That's when he gets a good look at Katie. She's pushed into a corner, half buried in hay, curled on her side in the fetal position, hands over her head, whimpering. Bethany stands over her like a victorious gladiator. Her hair is tangled, shirt torn around the collar. Long scratch marks, like crimson lightning bolts, stretch up her arm from elbow to shoulder. Her right cheek is red and raw. Katie has put up a good fight (*but, dear Lord, not good enough*).

Bethany points a finger at Katie. "You say one word about this to Mom or Dad and I'll tell them about your little make-out session with butt face. You were foolin' around in the loft, and both of you fell. Got it?"

With that, she spins around on her heels and stalks out of the barn, her cronies following close behind.

Clearing the cobwebs from his head, he climbs to his feet and stumbles over to Katie. She cowers in the corner like a whipped dog, whimpering and crying. Her hair clings to her bloodied face; abrasions mottle her arms and hands. She's been beaten good (*like a bad dog*).

He gently places a hand on her forehead and swipes away some of her sweat-soaked hair. Her left eye is almost swollen shut. Tears burn his eyes, and the rage is there again. He'll get them for this. (*Vengeance is mine, saith the Lord—no, vengeance is* mine.)

Then he smells it. Something burning.

A ribbon of smoke lifts off the hay and floats toward the loft above. He digs through the hay and feels a burning pain against his hand. It's on fire! Fat Girl must've flicked her cigarette at Katie.

Before he has time to react, a small flame springs to life, just feet from where Katie lies.

"Katie, c'mon. We gotta get outta here."

But she doesn't move. He doesn't think she *can* move. Probably has some broken ribs.

He grabs her by the wrist and tries to pull, but her dead weight is just too much for him. (*Dear God, help us.*)

The flame grows larger, billowing smoke now.

He tries to roll her, but there is no time left. The flame has reached his pant leg and singes the bottom of his jeans. He jumps back and swats at the hem.

By the time he looks up again, the flames have surrounded Katie in the hay. She tries to sit up, but it's too much for her. As the flames surround her, she screams in terror, her face twisting with the recognition that she's going to die, burn to death. (*Hell-fire surrounds the wicked, but there's nothing wicked here.*)

He has to do something, *knows* he has to do something, but his mind is stuck in mud; it won't work. He's paralyzed, helpless to rescue the girl that just moments before enabled him to feel real love for the first time in his life.

Judge snapped his eyes open. *Enough!*

He couldn't relive any more of the horrors in his tortured memory. He jumped out of his chair, reached over his desk, and ripped the snapshot from the wall, tearing it into a hundred pieces.

Tiny squares of paper floated to the floor.

That grin would haunt him for the rest of his life.

Mark lay on the sofa in his parents' family room, shoeless, wearing torn jeans and a faded Led Zeppelin T-shirt. After Dad slipped away yesterday, he'd spent some time with his mother, making the funeral arrangements, then headed back to her home, finally climbing under the covers of his old bed at a little after 1:00 a.m. Sleep only came in restless spurts, though. His mind was too active, and being in his old room in his old house brought back a scrapbook full of memories. At six o'clock he'd finally given up on any productive sleep and moved to the sofa in the family room.

He planned on spending a few days here with Mom, make sure the funeral went OK and she was settled in before going back home. The service was Monday, the day after tomorrow...at his old church. He wouldn't go back to work until

Wednesday or Thursday. The events felt like entries in some-body else's calendar book, scribbled engagements that had to be kept to keep life rolling on. And it did roll on, didn't it? People died, babies were born, couples wed then split up, but life just kept truckin' on, merciless, unforgiving.

He'd spent most of the night thinking about Dad and the things he'd said in those final minutes. Dad was a lot of things, and one of them was religious. Too religious. That's what drove Mark away. At the age of eighteen, he'd finally grown tired of all the Bible quoting and finger wagging. That was when he'd decided to tune Dad out. The old man could quote from the King James all he wanted; he could judge and condemn and testify until Mary had another lamb, and it wouldn't matter, because Mark didn't care anymore. It was all just background noise.

Boy, was he bitter back then. A rebel teen out to prove the self-righteous Christians wrong. And Dad was public enemy number one. Over the years he'd matured and settled down, lost his contempt for Dad and his overzealous ways, even tried a few churches here and there. But none were a good fit for him. The Episcopal church was too dead, the Assembly of God too happy, the Baptist too pious. He'd grown up hearing the Word preached, yelled, prayed, and sung. He knew the gospel message inside and out. Could quote Scripture with the best of them. What he needed, and to be honest, longed for, though doubted he'd ever find, was reality. Christians who walked their talk in the real world, fleshed it out in the midst of real people with real problems, trudged through the muck and mire of life with everyone else. That's what he wanted to see, that's what he'd searched for but never found.

But what Dad had said, lying there so close to death, had touched Mark in a way he'd never thought possible. It was honest and raw, right from the heart. It was the most candid and transparent he'd ever seen Dad, ever seen anyone, for that matter. Here was a man who'd spent his whole life trying to live up to the impossible expectations of the Bible—*bein' Christlike*, he'd say—and, faced with death, admitted it was all lies. Hypocrisy at its best. And worst.

What was Mark supposed to do with that? How was he supposed to process such honesty? Dad's words still rang in his ears—*My whole life was a lie. I'm lost.*

What a waste. What a horrible, tragic waste.

Tears leaked from Mark's eyes, and he let them come.

Dad's words continued to come as well. *I don't even know what's right anymore. What the truth is.*

Somewhere in those dreadful words was a warning; he was sure of it. Dad's words, spoken moments before death, tolled as a warning bell, warning, warning him to reevaluate life.

And then there was the look in Dad's eyes as death crept in and robbed him of life. The look would be forever tattooed on the inside of Mark's eyelids. It was the look of fear—pure, untainted fear.

A thought struck him then and tightened his scalp. The look in Dad's eyes was the look of those screams. If the screams had a face, Mark had seen it. And it was terrifying.

He had to talk to someone else about it. Someone had to know how to make sense of it.

But first he had to call Cheryl. She deserved to know. He sat up on the edge of the sofa, raked his fingers through his hair, then over his stubbled face. Picking up his cell phone, he flipped it open and dialed Cheryl's number. Her phone rang once, and a sudden weight of anxiety settled over him. What was he doing? She didn't want to talk to him. He couldn't just call her. It didn't work that way anymore. She hated him. She—

"Hello?" It was Cheryl. Obviously.

"Hi, uh...hi." His mind froze, locked up like dry gears.

"Mark?"

"Um, yeah. Hi."

Her voice turned cold. "What do you want?"

"Um, what are you doing? You sound out of breath."

"I'm jogging, OK? And you're interrupting me. What do you want?"

Just like Cheryl to have her cell phone with her while she was jogging. Never left home without it. "I, uh, just thought you should know my dad died yesterday."

There was a long pause. Heavy breathing. "Mark, I'm sorry." Her voice had softened some but still sounded labored and edged in steel. "How? I mean, what happened?"

"Heart attack. They did surgery, but it didn't take or something. I don't know. He went downhill fast. I was there when he passed. It was really hard on Mom." Why was he telling her this? Because she was still his wife, that's why. They used to tell each other everything. No secrets.

—*Hey, babycakes, since it's our first night as man and wife, let's make a pact.*

—*Anything for you, Cheryl. Name it.*

—*Let's agree to always tell each other the truth and never keep secrets from each other.*

—*That sounds doable.*

—*Pinky swear?*

—*Swear.*

—*Good. This solemn pact is hereby notarized and effective immediately to continue forever and ever.*

—*Forever and ever. Cross my heart—*

—*Hope to die.*

"I'm sorry. Really, I am. It must have been horrible," Cheryl said.

It was good to talk to her again without arguing. "It was. He looked so frightened. The funeral's Monday here in Virginia. Don't feel like you have to come."

He wanted to tell her about the screams, about everything, but she'd think he'd totally lost it. She already didn't think too highly of him. He was right up there with the mud caked into the tread of her sneakers.

There was an awkward silence for a couple seconds. Cheryl's breathing was slowing. A car rolled by in the background, gravel crunching under its tires.

"I miss you, Cher. Really." It was the truth too.

Cheryl didn't say anything at first, and Mark thought she wouldn't, then, "Why?"

Why? He tells her he misses her and she asks *why*? "Because. I still love you."

She snorted into the phone. "You love me, do you? You cheated on me. Is that how you show love?"

Her question was like a sword in the heart. He had no answer, no defense. She was right. He would admit his mistake, take the punishment. "No, it's not. Look, Cheryl, I was wrong. I know I was. And I'm sorry."

"Sorry doesn't cover the hole in my heart." She paused, and he could tell she was crying. It broke his heart. He wanted to just plead with her.

Please, baby, just accept my apology and forgive me and let's move on.

He knew what she looked like, hair pulled back in a ponytail, loose ends clinging to her damp forehead, eyes red, tears wetting her cheeks. He wanted nothing more than to reach through the phone and pull her close, stroke her hair, wipe her tears.

"Mark, all I had was your word. You promised me. And my

whole life was built around that promise. Then you broke it. Do you know how that feels?"

He swallowed hard. "No. I don't."

"That's right, you don't. So don't pretend like you do. Look, I gotta go." Then the phone went dead and Cheryl was gone. Again.

Mark shut his phone and dropped his head into his hands. When the sobs came, they came in waves, shaking his body uncontrollably. It was all he could do. He could never make Cheryl love him again. She wouldn't; she couldn't trust him. He'd lost her forever.

❺

The barn seemed to be shrinking, closing in on her.

After being there a week, Amber was getting desperate. What was Judge planning? He'd stopped by yesterday again and dropped off more food, water, and toiletries, even a hairbrush, deodorant, and toothpaste. No toothbrushes, though, but fingers did just fine. He seemed to want to keep them alive and comfortable. But for how long? And why?

Her health was deteriorating. Her sinuses constantly emptied down the back of her throat and settled deep in her chest, causing a residual burn every time she coughed. Her throat ached like an open wound. The sandpaper had turned to shards of glass. She was alive but anything but comfortable. But still, she was thankful for the food and blankets. She found it odd that she could be thankful for anything given the circumstances, but it was something. A pinprick of light in a dark room.

She leaned against the wall, forehead resting on her hands, and stared at the outside world. A falcon circled silently overhead, free to come and go as it pleased. In the distance, along the tree line, a family of white-tailed deer munched on something, the buck keeping careful watch over his ward. The trees were alive with color—reds, oranges, and yellows. Peak week. Her muscles ached to get out and run or hike along some winding trail as it wove through hills, a ribbon of hard-packed dirt shaded by the brilliant canopy. Her mind went back to a vacation she'd taken with her family when she was young. West Virginia in October. She'd never seen trees clothed in such vibrant colors.

When Judge stopped by yesterday, she tried to strike up a conversation with him, ask him some questions. She'd read that in abduction cases it was important to try to humanize yourself and make a connection with your abductor. Maybe he would see her as a person, with loved ones and people who cared about her. But he didn't say a word except to curse at the dogs. Just dropped the two bags of provisions on the floor and left.

She'd tried to talk to Ginny too. But she wasn't talking either. When the younger woman had first appeared, Amber had hoped the two of them could bond, find that solace in each other that only victims shared. They could be each other's support, keep each other sane. But Ginny wanted nothing to do with bonding or solace or support. Whether she was extroverted in the outside world or not was of little value. Here, in the barn, their wooden prison, she was as introverted as a box turtle hiding in its shell. Every so often she'd poke her head out and squint, realize again that nothing had changed and she was still entombed within the four plank walls, and immediately retract her head and go on hiding in her shell. A prison within a prison.

Amber turned and looked at Ginny. She was in the same spot she'd been an hour ago: hunched in the corner, knees pulled to her chest, face like stone. A turtle in her shell. She wouldn't eat, either. Amber had to practically force her to drink some water; and the only time she changed position or location was to relieve herself in the far corner, or, occasionally, to stand up, press herself against the wall, and scream for help until her voice went hoarse. It was a horrible sound, her scream, the sound of panic and fear and uncertainty balled up into a primal shriek. When she was either too exhausted or too hoarse to scream anymore, she'd collapse to her haunches and resume her position in the corner.

At different times, Amber had tried to make conversation with her. But Ginny only stared that blank stare, her hollow eyes focused on nothing. The first day, she did talk when Judge showed up. Asked him a string of questions: Why did you bring me here? Why me? Are you gonna kill me? Where am I? Who are you? Then, when it became quite apparent that Judge wasn't going to respond, she shot a long line of expletives at him and cursed him over and over. Other than that, though, she spoke not a word. But Amber talked to her anyway, held a running monologue. She figured it would do Ginny good to at least hear another human's voice, maybe keep her sane a day longer. And sane was good.

Amber lifted an apple and took a bite of it, letting the juices fill every cavity in her mouth. She held the meat of the fruit on her tongue, savoring the sugary sweetness that leached out of it and teased her taste buds. She marveled that anything could be enjoyed under these circumstances. But under these circumstances, even the littlest comfort, like the sweats she was wearing or the brush she ran through her hair this morning, things she usually took for granted, were a luxury to be enjoyed.

"You know, Ginny," she said, chewing her apple, "in all the years I've lived around here, I've never spent so much time admiring the beauty of nature." It seemed an odd thing to say. How could she be thinking about beauty in a place like this, a prison, a mausoleum for all she knew. But it was talk, and it was true. She swallowed the apple, forcing it down her raw throat. She might as well be swallowing glass.

She turned and looked at Ginny, but met only that blank stare, void of life.

"I've been so busy my whole life with school, friends, parties, work, and everything else under the sun that I've never stopped to really admire my surroundings. I know it's weird to be thinking about that kind of stuff in here, but I've got plenty of time to think, and a lot's been going through my head."

"I'll never see them again."

Amber snapped her head toward Ginny. She spoke! "What was that?"

Ginny shifted her eyes, still void but at least moving, and met Amber's. "I'll never see them again." Her lips barely moved as she said the words.

Amber walked over to her and knelt in front of her. "Who, dear?"

Ginny's eyes fell to the floor again. "Anyone. Brandon, my brothers, my dad..." She coughed up a sob and tears sprang to her eyes. "My mom. I'll never see them again. I haven't talked to my parents in a couple weeks. They've been on vacation." She looked at Amber, tears coursing down her cheeks, leaving trails in the dirt. "Do you think they miss me yet? Even know I'm gone?"

Amber ran a hand over Ginny's head, smoothing her hair. "Oh, honey, of course they do. They probably have the police looking for us right now. They'll find us. Don't worry." She cupped Ginny's face in her hands. "Look, we gotta stay positive, OK? We're in this together and we're gonna get out of it together. And we *will* get out. I promise."

"I want to kill him."

A chill spread over Amber's head and arms. She knew Ginny

was talking about Judge. She felt the same way, but for some reason she hadn't the gumption to actually form the thought yet, let alone verbalize it. "I know." She stroked Ginny's hair again, tears coming to her own eyes now. "I know."

❻

Sheriff Wiley Hickock had just returned to his car from issuing a citation to some moron doing seventy in a forty-five when Jess came over the radio.

"Yeah, Jess. Go ahead."

"You'll never believe this. We got another missing person. A Virginia Grisham. Last seen Thursday night, leaving work. Just For You Salon, off National Highway, near Red Hill. A co-worker said they locked the place up, got in their cars, and left. Said Grisham said she was going home to watch a movie. Her boyfriend called us about it. Said they were supposed to get together on Friday after her shift, and she never showed. They've only been dating a couple weeks, so he didn't press the issue, but then he tried calling her Saturday morning and again in the afternoon and there was no answer either time. Tried again to call her at work, but they said she hadn't shown up for two days in a row. The boyfriend got worried, so he called us. Said it wasn't like her to just up and disappear. Co-workers said the same thing. I'm heading over to her house now if you want to meet me there."

Wiley laid his head back against the seat's headrest, shut his eyes, and sighed. "Did you take my advice?"

"About what?"

"Getting a life."

"Sir, Virginia Grisham. Can you meet me at her house?"

Wiley lifted a hand to his mustache. "Yeah, sure. Where is it?" He hated missing person cases. Jess's personal life, or lack of one, was much more interesting. But probably not much more promising.

"42 Broad Court, near Homewood."

"OK. I know the area. Nice neighborhood. I'll be there in fifteen."

Pulling up along the curb in front of Grisham's house, Wiley killed the engine and climbed out of his cruiser. Jess's car was parked in the driveway and behind it, a white van with *Ned Tatum, Locksmith* stenciled on the side and Ned himself, wearing his trademark white long-sleeve T-shirt, tan overalls, and small oval spectacles, strolling down the sidewalk, toting a small gray tool box.

"Afternoon, sheriff," Ned said, tipping his baseball cap.

"Afternoon, Ned. Thanks for stopping by on a Sunday. Everything open up OK?"

"Piece a cake."

Ned climbed into his van, and Wiley turned back toward the house, a nice brick rancher sitting on a wooded lot. Jess met him at the door.

"Good thing we got old Ned to call on, huh?"

"Yeah. Ned's a good man." Wiley turned and nodded his chin toward the silver Ford Focus parked in the driveway in front of Jess's cruiser. "That her car?"

"Sure is. I checked the perimeter of the house while I was waiting for Ned. No forced entry anywhere. Why don't you look around and I'll go see if the neighbors saw or heard anything."

Wiley rested his hands on his hips and surveyed the neighborhood. A similar rancher sat to the left, no more than a hundred feet away, with a good view of the whole property, and a two-story colonial was to the right, but a row of Rose of Sharon blocked a clear view. Maybe from the second-story windows, though. "OK. Yeah. Do that. I'll check the place out."

Jess headed toward the rancher, and Wiley stepped inside the house. It smelled of rotten garbage and some kind of apple spice scent. Nothing looked disturbed, though. He walked through the house, checking each room for any sign of an intruder. Grisham was a neat freak. Or she was never home. The place looked like it had just been scrubbed and tidied, vacuumed and organized. Nothing was out of place. In the spare bedroom, which she apparently used as an office, papers were arranged on the desk in two neat piles: bills to be paid and papers to be filed. The bathroom sparkled like it had been waxed and polished. Not even a hint of mildew. No hair in the drain. No toothpaste on the mirror. Two towels hung from a wooden towel rack, equally spaced, mirror images of one another. He entered the master bedroom. It looked like a hotel room before the bed is slept in and the room is cluttered with dirty clothes and useless souvenirs. On a small dark-wood table beside the bed, the light on the answering machine blinked. Eight messages.

Wiley crossed the room and hit the play button.

A man's voice came on. "Hey, Gin, it's Brandon. I missed you tonight. Did you forget? Call me." His voice was slightly high-pitched, almost feminine, with a distinct lisp.

He hit it again. Same man. Same lisp. "Ginny, it's me again. Are you there? Call me. I miss you."

Isn't that sweet. Again. "Ginny, you're worrying me. Call me back as soon as you get in."

The next message was a woman. Masculine voice with a hard edge to it. "Hello? Ginny? Where are you, girl? Bonnie's ready to blow her top. I hope you get here soon."

He hit the button again. The woman. Smokey voice. "Ginny. It's Jody again. What are you thinking just not showing up today? Bonnie's ready to kill you, girl. Call me at home."

Wiley snorted. Lispy Brandon and smoky Jody should exchange voices.

The next two were more of the same. One was from Brandon with the woman's voice, one from Jody with the man's voice. Both wondering where dear Ginny was.

Wiley stepped outside the bedroom and paused in the hall. A faint tingling started at the top of his head and moved down his spine. He could feel her here, calling to him. The photo in the living room, her smell in the bedroom, the towels in the bathroom. They spoke to him, reminding him that she was a person, a living, breathing person with a life that would miss her. It chilled him to the bone.

He made his way downstairs to the first floor then down to the basement where a large family room, fully furnished but apparently never used, and a small washroom waited.

Fifteen minutes later, he heard Jess call from the living room. Stomping up the basement steps, he rounded the corner. "Tell me something, how does a single woman hair stylist afford a house like this?"

Jess shrugged. "Beats me. Maybe Mommy and Daddy helped her out. Maybe she won the lottery."

Wiley glanced around the well-furnished living room. "Find anything interesting?"

Jess held her trusty notepad in her right hand. She pointed her thumb in the direction of the colonial. "They're an elderly couple and said they go to bed around nine-thirty and didn't see or hear anything Thursday night. They've seen the new boyfriend a couple times, but that's it. Never talked to him and didn't talk to Grisham much. Said she was real quiet, reclusive."

She pointed in the direction of the rancher to the left. "They heard Grisham's car door shut just before ten. Said that's what time she normally came home. Now, here's something. They also said about forty, forty-five minutes later they heard a couple car doors shut and an engine start. They didn't think anything of it at the time. The husband said he talked to the boyfriend once while they were working in the backyard. Said he seemed like a nice guy."

Wiley grunted. "Aren't they all. There's seven messages on the answering machine. Four from *Brandon*, three from Jody. The co-worker?"

"Yeah."

Wiley looked around the living room. "Well, it looks like we're stuck with nothing again. Except another suspicious boyfriend. Put the pressure on this Brandon fella and grill him good. I want to know where he was Thursday night between ten and eleven. And if he wasn't with Grisham, he better have a good alibi."

Jess cocked her head to the side. "You think we have a serial thing going on here? Or just coincidence."

Wiley shoved his hands in his pockets. "No. I don't think this is the work of a serial. Heck, we don't even know if these two were abducted. They may have just run off somewhere. No one's gotten any ransom calls; we've got no leads. This Mann case is turning out to be a real dead-ender. No doubt this one will too." He dipped his chin and pinched his brow.

Jess had that look on her face. Pursed lips, tight jaw, dimple between her eyebrows right above her nose.

"You don't agree?"

Jess straightened up and brushed a few loose hairs out of her face. "I got an awful feeling this is a serial and there'll be more. I think we should treat it like it was. If we're wrong, we're wrong, but if we're right, we're one step ahead."

Wiley paused to think, combing his mustache. The whole

115

thing made him sick. No good would come of it. "Why don't you like to talk about your personal life?"

Jess gave him a sideways look. "What personal life?"

"Exactly."

"I have a personal life."

Wiley lifted his brow. "Really? You mean when you go home you don't sleep in your uniform and dream about catching Jack the Ripper? You need a man in your life."

"I have a man in my life."

Wiley feigned surprise even though she had caught him off guard. Deputy Jessica Foreman never talked about her personal life, let alone her love life. She was reserved, introverted, and thoughtful. Exactly why Wiley liked her. "You *have* a man? All this time I've been riding you about finding a boyfriend, and you already have one? What's his name?"

Jess turned her eyes to the living room and propped her hands on her waist. "Did I say he was a boyfriend? Can we get back to the case?"

"No. What's his name?"

Jess shot him a look that warned *change the subject.* "Are you gonna treat this like a serial or not?"

"What's his name?"

"Jesus. Happy?"

"Jesus? Like the *Son of God* Jesus?"

"The very one."

Wiley didn't say anything. Jess had succeeded in rendering him speechless. Either she was having some fantasy affair with the Holy One, or she was one of those born-again fanatics, the type he'd grown up with. Either way, it sure explained a lot. Jess never went to the bar with the other cops, never drank even a beer at the station summer picnic, never cussed, never laughed at the crude jokes that floated around the station, and never responded to any of the advances of the other deputies. He was beginning to wonder about her sexual orientation, but now he understood. All too well.

Jess was staring at him. "The case, sir. Can we get back to the case? Serial or not?"

Wiley ran a hand along his jawline, ending at his chin, and shook his head. "Sorry, Jess. Can't do it yet. The minute we declare this thing a serial, we'll have the Feds breathing down our necks, taking over the investigation, yappin' about what they need and what they want, telling me what to do in my own house. Not to mention the resources and expenses involved. I have to be sure before I go that far."

"Well, it's your call. I'll go along with whatever you decide; you know that."

Wiley smiled. "That's why you're my number one."

Chapter 6

❶

I T WAS A DAMP, LIFELESS EVENING. A STARLESS SKY HUNG overhead like a black blanket. A light mist drifted in the air, specks of shimmering dust in the lamplight, chilling to the bone. The campus of Frostburg State University was almost deserted. Barren sidewalks wove through manicured lawns, lighted only by the occasional light post dropping a tent of soft light on the darkened walkway. Benches sat wet and abandoned. Even the air was still and silent.

On the first floor of the Compton Science Center, a three-story brick structure, two windows glowed brightly. One Monday evening class, Chemistry I Lab, would soon be dismissing, and sixteen students, if Judge had counted right, would exit the double glass doors and go their separate ways, making a swift retreat to their dorm rooms. And if he planned correctly, Shelley Kurtz would be the last to exit, alone, and make her way to Westminster Residence Hall on the other side of campus, alone. And if he timed it right, she and he would cross paths at a particular spot along the sidewalk behind Tawes Hall, where there were no light posts and a sprawling maple cast a black shadow over the ground.

He would take her out there and drag her down the hundred-foot grassy slope, where his car would be waiting.

If he planned it right. And, of course, he had planned it right.

Judge glanced at his watch and pushed the light button. 9:55. Five more minutes. Unless Professor Ngyun dismissed early.

Three minutes later the first threesome pushed open the glass doors, followed by a couple holding hands, a group of five college joe types, three girls huddled under one bright pink umbrella, and one middle-aged woman, toting a professional-looking briefcase. Let's see, fourteen in all. Seconds later the door swung open again, and out came Shelley. Short, pudgy, loner Shelley.

Fifteen? Had he miscounted? Apparently he had, or someone had pulled a no-show. Shelley was always the last one out. She was as predictable as Mother's Sunday dinner—roast beef, mashed potatoes, cooked carrots, and dinner rolls.

She stopped just outside the door, turned her face toward the sky, squinting at the mist, then pulled out a pack of cigarettes. After tapping the pack on the palm of her hand, she slid a cigarette out and shoved it between her lips. Cupping a hand around the tube, she flicked her lighter and held it close. The glow of the flame illuminated her chubby face.

Judge tugged the brim of his Stetson a little lower, pulled the collar of his jacket up around his neck, and took off. He had to move quickly to get ahead of her. Fortunately, Shelley didn't move real fast.

Exactly one minute later he rounded the corner of Tawes Hall and waited for her familiar form to appear heading right toward him. There. That gait was unmistakable, sort of a hunchbacked waddle, ugly duckling style. He could even see the orange glow of her cigarette, hovering five feet off the ground like the first lonely star of night. He shoved his hands in the deep pockets of his coat and pulled out a white rag and the vial of ether. Dousing the rag with the chemical, he placed the vial back in his pocket and took to the sidewalk in long, even strides. This was almost too easy. To his right, the lawn sloped down a steep embankment and there, at the bottom, sat his car. He could see the shine of a faraway light post reflecting off the glossy hood.

When he was within thirty feet of her, he slowed just a little and spread the rag out in his right hand. He'd wrap her from behind with his left arm and press the rag to her face with his right. He'd visualized it at least a hundred times.

Twenty feet. She looked up and spotted him for the first time. He diverted his eyes and picked up the pace.

Ten feet. She slowed and blew out a puff of smoke.

Zero feet. As soon as he passed her on the left, he pulled up and began to turn to his left, lifting the rag. He had to make it quick.

"Hey, Shelley!" a woman's voice called and startled him.

Shelley spun around.

He dropped his hand in his pocket.

She looked at him, bewildered, then they both looked at the source of the voice. A thin Asian girl approached in a shuffled jog, a carryall draped over her shoulder. "Wait up."

He cursed to himself. Number sixteen. She must have lingered behind.

Both Shelley and the Asian girl looked at him as if waiting for an explanation. He forced a nervous laugh and smiled. "You startled me. Sorry." Then he turned to make a quick departure, cursing his carelessness, Shelley, and the Asian.

Amber slowly pried open her eyes, still stuck somewhere between dream and reality. Someone was tugging on her shirt...and talking. Instinctively, she pulled away and grunted. She tried to swallow, but her throat would not accept the saliva.

"Amber. Amber."

The voice was familiar. Ginny.

Amber opened her eyes all the way and moaned a groggy, "What?" then immediately regretted forcing sound through her wounded throat.

Ginny tugged harder. "Amber."

Ginny's face was right next to her cheek, and she felt the warmth of the younger woman's breath against her ear.

It was still dark, sometime during the night. The barn was black as tar. The darkness enveloped her like a fog, pressing down upon her like a heavy weight. Amber reached for the water bottle in the straw next to her, untwisted the cap, and took a slow swig. The tepid water felt surprisingly cool against her hot esophagus. "What, Ginny? What is it?"

Ginny leaned closer, so close her nose brushed against Amber's ear. "I hear noises." She said it slowly, fear hanging on every syllable.

Amber held her breath and listened. She heard it too. A faint scratching, like fine-grit sandpaper sliding over soft pine. Back and forth, back and forth. Steady.

"It's the dogs," Ginny whispered. "They're trying to get in. They've been diggin' for hours."

Amber sat up, ignoring the throbbing in her head, and wrapped her arm around Ginny's shoulders. Her eyes were wide, but all she saw was darkness. All she heard was that scratching. Against the dead silence of the night, it grew louder and louder—back and forth, back and forth.

Ginny whimpered. "They're gonna get in. They won't stop until they do."

Amber pressed her fist to her mouth, holding back her own cries of terror. "No. They can't get in. They can't." She said it for her own sake as much as for Ginny's, though she didn't fully believe it herself. She'd heard of dogs scratching through solid wood doors before. It wasn't impossible. And she had no idea when was the last time the dogs were fed. Judge had been bringing her and Ginny food, but what about the dogs? Surely he had to have brought them something. They would have starved to death by now. It had been over a week. How long could a dog go without food? How long until they were crazy enough with hunger that they would dig and scratch all night to get to food? Food that couldn't escape and was no match for their teeth and claws.

Ginny leaned into her and buried her face in Amber's hair. Silent sobs shook her shoulders.

"They can't get in," Amber said again. Her voice sounded weak and frail in the darkness. She coughed loudly. "They won't."

The scratching persisted, unrelenting, until Amber could hold her eyes open no longer and finally gave in to sleep.

Amber's eyes didn't open again until muted light filtered through the gaps between the wallboards. She started to push herself up to a sitting position, then froze and listened. No scratching. The dogs had stopped. She remained motionless for a full minute, eyes searching the interior, listening, half expecting the Dobermans to spring from the shadows and launch into a feeding frenzy. The bats were back from their nightly hunting spree, jostling for position, and squeaking quietly. A barn swallow chirped excitedly from somewhere just outside the barn. But no scratching. No back and forth sandpaper. And no Dobermans in the shadows.

She grasped Ginny's shoulder and shook it gently, still listening for even the faintest sound of those paws or the low, throaty rumble of a growl.

Ginny rolled over and moaned. Straw was tangled in her

hair, and her right cheek was reddened by a maze of indentations from the straw.

"Ginny." She held both hands over her mouth to muffle a cough. The burn in her chest was intensifying, lingering longer after each hack.

Another moan, then Ginny snapped her eyelids open and sat up, eyes wide, searching the barn. "The dogs."

"Listen."

Ginny sat perfectly still, lips slightly parted, hand at her throat, listening. Not even her chest moved.

"They're gone," Amber said.

Ginny shook her head slowly. "No. They're out there. Waiting for us."

Amber stood and walked around the inside perimeter of the barn, searching the outside world for any sign of the dogs. When she had come full circle, convinced that the dogs were truly gone, she knelt in front of Ginny and took both her hands. "Ginny, listen to me. The dogs are gone for now. This happened before. Before you came. They didn't come back until he showed up and called for them. I think they're off looking for food."

Ginny swallowed and looked through a gap in the wall. Her eyes darted back and forth.

Amber squeezed her hands. "Listen. I know a way out of here."

Ginny turned to face Amber again. Her mouth hung open, eyes wide. "Why didn't you tell me before?"

"The dogs were here. And you were so...I thought you'd try something desperate and...well, the dogs."

Amber stood and walked over to where the trapdoor lay covered with straw. She stooped and used her hand to sweep away the straw, revealing the outline of the door. "It's used to drop hay and straw into the stalls below." She slid her finger through an iron ring and lifted the door an inch off the floor. "It isn't locked."

Ginny climbed out of their bed of straw and walked over to the door. Getting down on all fours, she whispered to Amber, "Open it all the way. Let's take a look."

Amber pulled the door open, squeaking on its iron hinges, and laid it back against the floor. They both stared at the ground below.

"How far do you think it is?" Ginny whispered.

"About eight, nine feet."

Amber then got on her belly and dipped her head below the level of the floor. The pressure in her sinuses was almost too much to bear. The ache in her head throbbed like a jack-hammer. The stalls below were empty, of course, and quiet. No dogs. "Pssst." She listened. No dogs.

She pulled herself back up and knelt beside the opening, waiting for the pain in her head to subside. "I think we can do it. But we have to do it now. And fast. No telling when the dogs will be back."

Ginny's eyes were wide. She nodded. "OK. I'm ready."

"I'll go first—"

"Wait! Where will we go?"

Amber blinked, then looked in the direction of the dirt lane. "We'll follow the lane out. It's gotta lead to a larger road."

Ginny nodded again and glanced toward the lane. "Yeah. OK."

Amber scooted herself around and swung her legs through the opening so she was sitting on the edge. Placing her hands on either side of the hole, she slid herself off and dropped through the opening, landing with a thud and rolling back onto her rear. She froze and listened, half expecting the Dobermans to come tearing around the corner and rip her to shreds. But the dogs didn't come. She listened. Above, Ginny's face peered through the opening, framed by the aged boards.

Amber nodded to Ginny. "C'mon," she whispered. "It's OK."

Ginny's face disappeared, and moments later her legs dropped through, then she was falling toward the ground. She hit with a grunt and rolled to her side.

"You OK?" Amber said, helping her up.

Ginny brushed herself off and nodded. There were tears in her eyes and a look of determination Amber had not seen in her yet.

Amber said, "We have to get moving. And we gotta stay quiet. The dogs."

Ginny nodded again, tears now rolling down her cheeks.

Amber led the way, rounding the barn and heading down the dirt lane. On either side of the lane stretched acres of barren field, overgrown pasture, rolling gently like the undulation of the ocean. To the right, in the distance, lay the tree line and, behind that, who knows how many acres of wooded land. Most likely where the dogs were hunting for something to fill their bellies.

They walked quickly—at almost a jog—holding hands and kicking up dust in their stocking feet. Amber's eyes continuously scanned the landscape, looking for any sign of movement, watching for the bob of a Doberman's dark head above the high grass.

Ginny leaned toward Amber and whispered, "What will we—"

"Shhh." Amber put a finger to her mouth. "We'll talk when we get to the main road. Listen for the dogs."

So they jog-walked in silence, listening, watching, straining to hear the sound of grass rustling or barking in the distance. Amber fought the urge to cough, and when she could hold it back no longer, she resorted to burying her mouth in the crook of her elbow to muffle the sound. It would most certainly draw the dogs' attention.

When they had crested the hill over which Judge's white sedan had disappeared, they saw it. Less than a quarter mile ahead, at the end of the lane, lay a two-lane paved road. And freedom.

They both broke into a fast jog, still holding hands. Tears blurred Amber's vision of the lane. She kept her eyes on the beige path that fell in a straight line ahead of her, dividing two green smudges.

When they were no more than one hundred yards from the road, Amber pulled up. "Listen," she said, breathing hard, each inhalation wheezing like the air was being sucked in through a straw. A trickle of sweat broke from her hairline and caught in her eyebrow. Her pulse thumped in her neck.

Ginny stood still, mouth open, chest heaving, eyes going back and forth along the pasture. Her cheeks were bright red, forehead glistening with sweat.

Amber listened closer, wiping the tears from her eyes. She knew she heard something. A whine in the distance.

There.

Her heart kicked against her ribs. The sound of a car's engine.

Before she could form words to warn Ginny, the white sedan appeared on the paved road, slowed, and turned left onto the dirt lane.

Amber squeezed Ginny's hand and yanked her off the road, diving into the tall grass. The sedan's engine growled, wheels spun in the dirt. He'd seen them!

Amber jumped to her feet, grabbed Ginny's arm just above the elbow, and yanked her up too. "C'mon. Run." Then both of them took off across the pasture, grass slapping at their legs, rocks jutting into their feet.

Behind them, Amber heard the sedan's engine settle and a car door close.

She didn't dare look back. She wanted to, had to know how much of a jump they had on Judge, but fear kept her looking straight ahead. Her hand was still around Ginny's arm, and she gripped it tighter, practically dragging the poor girl along. Where she was headed, she had no idea. A thought flashed through her mind to cut to the left and head for the road. Maybe a car would be passing by. Maybe a house was nearby. She dug her feet into the dirt and made a sharp change of direction, yanking Ginny along with her.

Then she heard it. A gunshot, like a crack of thunder, echoing off the trees to her right. She instinctively ducked and hunched her shoulders, waiting for the impact of the bullet. Ginny started crying.

"Duke! Buck!"

Judge was hollering for the Dobermans.

They were doomed. If he didn't shoot them, the dogs would surely get to them. And the road was no more than fifty yards away.

Suddenly, from the tree line, the two Dobermans appeared, barking and cutting through the grass at full speed like black demons. Amber surged forward and lost her grip on Ginny. She swung her head around and saw Ginny sprawled in the grass, belly down.

She pulled up. She couldn't leave Ginny. She just couldn't. Either they both escaped, or they both stayed and took whatever fate held for them. The dogs were getting closer, barking and snarling. Judge was in a full run, barreling through the pasture, rifle in hands. It was over. The chase and maybe their lives. She fell on Ginny, who was now gasping for air between sobs, and covered her with her own body, tensing for the burn of the dog's teeth or the punch of a bullet.

The gun exploded in her ears. She flinched and let out a scream. The dogs had arrived.

"Back off!" Judge hollered. "Buck! Back off! Back!"

Amber held her eyes closed tight, clinging to Ginny beneath her, pulling in air through her raw, swollen throat. The dogs were right there. She could hear them tamping the ground with their paws, slapping their jaws, panting heavily and whining. Judge was there too. She felt him hovering over them.

"Well, well," he said, sucking in air between words. "We got a couple of runners." Amber felt something hard nudge her in the ribs. "Get up."

She lay still, unmoving, tears stinging her eyes.

The nudge came again. "Get...up. Or do I have to turn the dogs loose?"

Reluctantly, Amber pushed herself up and stood facing Judge. He was wearing his Stetson low as usual, faded jeans, and a red and yellow plaid flannel shirt. A large rifle rested comfortably in his hands, the barrel pointed at her. To her right stood the dogs, their dirt-brown eyes bouncing between her and Judge, waiting for permission.

Judge motioned toward Ginny with the rifle. "Get her up too."

Amber bent at the waist and grabbed Ginny under the armpit. She choked the words out. "C'mon, Ginny. Get up."

Ginny covered her head with her hands and screamed something. Amber couldn't make out what it was, but it was defiant. She wasn't getting up.

Redness crept up Judge's neck. His nostrils flared and upper lip twisted into a snarl. "Get up, woman!"

Ginny screamed again and shook her head.

Judge glanced at the dogs, his eyes on fire.

"No," Amber said. She was ready to beg. "Please, no. Let me talk to her."

Judge just glared. The dogs kneaded the ground impatiently, tongues darting in and out of their mouths, whimpering occasionally.

Amber knelt beside Ginny and whispered in her ear, "Ginny. If you don't stand up, he'll set the dogs on you. We'll get out of this alive. Trust me. Just do as he says."

For a moment it seemed she wouldn't cooperate, like she had chosen the fate of the dogs over the wrath of Judge. But after several unending seconds she wiped her eyes and nose with her sleeve and slowly stood. Her face was red and dirty, streaked with tears, smeared with mucus. Her hair was tangled and clung to her forehead in jagged bunches. She stared at Judge, lips thin, eyes narrow.

Judge's mouth parted in a crooked smile. "Good. You do know how to listen. Now, here's what we're gonna do. You're gonna march your little selves right back to that lane and back to the barn. I'm gonna follow in the car. Don't get any ideas about running again. Remember, I'm the only obstacle between you and the dogs. And from the looks of things, they're right hungry. Now move."

Amber reached down and grasped Ginny's hand. "C'mon. Stay close."

They shuffled through the grass in no hurry, Judge following close behind, poking them with the tip of the rifle's barrel. The dogs were somewhere back there too. Amber could hear them weaving through the grass, panting loudly, their paws falling softly on the ground.

When they reached the dirt lane, Judge nudged her with the rifle. "In front of the car." He then opened the back door of the sedan and ordered the dogs in. Slipping into the front seat, he fired up the engine and hung his head out the window. "Now, ladies. March. And remember the dogs."

Amber tugged on Ginny's hand and began walking. "It'll be OK. If he wanted to kill us, he would have done it already." But she didn't believe the words herself. She was sure they were marching to their deaths. What was the saying on death row? Dead man walking? A sense of doom settled over her then, and she almost broke for the road. Maybe it was better to die at the jaws of the dogs than the hands of Judge. Who knew what he had in store for them when they got back to the barn? Maybe something far worse than being eaten alive by a couple of ravenous dogs. If that was possible. Which she imagined it was.

Ginny plodded along in silence, head hung low, shoulders slumped, the picture of defeat. And that was just what Judge wanted, to defeat them. Amber straightened her shoulders, lifted her chin, and took deliberate strides, a sudden surge of stubbornness empowering her. She wasn't dead yet, and until that moment came, she would give Judge no indication of the vortex inside her that was swallowing her hope. No way. She had to be strong. Or at least *appear* strong.

When they arrived back at the barn, Ginny began to whimper and cry again. The very sight of the wooden tomb sent shivers through Amber. Judge cut the engine and exited the sedan, letting the dogs loose. "Stay!" he ordered, though Amber wasn't sure if he was talking to the dogs or them. She stood still, waiting for the death bell to toll.

Judge approached Amber and Ginny, his boots landing softly in the dry dirt. Amber noticed he was rifleless. He'd left it in the car. With arms hanging casually at his sides, he nodded his head toward the barn. "Inside."

Amber clutched Ginny's hand and pulled her through the cutout door in the side of the barn. Home sweet home. The first thing Amber noticed was the smell. Over a week of human waste. She knew it was bad before, but spending time in fresh air had made it seem even worse. She almost gagged but swallowed the bile that had risen in her throat. *Be strong.*

Ginny immediately headed for their corner nest and fell on her bottom, pulling her knees to her chest. Amber glanced at the open trapdoor then at Judge. He too was looking at it, eyes wide, mouth tight, jaw set, hands clenching into fists then relaxing, clenching and relaxing, like he was pumping the life out of two stress balls.

Finally, Judge shifted his eyes to Amber, held his gaze there for what seemed minutes, blinked twice, then sighed. He then spun on the heels of his boots and exited the barn, leaving the door open. Amber took a step to her left so she could see what he was up to. She saw him go around to the back of the car, the dogs circling his legs, and open the trunk. She had the sudden urge again to make a run for it. With the trunk open, she couldn't see him, which meant he couldn't see her. Could she slip out of the barn unnoticed and hide in the pasture? Maybe she could stay low enough to conceal herself in the tall grass, crawl on her belly all the way to the road.

She shook her head. Ridiculous idea. The dogs would track her down in no time. She had to think more clearly than that if she was going to survive this thing.

After a few seconds, the car trunk slammed shut, and Judge strode back to the barn with something in his right hand.

He marched over to the trapdoor, dropped it shut, and slipped a padlock through the iron ring, all without saying a word. When he was finished, he stood, glared at Amber, then at Ginny, and turned to leave again.

A scream pierced the still air of the barn. "Why?" It was Ginny.

Amber spun her head around and found Ginny standing in the corner, clutching her chest, eyes red and swollen, mouth turned down at the corners, an inverted U. She looked like she'd been through a war. And, in a way, she had.

Judge had spun around too and now stared at Ginny, a curious look on his face. Not anger or hate, not anything evil. More like...pain.

Ginny leaned forward and screamed again, "Why? Why did you take us?"

Judge took a step toward Ginny, then halted. His left eye twitched and his hands began pumping again. He opened his mouth, then clamped it shut and swallowed hard. His Adam's apple seemed to be stuck in his throat. When he opened his mouth again, his lips trembled ever so slightly. "Why? Because...because I watched her burn. *They* burned her, and I stood there helpless and watched."

Amber glanced at Ginny, who was staring at Judge with an open mouth and wide eyes. She obviously hadn't expected an answer. She then glanced back at Judge and for a moment thought she saw something glisten in his eye. Was it a tear?

Judge continued. "Then *I* took the blame while *they* walked." He shrugged his shoulders and frowned. And yes, there was a tear. It spilled out of his eye and ran a track down his cheek. Either he didn't notice or didn't mind because he did nothing to hide it. "Someone's gotta pay."

He turned without saying another word and headed for the door.

"How many were there?" Amber asked in a low voice. She was beginning to understand his motive. Peering into his mind reminded her of the time she paid two dollars at the county fair to see the "lobster people." Intrigue and curiosity had pushed her there, but once she saw that the "freaks" behind the curtain were no more than normal people with some odd deformity that had fused their fingers into claws, she felt a mixed sense of guilt and revulsion and pity. And she wished she hadn't looked in the first place.

Judge stopped with one foot through the door, turned his head to the side, and opened his mouth. He stood like that for at least three seconds, shifting his jaw side to side, then closed his mouth, turned his head away, and left.

Amber and Ginny stood in total silence as the door shut, the lock engaged, and the cinder block fell back into place. The car door opened, then shut, and the engine groaned to life. But the car didn't move. No sound of tires grinding over dirt or engine fading into the distance. It just sat there, idling.

"What's he doing?" Ginny asked.

Amber walked over to the door and peeked through a crack. The sedan sat in the dirt, white smoke puffing out of its muffler, the dogs circling it, noses to the ground. She could see Judge's silhouetted Stetson-less head above the headrest, unmoving. "Nothing," she said. "Just sitting there."

Judge eased the back of his head against the headrest, closed his eyes, and drew in a long deep breath, filling his lungs with cool air. His hands rested lightly on his thighs, fingers splayed. That hadn't gone so well. Did he actually cry in front of them? No matter, the outcome would be the same. And besides, they needed to know, they needed to see it firsthand—he wasn't a monster.

He thought about what he'd said in there. *I stood there helpless and watched.* He did watch too. Oh, he tried to turn away. The moment the flames licked at Katie's skin and she shrieked in both terror and pain, he tried to turn his head away, but he couldn't. Instead he leaned against the barn door, hugging it, digging his fingers into the wood until they bled, watching, watching the flames engulf her, watching her writhe in pain, watching her skin turn black like barbecued chicken. He hated himself for watching, knew he shouldn't, but he just couldn't tear his eyes away from the grisly scene. It was like some unseen hand was grasping his chin, squeezing his cheeks, holding his head there and a voice saying, *Look! Look! You have to watch this so you will never forget.* And he'd known then and there he would never forget. How could he?

It didn't take long for the flames to spread throughout the rest of the barn, and he had to flee. He ran through the cornfield until he could run no longer. Then he collapsed on the ground, exhausted, and cried. Oh, how he cried, like never before. The tears seemed to be sucked out of him, pulling every ounce of fluid in his body with them, until he was completely drained and dry.

He had no idea how long it was before he finally heard the wail of sirens. Then, after some time, the wail of Mr. McAfee when he found out his youngest daughter—Katydid, he called her—was in the barn.

Judge had curled into a ball and covered his ears to block out the sound of the grief-stricken father. It was the first time he'd ever heard a grown man cry, and it sent eerie chills racing along his body. Cries and groans and curses rose into the air with the black smoke and floated up to heaven.

Days later he was confronted with the awful conclusion. Bethany had told her side of the story, and he was taking the blame. They were blaming him! Not that he did it intentionally; nobody was saying that. They were saying that he was playing with matches and must have been careless. Just a stupid accident. By a stupid kid. But from then on, none of the McAfees would even look at him. Accident or not, they blamed him.

He pulled his thoughts out of the painful past and ran a hand over the vinyl seat. Tears blurred his vision, and a lump sat in his throat like a tumor. A deep sense of loss had settled over him. He thought of Amber and Virginia in the barn. They had nothing to do with Katie's death—murder—but, like he said, someone had to pay. They were like the lambs he'd learned about in Sunday school all those years ago. The ones the Israelites sacrificed. The lambs were innocent of the crimes of the people, but...someone had to pay. Virginia and Amber and the ones to come were like the lambs, a substitutionary sacrifice.

Justice had to be satisfied.

He sat a moment longer, thinking on that, turning it over and over in his head, like his grandmother used to churn butter. After a few minutes he reached up and turned the key, killing the engine.

Ginny looked up. "What? What is it? The engine stopped."

Amber returned to the crack in the door and pressed her face against it. "He's getting out." The car door shut, and Judge's footsteps drew closer to the barn. The cinder block tumbled away, the lock disengaged, the door opened. Judge stepped one foot through the door and stopped. His Stetson sat even lower on his brow, and his face remained turned toward the floor. His shoulders were slumped, arms relaxed at his side. Anything but killer-like.

"What do you need?" he asked.

Amber looked at Ginny, whose face was expressionless, a blank slate, then back at Judge. "Some clean clothes would be nice, underwear. Maybe some new socks." She looked again at Ginny, seeking a suggestion, but she still looked dumbfounded by Judge's request.

Judge dipped his chin in a shallow nod, still facing the floor. "Anything else?"

Amber waited a few seconds, trying to decipher the motive behind Judge's sudden interest in their well-being. Maybe he was softening some. Maybe there was some hope after all. Finally, she swallowed and said, "Something other than apples. Maybe some"—she looked at Ginny for help but got nothing but the same blank stare—"cereal or Pop-tarts or granola bars. And some tissues."

Judge nodded again, backed out, and shut the door. Minutes later, the engine fired up and the sedan rolled away.

When the engine's whine had faded, Ginny fell back in the straw, covered her face with her hands, and let the tears come, like a levy being breached. "He's toying with us," she sobbed, choking out the words. "He's gonna kill us."

Chapter 7

❶

MARK LEANED AGAINST HIS '73 MUSTANG, COLLECTING his thoughts. Dad's funeral yesterday had left him shaken. Depressing wouldn't even begin to describe it. The thin, balding preacher went on and on about what a pillar in the church Dad was, what a godly man.

A devout family man and model for all of us to emulate.

He ran down the list of ministries Dad had been involved in over his fifty-odd years of church participation, then waxed eloquent about the eternal glory Dad was experiencing.

In the presence of Jesus. Experiencing perfect peace. Glory. Amen.

But the look on Dad's face the moment before he crossed that line from life to death was anything but peaceful. It was one of terror and confusion. Panic. And it would stick with Mark for the rest of his life.

Then the testimonies came. And came and came and came. For over an hour people from the church—Grace Independent Baptist Church—stood behind the little wooden podium, wrung their hands, wiped their tears, and spoke about the virtues of the man they called Brother Ed.

If they had only known the real man, Mark thought. If they had only been there in the last fleeting moments, when reality finally set in, and Dad removed the mask and faced himself for who he really was: Edgar M. Stone, hypocrite for life.

The preacher said Dad's passing was a cause for celebration, a time of joy, but Mark knew better. In those last minutes when Dad was confessing like a man ready to be fried in the electric chair, when he had torn his heart wide open and let all the gunk show, no one was celebrating. There was no joy in that room. And Mark knew—he didn't know how, but he just *knew*—that Dad was not experiencing everlasting joy right now. The screams still echoed through his head, and if he listened close enough, he could almost make out Dad's baritone voice among them. It put a nauseating knot in his gut. Dad was there. *Weeping and gnashing of teeth.* A lifetime full of good works and playing the game of church as well as anyone had gotten him nowhere.

And that's what made it so depressing. So much *more* than depressing.

After the funeral, Mark had headed home and pulled out the phone book. He had had five hours on the road to think, and he had decided to talk to someone else about the screams. As he ran his finger down the long list of churches, one caught his eye—Mount Savage Community Church. It wasn't the name that interested him as much as the motto beneath it: Real Church for Real People in the Real World. The pastor's name was Tim Shoemaker.

So this morning Mark had gotten ready and headed over to the small town of Mount Savage. He didn't have an appointment, didn't call ahead. He was just going on a whim. He had nothing else to do.

The church was a quaint brick building with a steep-pitched slate roof; short, chunky steeple; flaking white paint around the windows and door; and one stained-glass window over the front door bearing the image of Jesus holding a lamb. A few scrubby shrubs nestled close to the building, and a handful of overgrown oaks stood behind the church. Other than that, any kind of landscaping was sparse. The church sat in the middle of a gravel parking lot, in the middle of nowhere. It was actually a few miles outside of Mount Savage, down a twisting country road littered with potholes. A faded gray trailer propped up on cinder blocks was parked beside the church with a sign that read *Church Office* on the door. Beside the trailer sat an early-model, steel blue Ford Taurus station wagon with a hood full of chipped paint and a cock-eyed rear bumper.

Mark pushed away from his car and walked over to the trailer, hands in the pockets of his jeans, gravel crunching beneath his sneakers. He climbed the three wooden steps to the trailer's door, knocked, and waited. It was a chilly morning, and the smell of burning wood hung in the air. Mark hadn't seen any other houses along this road, but someone obviously lived nearby. Maybe the parsonage was on the other side of the oak grove.

A few seconds later he heard heavy footsteps inside the trailer and the door swung open. A man stood there, no more than fifty but older than forty, trim and well built, dressed in khakis and a red short-sleeve polo shirt, untucked. He had a hard face full of sharp angles and hollow cheeks pocked with acne scars. His short-cropped brown hair was sprinkled with gray. Intense blue eyes, set narrow, peered from deep sockets.

"Can I help you?" the man asked, holding the door open with one hand, a pen in the other.

Mark shifted his weight. "Yes, uh, my name's Mark Stone. Are you the pastor?"

The man smiled. A nice smile, warm and inviting. His eyes

sparkled in the early morning light. "Sure am." He stuck out a hand and shook Mark's. "Tim Shoemaker."

"Nice to meet you, Pastor Shoemaker—"

Shoemaker held up a hand. "Tim will do."

Mark smiled. He liked this guy already. "OK. Um, I don't have an appointment or anything, but I was wondering if I could talk to you about something."

Tim's smile broadened. "Well, if that just doesn't beat it all."

"Excuse me?"

"Oh, I'm sorry. See, I usually don't come in to the office this early unless I have an appointment. I do most of my studying at home. But this morning I just had this urge, you know, a feeling right in here"—he tapped his sternum with his fist—"that I needed to come in this morning. Now I know why. So come in, come in. Looks like you had an appointment after all."

Mark stepped through the doorway into a small waiting area. Two upholstered chairs sat against one wall, and a dark wooden table sat across from them against the other wall. On the table were an assortment of magazines, a potted plant, and a lamp. An oval woven rug lay in the middle of the room.

"Follow me," Tim said. "My office is back here."

As Tim turned to lead the way, Mark noticed a spider web tattoo circling the preacher's left elbow and a circle of small skulls around his right elbow.

The office was a small room with a metal desk and wooden chair in one corner, a beige bookcase in another, and a potted tree in the other. Across from the desk sat two more upholstered chairs just like the ones in the waiting room. Nice. Quaint. And nothing like Reverend Mahoney's over at St. Agnes's.

Tim slipped in behind his desk and sat in the wooden chair. "Have a seat," he said, motioning to one of the upholstered chairs.

Mark sat and crossed his right leg over his left.

Tim leaned both his elbows on the desk and laced his fingers, and Mark now noticed a tattoo of a black widow crawling up his right forearm. Tim patted the spider. "I see you noticed my tattoos."

Mark blinked and looked away from spider. "Uh, yeah." Should he say more? What was there to say? A preacher with spider and skull tattoos? Maybe he came to the wrong church.

"Reminders of where I came from," Tim said, his smile forming deep crevices in his pocked face. "I lived a pretty rough life in my younger years. Got in with the wrong crowd and, you know, sorta went off the deep end. Thought I was really bad. Then one day I woke up in jail with dudes that *were* really bad and, you know, reevaluated my life. A couple weeks later I found Christ, and He changed my life." He patted the spider again. "But some things about your past don't go away so easily. That's why I call them reminders. Every time I look at my tats, I remember where I was and where I was headin', and where I am now and where I'm headin' now."

OK. Mark was intrigued. A preacher who had taken a walk on the dark side. At least he knew what it was like *over there*. "So how did you become a preacher?"

Tim chuckled and leaned his head forward until his fingers touched his chin. "College is free in prison, you know. So I made good use of my time in the slammer and went to Bible college. Graduated in three years too. Thank you, Joe Taxpayer."

Mark was starting to like this preacher. He was like no other he'd ever met. He wasn't pretentious or pious or high-and-mighty Reverend Father Almighty. He was just Tim, a man who had taken a stroll in the land of the forbidden, did time, and had a criminal record and tattoos to show for it. He was who he was, and he was comfortable with that. It had been a long time since Mark had seen a man, especially a preacher, who was comfortable in his own skin, no matter how inked up it was. He just might be able to get some answers from this guy.

"Are you from around here, Mark?" It was small talk, and Mark hadn't come for small talk, but something about Tim made it seem like more than small. Mark could tell this unorthodox preacher was sincere, probably sincere in everything he did.

"I live in Pineville. Grew up in Virginia."

"What do you do for a living?"

"I own a garage, Stone Service Center. Been doing it for ten years now." He'd opened the garage a month before he and Cheryl exchanged vows. They had such high hopes then, for the garage and their marriage. Ironically, the business was doing better than their marriage.

"I'm looking for a new mechanic," Tim said. He motioned out the window. "My beater out there likes the attention, I think. Spends more time in someone else's garage than my own."

"Why are you looking for a new mechanic?"

Tim wrinkled his forehead into a washboard and smiled. "It seems the guy I had working on it liked finding things to fix. Things that didn't necessarily need fixing, if you know what I mean."

Mark knew exactly what he meant. It was those kind of mechanics that gave the rest of them a bad rap. Most mechanics were hardworking, honest men, but there were a few out there who cast a shadow over the profession. When Mark got into auto work, he'd hoped to be one of the honest ones who changed the perception. "Unfortunately, they're out there. But not as many as you think."

"Stone Service Center, you say?"

"Yeah. Right in Pineville."

Tim smiled. "Mark, you just got yourself a new customer."

"Thanks. I hope I can give your car a comfortable visit."

Tim laughed, then glanced at Mark's ringless left hand. "You got a girlfriend or something?"

Mark was afraid the subject would surface sooner or later, and he didn't want to get into his marriage problems with Tim. That wasn't why he came here. With his thumb, he rubbed the empty space where his ring should have been. "No, I've been married ten years. Don't wear my ring, though. It's a safety thing. I met my wife, Cheryl, at a friend's birthday party. We dated a few years, then got married." The party was Jeff's. Mark knew him through high school, Cheryl through Wendy, who was dating Jeff at the time. Their first words came back to Mark like a torrent, sweeping up emotions he did not want to show to Tim or anyone else.

—*Great party, huh?*

—*Yeah. Good cake. Real ... chocolaty.*

—*My name's Cheryl. I'm a friend of Wendy's. We've known each other since third grade.*

—*Nice to meet you. I'm Mark. Friend of the birthday boy. Good cake.*

"What does she do?"

Tim's voice was like a lifeline, saving Mark from the flood of emotion carrying him off to that shipwreck of a memory. "She's a graphic designer."

"Any kids?"

"Not yet. Maybe someday." Mark swallowed to bury the tears that burned at the back of his eyes. This wasn't why he came here.

As if he could sense Mark's uneasiness, Tim said, "So what do you want to talk about, Mark?"

Mark uncrossed his legs, shifted in the chair, then met Tim's steady blue eyes. "Do you believe in hell? That it's a real place?"

"Whoa," Tim said, arching his eyebrows. He sat back in his chair and flexed his jaw muscles, narrowing his eyes. "It's not often I have a stranger show up on my doorstep asking me if I believe in a place of eternal damnation. That's deep stuff."

"I know it's an odd question, but..." He let the words trail off, hoping Tim would step in and finish whatever thought he had had and lost.

"But what?" No such luck.

Mark opened his mouth to say something, then clamped it closed. The explanation wasn't that easy.

Tim let him off the hook. "But it's something you've been pondering, wrestling with. How can a loving God send someone to such a horrible place? Is that it?"

Mark shrugged. "Sort of. I just want to know if it exists. If it's a real place."

"Do you go to church anywhere, Mark?"

Mark dropped his eyes to the floor. "Not recently. I grew up in a Baptist church. Left it when I was a teenager."

Mark didn't look up but felt the weight of Tim's stare. "Then you know what the Bible teaches about hell. Eternal separation from God. Weeping and gnashing of teeth. A place where the worm doesn't even die. Darkness. Fire. Unquenchable thirst. Does it sound like the Bible is describing a real place to you?"

"I guess. I mean, yes, it does. I always believed it was a real place, anyway."

Tim dipped his head so he could meet Mark's eyes. "So why the question? If you believe it's a real place, why does it matter what I think?"

Suddenly a lump rose in Mark's throat, and tears began to burn his eyes. He didn't want this to happen, but he'd been thinking about it a lot lately. Hell, that is. If the screams were really from hell, that meant Jeff, Jerry, and Dad were all there.

And if they were there, that meant Mark was surely headed there too. *If* it was a real place. And *if* the screams were real.

Tim leaned forward again and picked up a pen. "What is it, Mark? I know there's more to it than just wondering if hell is a real place." He twirled the pen through his fingers. "That's not the real reason you came."

Mark wiped at his eyes with his sleeve. "What would you say if I told you I've been hearing hell? The screams, the weeping, the agony."

The pen stopped twirling and fell to the desk. "What do you mean? In your dreams?"

"No. On the phone." Mark then told Tim everything, starting with Jeff's call and ending with Dad's death. He told him about the screams and the way they had sliced right through him like ice water in his blood and how they had always preceded death, like an eerie warning. Tim nodded occasionally and grunted frequently, but he never took his eyes off Mark. His jaw remained firm and his blue eyes intense, hardly even blinking. When he was done, Mark sat back and sighed.

Tim didn't say anything at first. He sat there behind his metal desk and stared at some papers, looking like he was deep in thought. Finally, he raised his head. "I thought you said you were raised in a Baptist church. Was your dad a believer?"

"I always thought so. And apparently he did too. But at the end he admitted it was all just a game, a show he put on, fooling even himself. Tim, if you could've seen the look on his face right before—" Mark pressed his fist against his mouth, holding back a sob that was pushing up his throat.

When he looked up again at Tim, there were tears in the preacher's eyes. "I'm sorry, Mark. Really, I am. I know it's hard. I lost my dad two years ago, and to my knowledge, he didn't know Christ. I know what you're going through. I do."

"What do you think they mean? The screams, that is."

Tim lowered his eyebrows and frowned. That intense look again. "Honestly, Mark, I've never heard of anything like this happening before. It gives me chills, you know? But my best guess is that they're a warning."

"A warning. So what should I do?"

Tim picked up the pen again and starting twirling it. "Let's start with this. Do you know where you will go when *you* die?"

Mark had never been asked that question before. Not point-blank like that, anyway. Growing up in a Baptist church he just assumed he was on the straight and narrow. After all, he was Brother Ed's son. Was there any question about the state of his soul? He'd always thought he was going to heaven, but then again, so did Dad. He needed some time to think about it. "I—I don't know. I'd like to think I'll go to heaven. I mean, I was born again as a kid. I said the prayer and went forward in church and everything. Was even baptized when I was twelve."

Mark remembered the day well. The baptism took place in a waist-high pool along Cody Creek. It was a muggy summer day, and the water felt cool as it soaked through his Wranglers and wrapped around his legs. He remembered standing next to Pastor Dickson and Pastor Dickson asking him several questions (all of which he had answered yes to), then saying something about the Father, the Son, and the Holy Spirit, then grasping him with one hand on his chest and the other behind his neck. He remembered the feeling of helplessness as he slipped under and the muddy Cody Creek water engulfed his face and filled his ears and nose. He remembered Pastor Dickson pulling him up and his feet slipping on the creek bed and the mixture of laughter and *hallelujahs* and *praise the Lords* from the onlookers. It had felt so good at the time. So *right*. The way the water ran off his face and the sun warmed his skin. But thinking about it now, was it just more of the game? Hollow, meaningless motions?

"—Mark." Tim was talking to him.

He looked away from his hands and found Tim's blue eyes.

"Mark, doing those things won't get you into heaven. It's gotta be in here." He tapped his chest with his index finger.

Mark knew he was right. After all, wasn't that really what Dad was saying? He had done all the right things, lived the right kind of life, but the truth of it never made it to his heart. And in the end, he didn't even know how to get it there.

"I know," Mark said. His voice sounded tinny and hollow in his own ears. "I—I need to think about this."

Tim leaned further forward on the desk and looked Mark right in the eyes. "Don't spend too long thinking about it. I think God's trying to get your attention. But before you can help anyone else, you have to help yourself. Trust Jesus. Mark, none of us is guaranteed tomorrow. Remember that. You *know* that. That's what this is really all about, isn't it? The screams and all? Life is like a vapor. Here today and gone tomorrow. You know what the Bible says: it's appointed unto man once to die. Everyone has an appointment with death. For some reason, you're being given a little heads-up. But when will *your* appointment come due?" He raised his eyebrows and tapped the desk with the palm of his hand. "Think about it. Pray about it. You'll find your answer."

By the time Tim was done, there were tears in Mark's eyes again. Tim's words had pierced him deeply. He knew they were true, every one of them. He'd known it all his life. But he wasn't ready to dig that deep into his own soul yet. Not here. There were things there he needed to confront in private. Things that needed to be wrestled with and brought out into the light. Dark things. Hurtful things.

"Thanks, Tim." He stood and headed for the waiting room.

"Hey."

Mark turned around at the doorway, one hand resting on the jamb.

Tim was still seated behind his desk, pen laced between his fingers. "You know you're welcome to join us Sunday morning. Ten a.m."

Mark smiled, but his heart wasn't in it. He knew he wouldn't show up, and from the look on Tim's face, the tattooed preacher knew it as well. "I know it."

The single naked bulb hanging from the ceiling cast a dull yellow hue over the room. The windows were covered with black cardboard. He didn't need any nosy kids discovering his lair and running home to mommy and daddy blabbing about the freak down the street.

Judge stood in the middle of the floor, hands on his hips, surveying the change he'd just made. The pictures of Shelley had been removed, shredded, and burned. She was a lost cause; she'd seen his face. There would be no element of surprise. Not to worry, though. She was replaceable. When it came right down to it, they were all replaceable. Really, wasn't everyone?

Everyone except Katie. There would never be another Katie McAfee.

But as far as Shelley was concerned, she was disposable. He had a backup. Kristen Willit. Twenty-five. Single. Average looks. Maybe below average. Second shift material handler at Exco Industries. Still lived at home with mom and pop. A leech.

He only had a few grainy photos of her leaving work, getting in her car, and taking a smoke break. She would do, though. But she'd have to get in the rear of the line. The face looking at him now from the wall behind the desk was anything but average. Now there was natural beauty. Thick, honey-blonde hair. Small, nicely shaped nose. High cheekbones. Full lips. And stunning blue eyes. But there was a sadness in those eyes. A woman so beautiful should have nothing to be sad about, he'd thought the first time he noticed the emptiness. He knew she was married but lived in a small apartment in Lonaconing while her husband lived in a Cape Cod outside Frostburg. Married but separated. Probably the source of that sadness.

She worked as a graphic designer for Prizm Printing in Frostburg. Eleven to seven shift. Picking her up after work would never do. She always left with three other employees who all parked together. Safety in numbers. Smart woman. But she jogged every morning along Jackson Mountain Road. Two miles out, two miles in. Of course, there was the problem of other traffic on the road. Nothing a few orange cones and the use of a service road that ran through the Dans Mountain Wildlife Management Area couldn't take care of. With a little preplanning, it would be easy.

He'd scope the area out once more tomorrow and time her so he knew exactly where she'd be along her course. He'd then wait a day and pick her up. *The girls will be happy to get some more company.*

Then hopefully, if everything went as planned, Kristen would follow a couple days later.

By this time next week, it could all be over.

Justice served.

Case closed.

Mark pushed open the glass door of Ray's Family Restaurant and heard the familiar jingle of bells overhead. He hadn't set foot in the diner since Cheryl found out about Rachel. He'd made every effort to put this part of his life behind him and forget about it...and Rachel. But the day had left him depressed and confused and vulnerable. He needed to hear Rachel's laugh, see her smile, smell her flowery scent.

After leaving Mount Savage Community Church and the tattooed preacher, he went home and spent the better part of the day milling around the house not really doing anything but thinking. Tim's words had hit him hard, like a sledgehammer to the chest.

Everyone has an appointment with death. When will your appointment come due?

An appointment with death. And what then? Heaven or hell? He had thought about it until his brain literally ached. Oh sure, he knew all the proper Christian jargon for such pondering. Saved. Born again. New creation. But what did it all really mean? He remembered Pastor Dickson, red-faced and drenched in a hot summer sweat, screaming from the pulpit, "Give your life to Christ! Turn it over to Him, you sinners. Confess and be saved!" But how? How does one come to Christ? And why would Christ even want him? He'd done nothing with his life. Nothing profitable, anyway. Just a series of bad decisions that wound up hurting others. *Here I am, Lord. Sorry my life is such a wreck.*

There had to be more to it than that. There just had to be.

He stood just inside the door of the diner and looked around. Nothing had changed. He could see Phil in the kitchen, hovered over the grill, forehead glistening. Wanda was waiting on a table, chewing hard on the gum in her mouth, and at the far end, with her back turned toward him, was Rachel. He took in the familiar shape of her body and allowed a subtle smile to play across his lips.

"Mark!"

He snapped his head around to find the hulking image of Jim Ray lumbering toward him. Jim was one of the largest, if not *the* largest, men Mark had ever met. He had a chest like a front-end loader and a belly like a cement mixer. His forearms were thick and wound tight like bunched-up steel cable. When he walked, he thundered forward with all the determination of an earthmover. Jim pulled up in front of Mark, a thick smile pushing his cheeks into balls of stubbled fat, extended his over-sized roughened hand, and shook Mark's whole body. "Good to see ya, buddy. Why don't you come 'round no more?" He had a distinct Maryland accent that clambered out of his mouth with no more gracefulness than a dump truck.

As far as Mark knew, Jim had no idea what had gone on between Mark and Rachel and Cheryl, and he didn't need to know. "Oh, I've just been really busy. Sorry I haven't stopped in lately."

Jim gave him a sideways look, one eyebrow cocked in skepticism, then laughed and slapped Mark on the shoulder. "That's OK, buddy. I know it's nuthin' personal. Hey, why don't you have a seat right over here and I'll hook ya up with some grub. Hot dog special, am I right?"

Mark nodded and laughed. "You have a good memory, but not tonight. What kind of pie is fresh today?"

"Ahh. Straight for the good stuff. Phil made up some lemon pies and his famous French apple. Personally, I'd go with the apple. Very good."

"Sounds good. The apple it is then. And is it OK if I sit in Rachel's section?"

Jim slapped Mark's shoulder again. "Sure, sure. Go have a seat, and I'll bring the pie myself. And coffee?"

"Great."

Mark headed down the aisle between booths on his right and

bar stools on his left and slid into a booth toward the back. Rachel was nowhere in sight. Seconds later, she backed through the swinging door from the kitchen, carrying two trays loaded down with dinner plates. When she turned, her eyes met his and she stopped, cheeks suddenly flushing a deep pink. She held his gaze for a few seconds then walked right by him without saying a word and served the family of five two booths down. When she was done, she stood by his table, one hand on her hip, the other tucking the two trays under her arm.

"What brings you here?" Her face was stone, and there was no emotion in her voice at all.

Mark looked at her, studying the sloping angles of her face. He knew them by heart. "I'm not sure."

She sighed and opened her mouth to speak but—

"Here ya go, sir," Jim said, swooping in from behind Rachel. He slid the pie in front of Mark and set a cup of black coffee next to it.

"Thanks, Jim," Mark said, then reached for the sugar.

When Jim had left to man his spot behind the register, Rachel sat on the bench across from Mark. "What are you doing here? I thought we agreed not to see each other anymore."

Mark dumped some sugar into his coffee and began stirring it. "Look, I—I don't know. I had a bad day, bad week. My dad died and his funeral was yesterday."

"I'm sorry to hear that. Really I am. But you shouldn't have come here. What did you think was gonna happen?"

Mark set the spoon on the saucer and lifted the fork. "I don't know. I guess I—I just needed...wanted to see you, that's all."

Rachel lifted both hands, palms up. "Well, here I am."

Mark let the fork drop to the table. "Look, I'm sorry, OK. I never even apologized to you. I'm sorry."

Rachel's eyes couldn't hide the hurt and guilt she'd probably carried with her since Cheryl caught them. "You never even told me you were married. If I'd known that, I never would have gotten involved with you. The last thing I ever wanted was to move in on another woman's man and wreck their marriage. I'm not that kind of person."

"I know you're not. I know. I was wrong. I know it, believe me."

Rachel leaned back and crossed her arms over her chest as if protecting her heart from more hurt. "Are you and your wife still together?"

"Barely. She moved out and got an apartment over in Lonaconing. I expect the divorce papers will show up any day now."

Rachel's face softened, a look that used to warm Mark on even the coldest days. "How are you doing?"

Mark blew out a sigh. Part of him wanted to play the role of victim, the poor husband who admitted he did wrong and only wanted to make amends with his wife who was too stubborn and bitter to even try to understand his true feelings, but part of him knew that even if it worked, it would only end in more heartbreak. And he'd broken enough hearts already. "I've been better. But I've got nothing to complain about."

Rachel slid out of the booth, stood, and smoothed her apron. "Enjoy your pie, Mark. I hope things get better for you." She hooked her thumbs in her apron and tilted her head to the left. Her facial expression said what her mouth would not: *Good-bye for good.* "I don't think you should come back here anymore. And go slow with your wife, OK? She's been through a lot too." She turned and, putting on a smile, asked the family two booths down if everything was to their liking. They nodded in unison, and she returned to the kitchen without even so much as a glance in Mark's direction.

His wife. Cheryl. Mark cut off a piece of pie and shoved it in his mouth. Why had he come here? What did he really expect to happen? He had no business ever setting foot in this place again, let alone coming here just to see Rachel. He needed to talk to Cheryl, to win her back. And he'd do anything to do it.

Chapter 8

❶

WEDNESDAY. THE DAY HAD TO COME SOONER or later, and it had come sooner. Mark unlocked the door of the garage and flipped the switch just inside. Four fluorescent overhead lights stuttered to life. He then flipped the switch to open the large bay door. He was gonna need some fresh air today. First day back since Dad's death, and a pile of work awaited him. A '95 Olds Cutlass sat on the lift, six feet off the ground, where he'd left it. Outside, an '01 Accord, a '97 Taurus, and a '99 Explorer all waited patiently, sitting like gentlemen at the barbershop. Two brake jobs and a *chunk-chunk-chunk* when the transmission shifted gears. Should be a busy day. And a long one.

He entered his office, hit the lights, and threw his keys on the desk. Looking out the large window, he eyed the Olds. What was he even doing to the thing? He glanced over his schedule book. Oh, right. New shocks. He'd gotten it last Thursday, before that call from his mom Friday. Fortunately, Mr. Kasino understood and didn't pressure him to get it done. Said he was very sorry for Mark's loss and not to hurry, he had a backup—a '69 Corvette. Mark tried to picture Mr. Kasino in a 'Vette, and it just wasn't happening.

An hour later the shocks were in place. He just needed to

tighten things up and drop her down. He looked at the clock on the wall—8:05. So far, so good.

Six miles away, along a secluded stretch of Jackson Mountain Road, Judge sat patiently among a stand of serviceberries, waiting. Waiting for her to jog past. This would be the place. Less than a tenth of a mile into the woods a service road ran parallel with Jackson. He'd slip in behind her, plant some cones along the road along with a Road Closed sign, then jump on the service road and get ahead of her. A half-mile ahead, the service road joined up with Jackson around a blind turn. He'd plant more cones there, another sign, and head straight for her, without interruptions. But his timing had to be perfect. That's why he was here, waiting.

Mark threw his wrench on the workbench and reached for a rag. The phone rang. Grabbing the rag, he wiped his hands as he walked into his office. He dropped the rag on his desk and picked up the phone.

"Stone Service Center."

"Mark Stone?" It was a woman. Husky voice. Definitely a smoker.

"Yes."

"Mr. Stone, my name is Andrea Kreiger and I'm calling from Pro Auto Parts. I understand you're in need of an auto parts supplier."

Oh, brother. Big-chain auto store moving in on Jerry's clientele now that he's gone. They didn't waste any time, did they? "Yeah. I guess I am."

"Mr. Stone, we'd like to offer you an introductory discount exclusively for repair shop owners. We call it our Gold Premium Plan. If you sign up now for a Pro Auto Parts account, you'll get 20 percent off all your auto part needs for—"

Out of nowhere, a steady chill buzzed down Mark's back. Andrea wasn't talking anymore; she was screaming. At least, it sounded like she was screaming, but Mark knew it wasn't her at all. It was *them*. The voices from hell. Wails and moans coming and going, rising and falling, crashing together like symbols and kettle drums bringing a symphony to its adrenaline-pumping crescendo. It was an orchestra of agony, the individual parts played by some of the most inhuman sounds to ever escape a mortal throat. Guttural groans clashed with sickening howls, and above it all, that scream, a full-throttle nerve-searing scream that pierced the air like a horn's howl.

Mark clenched the receiver. It was slippery against his wet palm. His hand was trembling, and a cold sweat had broken out on his forehead. Tim's words came back to him and jabbed at his mind: *For some reason, you're being given a little heads-up.* This woman was going to die, he was sure of it. He pressed the receiver against his ear and pounded his fist on the desk, waiting for the screams to die down. *C'mon. C'mon.*

After several more seconds the screams finally ceased, and the receiver was filled with silence. "Hello?" *What was her name? Angela?* "Angela?"

"Andrea. What was that?"

"Where are you?" His voice shook with each word.

"Pro Auto Parts. Are you OK?"

"No, I mean, where are *you*? Are you in the store?" He'd unknowingly grabbed a piece of paper off his desk and had it crumpled in his hand. His pulse was working overtime in his neck; he could feel the throb straight through to his spine.

"Yes. Mr. Stone? What's—"

"You're gonna die." Oh, that was good. She'd receive that real well.

"Excuse me? Look, if this is your way—"

"Listen to me!" Mark pressed the receiver harder against his ear. His whole body was trembling now; sweat leaked from his brow and upper lip. "Those screams. You're gonna die. That's what they—"

He heard a faint click on the other end followed by heavy silence. "Hello? Hello? Andrea?" Slamming the phone in its cradle, he cursed and slapped the desk with an open palm. This can't be happening. Not again. He tried to think, run through his options, but his mind was a blank, a void. He was in a dead zone. He stood there, leaning on his desk, staring at the phone for what seemed an endless minute, trying to formulate some kind of action plan. He had to do *something*! She was going to die. He was sure of it. Finally, a thought came. Call the police. They could get there quicker than he could. He picked up the phone and hit 911 with his index finger.

A male dispatcher answered.

"I need the police, and hurry."

"Is this an emergency, sir?"

"Of course it is!" His voice cracked. "Send the police to Pro Auto Parts on East Main Street."

"And what is the nature of the emergency, sir?"

"Someone's gonna die! Andrea. A clerk there. Just get someone there!" He dropped the receiver in the cradle. He didn't have time for twenty questions. Andrea didn't have time. There was no guarantee that she was going to die immediately, Dad surely didn't, but there was no guarantee she wouldn't either. Death didn't wait for the cops to arrive.

Everyone has an appointment with death.

He grabbed his keys and bolted from the office. His Mustang was parked around the side. Pro Auto Parts was on the other side of town. It would take him a good fifteen minutes to get there, what with morning traffic and all. But he had to go. What if the 911 dispatcher thought he was some kind of prank caller and never contacted the police? But he had to contact them, didn't he? Sure. It had to be part of their protocol. But what if the cops didn't respond? No, they would. If they received a tip that someone was gonna die, didn't they have to at least check it out?

He rounded the front of the 'Stang, slid in behind the wheel, jammed the key in the ignition, and turned. The engine rumbled to life.

Fifteen minutes later, Mark pulled onto East Main, tires squealing on asphalt. He'd stuck to side streets to avoid the traffic and lights on Main, running more than one stop sign. Fortunately, no cops were around to see his stunts. Hopefully, they were responding to his call.

When he got to the five hundred block he noticed lights up ahead, blinking lights, red and blue strobes. The light bars of more than one police car. His hands tightened around the steering wheel, and his throat constricted, the grip of death reminding him of the frailty of human life. *Please, no.* Maybe they were just responding to the call, being cautious, and everything was still OK. But when he got to the seven hundred block he noticed the ambulance parked at the corner of the building. His heart dropped right out of his chest. *No. No. No.* This couldn't be happening. Not again. The image of Jerry lying on the floor behind the counter, blue face, bulging eyes, flashed through his mind.

As Mark approached the building, he slowed his car and stopped along the curb. There were two cops in the parking lot. One was standing stiffly, writing in a small notepad while an elderly man in overalls talked, waving his arms like he was directing traffic. The other cop was standing by the door like a sentry.

There were about five people outside the store, huddled together, craning their necks for a view of what was happening inside and talking quietly to each other, shaking their heads.

Something was going on inside, and it wasn't good. Hopefully, the paramedics had gotten there in time.

Mark joined the crowd. "What's going on?" he said to a middle-aged man with a gray goatee, sharp nose, and small round glasses.

The man looked at Mark, then back at the building. "The clerk was choking on something. That guy over there"—he motioned toward the elderly gent in overalls— "tried to give her the Heimlich, but nothing happened. She turned blue and...and passed out, I guess. He tried to revive her, but she was gone. A minute later the cops showed up. They worked on her until the ambulance came."

Mark's body was numb. Choked on something? That was it? His mind swam in a pool of mud, unwilling to comprehend what was happening.

The man was talking again, shaking his head side to side. "—thing was, nobody in the store even called the cops. They just showed up. Like they knew they were needed."

If the man continued talking or not, Mark didn't know, didn't care. The cop standing sentry suddenly jerked the glass door open, and a gurney with two paramedics on either side, one at the head, and one at the foot, rolled out of the store, clanking through the doorway. A woman—Andrea—was lying on the gurney, her shirt ripped open. One paramedic, a stocky male with a thick chest, pumped away on her sternum with two hands, his body pistoning up and down like an oil rig. Sweat glistened off his forehead and cheeks. The other, a short female, worked a bag that fed air directly into Andrea's trachea, apparently bypassing whatever was wedged in her throat. The third paramedic, a slack-cheeked man with short-cropped graying hair, pulled the gurney from the foot, while the fourth, a pudgy baby-faced male, pushed from the head.

Mark swallowed hard. This wasn't happening. Not again.

When they reached the ambulance, the medics at the head and foot shifted to either side. The middle-aged one started to say something when Andrea suddenly sat straight up on the gurney. Her arms flailed about wildly, and she swatted at herself as if slapping at bees. Head, torso, legs, arms.

The paramedics started barking orders at each other while the two on either side tried in vain to restrain her. The bag came loose from her throat and fell to the ground. Her shirt hung open, exposing her bare chest to the world. But Andrea didn't seem to care. Her arms kept flailing and swatting, her legs kicking, like she was frantically fighting off some creature only she could see. Fighting for her life.

One of the medics, the baby-faced one, placed both hands on Andrea's shoulders and shoved her back into a supine position. And that's when Mark noticed the look on her face. Her eyes bulged and her mouth hung open in a silent scream, but there was more to it than that. There was a look of terror. *That* look of terror. The same one that twisted Dad's face right before he passed. A look like she was witnessing the horrors of hell, peeking into the inferno, or maybe being suspended above it. It sent chills right through Mark's body, head to toe, like someone had opened his skull and poured in a bucket of ice water. His skin crawled with goose bumps, his scalp tingled, hands went numb. This couldn't be happening.

Andrea continued to claw at herself while the paramedics

restrained her, fastening belts around her shoulders, waist, and legs. She wrenched and jerked about, eyes looking like they would pop right out of their sockets, tracheotomy sucking air like a hose. One of the paramedics, maybe the middle-aged one, yelled something, and they all lifted the gurney in unison, sliding it into the back of the ambulance. Within seconds, siren howling like a demon, the ambulance tore out of the parking lot and disappeared in the East Main Street morning traffic.

Mark stumbled back to his car, his mind spinning in a thousand different directions. He threw the driver's side door open and collapsed into the bucket seat. What just happened here? Again, the screams proved to be prophetic. And again, Tim's words echoed through the chambers of his mind:

For some reason, you're being given a little heads-up.

But what was the reason? He didn't even have time to save her! But she hadn't died. That was the weirdest thing of all. She should have, but she didn't. If Mark hadn't called 911, and if the cops hadn't been on the way when she choked, she would have. So he did save her...in a way. Then there was that look on her face when she came to. The look of someone who had just been to hell and back. He'd heard of people having near-death experiences, but they always talked about bright lights and soft voices and heaven, not hell. But the look on her face was definitely not that of someone who had just spent a few minutes in bliss. So maybe she had died, gone to hell, and was revived again. Was that even possible? He raked both hands through his hair and flopped his head back against the headrest. He was getting a headache.

Crouching in the serviceberries, Judge pushed a branch out of his face and glanced at his watch. 8:43. She wasn't going to show. She should have been there by now, should have been there fifteen minutes ago. He snorted, accepting defeat, and was about to stand when he heard the faint steady rhythm of footfalls on asphalt, like a ticking clock. He peered out of the shrub, looked right, and saw her coming on the opposite side of the road, about a hundred yards away. She was wearing navy blue jogging pants and a yellow loose-fitting T-shirt. Her hair was pulled back in a tight ponytail. As she drew closer he could see the redness in her cheeks, the sweat on her brow, the heaving of her chest. She was going at a pretty good clip too.

He suddenly had the impulse to do it now. Why wait? It would never work anyway; she was too irregular. He'd have to come up with some other way to take her, which might take days. And he didn't want to have to wait any longer. His impatience grew with each day. Now would be as good a time as any. He didn't have his ether with him, but he could subdue her easily enough with just his hands, drag her back to the car, and take care of things there.

He rose out of his crouched position, straightened the tightness out of his knees, and took one step out of the serviceberries when he heard a rumble coming from the left. He stepped back and pulled a branch in front of his face. Moments later, a semi loaded down with timber rushed by, its Jake Brake groaning through the turn. By the time the truck disappeared around the bend to his right, she was past him, her ponytail swinging like a blonde pendulum as she plodded on, steady, *tick-tick-tick-tick*.

He pressed his molars together and cursed under his breath. Stupid. Impulsiveness never paid. That's why he planned so carefully. But he'd have to come up with another way. This was too unpredictable, too risky. But he *would* take her. And soon.

Her clock *was* ticking, running out of time.

❺

After the excitement at Pro Auto Parts, Mark drove slowly back to his garage, his mind still saturated with questions, questions that no doubt would just have to go unanswered. He'd driven around for almost an hour wrestling with the questions, trying to sort out what had just happened, and searching, searching for anything that made even the remotest bit of sense.

Now he was sitting in his garage, in a stranger's car, trying to do his job but finding it almost impossible to concentrate. How was he just supposed to go back to work doing the same old mundane thing when *it* had happened again? The scream. A death. Well, an *almost* death. But he had to get back to work. The '97 Taurus behind whose wheel he was sitting was in desperate need of new brake pads. Probably needed them a thousand miles ago.

He was about to shut down the engine when a loud knock came from the back of the car, from the trunk. He spun around in the seat and saw two cops standing by the rear panel, a man and a woman, both dressed in brown shirts, beige pants, handguns hanging casually at their side. The woman wore her brown wide-brimmed hat sitting low on her forehead.

He killed the engine and climbed out of the car, dropping the keys in his pocket. "Hey, officers, can I help you?"

The man, middle-aged, tall, lean, and wiry, with a narrow chin and Frank Zappa thing going on with his mustache, extended his hand and shook Mark's. "Sheriff Hickock." He motioned toward the female cop. "This is Deputy Foreman. You Mark Stone?"

Mark looked from Hickock to the woman, a petite young gal, no more than thirty. She looked familiar, may have been the deputy that questioned him the night of Jeff's accident. Then it dawned on him. Andrea. He'd called 911, and they were prob-ably following up on his bizarre call. "Sure am. Is this about that woman Andrea at Pro Auto?"

Hickock hooked his thumbs in his belt and narrowed his eyes. "Andrea Kreiger. Almost died a little while ago. Did you make a 911 call from here, saying someone was gonna die at Pro Auto?"

Mark leaned back against the rear door of the Taurus and swallowed. Oh, boy, how was he going to explain this one? He nodded. "Yes, I did."

"Mr. Stone, I'm gonna be real honest with you," Hickock said, nailing Mark with a look that only a cop could get away with. The kind that made cocky kids and dumb criminals put on their best manners. "As you can imagine, we don't usually get calls of that nature. And it raises a little suspicion. More than a little, actually. Would you like to explain how you knew she would have a very close encounter with death?"

Foreman was jotting notes in a small notepad.

Mark shifted his weight nervously. Any way he explained it, it was going to sound absurd. Better to just tell the truth and let them interpret it however they wished. "Well, I, uh, have been getting some phone calls interrupted with these screams, see, and…well, it's weird, the people I've been talking to have all died."

Hickock jumped in. "Screams? What kind of screams?"

"Screams. Like full-out horror movie screams. Lots of 'em. Like a bunch of people all screaming at once. It lasts maybe five seconds or so, then stops."

Hickock glanced back at Foreman, who was standing a couple feet behind him and to the left. She nodded. She was getting it all down. Great.

"You said the people to whom you were talking when these…screams…occurred all died. How many times has it happened?" Hickock's face showed no expression while he talked. Either he was actually taking Mark seriously, or he was one heck of a poker player.

"Three. Four, counting Andrea. First a friend of mine, Jeff Beaverson—"

Hickock glanced at Foreman, and she met his look. "The auto fatality. Coopers Hollow," she said.

"You heard screams before Beaverson wrecked?" Hickock said.

"Yeah. He heard them too."

Hickock looked back at Foreman again. She shrugged and shook her head. "Did you tell Deputy Foreman about these screams then? When she talked to you at the scene?"

The evening was still fuzzy, a patchwork of memories, images, sounds, smells. "I don't know. I don't remember much from that night. Sorry."

Hickock waved his hand in front of him. "OK. Go on. Who else?"

Mark continued. "Then there was Jerry Detweiler. He was my parts supplier until…his heart attack. Then last Friday my dad died. He lived in Virginia."

Hickock remained motionless, his face like granite. "And they all screamed on the phone right before they died."

Mark shook his head. "No. *They* didn't scream. Other people—the screams—they came from somewhere else."

"Where?" When Hickock said *where*, his shoulders rose and dropped, and his eyebrows mimicked their quick movement. He then made a quick glance at Foreman again. Was that a smirk Mark noticed on his face?

"Well," Mark said. He wasn't going to dare tell Hickock the screams came from hell, though by now he was almost convinced they couldn't have come from anywhere else. Especially after his experience with Dad and Andrea. "I'm not sure. I just know they're there. And then the person dies."

"Dies immediately?" Foreman asked, then shot Hickock a look as if seeking his blessing on her interruption.

Mark nodded. "Jeff and Jerry, yes. Sounds like Andrea would have if I hadn't called for help. My dad was several hours later."

Hickock exchanged another look with Foreman. The corners of his mouth curled into a slight grin, and he pulled both eyebrows up, wrinkling his brow. This time the look on his face said exactly how he felt about Mark and his story—nut job.

"Look," Mark said. He knew he had to do some fast explaining and give them something they wanted or he'd find himself in the loony bin before the day was over. "I don't understand it either. I never had anything like this happen before. I get three phone calls interrupted by some weird screaming, and all three people die. Now I don't know if it was just coincidence or something else going on, but when I get another call and more screaming…well, what would you have done? I put two and two together."

Hickock unhooked his thumbs and gave Mark a long hard stare as if trying to decide whether or not to slap the cuffs on him and haul him away. Thankfully, he decided on the *not*. "OK. Thank you for your time, Mr. Stone. I hope you understand why we had to come here and ask some questions. It does seem a little odd when someone calls 911 saying someone else seven miles away is going to die. Then it almost happens. Most likely would have happened if our guys hadn't gotten there when they did."

Mark shrugged it off. "I'm glad they got there in time."

Foreman slid her notepad back into her shirt pocket and nodded at Mark. Hickock turned to leave, then stopped. A smile thinned his lips. "You'll call us again if you get any more of your screaming phone calls, won't you?"

"If you'd like me to."

Hickock lost his smile. "I would."

Back at the cruiser, Wiley dipped his head as he slid behind the wheel.

Jess shut her door and sighed, holding her hat on her lap. "Well, what do you make of that?"

Wiley didn't look at her; he was still looking at the garage, watching Stone through the open bay door. Odd fellow, that Stone. And his story, however far-fetched it seemed, was somewhat disturbing. "First tell me one thing."

Jess hesitated, then said, "Go ahead."

"Are you a born-againer?"

Jess sighed and rolled her eyes. "Do we have to keep landing on this topic?"

"Just answer the question."

"Why do I feel like I'm being interrogated?"

"Answer."

"Yes, I am."

Wiley snorted. He couldn't hide his disdain for the type. He'd seen enough of them in his lifetime to leave a bitter taste in his mouth for a very long time. Hypocrites, every one of them, as far as he was concerned. Jess didn't seem like a fanatic, or a hypocrite, but maybe that was just because she did a good job of hiding it. She probably talked all high and mighty on Sunday mornings. *Hello, Brother Morton, fine day the Lord's given us, isn't it? His mercies endure forever, don't they? Praise be to the Lawd Almighty! Amen and amen! Now please excuse me while I go memorize Paul's epistle to the Galatians.* Yeah, he knew the type.

Jess cocked her head at an angle. "Do you have a problem with that?"

"Not if you keep it to yourself and don't go thinking you're better than everyone else."

"You asked me about it, remember? And I don't think I'm better than anyone. We all have our problems. Now can we please get back to our guy Stone here."

Wiley ran a finger over his mustache. Jess was nibbling on a fingernail, watching Stone work. "You first," he said.

Jess stopped nibbling long enough to say, "Me first what?"

"You asked me what I think about Stone. You first."

"In a word? Crazy."

Wiley slowly shook his head and pressed his lips together. "No. I don't think there's anything crazy about him. Not yet, anyway."

"Then what was all that about screams over the phone? You think he's telling the truth?"

Wiley tapped the steering wheel, drumming out some unknown rhythm just to keep his hands busy. He continued watching Stone, who was busying himself with the right passenger-side tire of the Taurus, occasionally casting furtive glances at the cruiser. "Right now, I'm not assuming anything. He's odd, I'll give him that. And his story is even odder. Check Beaverson's and Detweiler's phone records. See if either of them talked to Stone right before they died."

"And if they did?"

Wiley brought his shoulders up and let them drop. "Then there might something to his screaming stories."

They sat in silence for several seconds until Wiley could feel Jess's eyes boring holes into the side of his head. "What?"

"You think he had something to do with the deaths?" Jess kept her voice low, like they were talking about some top-secret case.

Finally, Wiley pulled his eyes away from Stone and fixed them on Jess. "I'm not saying that. We need to cover all the bases though." He turned his head back to the garage and found Stone still fiddling with the front tire. "I don't like this."

"Like you don't like missing person cases?"

"Exactly."

The fifth floor of Frostburg Hospital was like any other floor on the hospital—cold, sterile, gray tile floors littered with black scuff marks, gray and white walls, harsh fluorescent lighting. The air held the aroma of rubbing alcohol and body odor so common in hospitals. Mark walked down the middle of the hallway, sneakers chirping with each step, in search of Room 547, Andrea Kreiger.

At the welcome desk adjacent to the lobby the receptionist had told him to take the elevator to the fifth floor, turn right off the elevator, follow the hall to its end, and make a left. Room 547 was on the right-hand side. "Odd-numbered rooms on the right, even on the left," she'd said, like she'd said it a million times a day.

While waiting for the elevator, Mark had studied the hospital's floor plan and discovered that the fifth floor was the psyche ward. They'd put her up with the crazies. He'd imagined her immobilized by a straitjacket, crouched in the corner of a padded room, ranting and raving about hellfire and demons, sweat matting her hair to her forehead, eyes blazing with hatred and fear.

Now on the fifth floor, he realized the psyche ward was not that kind of place. The rooms looked like normal hospital rooms. Most of them were private, had a bathroom, a TV, and a regular hospital bed in each one.

He came to the end of the first hallway, passed a nurse who gave him a slight smile and a cordial nod, and turned left. Andrea's room was the fourth one on the right. Mark paused outside the room and listened. The heavy wooden door was ajar by a couple of inches, allowing the tinny sound of the TV to escape. A woman talking, then laughter. Sounded like some afternoon talk show. Oprah maybe. He drew in a lungful of air and pushed the door open a couple more inches.

He then knocked and said, "Hello?"

Just then a nurse opened the door the rest of the way, pulling Mark off balance. He stumbled forward and almost fell into her. She was a heavyset woman with short dark hair, deep-set eyes, and baggy jowls.

"Oh, excuse me!" she said, placing a hand over her chest. "You almost gave me a heart attack."

Mark straightened and tried to smile. "Sorry. You startled me too."

The nurse smiled, her full lips thinning just a bit. "I was just leaving. Are you part of the family?"

"No. Just an...acquaintance...from work."

She finally took her hand off her chest and fanned herself. She was still breathing heavily from the encounter, and her cheeks had blushed. "Well, you just missed the family. They left maybe ten minutes ago." She leaned forward, peered around the door at Andrea, and shook her large head. "Poor girl. Family said she was perfectly normal until this morning. I guess you know she almost died. Choked on something. Now she won't stop ranting about monsters and fire. She thinks she's being burned alive."

Mark didn't say anything. He was certainly glad the family wasn't there. He'd have a heck of a time trying to explain who he was and how he knew Andrea. *Hi. I'm the guy who called the cops because I knew your daughter was gonna die because I heard the screams of hell while talking to her on the phone. Now, if you'll excuse me, I'll just go next door and get back in my bed.*

The nurse gave him a smile and patted his arm. "Don't stay too long, hon. She needs to get some rest soon."

"I won't," he said, returning the smile. "Just want to say hi and then I'll be on my way."

Mark entered the room and quietly closed the door. The lights were dim and cast soft shadows on the walls. Andrea was lying in the bed, sheet pulled up to her chest. Her hair had been pulled back in a ponytail, and she wore a blue and white flow-ered hospital gown, loose around the neck. She looked to be about forty or so, but hospitals always made you look older than you really were. Her skin was white like onion paper, and there was a bandage where the emergency tracheotomy had been done. Her wrists were fettered to the bed with canvas straps, and by the looks of the same straps anchored to the foot of the bed and disappearing under the sheets, her ankles were as well. She lay perfectly still, eyes fixed on some invisible spot on the ceiling. Mark took three light steps toward the bed and noticed the tenseness in her muscles. Her hands were clenched into tight fists, the cords of her neck taut. Her jaw muscles flexed rhythmically. Like a ticking time bomb, Mark thought.

He took one more step toward the bed so she was close enough to touch. He had no desire to touch her, though. Andrea didn't seem to notice him or, if she did, was ignoring him. She kept her eyes pinned to a spot directly above her, unmoving, unblinking. He didn't know what to say, hadn't even thought about it until now. He wasn't even sure why he had come. Curi-osity? Obligation? Guilt? Concern? They all fit, and, if he was being honest, all more than likely played a role to some degree or another.

But he should say something. He felt silly just showing up, standing there dumbly for a few minutes, then leaving. What purpose did that serve? Other than to satisfy his own curiosity. *Yep, she's nuts all right. Now I can leave and live my life in peace.* He shifted his weight to his right leg, slid his hands into his pockets, and cleared his throat. "Andrea? Hi."

Andrea finally blinked and turned her head toward him, her eyes trailing the movement of her head until they landed on his face. Her facial muscles were still tight, lips thin and white. Her breathing increased through her nostrils, and her chest began to rise and fall at a quicker rate.

Mark was uncomfortable and getting more so by the second. Her eyes seemed to look right through him, like they were watching the inner workings of his soul, curious to find the long-hidden secrets and forbidden desires that lingered there. He shifted nervously, planting his weight over his left leg. "How are you?"

Andrea's lips parted slightly, and Mark noticed a tremble come over them. Tears welled up in her eyes and spilled over, tracing polished rivulets down her cheeks. Her mouth turned down in a twisted frown, and darkness clouded her eyes. Her brow lowered, gathering in the middle and hiding her eyes in a dark shadow. Her nostrils flared wide. What was he looking at? What was this expression that had distorted her face? He knew what it was. Fear. And not just the run-of-the-mill scared-of-the-dark fear. What he was looking at was the face of *terror.* And it was disturbing. So much so that he had to take a step back.

Andrea's facial distortion continued, growing more and more misshapen. She looked as though she were about to scream when a low groan escaped from somewhere deep in her throat.

She opened her mouth wider. Dry and blistered lips peeled away from her teeth.

"Help me," she pleaded. "They're coming for me." Her voice was strained and hoarse and cracked on the word *coming*. A fresh wave of tears rolled over her temples and disappeared in her hair. "There's no escape."

Mark noticed he was holding his breath and let out the air in his mouth. "Who's coming for you?" he said in a shaky voice.

Andrea tried to lift her right arm before realizing it was tethered. She turned her head away from Mark and fixed her eyes on a darkened corner of the room. With her right hand she pointed at the corner. "They are."

Mark followed her eyes but saw nothing in the corner but a metal rolling cart. A chill tightened his scalp and buzzed down the back of his head. He looked back at Andrea, who was staring at him again.

"Go," she said, her mouth holding the *O* shape longer than it needed to. "They're coming for you too. You can't get away from them. They're everywhere."

Mark turned and looked back at the closed door. He needed to ask her something. He took a half step toward her and leaned his weight on his forward foot. Lowering his voice, he said, "What did you see when you died?"

Andrea shook her head side to side so violently he thought she'd snap her neck. She grimaced as if in tortuous pain. "No," she said, her voice choked with fear. "I can't. I won't." She pulled at the canvas straps, the muscles in her arms bulging beneath her pale skin, and moaned like a woman in labor. "Fire. Hot. So hot. Burning me. And"—she jerked her head to the left and glared into the corner again—"and *them*! Everywhere. Everywhere. Every*where*!"

She screamed the last *everywhere* like a warrior ready to

charge to her death. Mark started and stepped back. Not three seconds later the nurse threw open the door and rushed to Andrea's side. She pulled a syringe out of a drawer, fastened it to an IV line, and drained the contents into Andrea's blood. Andrea's eyelids fluttered and every muscle in her body seemed to respond in kind, relaxing like melting butter.

The nurse dropped the syringe in her pocket and looked at Mark. She had to have seen the fear on his face. "It's OK. She's OK now. She does that a lot, you know. Something put the fear of God in her." She rounded the bed and stood beside Mark. "Poor thing. She needs some rest now, hon. Why don't you come back later."

Mark nodded. "OK. Later," knowing he had no intention of ever setting foot in that room with whatever it was Andrea saw in the corner.

Chapter 9

❶

THIS WAS TOO RISKY. HE WAS GETTING DESPERATE, AND desperation led to mistakes, and mistakes led to failure, and he couldn't fail. Not again.

Judge sat behind the wheel of his sedan, parked a block from her apartment, uphill, waiting for the last light to wink out. His dashboard clock said it was almost eleven. Any time now. The one lighted window was the bathroom. She was probably doing a little washing up before jumping in the sack.

'Course, he'd have to wait another hour after that to make sure she was asleep.

Her apartment was on the ground floor, and a sliding glass door opened to a concrete patio, all of which added up to easy access. A patio door's lever lock was easy to disengage; any bloke could do it. All it took was a little know-how and a pinch of patience. The problem was going to be the neighbors. That was why he'd originally chosen to take her during her secluded morning jog. Homes were always risky business; too many things could go wrong. Too many variables and unknowns. Too little control. But he was here now, and risky or not, he was going for it.

He took a sip of his coffee—Dunkin' Donuts, cream, no sugar—and pulled in a long inhale. The steam filtered through his nose, clearing his head of everything and filling it with the full aroma of the premium blend. He let his eyelids fall shut and held the cup to his lips.

When he opened his eyes again the bathroom light was out. He smiled. Nighty-night.

Cheryl crawled into bed and pulled a red, white, and blue patchwork quilt up to her chest. Her great aunt Jennie had made it and gave it to Cheryl's mother. Her mother then passed it on to her. It was old, and some of the patchwork was torn in places, but it was warm and comforting in a sentimental way. She leaned back against two pillows propped against the headboard and laid her book on her lap. First things first. She'd promised her mother she'd call. The digital clock across the room read eleven o'clock. Should be fine. Mom always was a night owl. She flipped open her cell phone and punched the buttons with her thumb.

"Hello?"

"Hi, Mom, it's me. How are you?"

"Oh, I'm fine, honey. Just getting ready for bed. Your father is already asleep. Everything OK?" Mom sounded tired. She wasn't handling the late nights as well as she had when she was younger.

"Yeah, I guess."

Mom paused. When she spoke again, her voice was soft and quiet. "You don't sound like you're OK. Tough day, huh?"

Tears, unplanned, sprang to Cheryl's eyes, blurring her vision. A lump swelled in her throat. "Yeah." She couldn't say any more, or the sobs would burst forth like a geyser.

"Honey. I know it's hard. I know the pain is unbearable. Have you thought at all about what I talked to you about last time?"

Last time. Last time they talked—last week—Mom had gone

on and on about being *born again*. Apparently, some friends of theirs took them to their grandson's baptism, and Mom and Dad had "found Jesus"; that's how they put it. Where Jesus was or how He got lost, Cheryl had no idea, but they were different now. Especially Mom. Last week she rambled on about the peace and happiness she now felt. She'd told Cheryl she could have it too, if she only trusted Jesus with her life. She said Jesus would comfort her. Something about giving Him her burden and casting her cares at His feet. Cheryl knew Mom was referring to Mark and the separation, but she never came right out and said it. But Jesus comforting her? How could someone who lived and died two thousand years ago comfort her? She must have meant His teachings. But they were just words, black ink on white paper, and Cheryl was tired of words.

"—Cheryl? Honey?"

"Uh, yeah, Mom, I did think about it some. And—look, I just don't think it's right for me now. It seems like a lot of warm fuzzy stuff that really doesn't mean a whole lot in the real world, and I'm not in to warm fuzzies right now. I've had enough of them for a while." She braced herself for Mom's rebuttal.

"Cheryl. Dear. It's not warm fuzzies at all. It's real. Jesus is real. He's alive, and He loves you more than you could ever know. He only wants to have a relationship with you."

The lump in Cheryl's throat dissipated, and now a feeling of anger or frustration or both had settled in her chest. "If He wants a relationship with me so bad, why don't we have one? I mean, He's God, right? Jesus claimed to be God. So if He's God, why doesn't He initiate the relationship?"

"He did, honey. He became a man and came here to the earth and died on the cross in our place, your place, so you could have a relationship with Him. But He can't force you into it; it needs to be your choice."

"Why? Why does it have to be *my* choice?" Cheryl was aware her voice was growing in volume, but she didn't care. None of this made sense to her. It was religious mumbo jumbo for weak-minded fools, and it angered her that both her parents had been duped into believing it. "Why doesn't God or Jesus or whoever He is just say, 'Hey, you down there. Sorry your husband screwed your life up, but don't worry, I'll make it all better'?"

Mom sighed static into the phone. "Cheryl, He won't because love has to be...it has to be freely chosen. He won't force you to love Him."

The words bit into Cheryl's heart. *Love has to be freely chosen.* Or freely rejected. She knew what that was like.

Mom was still going. "...it isn't love then, is it? Cheryl, honey, the Bible says—"

"OK, OK. That's enough, Mom. I don't need to hear anymore." She sighed and calmed herself. "Look, I'm happy for you; I really am. It sounds like you found something that you're really excited about and that's great, but you have to understand, it's just not right for everyone, and it's not right for me. OK?"

There were a few seconds of silence, only Mom's breathing. "OK, dear. I understand. But won't you at least—"

"Mom, please. I'm tired. I'm going to hang up now. I'll call you again in a few days."

"OK. I love you, baby. I'm thinking about you...and praying."

"I love you too, Mom." And she did. Mom had always been her rock. And that's why this change, this *born-again* thing had upset Cheryl so much. Mom had changed, become one of those religious nuts, and there was nothing Cheryl could do about it. She flipped the phone shut and dropped it next to her on the bed. Picking up her book, she turned to the bookmarked page and began reading. Reading always calmed her and prepared her for sleep.

Twenty minutes later the words on the page began to blur, and Cheryl struggled to keep her eyes open. She read a little more, dozed off, lifted her eyelids, and read a few more lines. After a while, nothing made sense anymore. She'd lost her place and found it numerous times and struggled to keep the words together. Finally, she gave in and lowered the book to her chest.

An hour later the clock blinked to twelve. Midnight. Time to move. He pushed the brake pedal to the floor, shifted the car into neutral, and slowly released the brake. The car began to drift forward. Working the brake to control his speed, he allowed the car to coast downhill, slow and steady. When he came to her apartment, he gently depressed the pedal. The brakes protested with a high-pitched metal-on-metal whine; the car came to a complete stop. He shifted back into park and lifted the parking brake. Then he opened the car door, slipped out, and quietly pushed it closed again.

The sky was clear and deep, splashed with stars like grains of glistening sand. The almost-full moon hung high and bright, a single white eye watching with curiosity. With the stealth of a leopard he stole across an expanse of manicured lawns, keeping to the shadows, disappearing, becoming part of the landscape. When he came to her apartment complex he stopped at the corner and collected his thoughts, rehearsing every move that would get him into her bedroom, anesthetize her, and remove her, without so much as disturbing a blade of grass. There had to be no trace of an intruder, no hair, no fingerprints, no shoe prints, no clothing fibers. She must simply vanish. This was the challenge of a home invasion.

He pulled out a pair of latex gloves, slipped them on both

hands, and withdrew a simple credit card from his right back pocket. How resourceful the plastic could be. Never leave home without it.

Ten steps later he was crouched on her patio, feeding the card between the door and the jamb. Within twenty seconds he was inside her apartment, sliding the door closed again. He was in and hadn't made a sound doing it. Like he wasn't even there. He scanned the room. It was the living room, large and spacious, but sparsely furnished. A small television sat in one corner, watching quietly like an innocent bystander. A futon sofa rested against the opposite wall. Other than a brass torch lamp and wall-to-wall carpet, that was it. No chairs, no pictures. Nothing that would call the apartment a home.

He took the living room in five steps and entered a short hall that led to the bathroom on the right and two bedrooms, one on the left and one on the right, next to the bathroom. The bedroom door on the right was open and he could see that it was unfurnished. Not even a lamp. Empty. The bedroom door on the left was closed. And what lay behind door number one? Why, dear Cheryl, sleeping soundly, oblivious to the fact that when she awoke she wouldn't be in Kansas anymore.

Standing in front of the closed door, he placed his hand on the knob and turned it to the left without so much as a click or a squeak.

Slowly, silently, he pushed open the door. Another barely furnished room. Bed, dresser, lamp. The lamp was on, casting soft yellow light throughout the room. Cheryl was on her back, blanket twisted around her legs, mouth slightly ajar, one arm out to the side, the other resting across her stomach. Her chest rose and fell like the steady rhythm of a ship at sea. A hardcover—Janet Evanovich's latest—lay open beside her. No doubt about it, she was asleep.

He approached the bed and stood over her, removing the white cloth and vial of ether from his pants pocket. She looked so peaceful, like not a care in the world bothered her. Like nothing could wake her. For some reason his thoughts went again to Katie, to the day they put her in the ground. Nothing would wake her again.

1974

"Aren't you ready yet?" Mother calls from the living room.

He quickly adjusts his tie, smooths his hair, and dashes down the stairs, skipping two steps at a time. He hates wearing suits, too stuffy and stiff, and his are all tight across the shoulders and short in the sleeves. But for Katie, her funeral (*a final farewell to love*), he'll put up with it.

"It's about time," Mother says, straightening his tie and smoothing the lapels of his black blazer. "Just look at you. You still have your breakfast on your face." She licks her thumb and rubs at the corner of his mouth, leaving behind the smell of dried saliva and lipstick.

Patting him on the shoulder she says, "Come now, your father's waiting in the car."

On the drive to the cemetery, he sits in the backseat, head against the window, and watches the patchwork of fields float by as if in a dream. (*This can't be happening for real, no.*) It's a nice morning, sunny, blue sky. A few large cumulus clouds float by like parade floats, but a shadow hangs over him, like a rain cloud that follows him around wherever he goes. Katie died three days ago, and word has already gotten around town that it was his fault. Or so they say (*and maybe they're right*).

He tried to tell the police and the McAfees what really happened, but it's his word against Bethany's, and who's gonna believe a stupid kid over a teenager, and not just any teenager, it's Bethany McAfee, the most popular girl in her school.

When they arrive at the cemetery, he holds Mother's hand as they cross several burial plots to where a large crowd has gathered around a small green tent. As they near, he feels Mother's hand tighten around his own, and her palm moistens with sweat. His father places a large hand on the back of his neck and gently squeezes. They'd heard the talk too (*those lies that might not be far from the truth*) and no doubt are feeling the weighty stares of Katie's family. His stomach tightens.

During the short service, he doesn't hear a single thing the preacher says. Not that he *can't* hear; he doesn't *want* to. His mind is awash with memories of Katie—her voice when she said his name, the way her eyes crinkled when she smiled, the loose strands of hair she always tucked behind her ears, her laugh, her lips, the way her lips felt against his (*pillows where angels rest their heads*).

When the preacher says all he's going to say, the crowd begins to disperse. One by one they pay their respects to Katie's parents and Bethany and return to their cars, shoulders slumped, wagging their heads from side to side.

When all but a handful of mourners are left, he hears a woman's strained voice cut through the silence. "Why is he here?"

He looks up and sees Mrs. McAfee talking to her husband. He has his arm around her shoulders and is whispering something in her ear.

Then she looks right at him, and he sees the hatred in her eyes (*the devil eyes again*). Her stare burns like fire and paralyzes him. He feels Mother tighten her grip on his hand, and his father pulls him a little closer, but his attention is captured by those eyes, like she's willing him into the grave with her daughter. (*Fine, take me, take me!*)

Suddenly, her face twists into something that resembles a demon in some horror movie he once saw. She points a finger right at him. "You! How dare you show up here?" Her husband is patting her on the shoulder and whispering frantically in her ear. Dad is saying something, Mother is talking too, hurried voices, hushed and serious, but he hears none of it. He's a prisoner to the demon that sneers at him, begs for his soul. (*Take it, go on, you ole devil, take it and be done with it!*)

"Get out of my sight!" Mrs. McAfee yells. "Get out of here!"

The words rip through him like a saw, and he panics. He breaks away from Mother and Dad and runs across the cemetery, dodging tombstones and knocking over plastic flower arrangements. He doesn't know where he's going; he just runs. He runs until the funeral party and the McAfees are out of sight and his lungs burn like they've been stripped raw and his heart feels like it's made of lead, then he collapses against a gray tombstone and cries.

Judge stood over Cheryl, watching her sleep. If she only knew how drastically her world was about to change. He felt a sudden pang of guilt, or maybe just nervous jitters. Either way, he was having second thoughts. He could still get out of this. Leave the apartment without a trace, go and unlock the barn door, and drive away. Amber and Virginia had seen his face, though. No matter; he could hand in his resignation at work and be out of town by the time anyone suspected him. No, that was crazy thinking. It would never work. He was in too deep now. They'd seen his face. That was stupid, very stupid of him. There was no way out. Guilt or no guilt, jitters or not, he had to go on with the plan. For Katie. Always for Katie.

He reached out and took a strand of Cheryl's hair between his fingers. It felt like silk.

Sweet dreams, dear one.

He doused the cloth with the anesthetic and leaned over Cheryl. It satisfied him a little that at least he still had a conscience. There were those who did what they did with no conscience at all. Maim, rape, torture, murder, victimize, violate—all without even a bat of the eyes or flutter in the soul.

He wasn't like them. They were the monsters, not him.

Seconds later he was replacing the cloth and smiling. Cheryl's breathing had deepened; a puddle of drool collected in the corner of her mouth. Quickly, efficiently, he removed the book and placed it on the dresser, then returned to the bed and rolled Cheryl onto her stomach. He then gathered the quilt around her and rolled her back over so she was lying on top of the blanket. After gathering the four corners in his hands, he slung the quilt over his right shoulder and lifted Cheryl as if she were a duffle bag.

He managed to make his way back through the apartment and out the patio door without disturbing anything. Like he'd done it a hundred times. The only problem was locking the sliding door again. There was really no way to do it from the outside. It would have to be the one clue, the only sign of his presence. But there were other reasons why a patio door would be left unlocked.

With Cheryl concealed in the blanket and the blanket dangling from his shoulder, he shuffled across the lawn and popped the trunk of his car. He then backed up to the trunk and dropped Cheryl into it. Mission accomplished. Now to deposit her in the barn, safe and sound. For now.

❻

Amber started and opened her eyes at the sound of a car door shutting. *The* car door. She'd grown accustomed to the sound of Judge's car, the whine of its engine, squeal of its brakes, *tick-tick* of its engine cooling, click of its door shutting. Since the visit when he'd shown his humanity he'd stopped by once with more supplies—toilet paper, apples (always the apples), another box of Cheerios, two cases of water bottles, a six-pack of white women's briefs, four pairs of white athletic socks, and a box of tissues, the kind with aloe in them. The briefs were too small for Ginny, but with a little "encouragement," she made them fit OK. Seeing how Judge had brought them everything she'd asked for, she now regretted not asking for cold medicine, or a bottle of Tylenol at the very least.

Amber had tried talking to him, thanked him for the supplies, and asked him how much longer they'd be in the barn. The previous visit, she'd seen a glimmer of hope. He was human after all. He felt pain and sorrow, had feelings and emotions. If she could zero in on that and humanize herself and Ginny, make some kind of personal contact with him, their chances of surviving this ordeal would increase dramatically. But he'd simply dropped the grocery bag on the floor of the barn, spun around on his heels, and left without so much as a glance in her direction. He hadn't even spoken to the dogs.

Amber sniffed and tried to subdue a cough. Her condition was worsening every day. She was sure she had a full-blown sinus infection. Her sinuses felt like they were packed with lead, her throat protested at even the feeblest attempt to swallow, and her head felt like it was wedged in a vise, being squeezed tighter with each turn of the crank. The fever would come next, and

after that, if she didn't get out of here, pneumonia would probably set in and then...well, that was a long way off. Hopefully.

Amber heard another click and sat up in the straw. Sounded
like the trunk opening. She looked over at Ginny and could
barely make out her fuzzy form in the dark. She wasn't moving,
and Amber could hear her steady breathing. Still asleep. That
was probably good. Ginny still wasn't handling things well.
Most of the time she sat in the corner, head leaned against the
rough planks of the wall, staring out a tiny half-inch crack.
Her eyes were permanently bloodshot and swollen from crying
on and off all day. Her hair was still a tangled mess and every
day looked worse and worse. She barely ate, had noticeably lost
weight, and only spoke when Amber spoke to her first. It was
obvious she'd given up.

Outside, there was a rustle and a grunt. The dogs were there
too, around the car, whining and yelping. Ginny stirred and
propped herself up on one elbow.

Judge's heavy footsteps grew closer until they reached the
door. The lock disengaged with the sound of scraping metal
and a clink, the cinder block fell away, and the door opened.
Moonlight poured in through the opening, silhouetting Judge
when he stepped through the doorway. He was bent forward at
the waist, carrying something large over his right shoulder. He
took four or five steps and lowered the bundle to the floor behind
him, pausing for a few seconds to place his hands on his hips
and straighten his back. His dark, backlit figure seemed to be
staring at them. Amber could hear his heavy breathing, pulling
in the odor of the barn and then releasing it. She wondered if
he was about to say something. But her question was quickly
answered when he turned and left without a word.

Seconds later the trunk closed, the door slammed shut, and
the engine revved to life. Within a minute the rumble of the

engine disappeared in the distance, and she was once again surrounded by the silence of the night.

Amber turned her head and looked at Ginny. She was sitting up now, her head turned toward the bundle on the floor. Ginny just stared silently at the intrusion, as if she were waiting for it to introduce itself. Amber thought the bundle looked about the size of a woman. An eerie dread crept over her like an inky shadow. Another woman. She'd asked Judge, *How many were there?* But he hadn't answered her. Was this poor woman, bundled in what looked like a blanket, the last one? Or would there be more? God forbid there be more. And if so, how many more?

Amber looked at Ginny again, then stood and walked over to the bundle. Kneeling beside it, she saw that it was indeed a blanket, a quilt to be exact, white with red and blue patchwork. She ran her hand over the length of it and was surprised by the sudden sob that burst from her throat. It *was* another woman. She could definitely make out a shoulder and hip, tapering into thin, firm legs. Quickly she pulled the blanket back enough to expose the head. Blonde hair, pretty face, sleeping soundly. Probably drugged like Ginny was.

Amber turned to Ginny. "Help me with her. We need to get her in the straw."

Ginny stood and shuffled over.

"Grab the end there," Amber said, motioning to the feet. "I'll take this end and we'll drag her."

Ginny walked around to the feet and gathered the blanket in her hands. Amber gripped the other end. On the count of three they both leaned back and pulled. The blanketed woman slid surprisingly well over the straw-covered worn floorboards. When they reached their nest, Amber straddled the woman, slipped her hands under the shoulders, and lifted her onto the straw, between where she and Ginny slept.

"Thank you, Ginny," Amber said, hoping the younger woman would at least take an interest in the new arrival. But there was no response. Ginny lay down and turned her back to the new woman. And that was that.

Amber lay down on the other side of the new woman, facing her, and placed a hand on her shoulder. "I'm sorry," she whispered. "I'm so sorry. We'll talk in the morning."

Chapter 10

❶

BRIGHT LIGHT SWIRLED IN HER HEAD, SPIRALING toward her in convoluted waves, then spreading out in flowing tendrils until everything was washed in white. It was then that she realized she was awake. Her eyelids were too heavy to open, though, as if they were glued shut. She tried to move, and a grunt slipped past her tongue and escaped through her lips. At that moment three things registered in her foggy mind. One, her body felt like it was a hundred pounds heavier. Either that or the gravitational pull of the earth had suddenly increased. Two, something was poking the top of her head and her left temple. And three, she must be outside. She could hear grass rustling, birds whistling, geese honking. How had she gotten outside?

She lay motionless, straining to detect her surroundings through senses other than sight. Through her fingertips she concluded that she was lying on hay or straw. She felt no breeze, so she must be under some kind of shelter. And the odor seeping into her nostrils was foul. The smell of waste, either animal or human, she couldn't tell which. It wasn't revolting, but bad enough.

She drew in a long breath of the unpleasant air and slid her feet up so her knees were bent. She parted her lips and—

Wait a minute! Hay? Shelter? That odor? Didn't she fall asleep in her own bed in her apartment? What was wrong with her? Why hadn't that detail registered before? Was she dreaming? No, she wasn't. This was real. She tried again to pry her eyelids open. Suddenly a hand rested on her forehead and gently slid to the back of her head, smoothing her hair. That was certainly real. Mark? Mom? Then a woman's voice, calm and soothing: "Hey, are you awake?" The woman coughed, a deep-chested, raspy cough that rattled in her lungs.

She tried again, and this time her eyelids cracked open. Light blinded her, and she squinted hard.

"It's OK. Take your time," the woman said and brushed her hair again with a gentle touch.

Her eyelids fluttered then opened a little more. Still squinting, she could see the blurry outline of a woman's face hovering above her. At first, it was just a face, no neck or body.

Slowly, her eyes relaxed, and the image came into focus. Looking down at her was a woman she'd never seen before. Brown hair hung loosely around her shoulders, but the hair was limp and oily; hazel eyes, soft and kind, but sunken into deep, darkened sockets; full lips that curved upward into a motherly smile, but the lips were cracked and flaky and the smile...it wasn't real, wasn't genuine. Something was wrong with the way the woman looked at her. Something was wrong with the way the woman *looked*.

"Hey," the woman said. Her lips seemed to move in slow motion. She turned her head and barked out another throaty cough.

Above her, past the woman's head, Cheryl saw a ceiling arching upward and corrugated sheets of metal resting on large wooden beams. Shifting her eyes from side to side she realized where she was—in a barn.

The woman's hand was on her forehead again. "It's OK," she said. "You're OK."

Cheryl pushed herself to sit up. Her head spun, so she shut her eyes tight. Now the woman was rubbing her back. "Take some time. You're OK."

After a few seconds she opened her eyes again and looked around. She was indeed in a barn, and an old one from the looks of it. The plank walls were striped with lighted cracks; straw covered the smooth gray floor. Her blanket, the one from her bed back at the apartment, was wrapped around her legs. She raised a hand to her head and ran her palm across her forehead. None of this made sense. Where was she? How did she get here?

She opened her mouth, then shut it and swallowed. Her mouth and throat were dry, like the rotted boards enclosing her. "Where—where am I?"

The other woman continued rubbing her back. "That's a good question. For starters, you're in a barn, but you can probably see that. Other than that, I'm not sure where we are."

She looked at the other woman. A complete stranger, but beautiful features. She looked worn, though, tired. "How did I get here?"

"You were probably drugged. What's your name?"

She had to think about that. Her mind seemed to be stuck in quicksand. Drugged? Who would drug her? And why? Another thought struck her then and swept a wave of panic over her. What *was* her name? Her mind was a blank sheet of paper. Name. *Her* name. She didn't remember her own...Ah, yes. "Cheryl. Cheryl Stone." She rubbed her eyes with the back of her hands then looked at the woman. "What's yours?"

The other woman tilted her head to one side and smiled that motherly smile again. A crack on her lower lip split open, and she licked it. "I'm Amber Mann, and that's Ginny Grisham." She motioned toward another woman, smaller and chunkier, sitting in a far corner of the barn, knees pulled to her chest, head propped against the plank wall. Ginny didn't look at her; she kept her eyes fixed on something outside. "She's having a hard time with all this."

Cheryl blinked. "All what?"

Amber waved her hand around the barn in a circular motion. "This." She looked at Cheryl, that smile now replaced by a frown. "We've been abducted and put here in this barn. I've been here for two weeks. Ginny's been here a week."

Abducted? That would explain a lot, everything, in fact. Cheryl rolled onto her knees and slowly stood. She was a bit wobbly at first but quickly gained her equilibrium and oriented herself. She walked over to the wall to her left and peered through one of the cracks between the planks. They were in the middle of some sort of farm that, from the looks of it, hadn't been used in years, maybe decades. The sun had already cleared the tree line in the distance. A light breeze washed through a sprawling meadow, bending the tops of the grass in rolling waves. The sky was like blue crystal, dotted with big snowball clouds. "Is it just the three of us?" she finally asked.

Amber was behind her, her hand on the small of Cheryl's back. "So far. More may be coming. We can't be sure."

"Who did this?"

"We don't know. He comes by every couple days or so bringing supplies—food, water, even underwear and a hairbrush. For some reason he wants to keep us alive."

Heat spread down Cheryl's neck and radiated through her chest. She was being held against her will—they all were—by some sicko. She spun around and faced Amber. "Why haven't you escaped? How hard can it be to break out of this place?"

Amber took a step back but didn't seem the least bit surprised by Cheryl's outburst. "We did," she said, her voice low and serious. "There's a paved road at the end of the dirt lane"—she motioned to the other side of the barn—"and we almost made it there. But he showed up and caught us. And there's the dogs—"

"Dogs? What dogs?" Cheryl turned back around and looked through the crack again, scanning the meadow. "I don't see any—" There, a movement to the left. Before she could say another word, two Dobermans trotted out of the high grass, running their noses along the ground. One almost ran into the other and was sharply reprimanded with a low growl.

Dread sat in her stomach like a rock. They were in a wooden cage. Like three rats. Cheryl looked at Ginny, who was in the same spot in the same position with the same blank expression on her face. Then she looked at Amber.

"He knows we can't go anywhere as long as the dogs are there," Amber said. "Believe me, we—I—tried to think of any possible way out. But there just isn't any. And even if we did get out and got away without the dogs seeing us, we have no idea where we are. The dogs have our scent, and it wouldn't take them long to track us down."

Cheryl turned and pressed her face against the plank. High above, a vulture carved an arc in the sky. She slipped her fingers through some cracks and gripped the rough wood, a prisoner wrestling the bars that confined her. "Then we think harder and find a way out. There has to be a way. I'm not going to die in here. I'm not."

Miles away, in the bay of Stone Service Center, Mark Stone bent over the engine of a 1996 Ford F-150. It was Thursday, and he was hard at work. The owner of the truck, Gage Riley, a local brick mason, said it had been overheating. Mark's first thought had been the radiator, maybe the water pump. They were the usual culprits when it came to temperature issues. But first, he'd checked the thermostat. Easier to check and much cheaper to repair than a water pump or radiator. And, sure enough, the thermostat had been the villain.

Now, with hose removed, old thermostat resting in peace in the trash bin, he needed only to scrape off what was left of the old gasket, set the new gasket in place, drop in the new thermostat, tighten everything down, and reattach the hose. Simple as that. A twenty-minute job total. Riley would be thrilled.

Fifteen minutes later, Mark tightened down the last screw, securing the clamp to the radiator hose. He stood up and bent backward, stretching his aching back, then tossed the screwdriver onto the workbench. Wiping his hands on an already blackened rag, he headed for the office to check the mail. It was half past three; the mailman should have come by now.

Finding the mail in its usual spot on the floor, Mark picked it up and sorted through it. Two pieces: a credit card offer (0% Introductory APR!) and the state registration renewal for the Nissan. Cheryl's car. But it was still in his name.

Mark remembered when they bought the car. What a battle they had. He never liked foreign cars. Still didn't. Too pricey to maintain, parts too hard to come by. Sure, they had good track records as far as reliability was concerned, but there was nothing in the world like American muscle under the hood. For him, it was about American ingenuity, history, and national pride. For Cheryl, it was all about styling and colors and cup holders. From the moment she saw that Nissan on the lot of Valley View Pre-owned Cars she fell in love with it. Rushed right home and told Mark she'd found the car of her dreams. Never told him, though, that it wasn't American. Wise woman. He would have refused right then and there. He would have known better than to give way to her womanly powers of influence. Instead, he wound up standing on the cracked asphalt lot, fists in his pockets, chest tight and tightening, as Cheryl and Herman the toupeed salesman double-teamed him in a coup de sales pitch.

Mark tried to persuade her; for the next half hour he tried to deflect each of Herman's tantalizing scenarios and empty promises and tried to absorb each of Cheryl's pleas and puppy-dog looks, but it was useless. Cheryl had her heart set on the Nissan, the rice burner. Arguing was pointless.

And besides, he never could say no to her.

He sat in his chair, swung around so his legs slid under the desk, and pushed some papers (mostly customer work orders and bills) out of the way. Propping his elbows on the desk, he held the envelope in front of him and stared at it. He didn't open it, just stared at it, as if it would say something to him, tell him what he should do with it. He could pay it; in fact, he *would* pay it for her, but sooner or later he'd have to see her to give it to her. It belonged in the glove box of *her* Altima. But would she want him to pay for it? Maybe she'd be offended. The way she'd acted the couple times he'd spoken to her, she'd made it clear she wanted nothing to do with him, and that probably included favors.

—*Cheryl, Cheryl. Baby.*

—*What do you want from me?*

—*What do I have to do to prove to you how sorry I am?*

He set the envelope down and let his mind wander back to the first time he and Cheryl kissed. They'd been dating three months, and he hadn't been able to muster up the nerve to do it. Really do it. He'd wanted to. Oh, had he wanted to, from the first time his eyes found her in the crowd at Jeff's birthday party. And several times he almost had. There was the time at that same party, sitting next to her on the sofa, acutely aware of her arm against his. He'd imagined sliding his arm around her shoulders, tilting his head toward hers, and leaning in for the big move. Then there was the time, a couple of weeks later, when they'd gone to the lake for a picnic, their second date. The weather was perfect—cloudless sky, cool breeze—and a family of ducks paddled peacefully around the lake by the shore, occasionally dipping beneath the surface in search of food. There wasn't another soul in sight. And Cheryl was stunning. Her hair, tossed by the breeze, danced around her face; her capris and short-sleeve button-down shirt fit closely, accentuating her lean figure; her eyes sparkled in the sunlight like precious stones; her lips were full and inviting. Sitting on the blanket with their half-eaten lunch still spread out between them, he'd suddenly had the urge to lean forward and kiss her, really kiss her, but for some reason he didn't. Later, after berating himself all day for not seizing the opportunity, he'd come to the conclusion that he didn't because the day was too perfect. He didn't want to ruin it with an awkward kiss that he wasn't sure how she would react to. Better to leave well enough alone. But it had turned out to be a perfect day still, even without the kiss.

The actual first kiss happened at a more awkward moment. It was New Year's Eve, and she had invited him over to her uncle's house to celebrate. At five till midnight her entire family—parents, eight uncles and aunts, twelve cousins—gathered around the TV to watch the ball drop in Times Square. When the ball touched down, all the adults in the room leaned in for a kiss from their significant other. Except them. Mark and Cheryl stood frozen in the center of the room. He remembered the flush that settled in his cheeks when all her cousins started chanting their names then, "Kiss. Kiss. Kiss. Kiss." After a few seconds of the torment, he finally turned to Cheryl, smiled timidly, shrugged his shoulders, and planted one on her lips. It was nothing special. Just a peck, and then it was over. Not exactly the romantic lip-locked embrace he'd hoped their first kiss would be. But it was ecstasy nonetheless. For the mere half second their lips had touched, he had been raptured. His heart soared on a cloud of bliss. The moment—

Stop it! He had to stop letting his mind wander back to those days. They were over, long gone, and if Cheryl had it her way, dead, never to be resuscitated. That thought shifted the gears of his mind and shoved an image of Andrea to the forefront. She had died, hadn't she? And gone to hell? Was it possible? If so, it gave a whole new meaning to the phrase "been to hell and back." And if she did indeed go to hell, what was it that she'd seen in her room? The devil? A gaggle of old Lucifer's minions? The Grim Reaper or whoever it was that came knocking on life's door? Like the repo man, Mark thought. Coming to collect. Time to pay up.

The very thought of someone actually escaping hell's flames and living to talk about it put a knot in Mark's belly. What horrors must haunt the inner workings of her mind? It was no wonder she'd acted so strangely. He'd no doubt act the same way.

And then those words were there again, sitting in his mind like a hobo who simply wouldn't go away:

Everyone has an appointment with death.

Maybe the appointment can be postponed, but sooner or later death comes knocking.

Life's repo man.

His thoughts then shifted gears again and settled on Tim, the tattooed preacher. The preacher who'd spent time on the dark side and found Jesus in the slammer. He was odd. Odd for a preacher, that is. And yet Mark had found himself drawn to him. Why? Growing up around the performance of Christianity, Mark had grown cynical and calloused toward professors of faith in Christ. Did they really have faith in Jesus to save them, or was their faith in their own ability to play the game without a fault? But Tim was different. Way different. Not just in appearance but in...well, he was just different. He was real. Yes, that's what it was. Real. Transparent. It gave his words so much more credibility than some red-faced preacher in a polyester suit screaming about damnation while his comb-over flopped back and forth like a bird's lame wing. And what was it Tim had said?

None of us is guaranteed tomorrow. You know that. That's what this is really all about, isn't it? The screams and all? Life is like a vapor. Here today and gone tomorrow. You know what the Bible says, it's appointed unto man once to die. But when will your appointment come due?

The appointment. When *was* his appointment with the repo man? No one really knew, did they? That was life's greatest catch. No one knows when death will come knocking. Some never get a chance to live their lives before the flame is snuffed out; others get to live full lives and experience more than some whole towns experience. Why? Who makes the appointment? Of course, he knew the answer. God did. And again, Tim's words were there, knocking around in his head:

But when will your appointment come due?

But that was just it; he didn't know. But, of course, that was the purpose of Tim's question, wasn't it? We don't know, so we have to be ready. He'd asked Mark if he knew where he would go when he died, when that appointment came due and the repo man stood on his doorstep. And Mark had given the typical performance answer: *Well, I said a prayer, didn't I? Even got baptized. Full immersion, of course. The only way. Washed in the Spirit, cleansed by the blood.* And he'd gone to Sunday school and church, memorized Bible verses, learned all the stories, could repeat them forward and backward. But Tim said that wasn't enough:

Mark, doing those things won't get you into heaven. It's gotta be in here.

Mark could still see him lifting his tattooed arm and tapping his chest, over his heart, with his index finger. Of course it did. Mark knew that. But that was the problem, he *knew* what the Bible said—man looks at the outward appearance, but God looks at the heart—but for some unknown and bizarre reason it never sunk further than his head, never made it to his heart. Like there was some kind of levee there, holding back the truth from flooding his heart and really changing his life.

Mark shook his head and stared at the envelope in his hands. He'd think about that stuff later. Right now, he should call Cheryl while he was thinking about it and let her know he has the registration, give her a chance to claim it as her responsibility and pay for it. If she offered, he'd let her. If not, he'd pay for it himself. Heck, it was only a hundred and twenty-eight bucks. It was the least he could do.

After what he'd done to her, he owed her at least a hundred and twenty-eight bucks.

"So this was how you got out before?" Cheryl said, rattling the handle of the trapdoor. She lifted the padlock, inspected it, tugged on it, then threw it down so it banged hard against the metal ring to which it was attached.

Amber was pacing back and forth, arms folded across her chest, one hand gripping a water bottle. She took a swig of the water and winced as she swallowed. "Yeah. It was open. The dogs were gone. Off in the woods I guess, looking for food." She walked over to the wall and peered through one of the cracks.

She then looked at Ginny, still huddled in her corner, forehead pressed against a rough plank.

In the five or so hours since she'd awakened in this prison, Cheryl had done some quick deducing. Amber had it together. She'd been here two weeks and had not only survived but had kept her sanity. And some hope. And she'd escaped once; that was something. Really something. And from the way Amber told it, they almost made it too. But she was seriously ill. She hadn't complained at all, but Cheryl could tell. Her cough sounded horrible, like a bear's bark, and her face was flushed and glazed with a thin layer of perspiration. Sure signs of a fever. And when she talked, her words were measured and strained. She still showed signs of strength and spunk, but the facade wouldn't last much longer. If they didn't get out of here soon and get her some help, her condition would deteriorate quickly.

Amber had spent the last couple hours filling Cheryl in on everything she knew about the man called Judge, his tendencies, his mood swings, and his one almost-breakdown in front of them. She seemed to think he could be reasoned with, that somewhere in that demented mind was a soul that cared and knew right from wrong. Either way, they were going to escape again. Cheryl was going to make sure of that. It was just a matter of time. But how much time did they have? Amber said that Judge never said how many women he was going to stuff into this little penthouse. Was this it? Or were there more to come? And if so, how many more? Knowing was everything—it determined how much time they had to formulate a plan. But there couldn't be too much time left. Judge had to know the longer he waited to do whatever it was he was planning to do, the better the chances were of getting caught...of being found.

Oh, and then there was Ginny. She seemed young and was definitely scared (but weren't they all?), and Cheryl felt a little sorry for her. She'd be no help, though. In the past five hours she'd moved from her spot once, and that was to trudge over to the corner, relieve herself, and trudge back. She hadn't eaten any breakfast (Cheryl had a couple handfuls of Cheerios and an apple), hadn't spoken more than five words, and hadn't even hinted at having any real interest in getting out of here. She'd be no help when the time came. They'd take her with them, of course. But, as Amber had told Cheryl in a low voice in the far corner of the barn so as not to be heard by Ginny, she'd be a burden.

Amber turned from the wall and walked over, her feet shuffling through the straw. She lowered herself to her haunches and sat next to Cheryl, long legs stretched out in front of her. "Any ideas?"

Cheryl dropped to her backside, draped her wrists over her knees, and shook her head. "Not at the moment." There weren't a lot of options. They were in an empty barn, no tools, no weapons, and only the bare essentials for survival.

Amber covered her mouth with both hands and hacked loudly three times. Wiping her mouth with her sleeve, she smiled weakly at Cheryl.

"That cough sounds bad," Cheryl said. "You doing OK? I mean—"

"I'll be fine. It's just a cough. It gets cold in here at night, and I'm always having sinus problems in cold weather."

Cheryl glanced around the barn. Ginny was in her spot, glued to the wall, curled into a tight ball, hiding within herself. She'd have to face reality sooner or later, and when she did, it wouldn't be pretty. The bats were squeaking above them, jostling for position, opening and closing their wings. They gave Cheryl the creeps. She never did like bats. Now she had to share a barn with them. "Where are you from?" she asked Amber.

"Frostburg. You?"

Cheryl hesitated. "Near Lonaconing."

"You married?"

Again, the hesitation. How deep was she going to allow this woman to probe? Part of her wanted to protect her privacy, say, *Yes, I'm happily married and am sure my loving, devoted husband has nothing short of the National Guard looking for us,* but she wasn't sure that was even true. One, Mark probably hadn't a clue she was missing—how could he? And two, even if he did know, would he care? He might see it as an opportunity to finally be rid of her and fall into the arms of...Rachel. But another part of her wanted to pour out her soul on the straw-covered floor in front of Amber. She was cold, tired, scared, and homesick, and though she had tried to push the sentiment from her heart, she missed Mark. She needed someone to bond to, someone to connect with. Mark had always been that person, the one to whom she ran when life's worries and pains got too bad. Now Amber would have to do. She looked at Amber. "Are you?"

Amber smiled. A genuine smile this time. "I asked you first."

After a deep sigh and brief tug-of-war with herself, Cheryl decided that hiding her hurt forever would never ease the pain. "Yeah, I'm married. Barely."

"Barely? Sounds like you got a story."

"Nothing I enjoy retelling. My husband cheated on me and we're separated."

"Divorced?"

Cheryl shook her head and looked at her hands. "Not yet."

"Who was she?"

Cheryl shrugged. "Some waitress he knew." She looked up at the bats again, wishing she could fly away as easily as they could. "I caught them kissing. He...tried to apologize, said he was sorry and he'd never see her again. Said that was the first time he ever kissed her, ever even touched her. But it wasn't the kiss that hurt, it was that... it was that he *gave* himself to her. He bonded with her on a level that I thought only we shared. It was bad enough there was another woman in his arms, but it hurt worse that there was another woman in his heart." Tears puddled in her eyes, blurring the lines of the lighted cracks in the wall. There. It was out. It was the first time she'd told anyone what hurt the most. Mark had given his heart to her, and she didn't even know he was sharing it with some other woman.

Amber placed a hand on Cheryl's back and rubbed in a slow circular motion. "I'm so sorry. I wish it never happened to you. What a jerk."

Cheryl shook her head slowly. "No, that's the thing. Mark's not a jerk. I mean, what he did was jerkish, really jerkish, but he's really not a jerk. That's why it hurts so much. I hate him for what he did, and part of me never wants to see him again, but I still love him too. I miss him. I miss the feel of his arms around me, the smell of his cologne, the sound of his voice telling me he loves me when we're lying in bed in the dark. Is that crazy?"

Now Amber was crying. She slid the sleeve of her sweatshirt across her eyes and coughed again. She grimaced as she swallowed. "No, it's not crazy. I'm not married, but I have a boyfriend. I think I care more about him than he does for me. Everyone thinks I'm a bimbo, just running from boyfriend to boyfriend looking for a good time, but I'm not. I just want to love and be loved, that's all."

Cheryl forced a smile. "Looks like we're just two lost souls in search of real love. I don't know if that's romantic or pathetic."

Amber gave a little laugh, her hazel eyes sparkling through the tears. "I think I'll go with romantic. I like the sound of it better." She leaned closer to Cheryl and lowered her voice. "I'm gonna go check on Ginny. We need to try to keep her spirits up as much as possible." She stood and shuffled over to the corner.

Cheryl smiled. It felt good to talk to someone about how she really felt, to be transparent. But how she felt wouldn't get them out of the barn. The time for sentiment had passed; now she had to find a way out.

Cheryl stood, her knees popping as they unfolded. She placed her hands on her hips and looked around the barn, hoping for some hidden escape route to suddenly appear so she could say, *Why didn't we see this before?* She scanned the whole interior of the barn and came up with absolutely nothing. Sure, they could just bust through the wall; it wouldn't be that difficult. She'd noticed some of the boards were rotting.

But then there were the dogs to deal with. Amber said some nights she could hear them scratching, sometimes digging at the dirt around the barn, sometimes actually pawing at the wood. Whether they could actually claw through solid wood, Cheryl didn't know. She doubted it, but there really was no telling what starving dogs were capable of. And if they were smart enough and clawed at the same spot every time, eventually they'd get through. And then what? She didn't even want to think about it. Maybe they could somehow kill the dogs. But how? They had no weapons, and there was nothing in the barn except straw and the supplies Judge had brought.

Maybe they could use something in the supplies. She mentally ran through their inventory of belongings: apples, toilet paper, cereal boxes, dirty underwear, Amber's outfit she was wearing the night she was taken, her high heels, her...wait a minute! A thought suddenly materialized and bounded to the front of her brain like a child on a pogo stick yelling, *Look at me! Look at me!* She had to mentally run through it, check for loopholes, mistakes in reasoning, breakdowns in logic. What if—

What was that?

"What's that?" Amber asked, looking around.

There was a second of silence as they stood stock-still staring at each other and listening. Amber's hand was frozen in the air. In her peripheral vision, Cheryl could tell Ginny had lifted her forehead off the plank. She too was listening. Then it was there again. A musical tune, muffled, muddled, disjointed, but clearly "Sweet Home Alabama."

"Oh my gosh!" Cheryl shouted, running for the bed of straw. Her heart almost thumped right out of her chest. She scrambled through the quilt she was delivered in, fumbled, rummaged, looking, looking, all the while the tune, *that* tune, electronically garbled "Sweet Home Alabama," played on. Finally, she grabbed the quilt with one hand and lifted it, giving it a good shake. Something black and hard flipped out, rotated end over end in the air, then hit the floorboards with a double clank. The *something*. Their lifeline. Their way out of this cage. Her cell phone. She got down on her knees and scrambled for it. Her mind spun. How...?

The tune started over.

Suddenly it was in her hand. The plastic casing was cracked, and when she turned it over she saw that the keypad was busted in two places and the LCD display was shattered, a snowflake of cracked glass. Still, though, she could make out the caller's name. "It's Mark," she cried, tears dropping out of her eyes. "Of all people." She punched the talk button with a trembling thumb but nothing happened. The first notes of "Sweet Home Alabama" started over again. She pressed it again, mashing the tip of her thumb into the button. The phone beeped a weak electronic impulse. She pressed the speaker end against her ear. "Mark! Thank God. Mark!"

"Cheryl? What's wrong?"

She was never so glad to hear his voice. Never. Even if he was a cheating scoundrel. "Mark, I've been kidnapped." The words sounded foreign to her. Kidnapped? It suddenly seemed so real. The reality of it hit her all at once, and she started to sob into the phone. She cried so hard words would not come, only guttural grunts. He'd never believe her. Why should he?

"Cheryl. What do you mean *kidnapped*? Where are you?"

Finally, she was able to compose herself enough to talk. "I was taken last night while I slept. He drugged me or something—"

"Who drugged you? Cheryl, what is this?"

"Mark!" She meant to holler it, but it came out as a high-pitched scream. She choked out another sob then collected herself again. "I don't know who. I woke up in this...this barn, out in the middle of...of...I don't even know where we are. There's nothing around." She was talking fast and hoping he was getting it all. She could only imagine what it must sound like on his end.

"A barn? Are you OK? He didn't do—"

"I'm fine. OK, I mean. There's two others here too." She pressed the palm of her free hand against her forehead. *Think. Think. Be clear.* Mark was talking, but she really wasn't listening. "Mark, listen," she said cutting him off midsentence. "I think this phone's been on all night—"

"How'd you get your phone?"

"I don't know...I was in bed last night and called my mom...fell asleep...the phone was in the blankets when he...Oh, it doesn't matter! Listen! There's not much life left in this phone. Call the cops, OK?"

"Yeah, of course. Who's with you? You said *two others*."

"The other women here are..." She bounced the heel of her palm on her forehead.

Amber said, "Amber Mann and Ginny...Virginia Grisham."

Cheryl looked at Amber, her eyes were wide, tears streaming down her cheeks. She then looked over at Ginny, who was now standing, still in the corner, but at least standing. She was crying too.

"Write this down," she said into the phone. She was gaining some composure. "Do you have something?"

"Yeah. Go."

"Amber Mann. Virginia Grisham. Call the cops and tell them we're here. I'll try too."

"Cheryl, where's *here*? What am I supposed to tell them?"

Cheryl ran to the wall and looked at the outside world. "We're in a barn on what looks to be an abandoned farm. In a valley. Surrounded by hills. There's woods on one side, nothing but overgrown pasture all around. I don't know where, though. Could be Pennsylvania or West Virginia for all I know. Just call them, OK?"

"As soon as I hang up."

There was a moment of silence on both ends. "Mark?"

"Yeah."

"I'm OK. We're all OK. But..." She looked at Amber, then at Ginny. Ginny showed no sign of knowing how sick Amber was. If she did, she might withdraw even deeper into her place of despair. "Nothing. Just get us some help."

"Of course. And...Cher, I love you."

"OK. I'm gonna power down to save battery. I'll call you in an hour if I can." She depressed the disconnect button and held it down, praying the phone would reset itself. It did. She then pressed the 9, and an uncoordinated digital 9 appeared on the screen. But when she pushed the 1 button nothing happened. "No, no, no. C'mon." She pushed it again, harder this time and held it down. Still nothing. The LCD display looked back at her with that fractured face as if to say, *Is that all you got?* Panic gripped her throat and squeezed. She tried it again, pressing with both thumbs. But only the 9 remained, black on a white background. "No! Please, no."

Now Amber was there beside her. "Let me try," she said.

Cheryl cursed and slapped the phone into Amber's hand. With tears leaving pink trails in the dirt on her face, Amber fumbled with the phone for a few seconds then fell silent.

Ginny whimpered and let out a desperate moan.

Amber said in a low, defeated voice, "Only the nine and four work. That won't do us any good."

Cheryl took the phone back and hugged it against her belly. Her mouth felt like she'd been chewing on sawdust. She and Amber stood staring at each other for several moments. The barn was vacuous, like the air had been sucked out of it. Even the bats were silent.

"He'll call us," Amber finally said. "Won't he? When you don't call back, he'll call, right?"

Cheryl nodded. "He'll call. They'll find us." But she didn't believe her own words. How could they find them? An abandoned barn in the middle of nowhere. That really narrowed it down. She could hear the cops now: *Sure, great, we know exactly where that is. We'll just send a cruiser on over to pick 'em up.* They could be anywhere—Pennsylvania, West Virginia, the back hills of Maryland's panhandle.

Only one person knew.

Judge.

Mark dropped the phone back in its cradle and realized for the first time how badly his hand was shaking. Sweat pooled in his eyebrows, and his heart was pounding out a steady rhythm, double time, maybe triple. It felt like a Thoroughbred was racing through his chest. He glanced at his watch—four o'clock on the button. She'd be calling again at five.

He looked at the names he'd scribbled: *Amber Mann, Virginia Grisham*. They didn't mean anything to him, just names on a piece of paper, but they were people, real people, trapped in some barn with Cheryl. *His* Cheryl. He looked at the other notes he'd jotted down while Cheryl was talking. He'd tried to keep up with her and thought he'd done a pretty good job, but now the writing seemed like a foreign language. He picked up the scrap paper and studied it. *Valley* was there. Yes, she'd said they were in a valley of some sort. On an abandoned farm, or what *seemed* like an abandoned farm. But why did she think it was abandoned? *Overgrown pasture* was scribbled next to *valley*. But what if the farm wasn't abandoned at all? What if the pasture was just unused? What if the kidnapper was the farmer? More than likely he was. If there was a barn, there must be a house nearby. But she hadn't said anything about a house. Surely, if there was a house in view she would have mentioned that. His head was starting to hurt.

Focus, man, focus. This is Cheryl's life we're dealing with.

He stared at the paper, hoping the location would suddenly materialize, like one of those computer-generated picture-within-a-picture things that were so popular a few years back. He even let his eyes unfocus; it worked with the pictures.

A barn on a farm in a valley surrounded by fields and woods. That didn't give him much. *C'mon, baby. Give me something I can work with.*

After staring at the paper some more, trying to imagine what the farm would look like and remember if he'd ever seen such a farm around Allegheny County, he finally set the paper down and smacked the desk hard with an open hand. The jolt sent a shock of pain up the outside of his hand and into his elbow. He cursed and hit the desk again, this time ignoring the pain.

Picking up the phone, he pushed 911 with his index finger.

When the dispatcher came on, he told her he needed the police.

"Is this an emergency?" the woman asked.

"I have a crime to report," Mark said. "Just patch me through to the police. Please."

Moments later a man's voice, deep and gravelly, came over the phone. "Allegheny County Sheriff's Office, Deputy Franklin."

Mark froze. How to explain this? He hadn't thought about what he would say. Maybe he should ask for Sheriff...what was his *name*?...Hickock. No, he'd never believe him. That female deputy with him might, though. She seemed a little more open than Hickock. But what was her name? *Think!*

"Hello?" Deputy Gravel.

"Hello, uh, can I speak to...um"...*Her name?* "Deputy, uh"...*Yes!* "Foreman."

"Who's calling?"

"Um, Mark...Mark Stone. She knows who I am."

"Hold on one minute. I'll see if she's available."

Mark tapped his desk and bounced his knee while he waited. *C'mon. C'mon.* They needed to hurry. What if the kidnapper came back soon and did God-knows-what to Cheryl and the other two? *I'd kill him, that's what. With my own bare hands. Beat the life right out of him.*

"Mr. Stone?" It was Foreman all right. He recognized her voice immediately.

"My wife's been kidnapped. She's in a barn on some farm. We need to find her—"

"Whoa, whoa," Foreman said. "Slow down, Mr. Stone. Now what's this? Your wife's been kidnapped?"

"Kidnapped. Abducted. Last night while she slept."

"How do you know?"

"I called her on her cell. She's in a barn with two other women, but they don't know where the barn is. Only that it's on what appears to be an abandoned farm."

There was a moment of silence, then, "Mr. Stone, is this another one of your screaming calls? Because if it is—"

Mark shot out of his chair, ready to go head to head with Foreman, even if it was over the phone. "No! No, it's not. I didn't hear any screams. Thank God. Look, we have to do something. Who knows when this guy's gonna return and what he'll do when he does. We have to find them."

"OK, OK. Just hold on. Let me get something to write with. OK. Your wife called you from her cell phone."

"I called her."

"You called her. Why did you call her?"

"I got the vehicle registration info for her car in the mail and…what difference does it make? I called her and she answered."

Another pause. This time short. "She's been abducted, and she has her cell phone with her?"

"I guess. Something about falling asleep with it last night and not realizing she still had it until it rang. What are you gonna do?"

"Right now I'm trying to figure out exactly what's going on, OK? Work with me a little." Foreman sounded like she was getting irritated. Not good.

Mark sighed and sat in his desk chair. "I'm sorry. Look, I know you and Hickock probably think I'm nuts, but I'm telling you the truth. You have to believe me. She said they're in a barn in the middle of what looks like an abandoned farm in a valley.

That's it. That's all she could tell me. And that there are two other women with her. Both were also abducted."

"Did she tell you their names? These other women?"

"Yes." Mark picked the scrap paper up and read the names. "Amber Mann and Virginia Grisham."

This time there was a long pause.

"Deputy Foreman?"

"Mr. Stone, can you come over to our headquarters?"

"Sure."

"Do you know where we're located? Furnace Street in Cumberland?"

"Yeah, I think I know where it is."

"Good. Come right away." Her voice sounded urgent.

"Are you gonna help?"

"We'll do what we can."

"I'll be there in thirty minutes."

The sun was well into its downward afternoon arc when Amber pulled Cheryl into the far corner of the barn, out of Ginny's hearing. She couldn't believe the turn of events. To think that Cheryl got drugged in her own home, dragged here by Judge, locked up in this giant crate like some animal, only to have her cell phone with her the whole time, but the damaged phone could only receive calls and was sorely low on battery life.

Immediately following the call all three of the women were quiet and solemn. Ginny had slipped back into shell, her semi-catatonic state, and Cheryl was even showing signs of depression. She stood, clutching the phone to her chest, cheeks wet with tears, with a faraway look in her eyes. A look that screamed defeat.

Their lives were now in the hands of Cheryl's husband...

estranged husband...*cheating* husband. Would he call when Cheryl didn't call him in an hour? Of course he would. And he'd have the cops already looking for them. But really, what were the chances of the cops actually finding them? Sure, they couldn't be more than two hours away from Frostburg, but two hours covered a lot of land, a lot of farmland. And none of them knew how much time they had left. She had to try to convince Cheryl that they still needed to formulate a backup escape plan. Just in case. Which is what led to this secret meeting in the far corner of the barn. Ginny didn't need to hear any of this. She'd only fret more. And fretting more was not something they needed her doing right now. She was better off in the dark. They'd bring her into the light when the time came. And not a minute sooner.

"What is it?" Cheryl asked. Her eyes were wide, but no life was in them. Her lips were stretched thin over white teeth. She held the phone in both hands, pressed against her chest.

Amber took a gulp of water, swished it around in her mouth, and swallowed hard. She drew a hand over her forehead, mopping up the sweat that was now ever-present. The fever had started two days ago, low grade but enough to keep her up at night shivering. Her chest burned now with each breath, and coughing was like dragging razor blades up and down her throat. She forced herself to swallow again and kept her voice low. "I think we still need to talk about an escape plan. Just in case things don't... you know."

Cheryl blinked three times, and Amber thought she saw a spark of awareness in her eyes. "OK. Do you have anything— wait a minute." She snapped her fingers. Her eyes came alive. Thank God. "I had an idea before the phone rang." She thought for a moment, staring at her feet, bouncing her left hand on her thigh. "Yes. Your belt, from your skirt. The one you were wearing the night you got here."

Amber leaned in. This better be good. "What about it?"

"The dogs. They're the ones keeping us here, not this rotted old barn. We get rid of the dogs, and we're out of here."

"OK. So what about the belt?"

Cheryl held a fist to her chin. "If we can loop it through one of the gaps between the planks and lure one of the dogs in, we can use the belt to strangle it. Wrap it around the dog's neck and pull until...well, until—"

"Yeah, I get it," Amber said. The poor woman couldn't even bring herself to say it. *Until it snuffed the life out of the mangy mutt.* Amber thought about that for a moment, visualizing it in her head. It might just work. 'Course, they'd have to get the dog to come to a specific spot along the wall and hold still long enough to loop the belt around its neck without losing a hand in the process. Then, with it pinned against the wall, they'd pull with everything they had until the little beasty went limp. "It's a long shot, but there's a chance. Might be our only chance."

"We'll wait until five. See what happens with the phone. Then decide when."

"OK," Amber said. "And listen, don't say anything to Ginny until we're ready to do it. She's...you know."

Cheryl stole a glance at Ginny, and Amber did the same. Still doing the dead-man's stare. "Yeah. I know."

Chapter 11

❶

WHEN MARK ENTERED THE ALLEGHENY COUNTY Sheriff's Department headquarters, Deputy Foreman was waiting for him.

"Mr. Stone," she said, extending a hand and shaking his. She wasn't wearing her broad-brimmed hat, and her russet hair was pulled back in a ponytail. "Come this way."

Mark followed her back to a small room with two metal desks facing each other, each with a computer and monitor. Along one wall was a long table with papers and files spread out on it, orderly, like someone was in the process of organizing them. At one of the desks, a large man with a full face, short, thinning brown hair, and a large belly was wedged between the desk and chair playing with the computer's mouse. He wasn't wearing a police uniform, just khakis and a brown oxford that appeared two sizes too small.

Foreman entered the room first and motioned toward the bulky man. "This is Brinkley, our tech guy."

Brinkley looked up and squinted at Mark with clear green eyes that were entirely too small for his large head. He nodded, no smile, then went back to the monitor.

"Brinkley's going to help us find your wife and the others."

"Triangulation?" Mark had heard of cops and rescue personnel locating people using their cell phone signals by triangulating their position between three phone towers, but he had no idea how it worked. Regardless, a spark of hope ignited in his heart. Cheryl's phone could save their lives after all. *Just stay alive, baby. Just stay alive.*

Foreman bit off a piece of her fingernail and nodded. "Yeah. You know how it works?"

"I've heard of it but…no."

Foreman turned toward Brinkley. "You got a piece of paper and a pen?"

"Yup," Brinkley said. He took his hand off the mouse, pulled a pen from his shirt pocket, and reached across the desk for a small piece of paper. "Ready."

Foreman turned back to Mark. "We need your wife's full name, cell phone number, and network provider."

Mark gave them the information: name, number, provider.

"Got it," Brinkley said. He turned his attention back to the computer monitor, and his thick hand swallowed the mouse again.

"Good, Brink will work on that," Foreman said. "Now, triangulation. Cell phone towers are usually arranged across the country in a honeycomb pattern. In a rural setting, they're spaced maybe ten, twelve miles apart. When a phone is switched on, it sends out a check signal every so often to make sure everything is working as it should. All the towers within range will receive the signal, usually at least three. All we have to do is contact the provider, find out which tower is receiving the strongest signal, and triangulate it with two other towers. We should be able to pinpoint her location to within a few hundred yards. It's the same principle GPS uses except it uses satellites, not phone towers." She smiled a reassuring smile. "It's not so hard to find the needle in the haystack when the needle is screaming, *Here I am.* The only tricky part is that in rural areas, the towers usually follow roads, so they're arranged in straight lines instead of the honeycomb patter. Makes it harder to triangulate when the towers are in a line."

"Will it work if her phone is turned off?" Mark asked.

Foreman snapped her head toward Brinkley, who was already looking at Mark, lips slightly parted, eyebrows raised. "Her phone is off?" he said.

"She said the battery was low, so she was turning off the phone. She's going to call me at five."

Brinkley lifted his hand off the mouse in dramatic fashion and pursed his large lips. "Nope. No power, no signal. We need a signal to triangulate."

Mark looked at his watch. Four thirty. Half an hour. An eternity when your wife's life hangs in the balance. Maybe she'd call sooner. Maybe. Probably not. Cheryl was on time with everything, the most punctual person Mark had ever met. If she said she'd call in an hour, and an hour was five o'clock, then she'd call at five on the dot, not a minute sooner or later.

Foreman turned to Brinkley again. "I'll call Hickock and let him know. He told me to keep him updated."

"Where is the big guy?" Brinkley asked, a spark of humor flashing in his eyes.

"A domestic over in Keifers. Some woman threatening to take her husband's head off with a shotgun."

Brinkley snorted out a laugh, sounding like a hog rummaging for food. "Keifers? That's out in the boonies, isn't it?"

"Over by Green Ridge."

Brinkley shook his head. His full cheeks jostled back and forth with the same consistency as Jell-O. "Crazy rednecks."

"Well," Foreman said, turning to Mark, hands palm up. "We'll have to wait until five. Can you hang around until then?"

Mark felt anger—or maybe just frustration—rise in his chest

and spread heat up the back of his neck. "Hang around? Just sit on our duffs and not do anything while my wife is out there in some barn being held captive by a wacko? There's nothing you can do? Get the National Guard out there, for crying out loud, helicopters, troops, whatever. Comb the area."

Foreman's face softened. "What area? Mr. Stone, I know you're upset, really, I do. But we have no idea where that barn is. If we draw a circle around Allegheny County that spreads out what eighty, a hundred, and who knows how many more miles, we're covering most of Maryland, most of West Virginia, the whole southwestern corner of Pennsylvania, and some of Ohio. And Virginia all the way to the DC suburbs. That's a lot of land to cover and a lot of farmland. Do you realize how many unsuspecting barns we'd come across?"

"It's an abandoned barn in a valley, bordered by woods on one side."

Foreman sighed. "That describes most of the hundred-mile circumference. It's just too vague to call out that kind of manpower. We'll wait a half hour, and when we make contact with her, we'll be able to zero right in. Then we'll call in the big guns. I have the state police on standby. OK?"

Mark didn't like it, but there wasn't much he could do. This one was out of his hands. Frustration built inside him like carbonation in a shaken soda bottle. He was a fixer, a problem solver. It was why he was so good with cars. Find problem, diagnose problem, fix problem. Simple. But this was not so simple. It was the kind of thing his parents would have said to pray about. He could hear Mom now: *Pray about it, Mark. It's in God's hands now. God's able hands.* But he was in no mood to pray. He didn't want to talk to God. He wanted to scream. He wanted to grab Foreman and Brinkley by the collars and shake them until they understood the urgency of the situation. But of course they did. And Foreman was right; that barn could be anywhere, as close as his own backyard, as far away as Ohio. Pushing the irritation back and hiding it in some safe place in his mind, he lowered his head and shrugged. "Yeah. OK. Where's the coffee?"

"Down the hall, last room on the right. The lounge. I'll meet you there in a few minutes."

Mark shuffled down the black and white tiled hall, past what he assumed were two interrogation rooms, the men's bathroom, and another room that had the door closed. He could hear men talking behind the door, their voices muffled and serious.

The lounge was a small room equipped with a kitchenette to the left with all the usuals: stainless steel sink filled with plastic cups and ceramic mugs, blue Formica counter, microwave, toaster oven, coffee maker, oak cabinets overhead. Beside the counter stood a refrigerator, nothing special, just a beige, aging fridge. The rest of the room was furnished with a plaid sofa (well used and sagging in the middle), two upholstered chairs, a short oval coffee table covered with magazines, and a boxy TV on a spindly television stand. In the far corner sat a round oak table surrounded by six unmatched chairs.

Mark poured himself a cup of coffee, added two packets of sugar, and took a seat in one of the upholstered chairs. He wasn't really thirsty, and his stomach would probably protest the intrusion of hot liquid, but he needed *something* to do. Something to keep his hands occupied. Now if he could just keep his mind occupied. He stood again and meandered around the room, coffee in his right hand. On the wall, next to the door by which he'd entered, were two sheets of paper with the word *MISSING* across the top of each. In the center of each poster was a black and white photo of a woman. The one on the left was an attractive woman with shoulder-length brown hair, sharp features, full lips, well groomed. Very pretty; model material. The one on the right was a round-faced woman with short brown hair, cut just below the ears and pulled back with barrettes. She had a nice smile and a little upturned nose. Young. Looked like a nice kid.

He dropped his eyes a few inches on the poster and froze. A buzz started along his jaw and spread up both sides of his head. He looked at the other poster. It was them. The *other* women with Cheryl. Amber Mann and Virginia Grisham.

Amber disappeared two weeks ago. Oddly, that fact brought a strange sense of hope to him. Apparently, their abductor was in no hurry to get rid of them. But how much longer would it be before he did? Sooner or later he'd do *something*. Unless he was just collecting women for God only knew what reason. That sent a new wave of chills over his head, mixed with hot anger. Collecting women in some abandoned barn in the middle of nowhere. Sick, just sick.

"It's been two weeks."

Mark started and looked at Foreman, who had just walked into the room. "I saw. What are you doing about it?"

Foreman walked over to the counter and poured a fresh mug of coffee. She rested her hip against the edge of the counter and nibbled on her fingernail. "Not much we can do except let the right people know. Both of 'em just disappeared. Poof." She waved her hand in the air like a magician. "Mann left work and no one saw her again. Grisham disappeared from her house. No sign of forced entry. No fingerprints or shoe prints or tire prints. Nothing. Just two missing women. Up until your call I was starting to think they both just ran off."

Mark leaned against the wall. "Both of them?" He looked at the posters again, quickly doing the math. "A week apart?"

Foreman stirred cream into her coffee. "Hey, stranger

coincidences have happened. Believe me. I've only been on the force three years, but I've seen it all. Come. Sit down." She motioned toward the chairs, walked over, and sat on the edge of the sofa. She placed her mug on the coffee table.

Mark pushed away from the wall and eased himself into the upholstered chair he'd previously occupied.

Foreman rested her elbows on her thighs and interlocked her fingers. "So…did you hear the screams when you spoke with your wife?"

Mark looked at her, wondering at first if she was mocking him. But her face was as serious as his. "No. Thank God. Do you have any idea who the pervert is who's responsible?"

Foreman reached for her mug and held it with both hands. "Nope. Not a clue. Like I said, he left us nothing." She took a sip. "He's good. I'll give him that." She eyed Mark long enough that it made him uncomfortable. "Were you and your wife having problems? Is that why she had her own apartment?"

The question stung, but it wasn't unexpected. Mark knew sooner or later the subject would have to come up. After all, a normal, healthy couple in love didn't live in separate houses less than a half hour from each other. Mark shrugged, trying to appear nonchalant. "We've been having some problems. She thought it best if we split up for a while."

"Mind telling me what kind of problems?"

"Am I being interrogated?"

Foreman smiled and held up one hand in a half surrender. "No." She reached up and removed her deputy badge, setting it on the table in front of her. A symbolic gesture, Mark thought. "Off the record. Just 'cause I care."

Mark cupped his mug in both hands. The warmth spread through his palms like warm liquid. His eyes fell on the coffee, black, reflecting the fluorescent lights above. "I cheated on her."

Foreman set her mug down and flopped back against the sofa. "Wow. That was blunt. You don't seem like the type. Can I ask why?"

"And that was personal," Mark said.

"Sorry. You don't have to answer."

Mark thought for a moment then said, "No, it's OK. I need to own up to it sometime. Thing is, I don't really know why. There was this waitress, and we got friendly, and one thing led to another. It just all happened so naturally and...fast. Before I knew it, I was sharing my feelings with her. Stuff only Cheryl should have known. And she was doing the same with me. We got really close. Then, it just happened. We were alone. I walked her to her car after her shift. And..." He paused. Tears were building in his eyes. Reliving that moment, the moment that changed, no, more than changed, *ruined*, his life was painful. "And I kissed her. Took her in my arms and kissed her."

He forced a smile. A tear dripped out of his right eye and caught on the corner of his nostril. The lights danced in his coffee. "And wouldn't you know it? At just that moment, Cheryl was driving by on her way home from a friend's baby shower and saw the whole thing."

Foreman didn't say anything. Mark couldn't look at her, he was too ashamed, but he could feel her eyes on him. What must she be thinking? *What a pig!* That's what.

Mark thought back to that time, that moment, that instant when he looked up and caught the look on Cheryl's face as she drove past. It was the look of defeat—crushing, suffocating, heart-ripping defeat. She might as well have caught them in bed. He'd betrayed her, betrayed their love, betrayed his promise. He never did sleep with Rachel, but he was sure that if Cheryl hadn't caught them when she did, it would have been only a matter of time. The kiss, one kiss—one moment in time, one mistake—was enough, though. Enough to rip her away from him, to sever the love they shared. And now a gaping wound was all that was left. Could it ever be healed? He would do all he could to help it along, but the rest would have to be on Cheryl. Could she forgive him? Could she accept his repentance? Only time would tell.

"How long ago?" Foreman finally said.

"'Bout a month. Maybe a little more. I haven't been keeping records."

"You're sorry you did it, aren't you?"

Mark looked up and noticed her eyes were glassy. "Yeah, more than she'll ever know."

Foreman stood and placed a hand on his shoulder. "Hey, be real with her. She'll see how you really feel. OK?"

Mark nodded. It was all he could do. Tentacles of shame and regret constricted around his throat, choking off his words.

Walking over to the counter and placing her mug in the sink, Foreman said, "I'm gonna touch base with Hickock. Be back in a couple minutes."

It was 4:48 p.m.

Twelve minutes. Please, God. The prayer sprang from some deeply buried habit. It used to be instinct, when he was young and striving to be "Christlike," whatever that meant. He'd pray throughout the day: before meals, prior to tests at school, walking the halls, walking home, before bed, first thing in the morning. The Bible said to pray unceasingly, and that's what he had aimed to do. Whether he actually meant any of it or not, he no longer knew. There was a time when he thought he did, but so had Dad, and look where it got him. But still, the prayer he'd just spoken—*Please, God*—stirred something inside him.

It was simple and easy, not the flowery, eloquent, high-and-mighty King James prayers he used to send to heaven on a dove's wings. This one came from his spirit, groaning, naked.

Please, God.

Mark paced the lounge, hands cupped around his third mug of coffee, palms sweaty, heart tamping out an even rhythm. Butterflies danced in his stomach. He felt like a fifth grader right before his big part in the church Christmas pageant. But the Christmas pageant never had someone's life in the balance. Three lives in the balance. And one of them the love of his life.

God. Don't let anything happen to them. Please. "Call, Cheryl. Call." *Please, baby.*

There was a knock at the lounge door. Mark spun around, almost spilling his coffee, and found Foreman standing in the doorway.

"Hey," she said, one hand on her hip. "You looked deep in thought. I didn't want to startle you." She took a step toward him. "I just got off the radio with Hickock. He's in the eastern part of the county on another call but will be over as soon as he can."

"Did you fill him in on everything?"

She nodded. "Everything we know so far. You nervous?"

Mark looked at his coffee, studied the ripples and that fluorescent reflection wriggling in the dark liquid, like the moon's reflection on the open seas. "I'd be crazy not to be. I keep thinking, what if she doesn't call? What if we never find her and I never see her or hear her voice again?"

Foreman walked over to him and placed a soft hand on his forearm. "You have to stay positive. If there's one thing I've learned being a cop, it's that you can't give up. Ever. The minute you give up, all hope is lost. She'll call. And we'll find her."

Mark looked at the clock on the microwave: 4:50. *Please, God.*

The swollen sun hovered just above the horizon. The deep purple sky was streaked with pastel pink clouds, like claw marks across the heavens. For the past hour the mood in the barn was a mixture of defeat and nervous anxiety. Several times Cheryl had powered up the phone to check the time, and each time she tried dialing 911 again. One never knew when the winds of fate would change course and start blowing in their favor, at their back. But each time the phone responded with a weak beep when she pushed the 9 key and an empty stare when she pushed the 1. She tried different numbers, different keys, different combinations of keys, but got the same blank look from the LCD display. Even the 4 was no longer working. And there was now only a sliver of life left in the battery.

Little had been said during the past tense hour. They had agreed to wait and see if Mark called, then do something about the dogs. Neither of them was eager to give Cheryl's strangulation plan a go. For one, it meant sticking your hands outside the barn and having them frightfully close to the chomping jaws and knifelike teeth of the Dobermans. Second, it meant pulling off a Houdini trick to actually get the belt around said Doberman-with-the-chomping-jaws's neck. And third, it meant finding the strength to pull the belt hard enough to strangle the dog. There were no guarantees. The plan was far from foolproof. But right now it was all they had... if Mark didn't come through.

"What time is it?" Amber asked.

"Five," Cheryl said. "I'm gonna keep it on now. I'm guessing he'll worry when I don't call at five but wait until about five after to call me. Just hope there's enough life in the battery to last that long." She paused and looked at Amber, then at Ginny who was stilled curled into her turtle-shell semi-catatonic ball, soaking in the outside world. "Are either of you religious?"

Ginny shot her a quick look then broke off eye contact.

Amber shook her head. "Not anymore. My mom dragged me to Sunday school every week when I was a kid, though. Why?"

Cheryl snorted a short laugh. "I was just thinking we should maybe pray. It may be the only hope we have." She looked from Amber to Ginny. "Any volunteers?"

There was a moment of quiet between the three women before Amber said rather sheepishly, "I will." She wrung her hands and looked around. "Um, I guess I'll just start then. God, our Father who art in heaven, hallowed be Thy name...though I walk through the valley of the shadow of death...we know You're with us. Um, God, we need some help right now. We need Cheryl's...uh, Cheryl's husband to call us and for someone to find us. Help us, God. We could really use a miracle. Please send help. Um, amen."

Cheryl looked up and smiled at Amber. "Thank you." She then looked over at Ginny and noticed a tear had spilled from her eye and had a cut a single trail through the dirt on her face. "We'll get out of here," she said, trying to muster as much confidence as she could. "We will."

Mark was standing in the computer room again, Foreman by his side, Brinkley at the keyboard, and a couple other deputies he hadn't met standing on either side of Brinkley. Everything was ready to go. Brinkley said it would take about four minutes of airtime to locate them. Then Foreman would make some calls and the rescue mission would be in full swing.

Mark looked at the time on the phone's display for the umpteenth time: 5:03.

This was not like Cheryl at all. She was never late. Something had to have gone wrong. At 5:00 he'd tried calling her phone but got the answering service. Her phone was still turned off. Was Pervert there and that's why she hadn't called? Was she OK? Was she even still alive? Just before she hung up last time, she said she'd call in an hour *if she could*. What did that mean? Was she expecting Pervert to return? He didn't like this at all. He should have told her to leave the phone on. How many times had he tried to reach her in the past and her phone had been turned off?

—*Where've you been, Cher?*

—*What do you mean?*

—*I've been trying to call you all day.*

—*I had some errands to—*

—*Cheryl, you have to leave the phone on. What if I had to contact you? What if there's an emergency and I can't reach you?*

But if she left it on, the battery would be dead, and then there would be *no* way of contacting her, let alone pinpointing her location.

All these thoughts crowded and shoved their way through his mind in the couple minutes since he'd tried calling her. In two more minutes he'd try again.

He noticed Foreman looking at him. "You all right?" she said.

"She's late. Cheryl's never late for anything. It's one of the things that drove me crazy about her...in a good way."

Foreman rested a hand on his arm but didn't say anything, for which Mark was thankful. No amount of encouragement or positive thinking or platitudes could change the reality of the moment: Cheryl hadn't called, and it was now four past five. She was four minutes late, which for her was like an eternity.

With each passing second the tension in the little computer room built, like the pressure before a storm when it feels like the sky is falling and the air is rich with the smell of ozone. Brinkley annoyingly tapped a pen on the computer keyboard. The other two deputies looked mildly disinterested. One examined his fingernails; the other, with hands shoved in pockets up to the wrists, watched the screen saver on the monitor, the text *Serve and Protect* that slowly bounced around on the screen oddly reminding Mark of the old Atari game Pong.

Mark checked his watch: 5:05. "I'm trying again," Mark said— *Please, God, let it be on*—and punched in Cheryl's number.

Her phone rang, and his heart nearly stopped. "It's ringing," he almost shouted.

After one ring: "Mark?"

Tears sprung to Mark's eyes, and he had to hold back a sob. This sudden surge of emotion surprised him. He swallowed hard. "Cheryl. Baby."

"Mark, I'm OK. We're all OK."

"You sure? Because—"

"Yes. We're all OK."

"Has he come back yet?"

"No. Did you tell the police?"

"Yeah, I'm here at the station. They're going to triangulate your signal and we'll know exactly where you are. We're gonna get you out, babe. Just hang in there."

There was a pause on the other end, and Mark realized Cheryl was crying.

After a few seconds she said, "Hurry, OK?" Her voice was weak and broken. Mark could tell she was exhausted, physically and emotionally.

"We are. Just don't give up, OK?"

"O—" What came next dropped Mark to his knees. Screams. Wailing and crying. *Weeping and gnashing of teeth.* Hell's chorus drowning out his dear wife's voice. It was the last thing he wanted to hear. He collapsed to the floor and began to cry. "Cherrrylll!" He tried yelling over the screams, but it was useless. The cacophony only grew louder, drowning out every other sound. Then, as if a switch was thrown, it was gone. There was a moment of silence.

"Cheryl!" Then a dial tone, reaching through the phone and tearing at Mark's heart. She was gone. Just like that.

He looked from Foreman to Brinkley. Their faces were like granite, etched with hard lines of concentration...and maybe disbelief. "She's gone."

Foreman looked at Brinkley, who was on the phone with Cheryl's network provider. "Did you get it?"

"OK," he said into the phone, scribbling numbers as he listened. "Thanks." He dropped the phone into its cradle and frowned, his loose jowls sagging well below the line of his jaw. "We got the primary array. That's it." He looked at the piece of notepaper he was writing on. "Bedford County, Pennsylvania. Latitude, thirty-nine point seven-nine-one degrees north. Longitude, seventy-eight point six-six-two degrees west."

Mark turned to Foreman. "Did you hear it? The screams?"

She nodded, her jaw tight. "Try calling her. Maybe the signal just got interrupted."

Mark dialed Cheryl's number. Nothing. Dead. A feeling of dread swept over him and landed in the pit of his gut like a rock. Cheryl was going to die, and all he knew was that she was somewhere in Pennsylvania. Bedford County.

❺

Cheryl had heard the screams too. She didn't know what they were, but she'd heard them. And they'd given her the chills, top of her head right down to her tailbone. Sounded like hundreds, maybe thousands, of people in pain, awful pain, crying, screaming, moaning. She had been thinking it was probably just a bad signal when the cutout door burst open. Judge stood in the doorway, Stetson riding low on his brow, hands hanging loosely at his sides like a gunslinger.

Ginny screamed and scrambled on all fours to where Amber and Cheryl were standing.

Judge had moved quickly, taking the distance between them in five long strides, ripped the phone from Cheryl's hand, and stomped on it.

Now facing him, Cheryl saw the hate in his dark eyes. Anger, no, more than anger, *rage* burned in them like a fire. His chest rose and fell, drawing in deep breaths, nostrils flared. His lips twitched and jaw muscles flexed. They were going to die. He was going to kill them right here, right now. She was sure of it.

He turned his head and called over his shoulder. "Duke! Buck!"

Within seconds the Dobermans were there, swirling around his legs like two shadowy demons, panting heavily, pink tongues dangling between snarled lips.

A shot of fear paralyzed Cheryl. He was going to let the dogs have their way. She imagined what it would be like to be eaten alive, then pushed the thought from her mind. She had to stay alive. Stay positive.

"That was stupid. Really stupid," Judge said, drilling Cheryl with narrowed eyes. He raised a hand as if to hit her, stopped it in midair, then slowly lowered it to his side, fingers opening and closing. "Stupid."

With that he turned and headed for the door. The dogs stayed where they were, eyeing the women, snarling and snapping their jaws like two snakes tasting the air.

"Come!" Judge said. The dogs whimpered, chuffed, then obeyed and fell in beside him. At the door, Judge turned his head and drilled the women one more time. "I won't be gone long."

As soon as the door closed and the metal lock fell into place, Cheryl reached for the cell phone. The casing was now demolished, crushed and cracked, and a single white wire protruded through one of the fractures in the plastic. She tried turning it on, but nothing happened. She tried again, pushing the button repeatedly. Still nothing. It was dead.

And so were they.

6

"We have to go *now!*" Mark said. His hands were trembling, and a sickening nausea had settled in his stomach.

"Hold on, Mark. Just hold on," Foreman said. She took a few steps toward him, hands outstretched. "It's not that easy."

"What? What do you mean? You know they're somewhere in Bedford County. Get some people on it!" He couldn't believe they hadn't moved already. They'd been standing around for ten minutes. Why wasn't Foreman on the radio calling in the troops? Cheryl could be dead any minute. And he didn't even want to imagine how it would happen.

Foreman placed both her hands on Mark's shoulders. He pulled away. "Mark, listen," she said. "We only got one tower. It helps, sure. Really helps. But the fact is that one tower leaves us with"—she looked at Brinkley—"how many square miles?"

Brinkley shrugged, his thick shoulders rising and falling in rapid fashion. "Hundred and twenty, hundred and forty, max."

Foreman looked back at Mark and raised her eyebrows. "That's a lot of land. And mostly farms and wooded area. And the sun'll be down in a little over an hour. We're soon going to be out of daylight. Do you know how hard it is to search for a single barn in the middle of a hundred and twenty square miles in the dark? And besides, just because the tower is in Bedford County doesn't mean the barn is."

She walked over to a map of western Maryland/southern Pennsylvania on the wall. "What were those coordinates, Brink?"

Brinkley read the numbers to her again, and she quickly found the approximate location on the map. "Here, about eight miles north of the Mason-Dixon." She then drew a wide circle around the point with her finger. "That covers a lot of territory right here in Allegheny too."

Foreman turned and leaned against the wall, arms crossed over her chest. "This is a full-blown abduction. It's FBI territory now. We'll have to notify them and let them take the lead."

Mark smacked his palms against his hips. "Well, we can't just sit here and not do *anything*. I heard the screams! Do you understand what that means?"

"I think I do. Trust me, I want to do everything we can to get them out of there safe. But—"

"But nothing," Mark said. His face was hot. He began to sweat. Every minute they spent standing here arguing over whether they should go out or not was another minute they lost trying to find them. Another minute ticking off Cheryl's life. "Make the call, get the people out there. Who knows? Maybe we'll get lucky. Deputy—Jess—we can't just wait around all night. I'm telling you, it'll be too late in the morning. Cheryl will be gone, and probably the other two."

Foreman turned and looked at Brinkley, who only shrugged and arched his eyebrows. She paced the floor, index finger against her mouth. "OK," she finally said. "I'll call Hickock, get him to sign off on it, then start the wheels in motion. I'll need to call the FBI. Get them up to speed." She looked directly at Mark and pointed her finger at him. "I can't make any promises, though. Understand that. The chances of finding that barn, of them even still being *in* the barn, are…well, it's a long shot."

Mark nodded, feeling some sense of relief. "Thank you."

Several minutes later, Foreman returned to the computer room. Mark was studying the map on the wall when she appeared and leaned her shoulder against the doorjamb. She had a look of defeat about her. Her ponytail was loosening, and wild strands of hair hung over her ears; her eyes were tired, mouth drooped at the corners.

"What?" Mark said. "What did he say?"

"He's not going for it. At least not all of it."

Mark punched the wall. "What? Why not?"

Foreman sighed, then cleared her throat. When she spoke her voice was a little shaky. "He said we can't call in the Feds until we know for certain that we have an abduction on our hands and that the women are in immediate danger."

Mark punched the wall again and cursed. "Which means we have to find the barn?"

"Mark, listen. Here's what we're going to do. Hickock said he wants to search Allegheny County first, everything that falls within a fourteen mile arc from the tower." She went to the map and drew a line that covered most of the north-central part of the county. "About this much. Now, that's still a lot of land, about seventy, eighty square miles. If we don't find anything, then we'll contact the Pennsylvania troopers and get them in on the search. Either way we're still looking at hours. Two, maybe three just to search Allegheny."

"It'll be too late by then," Mark said. A lump had twisted his throat into a knot. He clenched his fists and closed his eyes tight, fighting back the urge to lash out at Foreman. "Why can't you call in the FBI now?"

Foreman placed a hand on Mark's shoulder. He shrugged it off.

"Hickock isn't convinced it's an abduction."

Mark's eyes flew open, and he glared daggers at Foreman. "What? Are you kidding me?"

"Mark!" Foreman snapped. "Get a grip, OK? Calm yourself. Look, after your little story about hearing screams on the phone and everything, Hickock isn't convinced you're playing with a full deck of cards." She shifted her eyes away from him. "He thinks you're the type to make things up...for attention."

"That's crazy! You heard the screams—"

"I did. And I told him that. That's why he's authorizing the search of Maryland. He wants to make sure we look in our own backyard first." She paused and ran her hand over her head, a look of fatigue and frustration deepening the lines of her face. "Look, I believe you, OK? I do. But he's the sheriff; he calls the shots. Besides, even if we did call in the Feds, it would still be hours to get them here, set up a base camp, and commence the search. You think something like that just happens? It takes time. The closest field office is Baltimore. Teams have to be assembled, briefed, transported, tactical stuff...do I need to go on?"

Mark was ready to pop. Cheryl was out there, somewhere, and the death bell had already tolled. It was just a matter of time, and time was one thing they didn't have (*forever and ever*). And these cops were playing around with bureaucracy issues. Red tape. People's lives were at stake. *Cheryl's* life was at stake. And the clock was ticking—*tick, tick, tick*. He couldn't just stand here and not do anything. His gut told him that the barn—Cheryl—was in Pennsylvania, and he sure as heck wasn't going to stand around and wait for Foreman and friends to comb their *own backyard* to find that out. He'd look for her himself. It was the least he could do.

"Then I'm outta here," he said, walking over to the desk and grabbing his jacket.

"Wait, Mark." Foreman stepped between him and the door. She squared her shoulders and looked like she was ready to go rounds with him. "Don't do anything stupid, OK? We can handle this. We'll find them. I don't need you going out there playing John Wayne and getting yourself into trouble."

"Handle it?" Mark said, leaning closer to her and raising his voice. "You can handle it? By the time you get done searching *your own backyard*, Cheryl will be dead. Now, am I under arrest?"

"No," Foreman said, looking surprised at the question.

"Then get out of my way."

Foreman didn't move. "Mark, I know you're upset and worried—"

"Upset and worried doesn't even scratch the surface." His voice was getting louder, and another cop suddenly appeared behind Foreman. A big guy, broad chest, square chin, thick neck, little beady eyes drilling Mark. Real Biff type.

Foreman turned her head. "It's OK, Markle."

Biff eyed Mark and gave him one last *watch yourself* look before disappearing down the hall.

Mark took the hint and lowered his voice. "Frantic is more like it. Something I'd like to see a little more of around here. Some urgency."

"This *is* urgent. We all recognize that. I may not agree with

Hickock's call, but he's got a point. We can't call in the Feds until we're sure we're dealing with an abduction case. And even at that, like I said, it'd be hours. This isn't a snap-your-fingers-and-get-results kind of situation. It's getting dark out there. We're dealing with over a hundred square miles of mostly farmland, and we're looking for one old barn. Really, given the circumstances, we're doing all we can do. *I'm* doing all *I* can do." Then she stepped aside.

"Then *I* need to do all *I* can," Mark said, walking past her and out the door.

Chapter 12

❶

J UDGE'S CAR RACED DOWN STATE ROAD 3003 TOWARD the Maryland line, the large swath of light cast by the sedan's headlights eating up the faded pavement. On either side, fields whizzed by, fading into an inky darkness. A thin cloud cover had moved in, coloring the starless sky black.

He gripped the steering wheel tighter and kneaded it like dough. His foot leaned on the accelerator. Things were unraveling quickly. How could he have been so careless as to allow her to make a phone call? How did she even get the phone? It didn't matter now. The damage was done. He should have just finished it there. He wanted to. For a moment, a very brief moment, he had the inclination to just let the dogs have them. It would have been a worthy punishment. But he hadn't. Why?

I'm not a monster, that's why.

But still, he needed to finish this, and fast. Tonight. He needed one more woman, didn't matter who now. It had to be four. Four did the crime; four must pay the time. He smacked the steering wheel with an open palm and cursed out loud. How could he be so careless?

Fortunately, he'd have a couple of hours before things started heating up. Still, he'd have to double-time it. And he knew exactly how to do it. It was perfect. Almost poetic.

He smiled in the darkness, reached up with one hand, and

stroked his soul patch. Finally, the night had arrived. Vindication was only hours away. Just the thought of it was like a balm to soothe his soul.

For you, Katie. Justice is near.

His mind then drifted to the final chapter in the creation of his life's mission.

1974

He stands by her grave, alone, hollow...angry. In the past week since being chased from this very spot by Mrs. McAfee, his sorrow has been replaced by anger. Not the usual superficial, I'll-get-over-it kind of anger a twelve-year-old boy is accustomed to feeling, but a deep-seated, gnaw-at-your-soul, all-consuming anger. Rage. It's more than a feeling, a fleeting human emotion that can be easily satisfied by simply waiting it out (time heals all wounds, his mother told him) (*nonsense if there ever was nonsense*). It was a passion, a driving force that will determine the course of his life, influence every decision, always be just under the surface, darkening every smile, casting a shadow across every blessed thing that ever enters his life.

The anger will become his sustenance, his god, his reason for existing. And it will consume him like a raging fire (*our god is a consuming fire*), the same fire that consumed Katie.

He slips a single flower, a daisy—Katie's favorite—from his pocket and drops it on the dirt mound that covers Katie's body (*or what's left of it*). An image of her charred figure frozen in one last scream flashes through his mind. He's had nightmares about it every night. No matter what he does, he can't get the image out of his head. It's like the fire seared it onto the backs of his eyelids, and every time he closes his eyes, it—the image, the horror—appears.

He closes his eyes tight and clenches his hands into fists (*squeeze it out, like dirty water out of a dish rag*), willing the image to flee, to retreat into some remote place in his brain where it will be lost forever. But it refuses. It will never leave him. He can never forget what happened. He *will* never forget who did it.

Justice has to be served.

So it's there, standing over the grave of his first love (*only love*) that Judge resolves in his heart to never rest until justice has been satisfied. They will have to pay for what they did. (*The wages of sin is death, fire and brimstone, forever and ever.*)

Someone will pay. *Someone* has to take the punishment.

He welcomes the anger now, knowing it will never allow him to forget. He will let it to grow and fester like a ravenous beast until the day comes when he can exact the appropriate punishment and feed the beast (*an eye for an eye, a tooth for a tooth*).

God won't approve, but where was God when Katie's flesh was melting off her bones and she was screaming for mercy? Where was God when he was being falsely accused of setting the fire? Where was God when he cried out for an answer, an explanation, anything that made some sense out of the horror that invaded his otherwise peaceful life? He wasn't anywhere. He wasn't answering prayers; He wasn't giving reasons; He wasn't offering consolation; He wasn't being the just God He was supposed to be...He wasn't doing *anything* (*wasn't doing a single thing!*). And for that, He will be ignored. He no longer exists.

The anger is his god now. (*My god is a consuming fire.*)

Tears well in his eyes and roll down his cheeks like streams of bitter water. He makes no attempt to stop them, doesn't even wipe at them. The tears are good. They are tears of rage, not sorrow.

"Katie, I'll never forget. I promise, if it's the last thing I do with my life, I'll make sure someone pays for what they did to you." (*If it's the last thing I do, I promise.*)

He knows with that one declaration he has sealed his fate. He'll give his life if he has to, if that's what it comes to.

And he's OK with that.

"I love you, Katie. I'll never love anyone else."

With that he turns and walks away, shoulders hunched, hands shoved in his pockets. It will be the last time he visits Katie's grave. He has no need to come back. He's said everything he needs to say.

Now he has to keep his promise.

The anger had subsided over the years; the fire had quieted to a lump of smoldering embers. It had to at some point, if Judge was to remain persistent and patient. The initial rage was like a burst of oxygen, whipping the flames into a roaring inferno, but sooner or later the fire must settle in to a steady burn, an even flame breathing just enough oxygen to maintain its luminous glow. Maturity had taught him that. And so he had to abandon the inferno and settle in to the rhythm of the flickering flame. What remained was a steady resolve, seared into his heart, to fulfill the mission, complete the job, see the task through to its end. And the moment was almost here; the end was in sight.

And the end was justice.

Mark slammed through the front door of his house and flipped on the living room light. Things were taking way too long. It had taken him almost twenty minutes just to make it here. Who knew how much longer Cheryl had? Or if it was already too—*No! Don't you dare think that. Don't you think that.* Anger and frustration bubbled inside him. A dismal feeling of helplessness had brought him to the point of fury. He wanted to strike out at someone, but who? He knew it wasn't Foreman's fault, wasn't even Hickock's fault. They could only do what they could do. There were protocols to follow, chains of command, jurisdiction issues, blah, blah, blah. Maybe deep down he wanted to turn his anger on God. He held death and life in His hands, didn't He?

He raced over to his gun cabinet, tried to shove the key in the lock, missed, and dropped it on the floor. "C'mon!" Picking up the key, he steadied his hand and tried again. This time it took. The glass cabinet door swung open, and Mark grabbed his .12-gauge pump-action shotgun and a box of shells. He then went to the hutch, pulled open the drawer, and sifted through a mess of papers. *C'mon. Where are you?*

There, the map of Pennsylvania.

Flipping the switch to light the kitchen, he spread open the map on the table. Now, where was that tower? Where had Foreman pointed to? He traced his finger around Bedford County. He remembered U.S. 220 was just to the west of it and...there, Buchanan State Forest was to the east. He'd head there first. Why? He didn't know. He just had a gut feeling, and right now that was the best he could do. He ran back to the hutch drawer, rummaged some more, and returned to the kitchen table with a drafting compass. Measuring out twelve miles, he placed the point of the compass on the map, some arbitrary location between 220 and Buchanan State Forest, and drew a large circle. It was a lot of territory to cover, all rural. Fields and forest.

A needle in a haystack, Jess had said.

And time running out.

He traced his finger along his planned route. He'd drive up Interstate 68 and catch 220 north. From there...he had no idea. The Maryland line was a good twenty-five minutes away. The estimated location of the phone tower, another fifteen, twenty minutes from there. He had to get moving.

Grabbing the gun, shells, the flashlight from the pantry, and the map, he headed back to his car. He'd stay out all night if he had to. He wasn't about to abandon Cheryl again. He looked at his watch: 5:51. Almost an hour since the call. Since the scream.

Please, God, keep her alive.

Hang on, baby. Just hang on.

Chapter 13

1

"WE NEED TO DO THIS NOW," AMBER SAID, WINDING her thin black leather belt around her hand. "No telling how long he'll be gone. And I think he wants to finish this tonight."

She looked from Cheryl to Ginny. They were both huddled close, and it was still hard to see the expression on their faces. Overhead, the bats were chirping quietly, getting ready for their nighttime feeding.

"We need to get out of here," she said. "No matter what."

"Any ideas on how to get the dogs close enough?" Cheryl asked.

Amber thought for a moment, tightening the belt around her hand until her knuckles blanched.

"I have an idea," Ginny said. Her voice was quiet and shaky.

Amber and Cheryl both looked at her. She had an idea? Did she even know what they were planning to do with the belt? She was standing there with them, not because she was invited, but simply because she hadn't left Amber's side since Judge left. Amber didn't remember ever discussing their plan to strangle the dogs with her.

As if she'd read Amber's mind, Ginny said, "I heard you talking about how we could get out of here."

Amber swallowed. Then she'd heard everything else too. "Sorry," she said, and meant it.

"It's OK. I just want to get out of here too."

"So what's your idea?" Cheryl said.

Ginny reached for the belt. Amber unwound it and handed it to her. Ginny held one end of the belt with her left hand so it dangled like a dead snake. "One of us reaches through a crack in the wall as far as we can and holds the belt like this. Someone else lures the dog close, so its snout is right up against the crack. Then you swing the belt like so"—she swung the belt like a pendulum—"and reach through the crack to grab the bottom end"—she pinched the bottom end with her right hand—"then pull hard and pin the dog's neck against the outside wall." She held the belt out to Amber, her mouth drawn into a thin, serious line. "That's it. I don't know if it would work or not, but that's the idea."

There was silence among them for at least thirty seconds. Amber ran through the scenario in her mind, visualizing it. It was a long shot and they'd get only one chance, but it *was* possible.

A voice from her past—her grandfather's—sounded in her head: *Anything's possible except squeezing toothpaste back into the tube. The real question is, is it probable?* Probable, Granddad? Yes, it is. The more she thought about it, the more she realized just how probable it was. "It might work," she finally said, breaking the silence.

"Yeah, I think we can pull it off," Cheryl said. "We'll need something for bait, something that will keep the dog occupied long enough to loop the belt around its neck."

Amber forked her fingers through her hair. "Well, we know they don't like apples and aren't that interested in the Cheerios either. It's gotta be something that gets them in a frenzy, something...wait a minute." She snapped her fingers. It was gross, but it would work. "I got it."

Jess sat behind the wheel of her cruiser, hands at ten o'clock and two o'clock. Her mind was spinning off in a hundred different directions. First, there were the abduction cases. Three women imprisoned in an old barn in the middle of who-knows-where. One of them for two weeks. The abductor must be feeding them, keeping them alive for...what? How weird was that? Then, there was the search effort. Their search in Maryland alone was like looking for a lost diamond in a wheat field. Then factor in the hundred or so square miles in Pennsylvania. Oh, they'd find the barn sooner or later. The area was big, very big, but not limitless. They'd find it. The question was, would they find it in time? The slimeball that abducted the women would most likely either move them or kill them. And probably within the hour. Not enough time. Especially if they were in Pennsylvania.

And then there was Mark. She wasn't sure what to make of the mechanic turned rescue hero. He was so sure that the screams he'd heard meant that Cheryl was going to die...and die soon. There was no telling what he was doing now. Probably scouring the Pennsylvania countryside looking for an abandoned barn. Finding *a* barn wouldn't be difficult, but unless he got extremely lucky, finding *the* barn was next to impossible.

Mark was odd, that one, but still she liked him. She couldn't put her finger on why that was, she just did. Maybe it was his passion or his determination. Or his love for his wife. Even if he did cheat on her, Jess could tell he still loved her. She didn't know how she would react if he was her husband, but knowing what she knew of him and hearing him tell his story, she could tell he was sorry. If she knew that part, she'd probably take him back. But, then again, it hadn't happened to her, and she really didn't know what it felt like to be betrayed by the one you love most in the world.

She still liked him, though. *Guide him, Father. Lead him to that barn.*

And now, there was Hickock. Shortly after Mark had stormed out of the station, Hickock had called saying he wanted to meet with Jess; he'd said it concerned Mark and was urgent. The way he'd said it, Jess wondered if Hickock suspected Mark was the abductor or, at the very least, was an accomplice of some kind. Did he have proof? Or was it just a scenario he wanted to entertain? If it was, having her drive all the way out here just to talk sure seemed odd. It had to be more than that. He had to have some evidence or proof he wanted to show her. He better have, anyway. The search teams were already gearing up to comb Allegheny County, and she wanted to be a part of it.

Steering her cruiser off U.S. 220, she headed down a winding well-beaten two-lane road that snaked through patches of farmland all the way to Rocky Gap State Park. Hickock said he'd meet her on the turn-off for the La-Ho hiking trail.

Five minutes later she pulled into the turnoff, gravel crunching and popping under her car's tires. Hickock's white, unmarked cruiser was there, in the far corner, facing the tree line. There were no other cars. She steered her car in behind his, the headlights silhouetting his form in the front seat. She then killed the engine and climbed out. The area was eerily quiet. It was a still night, and not even the creaking of dry branches or the rustle of leaves broke the silence. Only the sound of her boots on the gravel and the steady tick of cooling metal.

Hickock opened his door and stepped out, unfolding his lean frame to stand erect and face her. "Jess, thanks for coming," he said, his voice even and flat.

"Sheriff. What's this about?"

He approached her with a slow gait, boots grinding gravel. It was too dark to see his face, but Jess could tell by the position of his arm that he was stroking that mustache of his. "I need you to do something for me."

Something wasn't right. Jess's police instincts were screaming at her, warning her. *This isn't right! Get out of here!* But she brushed them aside. It was Hickock...*Sheriff* Hickock. If anything wasn't right, it was the news Hickock was about to share with her, possibly indicting Mark Stone in the abduction of his own wife and two other women. She didn't want to believe that Hickock would drag her all the way out here if it wasn't urgent...and if the evidence wasn't solid. But what evidence?

She hooked her thumbs in her belt. "What do you need?"

Hickock stopped maybe three feet away from her, his face still too dark to see any details, then walked past her toward the tree line. "Follow me. I want to show you something."

She followed close behind until they reached the edge of the woods where gravel met grass.

Hickock motioned her closer. "What do you think of this?" He was pointing to something on the ground. "I want your opinion before I go any further with this."

Jess moved closer, past Hickock, and bent at the waist to see what it was he was pointing at. It was too dark, though. She reached for her flash—

A bomb went off in her head, and she collapsed to her knees.

Was she shot? Had someone shot her? Someone waiting in the woods for them? Stone? She thought of Hickock. Had he been shot too? Clouds moved in and scrambled her thoughts. She had to move, find cover, but her brain wouldn't process the information, wouldn't send the order to her muscles. *Move!* She was on all fours, head hanging limp on the end of her neck. A warm liquid filled her eye, blurring her vision. Her head throbbed. She tried to move, shift her weight, push up, anything, but—

Another explosion in the back of her head dropped her to her stomach. Numbing pain radiated down her neck and back, over her shoulders and arms. Her vision faded to black. She could still hear, though...gravel biting. She tried to lift her arm, but nothing happened. Tried to move her hand, reach for her gun, but...nothing. Her fingers...nothing.

The pain eventually dulled, and all that was left was her hearing. Gravel crunched again, but it sounded far away, muted. A hand pressed into the front of the neck, gently. Then a voice, but it was distant and low, muffled. "Sorry...none...personal..." The voice was fading quickly. Something touched the back of her head, a light touch. "Sorry..."

Then it was gone. Everything was gone.

Wiley Hickock knelt beside Jess's still form, his hand resting on the back of her head. A lump was already growing there. Her hair was wet and sticky with blood.

"I'm sorry, Jess. It's not personal."

And it wasn't. He liked Jess, he really did. Best deputy he ever had. But that was a preference, and this, the mission, was bigger than personal preferences. He had to stay focused; he had to set emotions aside. Justice had to come first.

Katie had to come first.

He stood up, slid his baton back into his belt, removed a handkerchief from his back pocket, and wiped his hand clean. Bending over, he rolled Jess onto her back and pressed his fingers against her carotid artery. He had to hit her so hard to subdue her, he was afraid he'd killed her. But the pulse was there, weak, but there, tapping against his fingertips like a slow and steady drumbeat. Moving around to her head, he slid his hands under her arms and lifted her so everything but her heels was off the ground. He then dragged her across the parking lot, her heels leaving parallel trails in the gravel, and maneuvered her into the backseat of the car. He grabbed a jug of water from the floor in the back, shut the door, and retraced his steps, sweeping clean the trails left by her heels and dousing the ground with water to wash away the blood droplets. No need to leave any evidence behind. All they would find was Deputy Foreman's patrol car, sitting empty, with no sign of Jess. It would be as if she just up and disappeared, abducted by aliens maybe. Who knows what they would come up with?

He returned to his car, slid in behind the steering wheel, and turned the key. The engine revved to life.

He glanced at the backseat. Jess was lying on her back, her head dropped to one side, left arm hanging off the seat, right arm crossed over her chest. She was the fourth. The final piece to the puzzle. The time had finally arrived.

The time for justice.

"This isn't personal, Jess," he said again. But he said it more for himself than for her. He had to remind himself that it was about the mission, about justice, not about the individuals. It wasn't personal with any of them. He didn't even know them except by name and appearance and a few other personal markers like the car they drove, where they worked, and the schedules they kept. But it wasn't about the women. It wasn't about women at all. He wasn't one of those perverts who went after women like they were chunks of meat. He'd hunted jerks like that and caught them. He knew the type, and he wasn't like that.

"I'm not a monster." He said it aloud. For Jess. For himself.

4

Cheryl stood dumbly, holding Amber's black leather belt in her hand. She had been voted to strangle the dogs because she was the fittest—and healthiest—of the three. Amber would bait each dog and keep its attention long enough for Cheryl to loop the belt around its neck and pin it to the wall. Then it was all up to Cheryl. How it would all happen, she didn't know. She didn't even know if she could pull it off. Was she strong enough? Dobermans were big, muscular dogs. Could she kill a living, breathing beast with her own hands? She'd never killed anything before, and the question nagged her. Was she capable of killing even if it was to save her own life? One thing she knew: she'd soon find out.

Cheryl drew in a long breath of the barn's stale air, closed her eyes, and tried to focus on the task at hand. Ginny's idea was crazy, yes, but crazy enough that it just might work. Of course, there was no guarantee—anything could go wrong. And there was one major risk: Cheryl would have to expose both her hands to the dogs while she looped the belt. She didn't like that part. An image of the Doberman grabbing hold of her hand, clamping its razor teeth into her flesh, and shaking its head back and forth like it was playing tug-of-war with a hunk of rawhide had settled in her mind and wasn't leaving anytime soon. But this whole situation was one big risk. Judge could return anytime and kill all three of them, and then what?

And then what? The question suddenly struck her as odd but very valid. She could die tonight. These could be her last few minutes on this earth, breathing air...living. And then what? Obviously, then she'd be dead. But what did *dead* mean? Was there more? Was there an afterlife? Heaven or hell?

And then it struck her; she'd never even thought about it

before. How absurd. She'd spent her whole life living... *living*... but never thought about dying. What happens when the body dies? Is there a soul that lives on? She knew there was, had no idea how she knew, she just knew. There *had* to be more. She believed in God, and she believed in heaven, she'd always believed. But what about hell? If there's a heaven, wouldn't it make sense that there's a hell too? And where would she go? The question marched through her head in her own voice: *Where will you go, Cheryl? You could die tonight, and where will you wake up?*

"Ready," Amber said, her raspy voice coming out of the darkness. She had retreated to a far corner of the barn to "prepare the bait," she'd said. She returned, smelling like decomposed flesh.

"Ugh! What did you do?" Ginny backed away and held her hand to her nose. "Did you roll in a dead animal?"

Amber held up her hand. It was wrapped in a thick swath of toilet paper and held a lump of brown fur. "I told you it was gross. But it should keep the dog occupied long enough for Cheryl to do her thing."

"What is it?" Ginny asked.

Amber looked at the thing in her hand. "A dead bat. I found it a few days ago and buried it under some hay over in the corner. Smells ripe, don't it?" She looked at Cheryl. "You ready?"

Cheryl nodded and swallowed past a dry lump. "As ready as I'm gonna be."

Amber walked over to the wall and crouched down. It had taken the three of them almost twenty minutes to feel along the barn walls for the widest crack. It had to be wide enough for Cheryl to get her hand and at least half her forearm through. At least two inches wide. Ginny was the one to find it: an area about two feet off the floor where a knot had been knocked out.

It was a little tight, but with some encouragement, Cheryl could wriggle her arm through.

"Okay," Amber said. "I'll call 'em."

Cheryl looked at her and nodded. Her mouth was too dry to talk. This was it. This was the moment. She tried again to settle her nerves by taking a deep breath. Amber's little treat smelled awful, and Cheryl almost gagged. Either this would work or it wouldn't. Simple. She then looked at Ginny. The youngest of the three had made a remarkable turnaround since the phone call. Cheryl was proud of her. She wanted to tell her how proud she was, but her mouth felt like it was stuffed with cotton, her throat was constricting, and her stomach was in a state of its own rebellion.

Cheryl swallowed back the fear that pushed bile up her throat and looked at Amber. "I'll call them. Your throat can't handle it. It'll kill you."

Amber nodded and forced a thin smile. "Thanks. I'm right here."

Cheryl turned her face toward the outside world. "Hey! Duke! Buck! Here doggies." She whistled and knocked on the planks with her free hand. "Here, boys."

Within seconds they could hear the dogs' footsteps on the dirt, then their panting.

"Here we go," Amber whispered. She glanced at Cheryl. "Be quick."

The dogs drew closer, sniffing and growling.

Cheryl tensed.

"Here, boys," Amber said. She held her hand up to the crack, almost at ground level. Cheryl stood above her and slipped the belt through the crack with her left hand. Once the dogs were sufficiently preoccupied, she'd lower the belt on one of the dog's right side, slip her free hand past its face, and grab the other end of the belt under the dog's neck. Then yank with every ounce of strength she possessed. If the dog didn't have her hand by then.

She swallowed again. *Heaven or hell?*

The dogs approached, cautiously at first, sniffing from a distance of about three feet, their legs spread wide, necks craned, noses high in the air, curious eyes shifting back and forth. Amber punched at the crack with her wrapped hand. "Here, doggy."

The larger of the two came first, pressing his nose against the crack. He let out a low growl, then began pawing at the plank, pressing harder, his pink tongue flitting in and out of his mouth.

"Now," Amber whispered, teasing the dog with the dead bat. "Do it now."

Cheryl lowered her trembling hand so the belt fell on the right side of the dog's thick neck. With her right hand, she then reached through the crack and under the dog's neck. She couldn't see the belt, so she had to go by feel. Fortunately, the dog was so preoccupied with the bat in Amber's hand it didn't notice what she was doing. She groped some more, but still no belt.

"Hurry," Amber said. She was on her haunches, leaning away from the wall, her hand extended just beyond the reach of the dog's teeth. The dog was snarling and growling, pressing its muzzle through the crack, pawing at the ground and planks.

Cheryl pushed her arm farther through the crack. Splinters dug into the soft skin of her forearm. She grimaced and reached for the belt. It had to be somewhere—

There!

In one quick motion, she grabbed the free end of the belt and yanked back, falling hard on her rear end. The dog slammed against the wall and yelped. Cheryl placed her feet on the planks on either side of the crack and leaned back, gripping both ends of the belt in tight fists. This was it, the moment of truth. Ginny's crazy plan had worked... so far. Now it was up to Cheryl to finish it. Choke the life out of this devil. She braced herself, pushed against the planks, and leaned back. The belt slipped and cut into her palms, sending pain through her hand and up her forearm. But she wouldn't let go. She couldn't. She squeezed harder, ignoring the pain.

The dog writhed and wriggled, wheezed and choked, trying desperately to loosen itself from the death grip the belt had on its neck.

The Doberman was powerful and stronger than Cheryl had anticipated. It had managed to wedge its feet up against the wall and was using it as leverage to free itself.

Cheryl fought to maintain her grip and groaned under the strain.

"Don't let go," Ginny hollered. Her voice croaked with panic.

Cheryl let out a guttural grunt and jerked hard on the belt. It slid at least an inch through her hand. Any more and she'd lose her grip altogether. The dog coughed, a dry hack that sounded like it had just squeezed by taut vocal cords. She jerked back again. And again. And again. The dog coughed again, but its strength was not waning.

"Help me!" Cheryl screamed through gritted teeth.

Amber sprang into action, gripping the belt with both hands.

"Hold it so I can get a better grip," Cheryl said.

Amber held the belt at the point where it passed through the crack. Cheryl let go and quickly looped the ends of the belt around both her hands, locking it against her wrists. "OK."

When Amber let go, Cheryl pulled back hard, feeling the increased tension on the belt. But it did not slip. She pressed her feet against the planks, leaned back, and bore down like a woman in labor, contracting every muscle in her body. The dog wheezed and coughed, and Cheryl noticed it was finally slowing down. It had lost some of its fight.

Cheryl had no idea how long she pulled on that belt. It could have been five seconds or five minutes, but it seemed like five hours. Five hours of wrestling a great white shark with a leash.

When the dog finally fell still and its lifeless body slumped to the ground, Cheryl loosened her grip and let the belt fall to the floor. Her palms burned; her forearms ached; her legs shook with fatigue. But it was over. The beast was dead. She was victorious.

Cheryl fell back, breathing hard. All was quiet save for the distant sounds of the other dog alternating whimpers and growls somewhere in the distance. And the rapid thumping of her own heart in her ears. She let out a long, low moan and began to cry. A sudden wave of relief washed over her, and all the tension and fear and anger escaped through one loud choking sob.

But hidden behind it all was the reminder: there was still one more dog to go.

Mark raced down U.S. 220, his shotgun on the seat beside him, box of shells on the dash. The wheels of the Mustang hummed along the asphalt; the engine purred quietly. The speedometer read almost seventy, and his heart rate had to be at least twice that. He turned his wrist and glanced at his watch. The glowing hands read 6:25. He was running out of time, but Cheryl was still alive. He knew it. He could feel it. He didn't know how, but he knew she was still alive. That was the good news. The bad news was that he also knew—just knew—her time was expiring quickly. He had to find her, and soon. A sense of urgency gripped him, and he depressed the accelerator a little farther.

The engine revved louder, and the Mustang lurched forward. The orange pin on the speedometer crept toward seventy-five.

As he drove, Mark kept an eye on the sky to the right. He was traveling north, and he knew the phone tower would be on his right. Exactly where it was, well, that was the first hurdle. He had no idea what he would do once he found it, but that was the first item on his agenda: find the tower.

He pushed on for another minute, heart pumping as fast as the engine's pistons, all 320 horses working overtime. A blinking light caught his eye. Ahead and to the right, there was a single red light floating in the sky. It had to be the phone tower. Please, God, let it be the tower.

He slowed the car and looked for a turnoff, a road leading toward those lights. A half mile later he saw a street sign glowing green in the car's headlights. He slowed and made a right onto Narrow Lane. And narrow it was. It was more like a driveway, wide enough for one, maybe one and a half cars, with jagged shoulders that just kind of crumpled into gravel. He couldn't see beyond the swath of light cut by the car's headlights, but the occasional lighted window said there were at least a few houses in the area.

He worked the brake and accelerator through the sharp curves, keeping an eye on the red light still floating ahead, but looming closer. Within five minutes he was turning onto a dirt service road that led back to the tower. A couple hundred yards later, the Mustang's headlights fell on the base of the tower.

Mark stopped the car, left the engine and headlights running, and stepped out. The tower rose from the ground like a three-legged Cyclops, its head only visible by the blinking red light floating high above. It was surrounded by nine feet of chain-link fence crowned with three rows of barbed wire.

Mark walked around to the hood of the car, spread out the

map, and clicked on his flashlight. He found Narrow Lane and marked where the tower was. He had only been about a mile off when he estimated its location back at the house.

Now what? He'd found the primary tower that was receiving Cheryl's cell phone signal. She was around here, within twelve miles in any direction of this very spot, clinging to life by mere minutes. The thought struck him with the impact and finality of a guillotine: in this darkness, she might as well be on the other side of the world. *No! Stop it!* He couldn't, *wouldn't* allow himself to think like that. He *would* find her.

He looked at the map again, studying the lay of the region, the spiderweb of roads, the position of state forests and game lands. Really, according the description Cheryl had given, there were only a handful of locations that would work. There had to be enough open land, unmarked by roads, for a barn to be secluded, and there had to be wooded land nearby. That left some land to the northwest by the state game lands and some land to the southeast, near Buchanan State Forest. But what if the woods Cheryl mentioned was only a small stand of trees, a wooded area no more than fifty yards wide? That could be anywhere!

Mark let out a groan and slapped the hood with an open hand. It was impossible. *Impossible.* Suddenly, a thought occurred to him. No, more than a thought, a voice in his head, quiet and small. It was a voice from his past, a child's. He knew the voice, of course, because it was his own. He stopped and listened. An image flashed in his mind like an old home movie. He was seven years old, dressed in a light blue button-down shirt and navy blue pants. The top button of the shirt was fastened, and his hair was wet and parted neatly to the side. He was standing at attention, arms straight and rigid at his sides, shoulders back, chin tucked. A lady, elderly and very kind looking, sat in front of him. It was Mrs. Leatherby, his first grade Sunday school teacher. He opened his mouth and, in that same small quiet voice, said his Bible memory verse: *With men this is impossible; but with God all things are possible. Matthew nineteen, twenty-six.*

Mark blinked and the image faded, taking the voice with it. He swallowed past the lump that had risen in his throat. *With God all things are possible.* What brought that memory on? He hadn't thought about that for years. He looked at the map again.

The abductor would want to keep the women close enough that he could reach them quickly. Secluded but close. Probably within a half hour, forty-five minutes. He didn't know this for sure, but it was a guess that made sense. That meant the barn had to be south of the tower.

So south it was. He'd head south. Toward Buchanan State Forest.

❻

Cheryl was still lying on the floor, arms across her chest, legs extended, when Amber sat next to her and placed a hand on her shoulder. "You OK?"

"Yeah," Cheryl said. She turned her head to face Amber. "I don't know if I can do that again."

Amber gave her shoulder a reassuring squeeze. "You don't have to. I'll do the next one. Or maybe Ginny will."

Cheryl reached her hand up and covered Amber's. She'd only known Amber a few days, but the woman was like a sister to her already. Must be a captivity thing. The admiration she felt for Amber went much deeper than sisterhood, though. It was obvious the woman was suffering, and yet she had remained strong and determined. There was no way, in her weakened state, that she could wrestle the other demon to its death, and yet she had volunteered. And she'd give it a go too. But Cheryl couldn't let her do that.

"Thanks, but I'll do it. I just need another minute. Where's Ginny?"

"Looking for another crack that'll work. We can't use the same spot. The other dog ran off."

Cheryl laced her fingers with Amber's. "Thanks for helping me out there. I almost lost the belt, you know."

"But you didn't," Amber said. "You did it."

Cheryl smiled and felt another tear slip from her eye and trickle over her temple. "I'm glad I have you here. Help me up, and let's finish this."

Amber stood and offered her hand. Cheryl grasped it and hoisted herself up with a grunt. Her hands were still sore, and her back ached like someone had stuck a hot poker right into the base of her spine. She walked over to where she had strangled the dog and peered through the crack. The clouds had parted, allowing soft moonlight to wash the outside world in deepening shades of blue. She could even make out the tree line in the distance. At her feet, just on the other side of the wall, lay a dark lifeless shadow. The dog. But where was the other one?

Cheryl heard footsteps shuffling through the straw behind her. "I found another gap I think'll work." It was Ginny. "So...whenever you're ready."

Cheryl turned her head a quarter turn. "I'm ready." She wasn't really. She would never be ready to do that again. It had taken everything she had, physically and emotionally, to wrestle that beast and kill it. How many times could she do that? How many times could she turn herself inside out and drain herself of every ounce of energy and courage and faith and resolve?

Once more. That's all she had to do it. Once more. And what if it didn't work? It was pure luck, a miracle even, that Ginny's ridiculous plan had even worked once. What were the chances of the other dog falling for the same trick after watching its pal die? Luck or no luck, miracle or no miracle, it had to work again. It was as simple as that. They couldn't be wandering around out there in the open with even one of the Dobermans after them. She needed to finish the job. Then they would be free.

She tried to focus on that, on the end result. Freedom.

An image of the three of them running through the prairie in their stocking feet and sweat suits with the Doberman in hot pursuit, gaining ground quickly, flashed through her mind. It would be a terrible way to—

"—Cheryl." Amber's voice, followed by three loud coughs, brought her back.

Cheryl blinked and looked at Amber.

"Are you sure you want to do this again?" Amber said.

Cheryl brushed her hair away and ran the back of her wrist over her forehead. Despite the cool air, she'd already broken out in a sweat. "Yeah. Yes. Let's just get it over with, OK?"

Amber held up the belt. It hung from her hand like a black hangman's noose.

Cheryl was about to reach for the belt when she froze. What was that sound? Tires on dirt. In the distance.

He was back.

A tingle started at the top of her head and shot down her spine. Goose bumps peppered her arms and legs. Her pulse spiked. This was it. They were too late. Freedom had slipped from their grasp, and now they would die. And God only knew how.

Cheryl looked at Amber, and Amber met her gaze. They stood motionless for a second, staring into each other's eyes. Both knew what it meant. To her right, Ginny whimpered. She'd heard it too.

"I'm sorry," Cheryl whispered.

"What if it's the police?" Ginny said.

The police. Could it be? Could they actually have found them? Cheryl rushed to the wall and peered through a crack. The sound was getting closer, but she didn't see any flashing lights. But then again, maybe they'd turned the lights off so as not to announce their arrival. As much as she tried not to let it, a glimmer of hope worked its way through the gloom. Maybe they'd somehow traced Mark's call. She glanced at Amber and Ginny—both had their faces pressed against the gaps between planks, like prisoners longing for freedom—then back to the sound of the tires. The police. Freedom. Maybe—

The car came into view, and Cheryl couldn't hold back the sob that leaped from her throat. Moonlight glowed off the white roof and hood of Judge's sedan.

Chapter 14

❶

CHERYL STEPPED BACK FROM THE WALL. HER LEGS felt weak and her hands tingled. She tried to swallow, but nothing happened. Ginny crumpled to the floor and began crying. Amber kicked the wall and cursed.

He was back. Tonight they would die. If she could, if she was capable of such an atrocity and if she had the means, Cheryl thought she would end her own life now, before that sicko had a chance to get his hands on her.

And then what, Cheryl? Huh? Then what?

The sedan came to a stop, and the headlights winked out. Seconds later, the driver-side door swung open, and the familiar form of Judge climbed out. He donned his Stetson and walked around to the rear of the car. The trunk swung open. Cheryl lost sight of him until he rounded the corner again, hauling something large over his right shoulder.

Cheryl's heart dropped into her stomach. The moonlight distorted the image of Judge walking toward them but not enough that she couldn't tell the bundle thrown over his shoulder was another woman. Number four. Surely that was it. Four victims who would die tonight. She tried again to swallow, but her throat was still locked up. Her hands began to tremble.

Judge dumped the woman on the ground, kicked the cinder block out of the way, and unlocked the cutout door. He stepped through the door, dragging the woman by the wrists. When her feet cleared the doorway, he let go of her wrists, faced Cheryl and the others, and straightened his back. "She's alive, but don't bother with her. It's time." And with that he left, closing and locking the door behind him.

Cheryl and Amber rushed over to the new girl. The first thing Cheryl noticed was her uniform. She was a cop. A sheriff's deputy from Allegheny County. Her nameplate read *Foreman*. Was she looking for them and Judge intercepted her? If so, then maybe others knew where they were. Maybe they were on their way right now.

Cheryl looked at Amber then over her shoulder at Ginny, who was back in her corner, arms wrapped around folded legs, face buried in her knees. She turned back to Amber. "We have to stay alive a little longer."

Cheryl heard a rustling behind her, turned, and saw Ginny heading her way.

"Stay alive a little longer?" Ginny said. Her jaw was tight, lips pulled thin, a wild look flared in her eyes. "We tried that. First the cell phone, then the dog, and where did it get us? Huh?" Her voice was tight, and tears started falling from her eyes.

Cheryl stood up and faced her. Amber followed, standing shoulder to shoulder with Cheryl.

Ginny's lips began to quiver. "Tell me. Where did it get us? We're still going to die." She then covered her face with her hands, taking fistfuls of hair, and burst into sobs.

Cheryl reached out and pulled Ginny into her chest, holding her tight. The younger woman was broken and defeated and scared. Different people handled the imminence of death in different ways. Some fought it stoically, some with panic, and others surrendered to it. But either way, if death was coming, the end result was the same for all.

Outside the barn, the trunk slammed shut. Amber ran to the wall and put her face to a crack. Moments later, she returned to Cheryl, Ginny, and Foreman, who still lay unconscious on the floor. "He's coming back, carrying some kind of container."

Cheryl waited for the familiar sound of the cinder block falling away and the metal lock disengaging, but it never came. Through the gaps between the planks she could see the broken silhouette of Judge outside. He stopped at the door and crouched down. When he stood, he walked to his right, and Cheryl heard the sound of liquid splashing against the side of the barn. *What—?*

Then the odor filled her nostrils. Gasoline. He was going to burn them.

Ginny must have smelled it too. She broke away from Cheryl and ran to the wall where Judge was just on the other side, dousing the brittle barn with gasoline. "Stop! Please stop!" she screamed, her voice frantic. "Why are you doing this? What did we do?"

But Judge ignored her. He continued sidestepping slowly, swinging the gas container with each step.

"Listen to me!" Ginny cried. "Why? Why are you doing this?"

Suddenly, she jumped back and spun to face Cheryl and the others, mouth wide in a silent scream, hands raised on either side of her head. Cheryl knew what had happened. Judge had threaded some of the gas through one of the gaps and doused Ginny.

Ginny stumbled toward them. Amber caught her and wrapped her in a tight hug.

Judge continued his slow pace around the barn, rounding the far corner and working his way across the back. When he came to where the dead dog lay, he stopped. Cheryl held her breath. Seconds ticked by, silent except for Ginny's muffled cries; her face was buried in Amber's chest. Judge stood motionless, gas container at his side.

He turned then and let out a loud, long whistle. Then, "Duke!"

Within seconds, the smaller of the Dobermans was at his feet, sniffing the carcass of its companion. Judge turned and faced the barn. "You four women are hereby charged, tried, and found guilty of the murder of Katie McAfee. Your sentence is death. By fire."

With that, he doused the dead Doberman with gas and continued on his course around the barn.

Cheryl looked at Amber. They had to do something. This guy was insane. Guilty? Of murder? Who was Katie McAfee? He obviously had the wrong women. But then, he knew that, she was sure of it. Amber had told her what Judge had said, about a girl being burned to death and him watching the whole thing and then being blamed for it. He said someone had to pay. That someone was them—Cheryl, Amber, Ginny, and this poor cop, Foreman. She was the lucky one, though. Unconscious, she wouldn't feel a thing.

Mark slowed his Mustang and made a sharp left onto Dam Road. He'd decided to look in this area, a six-square-mile block of land light on roads and heavy on open field and woods. This is where he would put all his cards. It was all he had time for. He knew it was a gamble with Cheryl's life, but that verse...*that verse—with God all things are possible*—kept echoing through his head, giving him the slightest bit of confidence that this south-central chunk of Bedford County is where he would find his wife. And if it wasn't? Then he'd have to live out the remainder of his life cursing himself (and maybe God) for making such a foolish decision. But foolish or not, this is where he'd chosen, and he'd just have to go with it.

And pray that with God, all things really were possible.

When Judge had finished circling the barn, dousing at least three walls with the gasoline, Cheryl watched as he casually strolled back to the car, popped the trunk, and returned the gas container. Leaving the trunk open and leaning against the rear driver's side door, legs crossed like he was settling in for an evening of studying the stars, he reached into his pocket and drew out something. She couldn't tell what it was until he lifted a hand to his mouth and struck a match. Holding the match to his face, she saw the flame illuminate his sharp nose and angular chin. His mouth was hidden by a full mustache and tuft of hair beneath his lower lip. Moments later, he shook out the match, and an orange glow tipped the end of a cigarette.

He was smoking.

They were about to die a horrible death, and their execu-tioner was taking the time for one last smoke before lighting *them* up.

Amber came and stood beside Cheryl. "What's he doing?" she whispered.

Judge removed the cigarette and blew out a trail of smoke. With the sky now clear, Cheryl could see the blue-gray smoke curl upward and eventually disappear.

"He's smoking," she said.

Amber put her face to one of the gaps between the planks. "Hey!" she hollered. But Judge didn't acknowledge her, didn't even seem to hear her. He tilted his head back and blew out another plume of smoke, replaced the cigarette, and inhaled. The orange tip glowed brighter. "Hey! Did she suffer?"

If he heard her, which Cheryl was positive he had, he gave no indication of it. He simply crossed his arms and drew on the cigarette again.

"Did she suffer? The girl who burned? Katie?"

Cheryl jerked her head toward Amber. Was she nuts? What was she trying to do, infuriate him so he'd get it over with quicker? She opened her mouth. "What—"

Amber held up a hand and cut her off. "Wait." Then to Judge, "You loved her, didn't you? Katie was your girl. Your first love."

That got his attention. He pushed away from the car and walked directly toward them, his feet falling in even, determined steps. Stopping ten feet from the barn, he reached up and stuck the cigarette between his lips. The tip flared orange in the Stetson's shadow. He stood there for a few seconds drawing on the cigarette, removed it, and, holding it between his thumb and index finger, said, "Are you ready to die?"

"No," Amber said, her voice remarkably calm. "I don't want to die. Not yet. Not like this. I'm sorry she died. How did it happen?"

Judge paused as if contemplating how much he wanted to divulge. He took another long drag on the cigarette, blew out the smoke.

Amber didn't give him time to think about it for too long. "I'm sorry Katie died. I really am. It must have been awful. And I'm sorry they blamed you while her murderers walked free."

Judge didn't do anything. Cheryl expected him to strike a match at any moment and light the place up, but he didn't. He just stood there, hidden in the shadow of his Stetson, puffing away on that cigarette, while the Doberman sat at his side as man's best friend should. Was she getting through to him? Was she connecting with him on a personal level? Humanizing herself?

"We're not them," Amber finally said, her voice low and

innocent. "We're not the ones who killed Katie. Let us go. Please. We—"

"Enough," Judge snapped. He took two long steps forward, held the cigarette in front of his face, and flicked it with his middle finger.

"No!" Amber yelled.

Cheryl tried to scream, but the words got stuck in her throat. She watched as the cigarette flipped through the air, end over end. Her fingers dug into the wooden planks; an electric buzz spread over her whole body.

The cigarette landed on the ground six inches from the barn wall. Cheryl turned away and covered her face just as the wall erupted in a thunder of flames behind her. She scrambled to the far wall and frantically began using her hands to sweep the straw to the center of the barn.

"Hurry!" she yelled, lifting her strained voice above the roar of the flames.

Amber got the idea and sprang into action, clawing at the floor, shoving straw between her legs. Somewhere, Cheryl heard Ginny scream, a guttural, primal shriek, then a solid thump. She looked to Ginny's corner, but she wasn't there. The flames were eating up the perimeter of the barn at a quick pace. Another throaty scream sounded and another sickening thump. Where was Ginny—? There. To Cheryl's right, near where the dead dog lay. She was throwing herself against the back wall, hitting it with the force of a linebacker and bouncing off like a rubber ball.

Cheryl watched as Ginny picked herself up, scrambled back fifteen feet or so, let out a shriek, and launched herself at the wall again. *Whump!* She hit the planks and bounced off, landing on her backside. The whole display reminded Cheryl of a sparrow flying into a patio door.

Ginny got up, turned, and looked at Cheryl. And though

the temperature inside the barn was steadily climbing, Ginny's appearance made Cheryl's skin pucker with goose bumps. Her hair was matted to her forehead and littered with straw. Her face glowed red in the light of the fire and glistened with sweat and smeared blood. Her lips were twisted into a panicked frown, and her eyes were wide with fright. Cheryl had seen fear before but never like this. The look in Ginny's eyes wasn't fear... it was terror.

Ginny held Cheryl's gaze for a second, reared up, and threw herself at the wall again. *Whump!* She hit hard this time, crumpling into the solid plank wall and sliding to the floor. She rolled over and shook her head, obviously dazed by the collision.

Realization dawned on Cheryl like a black sunrise and sent a whole new wave of goose bumps over her flesh.

Ginny wasn't trying to get out. She was trying to kill herself.

Mark jammed the Mustang's brakes. The car fishtailed to a halt. Something had caught his eye. To his left, in the distance. He opened the car door and jumped out. Why hadn't he noticed it before? There, just over the crest of a sloping field, a thin pillar of black smoke rose into the twilit sky. He hopped onto the hood of his car for a better look. The source of the smoke was still out of sight, but it couldn't be more than a mile away.

His heart hammered away in his chest. It had to be them. Cheryl. The barn was burning! But why hadn't he noticed it before? Had he missed it? He couldn't have. It must have just started.

Mark jumped back into the car and stomped on the accelerator. The Mustang's engine roared, wheels squealed, and the car lurched forward, rear end fishtailing.

Mark sped down Dam Road in a reckless panic, keeping his eyes on the growing pillar of smoke. About a quarter of a mile down the road, he jerked the wheel to the left and turned onto an unmarked side road even narrower than Dam Road. It was more like a driveway, littered with potholes and debris from the last storm. On either side lay acres of meadow, fields that hadn't been farmed in years. This had to be it.

The plume of smoke was now directly in front of him. He gripped the steering wheel tighter and pressed the accelerator to the floor. *Please, God. Please let me be in time.* The Mustang bounced over potholes like a golf ball on pavement, abusing the car's suspension.

No more than a few hundred yards down the road a dirt lane split off on the left. Mark took the turn without letting up on the accelerator and almost lost control of the car as it slid on the packed dirt and nearly landed in a shallow gully that ran along the right side. The smoke now rose to his left again, and for the first time he noticed an orange glow flickering at its base. The Mustang rattled over the dirt lane, jarring Mark's eyes and blurring his vision. Within seconds, he crested a low hill.

The barn was in full view now, no more than a couple hundred yards away.

Orange and yellow flames licked at the old structure, climbing halfway up the front and side walls. Billows of thick smoke poured into the night sky like a black chimney.

Mark pounded the brake, and the car slid to a stop. He opened the door and fell out, landing on his hands and knees. He tried to scream, wail, anything to release the pressure in his chest, but nothing could get past his tight vocal cords. Tears spilled out of his eyes and dripped off his chin and nose.

Run.

The voice started as a whisper, somewhere in the back of his mind. He rolled over onto his butt, propped himself on one arm, and forced himself to look at the blazing barn. The fire roared and crackled and sent sparks shooting into the sky like fireworks. To the left of the barn sat a white sedan, glowing in the light of the fire.

Run. Go.

The voice was louder now, more urgent. But the barn was burning like dry kindling. Could anyone survive that?

Run to the barn.

Without thinking, Mark jumped to his feet and started toward the barn in a stumbling run. He pulled up, spun around, and dashed back to the car. Reaching across the driver's seat, he grabbed the shotgun, then tore off in a full sprint toward the barn.

It took him less than a minute to reach the structure, but the intense heat stopped him a good fifteen feet out. The roar of the flames was growing. A steady blast of heat buffeted his face. Mark fell to his knees, still holding the gun in his right hand. His heart felt like a lump of rock in his chest; his throat was still stuck in a vise. Beads of sweat popped out on his forehead and coursed down his face, mingling with the tears.

What was he doing? The thought occurred to him that he would also die here. And somehow, he didn't care. His life was over anyway. First he'd lost Cheryl's love; now he'd lost her. The urge came to rush the barn and die in the flames with her. It wouldn't be painless, but he didn't deserve a painless death. He deserved hellfire. The screams—*those* screams—came back to him and streaked across his mind. *Weeping and gnashing of teeth.* Utter torment.

But the screams were no longer coming from inside his head; they were coming from in the barn. Were they still alive?

"Cheryl!" He yelled her name into the roaring flames. His throat rebelled against the hot air, and he barked out a dry cough.

"Mark!"

He could barely hear her above the thunder of the fire, but it was definitely Cheryl's voice. She was alive!

Mark jumped to his feet and ran around to the back of the barn, where the flames weren't as intense. Sweat poured off of his forehead, pooling in his eyebrows and stinging his eyes. "Cheryl!"

"Mark!" His name was followed by a loud pop, then the sound of cracking wood. Someone inside screamed.

The barn was collapsing! He had to find a way to get them out. There had to be a way. What kind of God would bring him here—

Mark stopped dead in his tracks. Panic crept up his chest and gripped his throat like two bony hands. He couldn't do this on his own, he knew that much. And it scared him. Pastor Tim's words came back to him:

Trust Jesus.

Trust Jesus. That's what this was all about, wasn't it? Hell? He was being given a second chance, a heads-up, Tim had called it. He didn't want to die. He didn't want to suffer in hell. And he knew the only way to rescue Cheryl was to trust Jesus. It was all about Jesus. It always had been. An image of Tim, the tattooed preacher, tapping his chest—*It's gotta be in here*—flashed in his mind. He shut his eyes tight and cried out, "Jesus, help me! Save me!"

Surprisingly, the words came out of his mouth like a cool rush of water. He knew it was a foxhole prayer, but he didn't care because he meant it. Every word of it.

Mark opened his eyes and looked at the flames, past the flames. There, in the barn, he could see the outlines of three women huddled together.

"Mark!"

"Cheryl!" He started toward the barn, not knowing what he would do, then stopped. The heat was still intense. His face burned hot, and his clothes felt as if they'd spontaneously combust at any moment. The gun burned too, and he let it slip from his hand.

He shielded his face with his arms and backed up a couple of paces.

That's when he heard it. A voice. Not the child's voice he'd heard before, not Cheryl's voice, but a gentle, deep voice, so clear it could have come from someone standing right next to him.

When you walk through the fire,
You will not be burned,
And the flame will not scorch you.

From somewhere in the barn, wood cracked and popped. "Mark!"

Mark pulled his jacket up so it covered his face. He was going for it. And somehow, he knew he'd make it. *Jesus. Help me.* He ran at the barn, ducked his head, and hit the wall with his left shoulder. It gave out like a piece of cardboard. He tumbled through the flames, rolled twice, and stopped on all fours in the middle of the barn.

Cheryl and another woman he immediately recognized as Amber Mann were there, crouched low to the floor, finding what oxygen was left in the barn. A thick cloud of smoke roiled above them. Dazed, Mark pulled his shirt over his mouth and stood. He looked himself over. Not a burn on him. Not even his clothes were singed.

He quickly surveyed the situation. Cheryl and Amber looked well, red-faced and soaked in sweat, but well enough. The other woman with them, whom he recognized as Virginia Grisham (Cheryl had called her Ginny on the phone), looked like she'd been through hell already. Her hair was matted in clumps, her face streaked with blood, eyes swollen from crying. And on the floor was another woman, lying on her side, apparently unconscious.

"She's out but alive," Cheryl hollered above the roar of the flames.

Mark looked back at the wall he'd just busted through. There was a hole maybe four feet wide where the planks used to be. But it wouldn't last long. The building couldn't hold up much longer. He bent down and noticed the woman on the floor was wearing a police uniform. No, dear God. He turned her over. It was Foreman.

"Help me get her on my shoulder," he yelled.

Cheryl and Amber helped him lift Foreman to a standing position. Her head lolled to one side like it was attached by a string. Mark bent over and slipped her over his shoulder. Then, turning to Cheryl and Amber, he motioned toward Ginny, who was standing wide-eyed, hands partially covering her face, watching the whole thing. "Take her and go."

Cheryl grabbed Ginny by the arm and pulled her through the opening in the wall. Amber followed. Mark adjusted Foreman on his shoulder, covered his face with his left arm, and ran through the opening as well.

When he had cleared the barn, he was about to dump Foreman on the ground when Cheryl stopped him with both hands on his chest. "He's still here," she hollered.

"Who?"

"*Him*. Judge. He's still around here somewhere."

Mark scanned the area. No sign of anyone except Cheryl, Amber, and Ginny.

"Judge?" Must be the maniac. "Where?"

Cheryl gripped his arm. "I don't know. But he's here. We have to go."

Mark threw his head in the direction of where his Mustang

was. "My car's over there. Go. I'm right behind you." He bent over and scooped his gun up off the ground. It was still hot but had cooled some in the tall grass. "Go!"

Cheryl grabbed Ginny's arm again and turned to head for the car.

Suddenly a shot rang out, like a crack of thunder. At first, Mark wasn't sure if it had come from the inferno or not. Something may have exploded in the barn. But then he saw him, tall and lean, standing on the dirt lane by the Mustang, like a gunslinger from the Old West complete with a broad-brimmed Stetson. He stood facing them, legs parted, shotgun in one hand, its stock resting on his hip. Looked like Chuck Connors—the Rifleman. Judge.

Cheryl and the others froze. Ginny let out a loud whimper and started to cry again.

Judge stood still for a few seconds, facing them, then turned, pointed the gun at the rear wheel of the Mustang. A blast of fire exploded from the barrel. The Mustang rocked side to side; the rear tire sagged to the ground.

Mark's head throbbed. His heart was in his throat. He could stay and make a stand against this nut—he had six shots in his gun. But what about the women? They were defenseless. What if this was how Cheryl died? A thought struck him like a rock between the eyes: he'd saved her from the fire, spared her life, but for how long? The repo man may have been delayed, but he was still coming. He had to tell her about Jesus. She'd survived *this* fire, but if she died, she'd still have to deal with hell's fire. He had to tell her. But when? Here? Now? Not a chance. A wave of frustration and desperation swelled within him, and he let out a loud grunt.

Another shot pierced the air, above the roar of the fire.

Judge was on the far side of the car now. He'd just shot out the passenger-side rear tire.

Mark looked at Cheryl, who was staring back at him with wide eyes.

"The woods," he said. "Head for the woods. Go." They could find some cover there. He'd put up a stand if he had to.

Mark looked back one last time at Judge finishing off the last of the Mustang's tires, then, repositioning Jess on his shoulder, took off for the woods.

Cheryl and the others were a good ten yards ahead of him and opening the gap with each step. Mark lowered his head and pumped his free arm, trying to make up ground. Each heavy step sent a jolt through his back. His lungs burned, and he was sure his heart was going to pump right out of his chest.

He had no idea if Judge was in hot pursuit or not. An image of the Stetson-wearing outlaw, silhouetted against the glowing flames, gun raised to shoulder level, sat in Mark's mind like a lump. He kept expecting to hear the gun's loud retort and feel the impact of a slug against his back. But it hadn't come yet. Maybe Judge had been caught off guard. Maybe he had to reload. At any rate, Mark knew if he didn't make it to the woods, that would be it. His appointment with death would come due.

A new wave of adrenaline surged through his arteries like hot fuel, and he pounded his feet harder on the soft ground. Cheryl was now close to twenty yards ahead and almost at the—

Something hit Mark in the back of the leg and he went down, spilling Foreman onto the ground. She rolled once and lay motionless, face up in the grass, arms splayed to either side.

Searing pain started in Mark's calf and shot up his leg.

His calf felt like it was in a vise. A vise with teeth. He flipped himself over, still gripping his shotgun, and came face to face with the Doberman. The dog had a death grip on his calf and was shaking it like it was a groundhog. Mark let out a throaty scream and tried to kick the dog away. But the jaws on the beast were like iron. The dog growled and snorted and gnawed on the thick muscle, keeping itself low to the ground for leverage.

The pain was almost unbearable, like fire in his leg. Flashes of white heat blinded Mark, and his head swam. This was it? This was how he was going to die? Eaten alive by some crazed dog?

The gun.

The pain had been so intense, and he had been in such a panic he'd forgotten all about the shotgun his left hand still gripped. He quickly transferred it to his right hand, pumped it once, shoved the barrel against the dog's chest, and pulled the trigger.

The barrel exploded, the gun jerked in his hand, and the Doberman released its grip. For a moment the dog just sat there, looking at Mark with glassy eyes, jaws ajar, tongue dangling to one side like a pink ribbon as if to say, *Hey, I was only kidding. Why'd you go and do that?* All the while, the gaping hole in its chest vomited a pool of dark red blood.

Mark dug his legs into the ground and pushed away from the dog. It teetered once, then collapsed to its side. Dead.

Mark quickly scanned the area. The barn had collapsed in on itself and was a ball of raging fire, the Mustang still sat on its rims like a junkyard jewel, but there was no sign of Judge.

Mark turned and looked toward the woods. Cheryl stood at the tree line, hands covering her mouth. The tree line was no more than twenty yards away. He could make it. He reached down and felt his calf. The pant leg was soaked with blood. He tried to pump his ankle. The pain was intense.

"Mark!" It was Cheryl. He turned and looked at her again. She was bent at the waist, waving him in.

Cheryl. Baby. He had to go to her. He had to make it to the woods.

He pushed himself up, doing his best to ignore the pain that shot up the back of his leg like a lightning bolt. Dropping his gun, he bent at the waist and grabbed Foreman under both arms. He then hoisted her up with a grunt and dipped his shoulder, catching her at the waist before she toppled to the ground again. He had no idea if she was even alive or not. All he knew was that she was dead weight and, for a woman her size, felt like a sack of lead.

Turning toward the tree line, he squatted with his good leg and grabbed the gun. He wasn't about to go into those woods unarmed, especially with Judge's whereabouts unknown.

Keeping his focus on Cheryl, Mark limped his way through the pasture, left hand gripping the shotgun, right arm bracing Foreman's legs against his chest. With each step his left foot dragged on the ground like a dead fish and sent a new wave of nauseating pain through his leg. Several times the leg buckled, and he almost dropped, but one sight of Cheryl waving him in like a third base coach kept him reeling forward. His gait wasn't really a run; it was more a succession of falls, each one broken by his right leg and started again by his gimpy left leg.

At the edge of the woods, another shot rang out. Mark burst through the tree line and fell to his knees, dropping Foreman on the leaf-covered ground. Looking over his shoulder, he spotted Judge's black outline walking through the pasture. Not running, walking. His arms hung loosely at his side, one hand balancing the rifle, as he took long measured steps, head up, shoulders square. Like an outlaw, Mark thought. Wanted, dead or alive.

"C'mon," Cheryl said. "We have to move." She looked at Mark, and their eyes met.

Mark wanted to reach out to her there, take her in his arms, and never let go. She was a strong woman, he knew, but he'd never seen this side of her. God only knew what she'd gone through in the past several hours. He wanted to tell her he loved her, that he'd been a jerk, a cursed fool, and beg her forgiveness. He wanted to shut his eyes and wish all this away. But it wasn't going away, was it? It was no nightmare. And the screams that had cut Cheryl off on the phone were still ringing in his ears, reminding him that she still had an appointment to keep, an appointment with the repo man. Odds were, she wasn't going to make it out of this alive. There would be no morning.

Mark gritted his teeth and clenched his fists. He had to tell her. He had to make her understand. She had to believe, make things right with God, with Jesus. If she was going to die, so be it; there was nothing he could do about it. But he had to make sure she wasn't going to wake up in…the place of those hideous screams.

"We need to split up," Cheryl said. "Someone has to get out of here and get help." She looked at Amber, who had one arm around Ginny's shoulders. "You two go. Find help. Anybody. Just get help."

Amber didn't say a word. Her eyes were wide, lips parted. She glanced from Cheryl to Mark and back to Cheryl again, then nodded.

Mark watched as Amber and Ginny disappeared into the darkness of the woods, then turned his head toward the pasture again. Judge was now jogging, but even in the cadence of his trot there was a confidence that bordered on cockiness, as if he knew something Mark and Cheryl didn't.

"Mark!" Cheryl was right in his face now, speaking in a hushed tone. "Can you get the cop? Are you able?"

As much as he wanted to dismiss the pain in his leg, as much as he wanted to carry her to safety, and as much as it killed him to admit it, he could carry her no farther.

"I don't think so," he admitted.

Cheryl felt Foreman's forehead, then checked her pulse. "She's got a steady pulse; it's weak, but there."

Mark combed a hand through his hair. "What can we do?"

"Nothing right now. We have to keep moving. Maybe we can hide her under a bush or something. Somewhere safe. When help comes, we'll come back and get her."

Mark didn't like it. Too risky. Foreman's face was a chalky white; it looked like death was waiting behind the nearest tree. "I can't just leave her. She could—"

Cheryl sprang to her feet and closed the distance between her and Mark in two steps. She lowered her voice to a strained whisper. "Mark! That freak is after us. Either we do this or we all die. You can't keep going with her over your shoulder, you know that."

He did know it too. He hated it, but he knew it. "OK, OK. Just make sure she's well hidden."

"She'll be OK. She will," Cheryl said, but there was no conviction behind her words.

After quickly making a bed of leaves under a thick stand of serviceberries and making sure Foreman was well concealed, Mark stood and looked around. "We have to keep moving." He nodded in the direction they were heading. "Away from the barn."

So back at it they went, running through the woods, dodging trees and limbs and fallen goliaths that had lost their battle with gravity long ago.

❻

Mark crashed through the woods, pain numbing his leg, cool air like shards of glass in his lungs. Briars tugged at his clothes like Velcro. His chest was tight, and he was sure his heart would explode with the very next beat.

Cheryl was right on his heels; he could hear her lungs heaving over the crunch of leaves beneath their feet. Was there any end to this woods? They'd been running for a good five minutes at least, maybe even closer to ten, with no sign of anything but underbrush, fallen limbs, and half-naked trees reaching for the sky like bony fingers begging for food. Enough moonlight filtered through the thick canopy of branches to at least partially illuminate the leaf-covered forest floor.

Even while he ran, hobbled, stumbled—that same series of falls—one thought soaked into Mark's mind: he had to tell Cheryl. She had to know about the screams and what they meant. She had to know what horror this night might hold…and the eternal horror to continue after that. She'd think he was nuts; he was sure of that.

Cheryl knew of Mark's religious background. How could she not? His parents made sure to tell her every time they saw her that "Mark grew up in a good Christian home." But she had never expressed any knowledge of or interest in church things. She was a good person, better than most Christians Mark had grown up with, but not at all interested in any kind of religion. Oh, she said she believed in God and believed the Bible was God's Word, but that's as far as it went. Mark didn't even know if she believed in heaven and hell; they'd never talked about it before.

But he had to tell her.

Again, frustration twisted his gut into a knot. When? When could he tell her? They were running for their lives, for goodness' sake. And Cheryl had no idea how literal that was. He couldn't just spit it out in breathless bursts while they ran—*By the way Cheryl (heave, heave), you're gonna die (heave, heave) tonight and (heave, heave) go to (heave, heave) hell.*

Mark suddenly realized the futility of this night, of the search and this rescue attempt. Was he really rescuing Cheryl? Or was he just delaying the inevitable? But he'd rescued Amber and Ginny, hadn't he? That was something. They were probably safe by now, hopefully finding help.

Help may be on the way right now, Mark.

But when it came to Cheryl, was death inevitable? She had an appointment. Was he only delaying it? Shoving it back a few hours? Only time would tell, really. Meanwhile, he had a few extra moments with her, even if they were spent running half blindly and fully lost through these woods with some maniacal rifleman on their trail. That was a good thing, the extra moments, that is. Enough time to tell her he loved her.

And about the screams, the appointment. He had to say *something.* "Cheryl...I need to...tell you...something."

"Can it...wait?"

"No—" Suddenly the ground disappeared beneath Mark's feet, and he found himself tumbling down a steep embankment, logrolling like a kid down a hill.

Chapter 15

❶

AMBER PULLED GINNY THROUGH THE DENSE WOODS by her wrist. Thickets and shrubs tugged at her clothes; low-hanging branches slapped at her chest and face. The cold night air ripped her lungs to shreds, burning like rubbing alcohol in an open wound. Overhead, the moon kept pace with them, silhouetting the forest's barren canopy against the velvet night sky. Her heart was in her throat; her lungs were on fire; her legs felt like they were made of lead.

She had no idea where they were going; she only knew they were headed *away* from the barn, away from *him*. And she knew they had to keep moving. Sooner or later they would break free from the trees and find help.

God, help us; we have to find help.

She thought of Mark and how incredible it was that he'd showed up when he did. If he hadn't, they'd all be dead right now. And she thought of how he'd broken through the barn wall, tumbled through the flames, and stood before them without even so much as a singed hem. But he'd walked right through the flames, hadn't he? It wasn't her imagination. She remembered the words she'd prayed just hours ago, right before Cheryl had called Mark: *We could really use a miracle. Please send help.* And He had. He'd sent Mark.

Behind her, Ginny's labored breathing increased. Suddenly,

Amber felt a tug on her hand, and Ginny's wrist slipped from her grip. She turned and saw Ginny sitting on the ground, elbows on knees, head in her hands.

"Ginny, c'mon," Amber said, her voice just above a whisper.

Ginny shook her head. "I can't."

Amber walked back to where Ginny was sitting and crouched beside her. She placed her hand on Ginny's back. "Ginny, I know you're tired. So am I. But we have to get out of here. We have to get help."

Ginny started to cry. Her shoulders shook with violent sobs. "Just go without me then. I can't do it."

Amber put her hand under Ginny's chin and lifted her head. "Hey, listen. It's OK to be tired. It's OK to be scared. I'm scared too. But we have to stay alive. Cheryl and Mark and the cop are counting on us to get help."

Ginny wiped at her face, smearing dirt across her cheek. "I don't know if I can make it."

Amber was about to lose her patience with Ginny and drag her out of the woods by her hair if she had to when she heard leaves crunch behind her and to the right. She spun around and stared into the darkness but saw nothing but trees and dense shadows. A branch snapped to her left. Closer. Then behind her, more leaves crunched. Ginny was whimpering now, ready to lose it.

"Hello, ladies," a man's voice said. *His* voice.

A cold chill spread out across Amber's shoulders and chest. She turned and saw a man's figure from mid-chest up, black against the charcoal sky, with one distinguishing feature—the Stetson.

The best Mark could tell, he'd already rolled and slid maybe fifty feet. He tried to get his footing and groped with his hands for anything stable enough to catch on to, but it was useless. He might as well have been in a free fall. At the bottom, a large boulder stopped his slide, hitting him like a middle linebacker and knocking the air out of his lungs. He clutched at his chest, mouth wide open, and tried to swallow huge gulps of air. He looked up and saw Cheryl, still on her feet but sliding down the hill like an out-of-control skier. She was there in seconds, gripping his arm with one hand, slapping at his back with the other.

"Breathe, Mark. Relax and breathe. Take a deep breath."

Finally, air rushed in and inflated his lungs again.

"That's better," Cheryl said. "Take some deep breaths."

Mark heard the soft gurgle of water. Were they near a creek? He looked around the boulder and noticed a winding creek cutting through the woods and reflecting the moonlight like a rippled mirror. He had fallen down an embankment that met a creek.

Mark grabbed at his ankle and rubbed it. His sock and shoe were both soaked with blood.

"Can you still walk?" Cheryl asked.

Mark nodded. "I'll have to." He stopped then, held a finger to his mouth, and tilted his head toward the embankment. "Listen," he whispered.

They both remained still for a long minute before Cheryl broke the silence. "Think we lost him?"

Mark shrugged and forked a hand through his sweat-wet hair. "I don't know." He took a deep breath and looked up the embankment again, listening for the crunch of leaves or snap of a dry branch, any indication that Judge was on their trail. But the only sound he heard was the soothing movement of water and the distant chatter of a squirrel.

"What are you thinking?" Cheryl asked.

"I think we lost him. Maybe we should wait him out here until help comes."

"Maybe."

Mark reached for his gun and clutched it to his chest with both hands. "We can make a stand if we need to."

There was a pause while both of them listened again. The chatter had stopped, and the silence of the night air was now only broken by the soft warbling of the creek.

"Cheryl?"

"Yeah." She had lowered herself to her rear and sat with her legs extended. Mark could just barely make out the features of her face. Soft light played off her high cheekbones and smooth jawline. Her hair glistened like strands of honey.

"I need to tell you something. I—"

"Mark, don't." There was a hint of irritation in her voice. "This isn't the time for that."

Mark leaned toward her and lowered his voice. "It *has* to be the time. Let's be honest, Cheryl. Neither of us knows for sure if we're gonna make it out of these woods alive. I need to tell you this... there might not be another time."

She stared ahead quietly, lips drawn tight, flexing her jaw. It was her "look," the look she had whenever she was contemplating how best to dismantle one of Mark's arguments. And she was a master of it—both the "look" and the dismantling.

When she let out a deep sigh, Mark knew he had the floor again—her way of saying, *OK, go ahead.*

Mark scooted closer to her so he could keep his voice low. "Cheryl, first, I know you—I mean I deserve it and all, but I know you probably hate me for what I did. And I know..." He stopped and rubbed at his eyes with his fingers. "Cheryl, I'm sorry. I was wrong and I know it, and I don't expect you to ever love me again, but there's something I need you to know."

She turned her head and looked at him, and there were tears in her eyes. He'd hurt her more than he could have ever imagined. He knew that. But regaining her trust would take more than a simple apology; it would take time, months, maybe years, if they both lived that long. The only thing he could do right now was deal with the screams.

"You probably don't—"

"Mark," Cheryl said. "Stop assuming you know how I feel. You don't. You can't. And let's hope to God you never do."

Mark dropped his eyes away from her. "I'm sorry."

He waited a few moments, and when she said nothing more, he continued. "If we—I mean, if we don't make it out of here tonight...alive, I need to know you're going to be all right."

"What do you mean? That doesn't even make sense."

Mark took another deep breath, wiped at his eyes again, and listened to the darkness. Still no sound of footsteps. All was quiet. *Help me, God.* "I mean, if we die here tonight, in these woods, if *you* die...then what?"

Cheryl looked straight ahead again and pursed her lips. By the light of the moon, Mark could see her Adam's apple bob once; then, a single tear spilled out of her eye and, glistening like a diamond, ran a straight course down her cheek and dripped off her jaw.

After a few seconds, Cheryl swallowed again and shrugged. "I don't know." Her voice was tight and raspy, and Mark knew it was all she could do to say those three words without opening the floodgate and letting the tears pour out. He could see the inward struggle etched in the tight lines of her face.

Mark leaned a little closer to her. "I need you to know, Cheryl. OK? It really is a matter of life and death. I need you to know."

Cheryl's chin began to quiver. "How?"

"You have to give your life to Jesus. You have to surrender it all. There's no other way."

Cheryl snorted a sarcastic laugh. "That sounds great coming from a man who cheated on his wife. Doesn't God condemn adultery?"

Mark paused and wiped a tear from his own eye. "Yes, He does. And I know I've been a hypocrite, been one my whole life. I know it. But standing outside that barn back there I realized how helpless I really am and how much I need Jesus. I called on Him, Cheryl. I surrendered to Him. Cher, I love you. I do. I know I screwed up, but I do love you. And I want you to make sure you're going to heaven. Please, consider it. I know you're a strong woman; you more than proved that tonight. But you're helpless when it comes to life and death. That's in God's hands. Everyone has an appointment with death. You need to be ready when it comes due. Please, Cheryl. Please. Trust Jesus. Do it now before it's too late. You—"

Mark's cell phone rang in his pocket—*The Dukes of Hazzard* theme. In his panic, he'd forgotten all about it! He slapped at the pocket, reached in, and grabbed the phone, flipping it open just as the tune started over.

The digital screen displayed a number he did not recognize. He put the phone to his ear. "Who is this?"

"Stone?"

"Yeah. Who's this?"

"Sheriff Hickock. Where are you?"

Hickock. Did Amber find help that quickly and call the police?

Mark's heart jumped in his chest. He looked at Cheryl and forced a smile, then mouthed the word *police*. They might make it out of here alive, after all. Both of them.

"We're in Buchanan State Forest, I mean. In Maryland. I took—"

"I know where you are, Stone. Mann and Grisham are with me. They told me everything. I need to know where you are exactly. Where in the forest?"

Mark looked around. "By a creek. I fell down a steep embankment, and we're on the bank of a creek, by a big boulder. That's all I can give you."

"Is Deputy Foreman OK?"

"She's alive, but I don't know anything more than that. Her pulse is weak. We had to...we had to hide her in a safe place. I know where it is."

"OK. Listen, Stone. I'm coming in with a SWAT team. I think I know where you are. Hold tight, OK? Are you armed?"

"Yes."

"What do you have?"

"A shotgun."

"How many rounds?"

"Five. Six. I'm not sure."

"OK, here's what I want you to do so none of my men get shot at. Set your weapon—"

Screams drowned out Hickock's voice, crawling out of the phone and into Mark's head, boring a hole in his brain. The same screams—wailing, moaning, crying, gnashing of teeth—that he'd heard with Jeff and Jerry and Dad and Andrea and Cheryl. His skin crawled with a million tiny bugs, and a chill blew down his back.

Then the phone went dead. Silence. Except for the tumbling water behind him.

Mark shut the phone and stared at its silver casing.

"What was that?" Cheryl asked, her voice trembling. She reached out and grasped Mark's arm.

Mark looked at her. "The screams."

"What was it? I heard the same thing in the barn when we talked. When Judge came in."

"The sounds of hell, Cheryl. I heard them before. Right before Jeff died, and Jerry the parts guy, and my dad. Hickock's gonna die soon. Maybe tonight."

Cheryl's grip tightened on his arm. He knew what she was thinking. It was written on her face. She was doing the math. Two plus two. It was ludicrous, yes, but she was buying it.

"I'm going to die, aren't I?"

Tears filled Mark's eyes, blurring Cheryl's face. He wiped at his eyes with his wrist, set the phone on the ground, and put his hand over hers, looking her right in the eyes. "I don't know that. No one does. But that's why you need to make sure you're right with God."

Cheryl didn't say anything. She just sat there, tears making tracks down her cheeks, lips slightly parted.

Mark shifted the gun to his right hand and placed his left hand on the back of Cheryl's neck. Her skin was smooth and cool. He pulled her head toward him until their foreheads touched. "Cheryl, baby. I love you. I'm so—"

"Well, well, well." A man's voice—Judge's?—broke through the still air.

Mark released Cheryl and spun his head to his right. A buzz shot over his skull and down the back of his neck, making the hair on his nape stand up like a bristle brush.

There, no more than ten yards down the creek's bank, was Judge. And in front of him, hands bound behind their back, mouths gagged, were Amber and Ginny. Ginny's right arm was interlocked with Amber's left, binding them together. Judge stood behind them, his rifle resting on Amber's shoulder, the barrel pointed at Mark.

❹

Mark looked from Amber to Ginny to Judge. Judge's Stetson was pulled low, shading his face from the moonlight. Amber and Ginny looked like they'd been roughed up a bit. Amber's right eye was almost swollen and shut; dark blood was smeared across her forehead and cheek. Ginny was hunched over, bent at the waist, whimpering softly.

Mark slowly moved his left hand toward the shotgun in his right.

"Don't do it, Stone!"

It *was* Hickock! He recognized the voice.

"Put the weapon down and get up."

Hickock shoved Amber in the back, and she stumbled forward a few steps, pulling Ginny with her.

Mark started to rise, pushing himself up with his left hand and leaning on the boulder behind him. He still held the gun in his right hand.

"I said put the weapon down. Now!"

Hickock gave Amber another push in the back, and she stumbled forward again, almost losing her balance.

Mark brought his left hand to the action and raised the gun to his shoulder. He couldn't get a good look at Hickock; he was almost totally concealed behind Amber and Ginny. If Mark had the shot, he would have taken it right then.

Coward. Hiding behind two helpless women.

Hickock laughed. "What are you going to do, Stone? Shoot the ladies here first?" He moved the barrel slightly to his right. If Mark wasn't watching closely, he would have never even noticed the slight shift. But he had noticed. And now the rifle's barrel was trained on Cheryl.

"Put...the gun...down."

Whether out of fear or resolve—he wasn't sure which—Mark didn't move. Was this how it was going to end? How Cheryl would die? Mark saw himself pulling the trigger, Amber slumping over, and Hickock putting a bullet in Cheryl's head. It would never work. Hickock had him cornered. Game over. Checkmate. But still he held the gun against his shoulder. His pulse pounded in his ears, like a whitewater river of blood rushing through his head. A droplet of sweat broke from his brow line and ran down his forehead. His finger rested on the trigger, the fat pad barely depressed. If he only had an opening. He could pull the trigger in a fraction of a second and put a hole the size of a baseball in Hickock's chest.

"Stone, I'm giving you one more chance. Put the gun down or wifey goes."

No way. As long as he had the gun he had a chance. Without it he was dead, and so were Cheryl and Amber and Ginny and probably Foreman.

A thought struck him and sent a wave of heat over his face. Had he pumped the action since shooting the dog? He couldn't remember. His cheeks flushed hot, and beads of sweat popped out all over his brow. He didn't. He was sure of it. But did Hickock know that? Apparently not. Even if he didn't, the gun would do Mark no good unless a shell was in the barrel. It was a useless toy. He made up his mind then; he'd have to do it.

With one quick motion he slid the action forward and back.

What happened next seemed to unfold in slow motion and fast-forward at the same time. Amber lunged to her left, knocking Ginny over. Mark saw his opening and in that fraction of a second squeezed the gun's trigger. It was more reflexive than volitional. The barrel exploded in a blast of light, and the stock kicked back against his shoulder. At the same time, he saw a flash of light jump from the end of Hickock's barrel, then Hickock's Stetson flew off his head. He grunted and hit the ground like someone had punched him square in the chest, knocking his feet out from under him.

Time seemed to stand still for several endless seconds. Amber and Ginny were both lying on the ground, facedown and motionless. Hickock was flat on his back. He lifted his head slowly, looked at Mark, then let it fall as if it were a bowling ball.

Mark turned and looked at Cheryl. She had fallen backward and lay motionless facing the sky.

No! No, no. Please God, no.

Mark dropped his gun and fell to the ground beside Cheryl. Her eyes were closed, mouth open. He reached for her head and felt something wet and sticky in her hair. Pulling his hand away, he saw it was covered with blood. She'd been shot! Somewhere along the left side of her head, hidden by her hair, Hickock's bullet had found its mark.

Mark reared back and screamed at the sky.

Screamed at heaven. At God.

Chapter 16

❶

THREE WEEKS LATER

Mark stood by the grave site, hands clasped in front of him, shoulders slumped, head bowed so low his chin almost rested on his chest. The cemetery was still and quiet and void of living souls with the exception of the small assembly huddled around this one burial plot.

November had come in like a raging bull, bringing with it temperatures dipping into the twenties and the first light snow of the season.

Mark raised his head and scanned the cemetery, looking for a familiar figure to arrive. A thin blanket of white covered everything, skimming the surface of the ground so close that only the tips of assorted blades of grass poked through, like needles through a quilt. Rows of gray and white tombstones, some dating back to the early eighteen hundreds, stood like sentries, wearing soft white hats while they solemnly watched over the land of the sleeping. Scattered trees stood leafless and bare, their twisted branches reaching into the slate gray sky like upside-down roots. The meteorologist was predicting more snow, one to two inches.

A gust of bitter cold wind kicked up, biting Mark like icy teeth and sending a wave of shivers through his muscles. He reached out and put his arm around Cheryl's shoulders, pulling her close. She wrapped her arm around his waist and laid her head on his shoulder.

It was good to have her in his arms again. No, more than good. It was a miracle. He thought for sure he'd lost her. Back in the woods, with Hickock on one side of him and Cheryl on the other, Mark had lashed out at God, emptying himself before his Creator, questioning, bargaining...even cursing.

But Cheryl had not died. Hickock's bullet had not found its mark. The slug caught the side of Cheryl's head, penetrated the skin, but only grazed the skull, wrapping around the side of her head and exiting the back. The doctors said it was not unusual, that the skull was harder than most people gave it credit for. But to Mark, it was a miracle, plain and simple. In his heart he knew Cheryl should have died that night. Her appointment had come due. The repo man had knocked on the door and was waiting on the stoop.

And while Cheryl underwent brain surgery to remove a blood clot that had formed on her brain, then spent three days in an induced coma to ease the swelling, the question had burned in Mark's mind: Why hadn't she died? How had she escaped death's sure grip?

Mark's mind went back to the day in the hospital when he spoke to Cheryl for the first time since she had been brought out of the coma, and he finally received his answer. She was glassy-eyed and groggy. Her bangs were wet and stuck to her forehead. The left side of her head was shaved, and a long stapled incision arched over her ear like a railroad track, starting just behind the temple and ending beyond the ear. Skin puckered between shiny staples, and the length of the incision was crusted with dry blood. Her skin was pale and almost translucent; her cheeks were sunken and hollow. An oxygen tube snaked out from just above both ears and rested on her upper lip, pressed against her nostrils. Multiple IVs hung from her arms like power cords.

She smiled when she saw him. "Hey," she said in an almost inaudible whisper.

Mark pulled a chair to the side of the bed, rested one hand on top of hers, and smoothed back her bangs with the other. "Hey. Welcome back."

Cheryl just smiled again.

"How are you feeling?" Mark asked.

"Tired...and my head hurts." She grimaced as she swallowed. "My throat hurts too."

"I'm sorry." Mark leaned forward and kissed her on the nose. "You look beautiful."

Cheryl rolled her eyes. "You must be blind."

"I love you, Cher."

"I know." She smiled again and squeezed his hand. "I know."

"How's your memory?" Mark had been wondering if the trauma to the brain had caused any amnesia. He remembered hearing about people in accidents who didn't remember the accident or any of the events leading up to it. God's grace. Most people didn't want to remember the accident. He wondered if Cheryl would remember that night in the woods or even being in the barn with Amber and Ginny. He hoped not.

"Fine," she said. "I remember everything. I think anyway. I guess I wouldn't know if I didn't remember something, huh?"

Mark laughed.

Cheryl focused her eyes on the wall behind Mark. "I remember being in the barn and killing the dog. I remember the fire, the flames...it was so hot I thought my skin would melt. I remember you busting through the wall like some kind of superhero." She looked at him. "You weren't burned at all. I remember thinking that was very odd. I remember the woods

297

and Hickock and your showdown with him. And I remember Amber falling over. That's it. That's where it ends."

Tears were running down Mark's cheeks now. He sniffed and forced a smile. "You have a better memory than me. I can't recall half of what happened that night."

"How's your ankle? I remember that too."

"It's going to be fine. I had surgery on it and have to wear this boot for six weeks." He held up his foot to show her the bulky brace Velcroed to his leg.

"Stylish," Cheryl said.

"I'm sorry you have to remember all that. It would probably be better if you didn't."

Cheryl rolled her head from side to side. "No, it wouldn't. I want to remember it. I also remember you telling me about the screams." She swallowed again, and her Adam's apple bobbed up and down slowly. "You told me I needed Jesus."

The tears were coming harder now, and Mark wiped at his eyes with his sleeve. "Yeah. I did."

Cheryl smiled, and a tear spilled out of her eye and ran over her temple, disappearing behind her ear. "Well, while you and Hickock were playing cowboys, I did it. I trusted Jesus."

Mark coughed, and a sob escaped his throat. Of course! That's why she'd escaped death.

Back in the cemetery, Mark shivered again and squeezed Cheryl's shoulders. Light flakes had begun falling again. He heard snow crunching behind him and turned to see Pastor Tim, the tattooed preacher, making his way up the hill.

Tim came alongside Mark and placed a gloved hand on Mark's shoulder.

"Thanks for coming, Tim," Mark said.

Tim smiled and patted Mark's shoulder. He then leaned forward and nodded at Cheryl. "Good to see you up and about,

Cheryl." Then, walking in front of Mark and Cheryl, Tim approached the other two visitors and extended his hands. "Amber, Ginny, I'm glad you could make it too."

Tim exchanged some quiet words with Amber and Ginny, then nodded at Mark and fell in line beside Ginny.

Mark released Cheryl and stepped around to face the small congregation of four. Tiny white flakes speckled their hats and shoulders like a light dusting of confectioner's sugar on a cake.

Mark cleared his throat and stiffened his muscles against the cold. "I know it's cold, so I'll make this short and to the point."

He looked at Ginny, Amber, and Cheryl, meeting each one with a steady gaze. In the week following the *showdown*—as it had come to be called—Mark had talked with Amber and Ginny almost daily. Amber had been admitted the same time Cheryl had and given a healthy dose of antibiotics to quell the pneumonia that had overtaken her lungs. After a brief reunion with her family and boyfriend, Ginny had sat at Amber's side in her hospital room until the attending nurse told her she had to leave.

Mark took the opportunity to share with them his experience with the screams, telling them about death and eternity and challenging them to examine their own hearts and ask themselves one simple question: *Do I know where I'll go when I die?* There were always lots of hope-sos and think-sos and maybe-sos but never a know-so.

Until the following week—last week.

Amber had been discharged with an improving bill of health, and as soon as she and Ginny had walked into Cheryl's room, Mark could tell there was something different about Amber, something bright, something...new. It was much more than just the absence of infection. He knew right away what it was. She smiled, and light seemed to radiate from her eyes.

"I did it," she said, beaming with pride. "I trusted Jesus."

They hugged and prayed, and when he opened his eyes again, Ginny was crying. She had looked at Mark with wide eyes and trembling lips. "I want to, but I'm not sure I know how. Will you show me?"

"—Mark?"

Mark snapped his eyes over to Cheryl and blinked twice. "Oh, sorry." He looked again at Amber and Ginny, then at Tim. "Thanks for coming. I thought this would be an appropriate place to meet." He glanced at the grave marker before them, a slab of cold gray granite with the name "Jessica Anne Foreman" etched in big bold letters. With the exception of Hickock, who hadn't escaped his appointment with death, she was the only one who hadn't survived that night.

He sighed and wiped a tear from his cheek. "Tim, she went to your church, so you knew her better than any of us, but I'm confident we'll see her again. And for that I thank God."

Tim nodded and wiped at his own tears.

Mark looked down the row again, meeting each one of them eye to eye—Cheryl, Amber, Ginny. They were all crying. "You are my family now, and I wanted you to be the first to hear this. Cheryl and I have decided to sell the garage and go into the ministry full-time. I have to tell people about Jesus. It's not that I want to; I *have* to. It's like a fire in my bones."

He shifted his gaze to a flock of blackbirds perched in a mess of tangled oak branches and let his mind drift to Jeff, Jerry, Dad, Andrea, and, yes, even Hickock. "You never know when you talk to someone if it will be the last time you ever hear their voice."

He then looked to his left at the sprawling town of Frostburg, Maryland. Homes and businesses squatted close to the ground like neatly arranged milk cartons separated into even grids, all covered with an untouched white blanket of fresh snow.

Somewhere in the distance a child let loose a playful scream that carried through the air on the tails of a gust of wind. The screams. He hadn't heard them since that terrible night. And he hoped he never would again.

"I have to tell them. I have to tell them all. And I won't stop until I do...until I've screamed it from the top of every mountain."

A Note From the Author

EAR READER,

There is nothing that humbles and honors me more than knowing that someone took time out of their busy schedule to sit down and read my book. Thank you. I hope you enjoyed the story.

But it's so much more than a story, isn't it? It's a call to action.

I wrote *Scream* to entertain, yes (and I hope I succeeded in that), but more so I wrote it to challenge, to challenge you to think about life and death—the brevity of life; the imminence of death—and then, by golly, to *do something* about it.

It's no lie; death is one of the only sure bets in life.

Think about that for a moment; let the reality settle in. The morbidity rate for men and women everywhere is 100 percent. You *will* die. Sooner or later.

Oh, I know most of us don't like to think about that. It's morbid, morose, melancholic. But necessary. Death is an appointment that cannot be canceled.

Now, since death is imminent, I want you to think about what happens *after* death. Where will you spend eternity? There's only two choices, heaven or hell. And the choice is yours. You decide. If heaven is your choice, there's only one requirement (and it doesn't include going to church or clean living or helping little old ladies cross the street); it's trusting in what Jesus did on the cross to satisfy your debt. You see, the Bible says we are all sinners and the wages for sin is death. It's a debt we've incurred but can never repay. Out of His love for each of us, Jesus volunteered to pay that debt on our behalf and now offers us the gift of eternal life. Entrance into heaven only requires that we acknowledge our fault and humbly accept that gift.

So, the call to action. If you've never accepted that gift, I implore you to do so. Admit your sinfulness, ask Jesus to forgive you, and accept His gift of eternal life. If you have accepted His gift, the responsibility is yours to tell others about it. Think about it: when you talk to someone (a friend, co-worker, neighbor, family member), you never know if it will be the last time you ever share words with them. Take advantage of every opportunity you're given. Tell them before it's too late.

If you're interested in knowing more about this or want ideas for sharing this good news with others using God's Word and *Scream*, log on to www.MikeDellosso.com. I look forward to seeing you there!

Humbly and with much appreciation for you, the reader,

—MIKE

FREE NEWSLETTERS
TO HELP EMPOWER YOUR LIFE

Why subscribe today?

☐ **DELIVERED DIRECTLY TO YOU.** All you have to do is open your inbox and read.

☐ **EXCLUSIVE CONTENT.** We cover the news overlooked by the mainstream press.

☐ **STAY CURRENT.** Find the latest court rulings, revivals, and cultural trends.

☐ **UPDATE OTHERS.** Easy to forward to friends and family with the click of your mouse.

CHOOSE THE E-NEWSLETTER THAT INTERESTS YOU MOST:

- Christian news
- Daily devotionals
- Spiritual empowerment
- And much, much more

SIGN UP AT: **http://freenewsletters.charismamag.com**